Praise for *The Innkeeper's Daughter*

"A gritty, steamy series opener full of dark twists and
hot trysts."

— Grace Burrowes,
New York Times bestselling author

"From the brutal opening pages, to the tenderest of
love scenes, *The Innkeeper's Daughter* took me on
a ride of contradictory emotions. Sadistic villains
paired with beautiful regency details made this story
unforgettable, but it is truly the characters who steal
the show. Eliza is a delight, Sir Henry March has my
heart, and our author, Bianca M. Schwarz, has me
eagerly awaiting the next book."

— Amanda Linsmeier, author

"Historically well-researched with enthralling
characters and excellent storytelling. Absolutely
wonderful."

— C. H. Armstrong, author of
The Edge of Nowhere

THE GENTLEMAN SPY MYSTERIES

BIANCA M. SCHWARZ

central
avenue
publishing

2021

Published by Central Avenue Publishing, an imprint of Central Avenue Marketing Ltd.
www.centralavenuepublishing.com

Published in Canada
Printed in United States of America

1. FICTION/Romance - Historical   2. FICTION/Historical

THE INNKEEPER'S DAUGHTER

Trade Paperback: 978-1-77168-210-7
Epub: 978-1-77168-211-4
Mobi: 978-1-77168-212-1

1 3 5 7 9 10 8 6 4 2

To my mother, who didn't live to see my work in print.
Thank you for sharing your love of books and your
ability to see the beauty in everything.

SETTING: HAMPSTEAD AREA, ENGLAND · LONDON / CAVENDISH SQUARE

YEAR: 1819

CAST OF CHARACTERS (IN ORDER OF APPEARANCE)

ELIZA BROAD

HORACE (Eliza's Stepfather)

LYNN (Married to Horace)

SIR HENRY MARCH

ROBERTS (groom)

WILLIAM (footman)

MRS. TIBBIT (housekeeper)

DR. HARTCASTLE

HIGGINS (Arthur's butler)

ARTHUR REDWICK (Duke of Avon, Henry's cousin)

WILKINS

HOBBS (Pimp, Wilkins' associate)

ELLERT (Henry's former classmate)

ROBERT PEMBERTON, (Viscount Fairly, Henry's friend)

DUKE OF ELRIDGE (Suspected Traitor)

MILLIE (actress; Henry's former lover)

DAISIE (Henry's Chambermaid)

ALLEN STRATHEM (Henry's friend)

LORD ASTOR (Duke of Elridge's son)

EMILY (Henry's daughter)

JULIAN, ANDREW, AND BERTIE REDWICK (Arthur's sons)

THOMAS (footman)

JACK (Thomas's brother)

LADY GREYSON (Henry's godmother)

EARL OF YORK (Henry's friend)

SARA DAVIS (Earl of York's mistress)

ELIJAH (former soldier under Henry's command)

CHARLIE (messenger boy)

RILEY (Henry's friend)

RUTH REDWICK (Prussian Princess, Dowager Duchess of Avon, Henry's grandmother)

CECILIA (Emily's mother)

THE
INNKEEPER'S
DAUGHTER

CHAPTER ONE

"OY, MISSY . . . "

Horace's harsh voice came from behind her, raising the hair on the back of her neck. Eliza had made it to the top of the stairs leading to the back door, but there was no way she would make it out now.

"Don't ya run from me. I told ya t' go pack yar crap. Wilkins will be 'ere in an hour."

With Horace breathing down her neck, there was nothing to be gained by running. Eliza swung around to face him and did her best to stand her ground. "I told him no, and I'm telling you again: I'm not going with him!"

She braced for the backhand she knew would follow. Sure enough, pain exploded down the right side of her face, and she flew against the wall three steps behind her. God, how had her mother put up with this for six years?

Horace was of medium build, thickly muscled and broad-shouldered. If one didn't know what a brute he was, one might even think him handsome. But all Eliza could see was his lust for violence. She tried to straighten, but he pushed her back against the wall and ground his groin into her belly. He smelled of stale ale and sweat, and she could feel his manhood swelling as he rubbed against her.

"Wilkins paid me twenty quid for yar li'l virginal cunt, so 'e owns ya now."

Outrage overrode pain and disgust, and she pushed at him hard enough to force him back a step. "You sold me to Pig Face? You truly are despicable!"

His face twisted with hate and his open hand connected painfully with the other side of her face. Wilkins and Horace were birds of a feather, best mates so to speak, and calling Wilkins "Pig Face" was sure to get his goat—she should have thought of that.

"Always with the big bloody words. Ya're nothing but a tavern wench, but ya won't go with the customers and ya won't let me between them lily-white thighs. What the fuck did ya 'spect me ta do with ya?"

He was screaming at her at the top of his voice now. Through the haze of pain, Eliza heard Lynn chime in from the bottom of the stairs.

"Just lock 'er in the cellar, love. Let Wilkins deal with 'er when 'e gets 'ere."

Eliza ignored her. In for a penny, in for a pound. She might as well get him good and mad now—maybe Wilkins wouldn't want her if she was all bruised up. Correcting his pronunciation, she countered, "I *expected* you to ignore me, but even that was obviously hoping for too much."

Grabbing her by the hair, he dragged her down the stairs and along the corridor toward the store cellar door. "Ignore a bit of all right like you? Not bloody likely. But I 'ad enough of ya stalking about the place like ya bloody own it and looking down yar nose at me."

The cellar door loomed before her. Eliza tried with one hand to yank her hair out of Horace's grip and braced herself with the other against the door frame. She could not let him lock her up down there.

She knew why he was so keen to get rid of her—she was the only obstacle to his full ownership of the inn. Her father had left the inn to Eliza and her mother in his will. That meant, now her mother was gone, it should be hers. But if it bought her freedom from Wilkins, she would give up all claim to it. "You can have the inn. Just don't make me go with Pig Face."

Eliza couldn't quite keep the desperation out of her voice, and the way he chuckled in her ear confirmed how much he liked hearing it. "Too late, Liza, he paid me coin for ya."

Lynn cackled behind her. "He owns a mill and 'e's willin' ta marry ya. What the fuck's yar problem?"

With that she kicked Eliza hard in the small of her back, sending her flying down the short flight of stairs into the cellar, where she landed on a heap of coal. She heard something crack inside her, then a strange kind of prickly sound accompanied the darkness trying to claim her before she was pulled back by Lynn's shrill laughter. "Prince Charmin's all out of glass slippers, ya stupid cunt."

Eliza got up, white-hot rage giving her the courage to taunt them into killing her right then. A quick death would be better than having to endure Wilkins and dying at his filthy hands. "I'm gonna make you pay for this and everything you ever did to my mum, you greedy, wife-murdering clods."

Something solid slammed into her arm with such force it lifted her off her feet. She heard another crack and pain exploded all through her. This time she didn't think she would be able to get up again. She lay limp, waiting for Horace to deal her the deathblow. But it didn't come.

Instead she felt Horace's fetid breath fan over the side of her face as he whispered in her ear. "I wanna fuck ya and kick the living shit out of ya all at the same time, but Wilkins paid to be the first in yar snatch and 'e wants ya still breathin', so I'll leave ya to contemplate yar future . . . see, I know some big words too."

She heard him climb the stairs, slam the door, and throw the bolt. And then, when she was sure she was alone, she gave herself up to despair. Hot tears streaked down her aching face as she let herself rest against the mountain of coal at her back. Something warm and sticky seeped into her collar, and she wondered if the cut was big enough for her to bleed out.

"I'm sorry, Mum. I tried."

She lifted her eyes to the ceiling, wishing she wasn't so completely alone in the world. "But how do you expect me . . ." She frowned at the usually pitch-dark upper left corner of the room and caught her breath. The coal chute had been left open and the mountain of coal reached almost to the top. Horace couldn't have known. They certainly hadn't noticed it before. It was growing dark out, and the opening did not add much light. Could she get up? Did she dare to hope she could make it out of the cellar, away from the inn and the fate Horace had arranged for her?

She might as well try. She had nothing more to lose.

CHAPTER TWO

The last pale light of the day filtered through the bare trees onto the road and the two men traveling it in an elegant open sports carriage. The jingle of the harness preceded their passage, the sound of the horses' hooves muted by the leaves blanketing the road. One man did his best to nap on the high seat, but the vehicle's driver seemed to thoroughly enjoy his occupation and the way the gathering darkness drained the color from the forest around them. A light rain had fallen earlier, and the damp soil smelled rich and fertile. It was a perfect evening to drive the last remaining miles to London.

The driver was Sir Henry March, knighted for his services to the crown during the campaign against the Corsican megalomaniac—although nobody cared to speculate on what exactly he had done to warrant that knighthood.

Beyond being a knight of the realm, Henry was a classical scholar, a notorious libertine, and the responsible owner of four estates, who could trace his lineage to William the Conqueror.

He was a handsome man. His nose was straight, his sandy hair was cut short and reached down into short-cropped sideburns, and his lips were neither too thick nor too thin. However, his jaw had a determined set to it, and even when he was otherwise relaxed, his blue eyes were intense.

His person was presently obscured by a calf-length, multi-caped greatcoat and a carriage blanket thrown over his knees against the November chill. But it was generally agreed that he cut an impressive figure, even if his clothes tended to be comfortable rather than fashionable.

They had just left the lights of a small roadside inn behind them and were turning up the hill toward Hampstead Village when Henry became aware of a shadowy figure scurrying along the road in front of them.

At the sound of the horses, the woman visibly startled, then ran as if the hounds of hell were nipping at her heels. She was bent forward as if aged, and her gait was unsteady. But the face that turned over her shoulder to see who followed her was young and utterly terrified. In her haste to get away from whomever she was trying to outrun, she stumbled over the hem of her soiled and tattered skirts and yelped in pain when her knee hit the gravel on the road.

Henry found it impossible to ignore the woman's obvious distress. He stopped just ahead of her, handed the ribbons to his groom, and jumped down to see what he could do for her.

Even once he was standing next to her and she could see him clearly, she continued to look behind her as she tried to get back on her feet, as if unafraid of Henry but terrified at what could still be behind. Henry put a hand under her arm to help her up, but she winced and drew in a sharp breath. He tried gently placing his arm around her waist to steady her, eliciting another pained noise as she sagged against him.

She was small and light, and a sense of unease crept over him as he examined her more closely. Her waist was trim under his hand, and luscious dark curls framed her face—a face that showed unmistakable signs of a beating. Her lip was split and her jaw had begun to discolor. There was a welt on her forehead and her left eye was almost swollen shut. Her hands and clothes were blackened with what appeared to be coal dust, and she was clad in only a simple peasant skirt and blouse, while her shoes were missing altogether.

"Good God," Henry breathed. He quickly decided, whatever her story was, he could not turn his back on her. "You're injured; can I take you somewhere? To someone who will help you?"

She shook her head, which obviously hurt, and squeezed out between clenched teeth, "I just need to get away."

The girl obviously wasn't thinking clearly, so Henry probed for more information. "From whom or where?"

She was barely holding herself upright now, but her voice was full of contempt. "My stepfather at the inn." She indicated behind her and sagged farther against him as she lost her footing again. Henry could feel as well as see her injuries were serious.

"Did he do this to you?"

She almost spat out her next words. "Him and his new missus. But I'll not marry that bastard Wilkins. I'll die first."

She then truly spat on the ground for emphasis, her eyes blazing with a need to defy her fate that struck a chord with Henry.

He answered her with a calm he did not feel. "Well, if you stay out here alone and in this state for much longer, you probably will." He smiled down at her, hoping to reassure her. "You had better come with me so my housekeeper can have a look at you."

She twisted to look at him for a moment as if to assess whether she would get herself into even worse trouble by going with him, then shrugged. "I think I'd rather the devil I don't know."

Henry couldn't suppress a wry grin. "That's the spirit."

He led her to the curricle without further delay, and when her knees buckled, he simply lifted her into his arms and boosted her up to Roberts on the seat. She was too light for her frame, and he wondered what other methods her stepfather had employed to bend her to his will.

Pulling himself up onto the driver's seat next to her, he realized he had neglected to introduce himself.

"I'm Henry March, by the way. Can you tell me your name?"

"Eliza." Her voice was weak now, the fight having gone completely out of her.

Henry wrapped the carriage blanket around her before he took the ribbons from his groom, Roberts, who then swung himself around onto the box seat behind. Henry urged the team into a trot, despite the gathering darkness and the girl's unsteady hold on consciousness. He tucked her uninjured arm through his and urged her to lean on him as he drove them toward London and his Mayfair home.

THEY ARRIVED AT THE TOWN house on Cavendish Square a little over an hour later with the girl barely conscious. Roberts jumped down first to knock on the door, then took the horses' heads, while Henry nudged Eliza awake. She straightened enough for him to climb down to the pavement, but as he turned to assist her, she almost fell off the high seat, so he lifted her down.

The door opened as Henry carried the girl up the front steps. William, the footman, had no trouble comprehending the urgency of the situation and preceded his master and former captain to the first available guest room on the second floor. There, Henry entrusted Eliza into the care of Mrs. Tibbit, his housekeeper, who had appeared at his side halfway up the stairs.

Mrs. Tibbit was an efficient woman with a kind heart and a serious dislike of anybody who treated another female with violence. Having left the girl in such capable hands, Henry retreated to his private sitting room down the hall to pour himself a stiff drink.

MRS. TIBBIT FOUND HIM THERE less than half an hour later, slouched into one of the big leather armchairs by the fire, visiting with his old friend Shakespeare. She spared a disapproving glance for the tomes littering the floor around him and the booted feet comfortably propped on the chair opposite. Looking up from his book, Henry grinned at the old retainer's obvious disapproval, secure in her affection for him. Mrs. Tibbit shook her head, acknowledging that at thirty-one years of age he was too old for her to scold, and heaved a heavy sigh. "I think we best call the doctor, if you don't mind, sir."

"Oh, are the girl's injuries beyond your capability, Mrs. Tibbit?" he teased gently.

The narrow-eyed look his housekeeper bestowed on him said much about what she thought of him questioning her abilities and teasing at a time like this. "Well, sir, we cleaned her, and I patched her cuts and bruises as best I could with basilicum powder and arnica cream, and I'm making her an infusion for the pain. But I can't set any broken bones, and the gash to the back of her head is too big for me to stitch."

Henry winced at this matter-of-fact description of Eliza's injuries. "By all means, call for the doctor, but make sure nobody mentions I brought home an injured girl. The brute who did this to her may well be looking for her."

Mrs. Tibbit's round eyes blazed with indignation and the desire to protect the mistreated girl. "I'll send William to the doctor and make sure everybody keeps their mouths shut down at the pub. The poor mite! Do you know who did this?"

All hints of playfulness had left Henry's demeanor. "She says it was her stepfather and his wife. And she mentioned a man called Wilkins they want her to marry."

The housekeeper nodded as if that explained everything and turned toward the door. "Well, they won't find her here. I'll make sure of that."

Henry knew she ruled her kingdom belowstairs like a benevolent queen, so he didn't doubt their guest's safety. "Thank you. And send the good doctor to me after he has done what he can for Miss Eliza."

Mrs. Tibbit headed for the door without being dismissed and threw her next words over her shoulder with complete disregard for proper address and ceremony. "Will do."

Henry grinned and mused—not for the first time—that her familiarity would not be tolerated in any other household. But then again, they had known each other since he was five months old, and he supposed it was progress she no longer told him to sit up straight and pick up after himself.

Two hours later, Henry was lingering in the dining room over his after-dinner cigar when Dr. Hartcastle found him. The good doctor took the glass of port Henry offered, confirmed Mrs. Tibbit's assessment of the broken arm, and lamented that it had taken seven stitches to close the gash at the nape of the girl's neck. Beyond that, the doctor reported two broken ribs and revealed Eliza's dizziness was caused by a concussion. Recommending she stay abed for at least a fortnight, he informed Henry he had given Eliza laudanum for the pain. He also left arnica drops to be taken three times daily, to combat any internal injuries.

Henry was assured he would return the next day to check on the girl's progress. Before he left, the good doctor took it upon himself to tell Henry earnestly that, in his opinion, Henry had saved the young woman's life.

Dr. Hartcastle said it as if Henry ought to be congratulated, but having noticed her at the side of the road, Henry could not have left her to her fate; and now that she was under his roof, he felt responsible for her. It seemed she had no one else. Henry resolved to find out Eliza's full story as soon as possible.

ONCE DR. HARTCASTLE LEFT, HENRY climbed the stairs to look in on his guest. He entered the comfortable second-floor bedroom quietly and found Mrs. Tibbit sitting by the fire doing her mending. The bed in this room, although big enough and made of rich, dark cherry wood, had no curtains to be drawn around it. In order not to disturb the girl's slumber, Mrs. Tibbit had angled her armchair to shade the single candle she had lit so she could work.

She smiled up at Henry. "She's resting easy now."

Henry stood next to the bed and gently brushed a dark brown curl out of the girl's bruised and battered face. "I have seen some truly horrendous things on and off the battlefield in Spain and France, but this somehow seems worse."

Mrs. Tibbit snorted her disgust. "Ay, there's no justifying this one. Can't blame it on war or hate between enemies. The person who was supposed to keep her safe did that."

Henry nodded and idly fingered a silver locket that had been placed on the nightstand. "Is this hers?" he asked, holding it up.

"Ay, I found it pinned to the inside of her corset. It's nice work and there's a lock of hair in it."

He studied the fine floral motif engraved on both sides of the ornament and opened it to look for an inscription. It was a long shot, since only people who could read and write bothered to inscribe their possessions, but when he lifted out the lock of coarse brown hair, he found a dedication: *All my love, Ted* and the date *1799*.

Had it been a betrothal present? Perhaps Ted was the girl's father and the locket had belonged to her mother. It seemed likely. When had things started to go so terribly wrong for Eliza?

He placed the locket back on the night stand. The more he found out about the girl, the more curious he became. Turning to Mrs. Tibbit, he instructed softly, "Make sure she knows it's safe as soon as she wakes up. She obviously went through some trouble to keep it from her despicable stepfather."

Mrs. Tibbit nodded without bothering to glance up from her stitching as he moved to the door.

"And get one of the girls to sit with her so you can get some rest. Good night, Tibby."

She smiled at the use of his childhood name for her. "Will do. Good night."

WHILE ELIZA SLEPT THE NEXT day away in a laudanum haze, Henry caught up on his affairs. The autumn round of his estates had taken him from Brighton in the south, to Berkshire and Lincolnshire, all the way to Norfolk, and back to London. It was no small thing to oversee the running of four prosperous estates, but besides his land, Henry had several financial investments also demanding his attention. In the six weeks of his absence, a veritable mountain of mail had accumulated on his desk, and Henry promised himself he would give it its due attention right after he had completed his duty to the crown.

In that spirit, a summons from his superior to give his report in person was heeded first and without delay. Once the Old Man was satisfied everything had been done to strike yet another suspect off their list, Henry made his bow to his godmother and then paid his man of business a visit to discuss his finances.

The following day, after checking on his houseguest and finding her still deep in slumber, Henry cloistered himself in his library to sort through his mountain of mail. His spectacles on his nose, he worked systematically through the pile, answering queries as needed, and was glad when he reached for the last missive around four in the afternoon. Recognizing his cousin Arthur's handwriting as well as his ducal coat of arms on the seal, Henry smiled at the thought the missive might contain news of his daughter, Emily. But instead it was an open invitation to dine at his cousin's residence as soon as Henry returned to London. Henry buried his disappointment and sent a note to the ducal palace on St. James's Square, informing his cousin of his return. Two hours later, Henry strolled through the now-dark but still bustling streets of Mayfair to join his cousin Arthur, the Duke of Avon, for dinner.

A BLUE- AND SILVER-LIVERIED FOOTMAN ushered Henry into the magnificent marble foyer, illuminated by the refracting light of a chandelier. There he was greeted by the family's butler, Higgins.

"Good evening, Sir Henry. His Grace awaits you in his study."

Henry handed his hat, walking stick, and greatcoat to the aging retainer and let his eyes wander over his mother's ancestors lining the walls. "Thank you, Higgins. No need to announce me, I know my way."

Higgins bowed. "Of course you do, sir." But he still preceded Henry down the hall to announce him. "Sir Henry, Your Grace!"

Arthur Redwick rose from behind his desk and strode forward with his hand outstretched in greeting. "Henry, I'm so glad you could join me tonight."

Henry smiled warmly and shook his cousin's hand. "Hello, Arthur. How is everyone at Avon?"

The Duke of Avon was a somber man by nature, his countenance perfectly suited to his political aspirations. He was a decade older than Henry, but the years had been good to him. The duke had hazel eyes and was perhaps an inch shorter than Henry, but shared his broad shoulders, sandy hair, and even features.

"Last I heard, everyone was in excellent spirits. Did Emily forget to write again?"

Henry followed his host to the sofa in front of the fire and took the brandy Arthur poured for him. "I had a letter from her in Norfolk, but that was two weeks ago."

"Ah, my information is only three days old. Your trip seemed rather longer than usual."

Henry heard the underlying question and contemplated how much to tell his cousin. Arthur was one of the few people who knew what Henry had done during the war, what he still did for the crown, but for everybody's safety, it was better to keep his own counsel in this instance. "I just had to stop off in Norwich to tie up a few loose ends."

The duke shot Henry a sharp look but only nodded, and a moment later, Higgins entered to announce dinner was ready to be served.

They shared an excellent meal and pleasant conversation, but never ventured beyond the commonplace, until the dishes had been cleared away and the servants had left them alone with their brandy and a box of fine cigars.

Arthur took a sip of the amber liquid in his glass and lifted his finger. "By the bye, Henry, you may have to write to your Emily again concerning her tendency to outwit her groom. The poor man does his best to keep up with her, but he reported last week that she had gotten away from him three times in the last month. Bertie is usually a willing participant in her adventures, but he is only two years older than she, and at fourteen he is not capable of protecting her, nor himself for that matter."

Henry watched his cousin carefully. His daughter's regular bids for freedom were nothing new, and neither were the duchess's pleas to curb her wild streak, but for the request to come from the duke piqued his interest. "Oh, any particular reason for your concern?"

The duke shot him a wry smile. "Not much gets past you, does it?"

Henry grinned in response and waited patiently for his cousin to come to the point.

The duke rested his elbows on the linen-covered table, steepled his fingers in front of him, and weighed his words like only a politician could. "Under normal circumstances I would not be concerned, but I am working on a bill that will be contentious, and it has come to my attention that questions have been asked about my family, particularly the comings and goings of the children."

Henry didn't move, his brow slightly furrowed in concern. "You think someone is trying to intimidate you by threatening our family?"

Arthur shook his head decisively. "No threats have been made. Just a few questions strange enough to prompt my stable master to report them to me."

Henry moved forward, mirroring his cousin's pose. "How strange are the questions, and who is asking them?"

Arthur met Henry's gaze steadily. "The questions are about the children. Where they go and when, and if they ever do it alone. As to who is asking: a groom from the livery stable in Woodborough. He is related to one of my footmen and therefore a fairly frequent visitor."

Henry considered that for a moment. "And you couldn't just put a stop to his visits?"

Arthur tapped his steepled fingers against each other and pursed his lips. "I would rather not curtail visits to the estate, especially so close to Christmas. Happy servants make for a well-run house, after all."

Henry's mouth quirked up in a crooked smile. "Besides, that wouldn't stop them from meeting in the pub. I see what you mean; it's best to tell the children not to venture out alone. I don't suppose you want to tell me what your bill is about."

"I would rather not," was the duke's only response.

Henry knew his cousin well enough to know he had said as much on the subject as he was willing to, and Henry respected that. The whole thing was probably nothing more than a few gossiping servants. He wasn't worried about his daughter's safety, but he would write to

Emily all the same. There was no point in tempting fate.

The two men enjoyed their smoke and each other's company for a while longer until the duke pleaded fatigue and Henry went home to write a letter to Emily.

CHAPTER THREE

THE THIRD DAY AFTER HENRY BROUGHT ELIZA to his house, she seemed somewhat improved, but her mind was still clouded by the laudanum, making conversation almost impossible. Henry sat with her for a while in her darkened room and gently tried to ask her a few questions, but when she nodded off on him for the third time, he admitted defeat.

On the fourth day, however, Mrs. Tibbit sought out Henry in the breakfast room at the back of the house to inform him their guest had refused the morning dose of laudanum and was sitting up in bed. Mrs. Tibbit further reported proudly that Eliza had consumed a sizable breakfast, and then left him to his morning coffee.

Encouraged by the news, Henry decided on a visit to his charge.

WHAT HE FOUND WAS A young woman so remarkably pretty, despite the bruises in various shades of yellow and green, that Henry paused on the threshold, admiring the picture in front of him.

The two tall sash windows let in autumn's golden sunlight and gave the chamber a bright and airy feel. Lace curtains added a feminine touch to soften the effect of light green drapes, white walls, and cherry wood furniture. Mrs. Tibbit sat by the window with her mending, chatting to the girl.

Smiling, Henry leaned against the door frame in his shirt sleeves, tan-colored breeches, and waistcoat. Eliza's shiny dark brown curls tumbling all around her were in stark contrast to the crisp white of the pillows she was propped up against. Her features were delicate and animated, and her eyes, as they turned toward him, were a clear and luminous brown. She reached out her hand with an answering smile.

"You are Sir Henry, aren't you."

It was more of a statement than a question, and he nodded in answer.

"You brought me here, and the doctor says I would've died if you hadn't found me, so I guess I owe you my life." She extended her hand farther to offer it to him, the gesture clearly an effort. "How can I ever thank you? Just saying it hardly seems enough."

Henry moved across the room and took her outstretched hand, uncomfortable with the signs of pain on her beautiful face. Eliza shook his hand, but was at a loss as to what else to say, so she lifted his hand and kissed it.

Taken aback by the gesture, Henry retracted his hand and hastened to assure her, "You don't owe me anything; I only did what any decent human being would have done."

A fierceness entered her eyes he didn't know how to read. "No, you saved my life."

"I'm sure—" he started.

But Eliza shook her head, suddenly looking utterly desolate, her voice barely a whisper. "Nobody helped me when they did this to me. Not even the people I've known all my life, the people I thought were my friends."

Henry was close enough to hear the hitch in her voice and leaned down to place a gentle hand on the crown of her head. She raised her eyes, bright with unshed tears, then swallowed hard and managed a tiny smile. Henry could not help but admire her courage and spirit, and wondered what it would be like to see that spirit fly.

"From now on you have friends willing to defend you, should the need arise again."

Mrs. Tibbit seconded the notion with a resolute nod, but Eliza searched his face for a moment, as if unsure whether he meant what he said. Evidently there was nothing in his expression to urge caution, so she relaxed back into her pillows.

Henry pulled a chair next to the bed and seated himself. "You told me your stepfather beat you in order to force you to marry somebody by the name of Wilkins. Can you tell me how you came to be in such a wretched situation?"

She shook her head in resignation and looked up at him. "It's not so unusual a story. Are you sure you want to hear the whole sorry mess?"

He held her gaze, and his expression softened. "I find I have a need to know."

Eliza had no reason to trust people, but his eyes held a smile, and she felt safe with him in his house. She found she wanted him to know her story, but where to begin? She decided on her name. "My name's Eliza Broad. Everybody calls me Liza, but I like Eliza better."

Henry grinned at the hint of challenge in her statement. "Duly noted, Eliza."

She smiled her appreciation, and he nodded for her to continue.

"I was born in The Cat and Fiddle just outside Hampstead, and I remember being happy there before my dad died when I was ten. He left the inn to my mum, and from what I could see, she made a good go of it. But it's hard for a woman alone to keep order in a busy taproom, so she hired a man who took care of all the rowdies and the heavy work."

Henry noticed Eliza made a credible effort to keep the countrified lilt out of her voice and silently commended whoever had taught her.

"He was always respectful to her, did his job well, and was even nice to me, so when he asked my mum to marry him, she said yes, thinking it would be a good thing for us." Eliza's jaw set in a hard line, and all joy was sucked out of her eyes. "It didn't take Horace long after the ceremony to show his true colors. He didn't like that my mum knew her letters and was teaching them to me. He didn't like that she was better at keeping the books. He didn't like when other men looked at her, and most of all he didn't like me."

Her voice dropped to a monotone, and she seemed completely absorbed in ironing pleats into the bedcovers with her fingernails. "And then the beatings started. I could stay out of his way, mostly. But my mum, she was his wife and had the inn to run, which of course he now considered to be his. Six years of dodging his fists and listening to him do things to her in the room next to mine."

Eliza swallowed hard before she pushed out the next sentence. "Her eyes were dead long before he pushed her down the stairs and broke her neck."

Henry's jaw clenched tight, his fists itching to seek revenge for her. But when he looked across the room at Mrs. Tibbit, whose eyes were filled with the kind of bitter comprehension that came from experience, he quelled his violent thoughts in favor of turning his attention back to Eliza.

Eliza's head was bowed, and a tear had found its way down her nose. She wiped it with the back of her hand, took a deep breath, and continued. "I half expected Horace to start in on me, but he took up with one of the barmaids before my mum was even buried. Not that that would stop him from tupping someone else, but he is always quick to see a chance to make a few bob. When Wilkins asked him for me—even though I had told him 'no' more than once—he apparently sold me to the sod."

Henry briefly wondered how much experience she might have with the opposite sex, but dismissed the thought as unimportant at the moment.

Eliza's eyes blazed with anger when she looked up at him again. "I kept refusing to go with him, and that made Horace stinking mad. Turns out he had already taken Wilkins's coin and had no plans to give it back on my account, so he and Lynn beat me and locked me in the cellar. I guess they thought when Wilkins came for me, I would go with him just to get away from them. But I know Wilkins. He's a big burly brute who's already buried two wives. Beats his horse and his dog too. I wasn't going to stick around to wait for him to come and use me as a punching bag and God knows what else. I climbed up the coal chute and stumbled away as fast and best I could, and that's when you found me."

Eliza met Henry's gaze with gratitude in her eyes, but also weariness. The telling of her story had taken its toll, and she obviously worried they might be looking for her. Henry covered both of her hands with his. "It's all right, they won't find you here."

It seemed a woefully inadequate thing to say in light of what she had suffered, but she smiled her appreciation and held on to his hand when he rose.

"Rest now! I'll come back this afternoon, and we can play a hand of cards, or perhaps you would like me to read to you."

Her eyes lit up. "Oh, do you have any books other than the Bible? That's the only book my mum had."

Henry smiled at her excitement, eager to share his beloved books with her. "I might have one or two."

At this Mrs. Tibbit gave a shout of laughter. "Ha, one or two thousand he means. I have to keep the bloody things dust- and mold-free."

"Come now, Mrs. Tibbit, you like the occasional novel!" he teased as he strolled out of the room.

WHILE ELIZA POURED HER STORY out to Henry, across town, in a little street just off the Strand, a burly, surly-looking man pulled up outside a busy pub, climbed off his cart, and handed the reins to a street urchin with the promise of a penny. He stepped into the dark interior of the bar and headed straight for a table in the back.

The dapper-looking gentleman who sat there nursing a pint eyed him with polite inquiry. "What brings ya to town, Wilkins? It ain't market day, and I don't recall sendin' for ya."

Wilkins sat without waiting for an invitation, causing the other man to raise a displeased eyebrow. "I 'ave to talk to ya, Hobbs! That's what."

Hobbs made a gesture as if to invite Wilkins to sit. Wilkins's brow wrinkled in confusion, which made Hobbs smile. "By all means, mate, talk!"

Wilkins pulled on his less-than-pristine neckcloth and tried to get the barmaid's attention. "Got t' wet me whistle first."

Hobbs, with growing impatience, snapped his fingers and commanded, "Bets, get the bloke a pint."

Wilkins, oblivious to Hobbs's mood, nodded his thanks and

geared up to unburden himself. "Remember you tellin' me to come to ya if I ever 'ad a favor to ask?"

Hobbs declined his head slowly, a sly smile taking up residence on his lips. "Ya want that virgin we talked about?"

Wilkins scratched the stubble on his chin. "Well, I got me own, but the stupid bint ran away before I could pick 'er up, and now Horace won't give me twenty quid back. Says if I want it I should get it off the toff that picked 'er up off the street. But all I found out from the lads in Hampstead is that some Sir somethin' or other picked 'er up and that 'e lives somewhere in the posh parts near the park. I need ya to 'elp me find Liza."

At the mention of the girl's name, sudden interest flickered in Hobbs's eyes. "That wouldn't be the same pretty li'l package with the dark curly 'air you told me to stay clear of, would it?"

Wilkins just nodded while Hobbs fiddled with one of the many fobs on his watch chain. His eyes were cold and calculating. "If I know anythin' about them rich pricks, then she ain't no virgin no more. You still want 'er anyways?"

Wilkins smiled a rather disturbing smile. "Horace gave 'er a good beatin' before he locked 'er up. She won't be pretty enough for anybody to want 'er for a while."

Hobbs assessed Wilkins for a moment and then adjusted his cuffs and sleeves with an air of finality. "All right, mate. I'll send me boys out and 'elp ya find 'er. But if it turns out she spread 'er legs for 'er knight in shinin' fucking armor, I'll give ya yar twenty quid and let ya 'elp me introduce 'er to the trade. Sound good?"

Wilkins grinned. "Too right, it does."

The two men shook on the deal and called for another pint.

As promised, Henry returned to Eliza's bedroom in the afternoon with a selection of books and a deck of cards. He deposited these treasures on the bed, and Eliza immediately seized Henry's beautifully bound and illustrated copy of *The Arabian Nights*.

It was a heavy book, leather-bound and oversized. Eliza would have had trouble holding it at the best of times, let alone turning the pages and reading it, but with two broken ribs it was impossible. She made a valiant effort, but had to admit defeat when the pain radiating from her ribcage threatened to take her breath away. Realizing her dilemma, Henry took the book from her and arranged his chair so he could hold up the volume while she studied the pictures gracing each page.

Completely fascinated, Eliza trailed gentle fingers over a picture of Aladdin in his cave. "I didn't know books like this existed. Look at the way the picture is drawn, and the colors so bright."

Henry corrected her gently, hoping she would be as interested as he was in finding out how things were made. "It's a print, in fact. The drawing is carved into wood, then dipped in ink and pressed on the page, and then other carved blocks of wood are used to fill in the colors."

Eliza looked at him with wide eyes full of longing. "That's amazing. It's the most beautiful thing I ever saw. Would you let me read the stories when I'm well enough to hold the book?"

Henry saw no reason for her to wait that long and took it upon himself to read the first story to her. She listened with rapt attention, her eyes sparkling with excitement, her lips parted in awe, and Henry could not think of a place he would rather be. When she finally fell asleep, he left the book on her nightstand and tiptoed out of the room.

Having already attended to his urgent business, and with

most of his friends out hunting in the country, Henry was at leisure to spend a considerable amount of time with his intriguing houseguest. They whiled away many hours together, during which Henry shared some of his favorite stories with Eliza. Scheherazade's beguiling tales were followed by *Rob Roy* and then the charming characters populating Miss Austen's work.

When they could find a third player for commerce, or even a fourth for whist, they played cards, and so the days of Eliza's convalescence were spent happily enough.

Once Eliza could sit up for longer periods of time, Henry taught her how to play chess, finding her a worthy opponent. For the times when he had to attend to his affairs, he found lightweight volumes of popular novels, which she devoured with increasing speed.

She loved Shakespeare and laughed at Byron. Mrs. Radcliffe's overwrought romantic heroines made her huff with impatience. But when Henry brought her a copy of *Frankenstein*, she read through the night in spellbound horror and bombarded him with questions concerning the scientific feasibility of the book's premise the next morning. Henry did his best not to laugh and reassured her that, to his knowledge, no one had attempted to make a monster out of body parts yet. He introduced her to the literary notion of an allegory, and from there they went on to discuss the Greek myth of Prometheus. Eliza concluded that both tales were not unlike that of "The Sorcerer's Apprentice," a story she had heard from her father many times.

In short, she showed intelligence and understanding, and Henry felt more drawn to her each day.

CHAPTER FOUR

IT TOOK TWO MORE WEEKS BEFORE THE DOC-
tor allowed Eliza out of bed. She was positively giddy at the prospect
of ending her confinement and exploring Sir Henry's house beyond
the beautiful chamber in which she had spent the past fortnight and
more.

Having ventured to the window once or twice on her way back
from a trip to the chamber pot, Eliza had watched a few red-golden
leaves fall in the square below, but she had never lingered long.

She would have liked to sit on the dainty chair in front of the
writing desk between the two windows to watch the children at play
below, but sitting had proved far more uncomfortable then standing
or even walking. What she had glimpsed, however, had convinced her
the houses around the square were rather grand, and it made her all
the more curious about the house she was in.

Henry, always willing to abet her curiosity, suggested she come
downstairs for afternoon tea and perhaps a turn about the garden if
she felt strong enough. But by the time Henry knocked on Eliza's
door to escort her to the drawing room, a cold and gloomy drizzle had
replaced the earlier sunshine.

Eliza had dressed with the help of the maid, donning one of the
gowns Henry had urged Mrs. Tibbit to buy for her. The soft blue wool
dress Eliza had chosen for the occasion was the most luxurious gar-

ment she had ever worn, and she couldn't help but feel pretty in it. Dressing had been an adventure in itself since her arm was still in a sling, but her ribs for the most part felt better.

According to the doctor, it would take no longer then six weeks for her to be healed completely, and Mrs. Tibbit had promised to help her find a good position in a respectable house, but whether that would be enough to keep her safe from Wilkins and Horace was anybody's guess.

Eliza wasn't naïve enough to think she could remain in a single gentleman's household beyond her recovery from her injuries, so she was grateful for the offer of assistance in finding work. With an uncertain future ahead of her, Eliza intended to fully enjoy the situation in which she presently found herself. After all, Sir Henry was handsome and kind, and for Eliza from The Cat and Fiddle to be convalescing in his Mayfair home with him for company was a tale almost worthy of Scheherazade telling her bloodthirsty sultan.

Eliza opened the door to Henry, hoping to please him with her appearance as much as with her progress in regaining her health.

Henry, for once wearing a full suit, was resplendent in an exquisitely cut dark blue jacket, a gray waistcoat, and gray pantaloons. His pristine white neckcloth was held together by a gold pin, and gold cufflinks winked from his wrists. He sketched her a little bow and offered his arm for the walk downstairs, surprising her with his courtly manners. "Good afternoon. Are you ready to depart, Miss Broad?" Henry smiled down at her, acting like a proper escort while letting an admiring eye roam over her figure in the form-fitting gown. "And may I just say how well you look in blue."

Eliza attempted a small curtsy, her eyes sparkling with amusement as well as appreciation of his gallantry. "Why, thank you, Sir Henry! And may I remark how respectable you look with your necktie all tidy and your jacket all buttoned up."

He grinned at her with the easy camaraderie they had built over the past fortnight. "Cheeky! Is it so wrong to want to be comfortable in my own home?"

She grinned right back at him. "It's a good thing I'm not some simpering society miss. I might have fainted seeing you strutting about in your shirtsleeves in my bedroom." She gave him the same kind of surreptitious once-over he had indulged in earlier. "But you do clean up rather nicely."

Henry's laughter filled the corridor as they strolled toward the front staircase. He stopped, stood back a step, and took another appraising look at her.

She was slender and of medium height; her breasts sat high and filled out her dress to perfection. The bruises were all gone now, and the big brown eyes dominating her face held a hint of mischief. Her dark curls shone in the light of the sconces on the landing and were held back off her face with two combs at her temples and then left to fall down her back in a luxurious cascade.

Her gown tied at the front left side with three bows, the high V-neck collar revealing only the dimple at the base of her throat, and the soft white cotton underdress spilled from beneath the hem and sleeves. Tan kid half-boots peeked out from under her gown, and the white ruffle at her wrists fell almost to the base of her long fingers. It was a dress infinitely suited to a chilly late November day, but somehow the sheer modesty of it made the girl inside it all the more enticing.

"So do you, Eliza. So do you."

He raised her hand over their heads and twirled her in front of him, and she let out a startled burst of laughter. It was a beautiful sound, clear as a bell and warm as sunshine, and he resolved to make her laugh again before the day was done.

"Shall we, Mademoiselle?" he said, indicating the stairs.

"By all means," she replied, copying his accent and manner, laughter still shining bright in her eyes.

He wrapped her hand around his arm once more and led her downstairs, across the black-and-white checkerboard marble of the foyer and into the drawing room where Mrs. Tibbit had prepared tea.

AFTERNOON TEA WAS ALL ELIZA had imagined it might be. The silver teapot had a candle beneath it so the tea never cooled, and it pivoted on hinges so one didn't have to pick up the heavy pot in order to pour tea into delicate china cups. The food was laid out on a three-tiered silver platter with an ornate handle on top and ranged from tiny, crustless cucumber sandwiches to warm scones with clotted cream, to dainty little custard tarts that concealed a juicy plum in their center.

The food Eliza had been served in her room was no less delicious, but the luxury of eating a meal in the afternoon, when she had had lunch and would no doubt be eating dinner, turned it into an indulgence.

Henry fell into the role of the visiting gentleman, keeping up a stream of inane small talk about the weather and what flowers one might still find at this time of year. Eliza played the prim little society miss, doing her best to pour tea for Sir Henry just as it had been described in one of the novels he'd lent her. It was easy to imagine herself a lady in Henry's exquisite drawing room, and easier still to enjoy his gentle teasing.

"That is one splendid cup of tea, my dear."

Eliza thanked him with a little nod of her head. "Can I interest you in a cucumber sandwich? They are delicious."

Henry surveyed the food tray carefully before he turned back to Eliza. "I shall indulge my sweet tooth. Those custard tarts look rather good."

Considering the size of the tiny tartlets, Eliza placed three of them on a dainty blue-and-white china plate matching their tea cups, added a small silver dessert fork, and placed a napkin under the dish before she presented it proudly to Henry.

Henry took the plate and spread the napkin over his knee, but discreetly placed the fork back onto the tray. He leaned in and whispered conspiratorially, "Tarts are considered finger food, no fork required." Then he winked at her and bit into one of his treats.

Eliza blushed at the mistake, but smiled at his antics and helped herself to another cucumber sandwich. A thought occurred to her. "Sir Henry, if you could, who, out of all the people we read about, would you like to have to tea?"

Henry didn't even hesitate. "Rob Roy! He seems an interesting fellow."

She laughed. "You might have a difficult time getting him to take you up on your invitation; you are English, after all!"

He leaned his head to the side for a moment, considering. "Good point! Who would you want to ask to tea? Mr. Darcy?"

Eliza shook her head in dismay. "Too broody. He would scare me."

"Mr. Bingley then?"

She shook her head again, but a tiny smile played around her lips. "Too fickle!"

Henry raised an eyebrow and tapped his lip, trying to think. "Dr. Frankenstein?"

Eliza made a big show of swallowing hard but couldn't quite stop the smile from broadening on her face. "I'm not sure he would be fit company for tea. He seems a little unhinged."

Henry huffed, feigning impatience with the game. "Don't tell me you want to have William Collins for tea?"

Laughing out loud, Eliza crossed her eyes at him, which made him laugh.

"Well, who then?"

She smiled and spread her hands out to the side, a little surprised Henry hadn't guessed. "Colonel Brandon, of course."

"Ah, the sensible choice."

It was Eliza's turn to huff a little. "Sensible maybe, but he is trustworthy and steadfast, a good friend to all around him." Eliza gave a triumphant nod, believing the subject closed, and helped herself to a scone.

Henry was surprised by her choice, but had to admit he liked it. He, too, would have picked the colonel as the best man out of all the characters they had encountered over the past weeks. Eliza might have been young, but her upbringing had obviously given her a unique perspective on life—and on men.

With their attention back on their food, Henry watched Eliza's fascinated awe as she took in her surroundings.

The chair Eliza sat in was of dark mahogany. Its legs and dainty arms were inlaid with ivory, and the seat and back were upholstered in a light blue velvet. Two sofas and the side tables were made in the same style, with clean, elegant lines. The exquisite furniture was arranged before a white marble fireplace that had a twin on the opposite side of the room with a writing desk close to it. Above both fireplaces hung huge eight-paneled, gilt-framed mirrors, seemingly extending the room into infinity.

There were three almost-floor-to-ceiling windows facing out to the square, bracketed by silver-blue drapes, and the greenery on the outside was mirrored by a few evergreens in brass containers placed here and there around the room.

The intricate parquet floor was partly covered by a large blue-and-cream Berber carpet. The walls were covered in light blue silk and adorned with painted scenes from around London. Studying them as best she could from her seat by the fire, Eliza declared the Thames at moonlight her favorite.

It felt as if she had stepped into her very own fairy tale. They enjoyed their tea and cakes, bantering back and forth, and Henry did his best to make Eliza comfortable in his stately drawing room. But had Eliza not been as comfortable as she was with Henry at this point, she would have been utterly awestruck by his elevated station in life, brought home by the sheer elegance of his home. She had nothing to compare this room to, but she couldn't imagine anything more beautiful. That was, until Henry decided to show her the rest of the reception rooms on the first floor, since the rain now falling made a walk in the garden inadvisable.

There was a rose-themed sitting room at the front of the house, also overlooking the square. It was a much more feminine room with its floral prints and rounded furniture, but it was no less elegant than the formal drawing room.

A yellow-and-cream breakfast room at the back of the house

looked cozy and promised to be full of sunlight in the mornings. There was also a formal dining room with a table so big Eliza thought it likely thirty people could comfortably be seated around it.

From the music room, French doors led out to a terrace and the garden below, giving the room a light, open feel. Eliza couldn't help but marvel at the pianoforte, never having seen one before. So Henry sat and played a Beethoven sonata for her while she rested, leaning up against the instrument.

But the library was the room that really took Eliza's breath away. The place was huge, running from the front of the house all the way to the back. It was also three windows wide on either side. There were two doors into the room, one from the short corridor running parallel to the front of the house and one from the back corridor. Opposite each entrance was a gleaming black marble fireplace with a jewel-like landscape painting above it while the rest of the walls were covered floor to ceiling with oak bookshelves.

The whole room was held in browns, ocher, and reds, with hints of brass and burnished gold. There were sofas and armchairs, upholstered in leather, grouped by the front windows and on either side of the fireplaces, as well as a large table in the center of the room. A big desk and the most voluminous wing-back chair Eliza had ever seen sat by the back windows. The floors were covered with red, cream, and black patterned Persian rugs, and the windows were draped in ocher velvet held in place by silky tassels.

Despite its size, the room was warm and inviting, and the moment she entered, Eliza knew she would spend most of her time in it, if she were allowed. Henry watched her intently as she turned about the room, inspecting some volumes on the bookshelves and looking at a book of prints of exotic animals he had left on the table for her to find. But what really drew her attention was the globe standing in the corner by the back window. Her eyes found his. "What's this round thing?"

Henry abandoned his post by the door and strolled over to join her. "A globe. It shows you where places are in the world." He turned it and found England. "This is where we are."

She leaned closer to see where he was pointing: the picture of a town on an irregular brown and green shape. "You mean that tiny little town here is supposed to be London?"

Henry smiled at her wide-eyed disbelief. "It's a representation. All the green and brown parts with the towns and mountains painted on them are land. And all the blue area with the ships and fish in it are oceans."

He circled his finger around the British Isles, naming places as he went. "That's Ireland, that's England, and here is Scotland, where *Rob Roy* is set."

Understanding dawned as Eliza's gaze followed Henry's fingers across the globe. All the places in the world could be found on this painted wooden ball. "Can you show me Italy? You told me Romeo and Juliet's Verona is a real place."

Henry turned the globe and pointed to the north of the Italian Peninsula. She studied the area for a moment, then another city caught her interest.

"Venice is in Italy?"

"Yes, it is a city state on the Italian Peninsula."

"Amazing, I had no idea. Where is Arabia . . . or is it a made-up country like the stories?"

He smiled at her and turned the globe again. "No, indeed, Arabia is rather a big country full of sand and Beduins. They make nice carpets," he indicated the floor, "and tell good stories."

She took a closer look at the floor coverings, then turned to him with a mixture of awe and yearning. "You have all these things and you know what they are and where they come from and how to use them." She let her fingers trail over the continents on the globe, then ran her eyes over the volumes lined up along the walls. "I wish I knew more about the world. Do you think I could come back here tomorrow, find out some more?"

Delighted with Eliza's quick mind and hunger for knowledge, Henry didn't hesitate. "By all means. You're welcome here whenever you please, and if you have any questions about the things you find here, just ask." He hesitated a moment and then offered, "When the weather clears up, I might be able to show you a little more of the world too . . . at least, what there is to see of the world here in London."

Her smile beamed with barely contained anticipation. "Really, could you? My da' took us to London once to see the lions at the Tower, and then we watched the fine ladies and gentlemen driving in the park. But apart from that, I've never been anywhere."

And then her face fell. Henry felt it as keenly as if the color had drained out of the world around them.

"Oh, we better not. Wilkins is probably still looking for me." She put on a brave smile. "I'll just find out about the world from right here."

But she couldn't hide forever. It occurred to Henry it might be better for Wilkins to find her while she was still under his protection. After all, she wouldn't be staying in his house indefinitely, much as he might like that. He was a bachelor—with a certain reputation, no less—and she was far too pretty for people not to start assuming her to be his mistress, if she stayed beyond her recuperation.

Not that Henry didn't want her. He wanted her more every day. But by now he was fairly certain she was still innocent, and he had no intention of depriving her of any future prospects by ruining her. But all he was really contemplating was whether or not to take her for a drive in the park. And if this Wilkins, or Horace the abhorrent, turned up, and he got to break a few bones on her behalf, so much the better.

"I don't think he is looking for you in Mayfair. As long as we don't venture into the seedier parts of town, I expect we can go out."

She brightened at that. "You think? I don't want him coming after you either, because I'm with you, you know."

Warmed by her concern for him, he assured her, "We will take Roberts or William with us wherever we go. Would that make you feel safe?"

She smiled at him despite her misgivings. "If you think it's safe, that's good enough for me."

Henry felt a twinge of guilt for not telling her all his motives, but she truly couldn't hide out at his house forever.

"That's my girl. So if it doesn't rain tomorrow, we will go for a drive in the park. And now off to bed with you. No sense in tiring yourself out too much."

He led her back to her room, where Mrs. Tibbit made her feel comfortable for the evening. He, however, changed into evening attire, and went to meet his friend for dinner at White's.

CHAPTER FIVE

HENRY WALKED UP THE FEW STEPS TO THE FRONT door at White's, waving jovially to the dandies in the great bay window. Amazing how some things never changed. A hundred years or more the club had existed, and ever since they put in that bay window, the most outrageous dressers of each generation had claimed it for themselves to see and be seen.

Thankfully, those gentlemen were usually satisfied with a wave for a greeting, but as soon as Henry had handed his beaver and gloves to the attendant and asked where he might find Viscount Fairly, one of them separated from the group, seemingly intent on speaking with him.

"March, wait up a moment."

Henry turned toward the speaker, inwardly groaning. The man really had no redeeming qualities except his ability to tie a perfect waterfall. But one had to acknowledge one's former classmates, particularly the ones that helped maintain one's cover. "Ellert, what brings you to town at this dreary time of year?"

Ellert affected an exaggerated eye roll. "Woman trouble, don't you know. Lissa is getting too clingy. You wouldn't want to trade, would you?"

The man referred to Henry's former mistress Millie. How or why Ellert thought he could do better than his current mistress was beyond Henry. The girl was pretty as a picture and inexplicably devoted to Ellert. Henry contemplated for a moment whether he should let the man know he no longer considered himself Millie's protector, but decided against it. Better to play along and keep the mystique going.

"Tempting, Ellert, tempting. However, I doubt Millie would stand for being traded, even by me."

Ellert shrugged and laughed at Henry's crude joke. "Worth a shot, Henry. Worth a shot!"

With that he stalked back to his group, leaving Henry to make his way up the stairs to the dining room where the attendant had indicated he would find his friend.

As soon as Henry entered the room, Robert Pemberton, the Viscount Fairly, beckoned him from the far side, where he had reserved a table by one of the tall windows overlooking St. James's Street.

The viscount was the tall, blond, blue-eyed, heroic type, too pretty for most people to take seriously, but Henry knew better. Robert was honorable, courageous, and loyal, and could even be ruthless if need be. The two of them had been the best of friends ever since Henry's first year at Eton more than twenty years ago, and serving together under Wellington had only strengthened their bond.

Robert stood at Henry's approach and shook his hand with a warm smile on his far too beautiful face. Henry returned the smile and the handshake and dropped into the chair opposite the viscount.

"How is the fair Millie?"

"Expensive," Robert said dryly. Then a naughty grin spread across his classic features. "But Lord, does she know what to do in the bedchamber."

Henry grinned right back. "I told you. Worth every penny."

Robert assessed him with a shrewdness few knew he possessed. "That begs the question why you steered her my way. I know you can handle the expense."

Henry shrugged and looked out the window. "The skills of a practiced courtesan only go so far. I just couldn't bring myself to like her."

Robert was familiar with the sadness in Henry's eyes and hoped someday soon Henry would find a woman who could be a true companion to him, not just a momentary distraction. But as long as he couldn't bring himself to trust a woman, the viscount knew that hope to be futile.

Both men were grateful the waiter chose that moment to deliver their meal. The roast beef was pink just as they liked it, the Yorkshire puddings plump, and the roasted turnips crisp. They assembled their plates and doused them with gravy before resuming their conversation.

"How was your trip north?"

Henry answered between bites of succulent beef. "Productive."

Robert shrugged dismissively and shoveled a forkful of gravy-soaked Yorkshire pudding into his mouth.

"Profitable," Henry offered with a glint in his eyes, knowing full well Robert had no interest in knowing how much his estates had brought in this year.

Robert just glared at him and returned his attention to his beef.

"Informative," Henry said, and waited for Robert's lips to twitch with amusement.

The viscount did not disappoint: he pinned Henry with a curious stare. "Do tell."

Robert's voice had been low, but Henry threw a quick glance at the gentlemen being seated at the table behind them, gave an almost imperceptible shake of his head, and launched into a description of how crop rotation had doubled his profits over the past five years.

By the time they finished their meal, they were discussing Prinny's latest excesses, but when the waiter offered them port, they opted instead to enjoy a brandy in the smoking room. Henry stood and bowed deeply to the two gentlemen at the table behind them. "Your Grace. My lord."

Robert turned as well and made an equally respectful bow. "Your servant, Your Grace. Jennings."

Bowing again, they made their way to the smoking room, where they situated themselves in a corner opposite the entrance, both looking out into the room as they relaxed in the comfortable leather chairs set at an angle so no one would be able to stand behind them.

The smoking room was easily the most comfortable room in the club. The high ceilings let the smoke dissipate somewhat, the burgundy drapes and dark walnut paneling rendered the room cozy despite its size, and the leather armchairs were supremely comfortable.

The two friends ordered brandy and cigars and settled in.

"So you still think Elridge is involved?"

The din in the room was moderate so early in the evening. Henry let his eyes travel lazily across the room, making sure no one listened in on their conversation. "More likely someone close to him. I have never had any personal dealings with him, but I doubt a peer of the realm as politically active and powerful as he would knowingly resort to treason."

He paused as a waiter approached with a box of cigars and lit them both. Henry puffed fragrant blue smoke in the air in front of them, the very picture of genteel contentment.

"You know we narrowed the leak down to Elridge or Davenport. Well, the Old Man sent me north to investigate the latter, and although the fool definitely talks too much, he is not a traitor. Neither do any of his cronies fit the description we got in France."

Robert's voice was grave, in total contrast to the nonchalant pose he presented to any onlookers. "Back to the drawing board then, so to speak." He elegantly sipped his brandy. "It is a perpetual mystery to me how the bastard has managed to elude us all this time."

Henry grunted, the rough sound the only evidence that he agreed with Robert. "We would have got to him by now if we didn't have to tiptoe around major titles. But patience, my friend. He will slip up sooner or later, or perhaps he already has and we just haven't found the evidence yet."

Robert was about to reply, but deftly changed the subject when His Grace, the Duke of Elridge, appeared in the doorway and stopped to survey the room. Henry scrupulously avoided looking at the duke, but could feel the man's eyes on him and wondered at the sudden interest.

THE FOLLOWING DAY BROUGHT PALE sunshine and clear skies. Henry sent word to Eliza to get ready for their drive in the park. Eliza donned her blue wool gown without delay and came downstairs, but left her cloak draped over the banister to follow the faint strains of music to the music room. There she found Henry at the piano, looking intently at his sheet music while his fingers played the tune.

Eliza stopped at the open door and enjoyed the music. He was in his shirtsleeves again, having carelessly discarded his hunter green jacket on a nearby chair. Tall boots and buckskin breeches and waist-coat marked him as a sportsman, not at all the kind of fellow you might expect to play the piano with some skill. But there he was, absorbed in studying this piece of music.

Henry played his way through the entirety of the song, humming along as he went, and didn't turn around until he heard the soft rustle of Eliza's skirts as she moved away from the door.

"Good morning, Eliza."

She smiled brightly, walking farther into the room. "Good morning to you too, Sir Henry. That was lovely. What's the song called?"

Henry turned back to look at the sheet music. "*Heidenröslein.*"

Eliza's entire expression was a question mark as she waited for him to elaborate.

Henry's face split into a wide grin, enjoying her reaction to his tease. "It's German and means 'little rose of the field.' Don't ask me how Germans get that much information into one word."

"Oh, that of course explains everything." She nodded wisely, which made his lips twitch again.

"It just came in the post. My cousin Anton sent it to me. It's by a man called Franz Schubert, who is apparently all the rage in Vienna at present."

She dropped the game, curiosity getting the better of her. "So you have a cousin in Vienna and you can speak German?"

His smile turned rueful. "Yes, well, my grandmother is German, and Grossmama insists we all speak German in her presence. And believe me, you do what my grandmother says; after all, she is the Dowager Duchess of Avon."

Eliza's intake of breath was audible as she let herself flop onto the piano bench next to him. And then, for the first time in his hearing, she fell into a broad cockney accent. "Christ a'mighty! Your grandma's a duchess?"

Henry chuckled at her loss of decorum and couldn't resist prodding her just a little more. "Oh, she is more than that. She started off as the Princess Ruth of Prussia before my grandfather took her down a peg or two and made her his duchess. The Avons are not royal dukes, you see."

Eliza shook her head in bewilderment. "A duke's a duke from where I stand."

Henry gave her a quizzical look and decided he needed to put her at ease again. "Eliza, even a duchess is just a woman in the end. As it happens, you would like her, and she would like you."

Eliza's eyes went wide. "She would, you think?"

Henry repeated a few chords of the song he had just played, mostly to give Eliza time to compose herself. "She likes strong women, and she has no time for men who think they can bend her to their will, to my cousin—the duke's—chagrin, I assure you."

"Oh dear," Eliza winced, "of course the duke is your cousin. So what did your grandmother do to earn his displeasure?"

He was glad she had recovered enough to ask about his family. Even so, he wasn't sure this was the time to answer her question. Henry shrugged. What he was about to say would most likely lead to a barrage of questions from his fair companion. But Eliza had trusted him with her story, had in fact entrusted her life to him. He wanted her to know about his past. "She bullied my cousin into taking in my daughter. Emily is being educated with her cousins in the country, surrounded by her beloved horses and dogs and under the influence of respectable women."

Despite her shock, Eliza didn't lose her composure again, her agitation only evident in her white-knuckled grip on the piano bench and the questions pouring out of her. "You have a daughter? But then you must be married. Are you married?"

Henry smiled, but looked her straight in the eyes so she might see his sincerity. "Yes, I have a daughter, and no, I'm not married and never have been. You see, my daughter, Emily, is illegitimate, but that doesn't mean I love her any less. And since her mother saw fit to send her to me less then twenty-four hours after she was born, with nothing but a verbal message saying she would be better off with me, I've taken it upon myself to do the best I can by her."

Eliza nodded, searching his eyes, slowly calming as the full implication of what he had revealed settled between them. "Of course you did. I can't imagine you doing anything less, even if most other men would have taken her straight to the workhouse. But her mother giving her away, that I can't understand."

Henry shrugged again, uncomfortable with having to make excuses for Cecilia. "Well, in her defense, her husband probably insisted upon it."

Eliza's lips formed a silent whistle. "That must be quite a story. Will you tell me?"

Henry stood and picked up his jacket, eager to get outside. "Yes. But it's a long story, so I'll tell you whilst we are driving in the park." He surveyed her quickly, noting she wore the blue wool again. "Where is your cloak? It's cold, even with the sun out."

"Oh, I left it on the banister in the hall."

Henry led her to the foyer, where he picked up her cloak, put it around her shoulders, and fastened the toggles for her since she couldn't do it herself with only one hand. Eliza blushed, knowing it wasn't proper for him to help her, but relishing his nearness.

By the time he was done, the curricle had pulled up outside; and William, the footman, held the door for them.

ELIZA ADMIRED THE BEAUTIFULLY MATCHED grays, whom she couldn't remember from the first time she'd been in this conveyance, and enjoyed the sun on her face.

They turned from Cavendish Square into Holles Street and from there right, into Oxford Street toward Marble Arch. There they entered Hyde Park and followed Park Lane all the way to the Serpentine.

Eliza marveled at the stately homes along the way and gawked at the hustle and bustle of Oxford Street, where the fashionable shopped and the traffic was brutal. But once they entered the park, where it was quiet at this time of the day, she turned her attention to Henry and his story once more. "How old is Emily?"

Henry let the horses trot a little faster, now they were out of traffic. "She is eleven, almost twelve." His voice turned soft with affection when he spoke of his daughter.

"You must have been about my age when you had her."

Henry glanced at her, then refocused on the horses. "I was nineteen. Her mother was two and twenty, and I was madly in love with her."

He kept his tone light, but it was clear he had come to regret his folly. "And she was married," Eliza prompted.

"And she was married. I was an underage student with no independent income." He sighed. "Not that that stopped her from having an affair with me. I should have known from that alone she had no integrity. But I was young and stupid and in love. She was beautiful, her husband much older, and she gave me the impression he was less than kind to her."

His voice had grown bitter as the memories crowded in on him.

"In any case, he found out and threatened to bury her in the country, so I persuaded her to run away with me. We made it all the way to Brussels before my very limited funds ran out, and I took a position as a clerk in a shipping office. I didn't mind really, I quite liked the independence of earning my own money. But Cecilia hated it. She hated not having money to go shopping. She hated not having her maid. She hated living in the two small rooms I had thought so romantic. She hated that I had to work. And by the time her husband and my father caught up with us, I think she hated me."

He paused there, his face stark with remembered pain, his eyes trained resolutely between the horses' heads. He swallowed, but when he continued, his voice was steady. "In any event, she chose to go back to her rich husband and the comfortable life she had had in Oxford, despite the fact she had just found out she was pregnant, or maybe because of it. I don't know, I never got to talk to her about it, or anything else for that matter."

Henry's jaw was clenched with the impotent fury he still felt after all these years. "My father forced me to come back home with him. He had me transferred to Cambridge and made my allowance dependent on staying away from Cecilia. Not that I wanted to see her at that point. She had deserted me for money, after all."

Straightening his shoulders, he braced himself for the telling of the next part of his story. "I had even resigned myself to another man raising my child, when I got a message from her maid asking me to come to a crossroad outside Oxford, and not to leave until I had spoken to her personally."

He fiddled with the reins, his voice now rather hoarse. "It was all rather mysterious, but I calculated that the baby should have been born by then, and I dared to hope I would be allowed to see my child, perhaps even finally talk to Cecilia."

Henry took a deep breath before he continued. "There was an inn close by, so I waited in the crossroad from morning to night for two days before the maid showed up with my tiny newborn daughter. She didn't even get out of the coach. She just handed me the crying bundle, told me her mistress said she would be better off with me, and told the coachman to drive on."

He shook his head. "I couldn't believe the callousness of it. It was January and freezing. Emily was wrapped in only a thin blanket, and there was no wet nurse. I had no idea what to do with a screaming infant, but I figured she was cold and starving, so I tucked her under my coat and took her to the inn, where I begged the landlady to help me. She sent me to her sister, who was nursing her own infant."

Henry wiped his gloved hand over his face, glad he had made it through the worst of his tale. "She fed Emily until I could engage a permanent wet nurse. I took her to my father's house, but he refused to take my bastard in, so I learned to take care of her myself. Emily turned out to be all right with the help of my grandmother, but as far as Cecilia is concerned . . ."

Henry shrugged and gave her an almost apologetic smile. Eliza smiled back and nodded. She understood—his feelings for the opposite sex had been marred by Cecilia's betrayal. She knew how trust was easily lost and difficult to regain.

"Thank you for telling me."

He shook his head and reached for her hand, gratified when she didn't shy away. "No, Eliza, thank you for listening. I know it's not a pretty tale."

He caught her eyes, and she held his gaze. There were so many questions. She knew how bastards were treated in her parish and could only hope the rich had more compassion. After all, it wasn't the child's fault. "What will happen to Emily? Will your circle accept her?"

Henry was further encouraged by Eliza's concern for his daughter. "Well, she will have a lady's education and she will be an heiress. I became a very wealthy man when my father died ten years ago. But my grandmother informs me that if I truly want to give Emily a chance and make the haut ton overlook her illegitimacy, I will have to marry a lady of impeccable lineage and repute. And I will have to marry in time to rehabilitate myself in the eyes of society before Emily can be brought out."

Eliza raised one eyebrow. "Have you anyone in mind?"

Henry released a short bark of laughter. "Indeed not. The usual society debutantes remind me far too much of Cecilia to give them a second glance. But I suppose in a couple of years I will have to start my search in earnest."

She shook her head. It seemed money and privilege didn't make life any less confusing. "There has to be a woman out there you can at least respect."

He squeezed her hand, and his warmth relieved some of the chill lingering under her cloak.

"Yes. You," he said quietly.

She laughed out loud; she couldn't help it, despite the compliment. "That won't do Emily any good."

Henry joined her laughter. "Not Emily, but me perhaps."

That at last made Eliza blush. She so hoped she could do *something* for him, even though marriage was completely out of the question. He had done so much for her.

Eliza took a moment to look around Hyde Park as they drove under the winter-bare trees along the Serpentine. It was a beautiful expanse of green even in this season, and she savored the intermittent sunshine after all the time she had spent indoors. The good weather had brought out a number of walkers and riders despite the unfashionable hour. There were children at play, watched over by governesses and nursemaids with prams. Rotten Row, some ways to the right, was busy with riders, and the paths were populated by a few ladies walking in groups and the occasional gentleman walking alone.

One particular gentleman caught her attention. He was tall and well-dressed in a black coat and top hat, and stood to the side of a path observing them. At least, that was what she thought at first, but once she looked a little closer, she realized the gentleman was positively glaring at Sir Henry. The intensity of the man's cold gray stare was somewhat disturbing, but just when Eliza decided to make Henry aware of it, the man turned abruptly and disappeared behind a stand of evergreens.

The whole thing had happened so quickly, Eliza couldn't be sure of what exactly she had seen, and since there was no longer anyone to point out, she turned her attention back to Henry. She pulled her hand from under his and threaded it through his arm in a gesture of friendship, and he leaned in a little to touch his shoulder to hers and smiled down at her. That smile turned into a frown when he noticed her bare hand. "Good Lord, Eliza, where are your gloves?"

She looked at her hand in some confusion. "I don't need gloves."

The line between his eyebrows deepened. "Of course you need gloves, it's bloody freezing. Wrap your hands in your cloak and we shall stop on the way back and get you some." With a decisive nod, he took up the reins with both hands again and encouraged the horses to increase their speed.

"You don't have to buy me gloves. I survived eighteen years without them, I'll be fine," Eliza protested. But she stuck her hands back under the cloak when he turned to her with mock severity.

"You need gloves. In fact, I'll take you to Covent Garden tomorrow and buy you a muff as well."

She had heard of Covent Garden, and was pretty sure Wilkins would be familiar with it too, which made her nervous about going there.

But Henry nudged her shoulder again and grinned down at her. "Come on, it will be fun. There is a market hall as well as an open air market. Both have dozens of different stalls where you can buy almost anything you can think of. Not to mention all the street performers outside the Opera House."

Eliza grinned back at him, unable to conceal her longing to go to such a place. "I would like to see that."

"Then you shall." Henry, having decided on a course of action, turned back into Oxford Street and headed toward home. Eliza, however, felt a prickle of apprehension as soon as they left the park. She wasn't sure if she should attribute the raised hair on the back of her neck to the planned trip to Covent Garden, or if someone had spied her already. She carefully scanned the faces on Oxford Street, but saw none that were familiar.

Henry felt the nervous energy coursing through her. "What is it?"

She rubbed the back of her neck. "Nothing, just a feeling."

Henry gave her a sharp look, then carefully scanned the street around them, but couldn't see anything out of the ordinary. "We will take both Will and Roberts along, if that would make you feel better."

She nodded and smiled up at him, grateful she didn't have to explain.

BEHIND THEM, A DAPPER-LOOKING GENTLEMAN in a gaudy polka-dotted neckcloth appeared to be studying the display in the window of a tobacco shop, but turned to look after the curricle as it passed. "Cozyin' up in an open carriage? With Sir Henry no less? Wilkins won't be 'appy about that." He chuckled and signaled a shifty individual lounging outside a nearby pub. "Keep yar peepers on them two. I wanna know if they sneeze."

He then turned and sauntered down Oxford Street, twirling his walking stick and whistling a merry tune.

"Revenge is sweet. Ain't that right, Sir Henry?"

CHAPTER SIX

THE NEXT MORNING DAWNED RAINY AND COLD and brought dispatches from one of Henry's estates demanding his attention. The outing to Covent Garden was postponed to a more hospitable day, and Henry departed to attend to business with his solicitor.

Eliza, left to her own devices, elected to spend the day in the library, where a fire made the room cozy, and the light by the back windows was good for reading.

Henry found her there sometime after lunch, when he came into the library to deal with the rest of the mail on his desk. He only noticed her once he was seated behind it. She had made herself comfortable in the enormous wing-back chair facing the rear window, with her legs tucked up under her and the skirts of her blue-and-white striped dress tucked around her feet. In fact, someone standing in the middle of the room would have no clue there was another person present, except for the slippers she had kicked off and left under the chair.

She was the picture of contented comfort, with a soft white knitted shawl draped around her shoulders and her elbow propped on the armrest so her hand could cradle the side of her head. Her dress had a square-cut neckline and three-quarter-length sleeves. The bodice was form-fitting to the waist and then opened into a full skirt, which allowed for her legs to cross beneath. It wasn't a terribly fashionable gown, but she loved the penny-sized silver buttons down the front and approved of the vertical stripes that made her look taller.

Eliza lifted her nose out of her book and smiled at Henry. "Good afternoon, Sir Henry. Did you get all your work done?"

Henry grimaced at the stack of letters before him. "Not quite, but the rain has stopped, so once I have dealt with what is in front of me, perhaps you would like to go for a turn about the square?"

Eliza's eyes twinkled with mischief. "Oh, don't worry yourself on my account, I'm in excellent company." She held up her book so he could read the title.

His eyes sparkled when they returned to hers. "*Tom Jones.* Indeed I am surprised you tore yourself away long enough to acknowledge my presence."

Eliza smiled wickedly, in total contrast with the blush staining her cheeks. "He is just about to climb into some lady's boudoir. So, no rush!"

"I'm not sure I should allow you to pollute your mind with all that debauchery," he commented, only half in jest, but she had already turned her attention back to the book.

"It's very educational," Eliza quipped.

With an appreciative laugh, Henry left her to her book and turned his attention back to his correspondence. The companionable silence descending over the library was new to him, but so very, very welcome.

AN HOUR LATER HENRY HAD worked himself down to the last of his letters and was looking forward to teasing Eliza about her risqué reading material, when he became aware of a commotion in the front hall.

A shrill female voice demanded to be taken to Sir Henry. In fact, the lady refused to take no for an answer, and the staccato of her heels accompanied her demands as she opened doors to look for him.

Henry, in the meantime, had matched the voice to his not-yet-officially dismissed mistress, Millie, and rose to take care of the situation when his eyes fell on Eliza. All color had drained from her face, and she was looking around in a panic trying to find a safe place to hide. Henry held her gaze for a moment. "What is it?"

Eliza motioned wildly to the door. "Sounds like Horace's missus. They found me."

Henry moved to her side and grabbed both her hands to calm her. "No, I know who it is. Calm yourself, I'll go and take care of it."

Eliza was not convinced. "Who is it then? I don't want you to get hurt on my account."

Henry couldn't help a wry chuckle. "Don't worry, I won't. Her name is Millie and she is the reigning queen of Drury Lane." He smiled apologetically. "She may also still consider herself my mistress."

Eliza's eyes went wide, her lips forming a perfect O, but the tension went out of her body. She sank back down into the wing-back chair and refolded her legs beneath herself before cocking her head up at him. "In that case, you better go talk to her before William has an apoplexy."

Her cheeks dimpling, Eliza used a silk ribbon to hold her place in Mr. Fielding's lusty tale, in expectation of a scene at least as entertaining as Tom's antics.

BEFORE LONG, THE DOOR SWUNG open, and a determined Millie made her entrance. Her sky-blue eyes swept the library with the efficiency of a Bow Street detective, despite her obvious fury at being treated as less than a lady by the indignant doorman who followed on her heels.

"You can't just barge in there!" wailed William from the hall.

"Oh, go f . . ."

The vulgar expletive died on Millie's lips as she realized she had found her quarry. She proceeded to demonstrate why she was considered one of the more talented actresses of her generation.

Millie immediately checked her temper, infused her face with a slow smile to indicate her pleasure at seeing Henry, and slowed her walk to a seductive swing of the hips. By the time she spoke again, her voice had lost its shrill tone and hard East End edge. Now it rippled like velvet.

"Henry, my dearest, sweet, sweet man, have you been working all this time? Is that why I haven't seen you, my love? The last time you came to me, you told me you had to go to one of your estates to work, and now I find you still working." She shook her head sadly, which made her blond corkscrew curls dance most enticingly around her neck and over the top of her pushed-up bosom. "I'm so glad I came. You need a break and I know just how to relax you." She purred and smiled invitingly, her eyes widening with the promise of passion.

Henry could still see Eliza out of the corner of his eyes and shot her a quelling look as she clamped both hands over her mouth to contain her mirth. She couldn't see the woman, but the change in her voice, what she said and how she said it, had Eliza in stitches. Henry, too, couldn't quite hide his amusement as he moved past Eliza and into the room to greet his neglected mistress.

Millie, meanwhile, leaned slightly forward to display the luminous expanse of her pale bosom in the most outrageously low-cut red satin dress he had ever seen anybody wear in broad daylight. She was clearly on a mission, and it behooved him to find out what it might be.

"Millie, my darling, you look simply ravishing. Did I buy you that dress? I must say it was worth every penny."

She followed the ample curves of her body with both her hands and replied, "Oh no, my love, that was Fairly." And shrugging somewhat apologetically, she added, "You haven't been around, and I didn't have a stitch to wear."

The sting of the revelation was considerably dulled by the fact that it had been his idea to hand her off to Robert. But Henry was aware of a suppressed giggle from behind the wing-back chair, so he moved past Millie to the wine decanter by the front fireplace, to make her turn back into the room. Satisfied Millie now had her back to Eliza in the wing-back chair, he filled two glasses with claret and handed one to Millie.

It may have been his idea to tell Robert to make a play for her, but that didn't mean he couldn't make her sweat a little for her faithlessness. "So, Fairly, hm? Where is the strapping young viscount now?"

Millie, encouraged by his apparent need for alcohol, fluttered her eyelashes with what she liked to think of as charming innocence and walked her fingers up his chest while she took a sip of wine.

Eliza, her hilarity having given way to curiosity, risked a peek around the side of her chair. All comparisons to *Tom Jones* forgotten, it was suddenly imperative to know what kind of woman held Henry's interest.

Millie set her glass on a side table and presented her claret-stained lips to Henry. When he showed no signs of taking the bait, she slowly licked the claret off her lips and pouted. "Out of town."

Henry nodded and granted her a sympathetic pat on the rump. "Ah, you find yourself at loose ends, my dear? Surely it isn't another wardrobe you need, so what brings you here?"

Millie gave him a little smile as if to say, *I know I'm naughty, but I also know you will forgive me because I'm adorable and you want me.* All the while her hips brushed against his groin in a slow circular motion that made him hiss in a breath between his teeth. When she was certain of his favorable reaction, she let her hands trail down his chest and around his waist, down to his buttocks, and pulled herself closer into his erection. "Why, Henry, I am making sure you are not working too hard, of course."

She let her hands slide to the front of his breeches, where she caressed him and opened the first button. "Why don't you sit down and let me take care of you . . . and then you can take me shopping. I found the most delicious little hat to go with this dress."

Henry caught her hands before she could open another button and thanked the heavens she had finally come to the point. His body urged him to take Millie upstairs and make her work for that hat, but he was keenly aware of Eliza in the wing-back chair, and that it wasn't Millie he wanted. "Much as I appreciate your talents, I don't think we should go behind the viscount's back. He is a friend, you know. Now he has taken my place, he might as well keep it, don't you think?"

Millie's eyes came up slowly to meet his, and comprehension dawned in them. She had overplayed her hand and this was to be goodbye. Her hands went to her hips in a decidedly unladylike stance and she narrowed her eyes at him. "You dirty, loathsome...."

His raised hand stayed her. "Now, now, Millie, no need to get into a temper. I tell you what, why don't you go shopping for that hat and have them send me the bill. Call it a parting gift."

At that, the smile returned, but she was still pouting. "What will I do till Fairly gets back?"

Grinning at her antics, Henry retrieved a fifty-pound bill from his box on the desk. But when he looked over to the wing chair, Eliza was glaring at him. She had obviously seen and not just heard some of what had passed between Millie and him, and did not approve. He tried to reassure her by holding her gaze and giving his head a tiny shake, hoping Eliza would understand he was just trying to part amicably with the lady, that he didn't want Millie. He wanted *her*.

Henry folded the banknote as he walked back to Millie and tucked it into her bodice. "I'm sure you will think of something." Then he turned her around and marched her toward the door.

She sighed heavily and sent him a dramatic glance over her shoulder. "Goodbye, Henry. It was fun while it lasted."

Smiling, he winked at her. "It certainly was. Goodbye, Millie. William will show you out."

Holding her head high, Millie made her exit in style, while William sprinted ahead to open the front door for her.

Eliza let out a relieved breath and chuckled. "So much for the tart."

HENRY CLOSED THE DOOR AND stood there for a moment trying to call his aroused body to order, but Eliza stirred in her chair, and her presence drew him like a lodestone.

Moving closer, he leaned over the back of her chair in an attempt to spare her the sight of his erection. Eliza glanced up at him and raised an eyebrow. The thought she'd been jealous of Millie made him happier than he cared to admit, but he also felt the need to explain.

"Try not to judge me too harshly. The woman is skilled, and I'm only human."

Eliza's face was tilted up to him; her eyes mocking him gently. "Oh, you poor, dear, sweet man," she said, imitating Millie's purr, "is that why you are hiding behind the chair? Did she put a bulge in your pants?"

Henry let his hand drop over the back of the chair to tease one of her curls, and was just about to ask if she knew what to do with a bulge in a man's breeches when she added, "At least you're not chasing me around the room trying to rub it against me."

There was a bitter note in her voice, and the comment was such a stunning mix of crude awareness and innocence that Henry felt ashamed of his urges. "We're not all like that. It can be beautiful, you know, what lies between a man and a woman."

They had both sobered, aware something had just changed. She met his eyes and nodded despite the blush staining her neck and face. Her eyes held a question, and she looked so beautiful with her face tilted toward him and the gentle curve of her breasts beyond, he couldn't help himself. He traced the curve of her neck with the curl he still held between his fingers.

When the pad of his index finger started to follow the same path, he felt her shiver, but she held his gaze. He let his finger follow her collarbone to the square-cut décolletage of her blue-and-cream striped dress and, from there, dip to the soft swell of her breast.

His eyes were dark and smoldering now, and Eliza realized he had sent Millie away because of her. She wanted to believe him, part of her even wanted him to show her. But all she had ever done was run from the unwanted attention of the men around her. Even as her breath hitched in her throat at the touch of his finger, she lost her nerve and lowered her gaze.

Henry silently cursed himself for frightening her. He could readily imagine what kind of men she would have had to fend off at the inn. The crude jokes, the lewd comments, the rough, dirty hands grabbing at her. It was enough to make him ill.

He lifted his hand away from her, flashed her a rueful grin, and attempted to make light of it. "Easy, sweetheart! No need to worry, I'll be civilized again soon enough."

He waited till she met his eyes, and smiled his apology. "I'll see you at dinner." Then he headed out of the room.

ELIZA SAT THERE FOR A while, watching the bare branches of the elm tree outside the library window sway in the breeze, and tried to make sense of what had just almost happened.

Henry rarely dined at home, preferring his club and the company of his friends. She wondered whether he would come to her room and eat with her there, or if she was meant to meet him in the dining room.

And after their almost kiss, did he mean to take things further?

What would he do if she said no? His caress had been soft and gentle, but she knew how fast a man's hand could turn into a fist. Would he hurt her too if he didn't get what he wanted?

He had saved her, housed her, clothed her, fed her, entertained her, and, more recently, confided in her and flirted with her. Did he expect her to give him her body in exchange for these kindnesses? It was a reasonable assumption and one she understood. That was how the men she had known so far would see the situation. And human nature remained the same whether you were born in a Mayfair mansion or a cramped roadside inn.

Did he know she had wanted him to kiss her, and now thought her a wanton, no better than Wendy the barmaid who brought in customers because she lifted her skirts for a shilling?

The old panic she had lived with at the inn seized her and she rose, resettling her arm in the sling. She paced the length of the library twice before she could calm herself enough to think rationally. Not every man was crude and brutal; her father had been proof of that. She had just been keeping the wrong company.

Eliza knew Henry to be kind and considerate, so she saw no reason to be afraid of him. But was he waiting for her to come to him, or did he really not expect anything from her like Mrs. Tibbit insisted? She had told Eliza he never dallied with anybody living under his roof.

But she didn't really live under his roof. She didn't work for him and therefore didn't depend on him for her livelihood. He had picked her up off the side of the road, where she would have died had he not intervened. She was staying in his house temporarily, and no matter what he or Mrs. Tibbit said, or how much he treated her as a friend, there was no way around the fact that she owed him.

Then there was the small matter of him being the most handsome, most intelligent, most amusing, and cleanest man she had ever met. She thoroughly enjoyed spending time with him. She wanted to know the things he had to teach her, and she suspected being kissed and touched by him would be exciting, pleasurable even, rather than repulsive.

She merely didn't like the idea he might expect it of her.

Her ruminations were cut short by Mrs. Tibbit, who came to tell her Sir Henry had indeed ordered dinner at home and had extended an invitation to her to join him. In the meantime, he had taken off for a ride in the park, and Eliza joined Mrs. Tibbit in her parlor for a sewing lesson.

Eliza was grateful for the activity and the chance to think of a future she could build without the undue influence of men.

THE FIRST THING HENRY DID when Eliza came downstairs for dinner was to apologize to her.

He met her at the bottom of the stairs, waited until she stood right in front of him, and took both her hands in his. "Eliza, I am so sorry I took liberties with you in the library earlier. Please forgive my behavior."

Taken aback, she nodded her acceptance. Seeing the sincerity in his eyes, she felt ashamed she had thought Henry capable of being as base and coarse as the men she had known so far. Pushing aside the painful feelings the earlier incident had dredged up from her past, she decided to make light of the situation.

The dimple in her cheek appeared and, letting a trace of the inn color her voice, she observed, "That Millie did have you riled up good and proper."

Henry's self-effacing chuckle ended in a shake of his head. "Yes, she did. But if I didn't find you attractive, what happened between you and me wouldn't have happened." He smiled another apology, but remained serious. "Eliza, you are a guest in my house and you have a right to feel safe here. I like spending time with you, and I want you to feel comfortable in my company, so I promise I will never take advantage of you. And," he said with a crooked smile, "I will do my best to keep my hands to myself."

Eliza, her eyes lowered, blushed a lovely shade of crimson at his rather forward declarations. Then she blushed even deeper as she found herself oddly disappointed he would never again touch her ever so softly as he had done in the library.

She managed a steady enough, "Thank you," and finally looked up at him and smiled.

Satisfied they had cleared up any misunderstanding between them, Henry took her arm and led her to dinner.

CHAPTER SEVEN

IT WAS A FULL WEEK LATER AND EARLY DECEM-ber before the horridly soggy winter weather lifted. Sir Henry was soon to depart for Avon to spend time with his daughter and celebrate Christmas with his family.

To that purpose, a beautiful dappled gray two-year-old filly, who was to be Emily's Christmas present, had been delivered and duly admired on Tuesday afternoon. But when Wednesday dawned crisply cold and sunny, it was finally time for their outing to Covent Garden. They took the town coach since it was too cold for the curricle, and both William and Roberts were to accompany them for security.

Eliza was clad in a high-waisted, claret-colored wool dress, the skirts of which flared out rather voluminously due to the extra petticoats Mrs. Tibbit had insisted upon. She was wrapped in her gray cloak and had pulled on the tan-colored kid gloves that had magically appeared on her dresser a couple of days ago. Her hair was held back by two combs and uncovered apart from the hood of her cloak.

Traffic slowed their progress as they traveled along Oxford Street and then down Regent Street to Piccadilly Circus. The sidewalks of the big avenues were full of shoppers so close to the Christmas holiday, and Eliza marveled at the decorations the various shopkeepers had put up in their windows.

A confectioner had fashioned a nativity scene out of marzipan, and a baker had made icing-frosted gingerbread snowflakes and hung them on red and green satin ribbons in his window. A boot maker had stuffed his boots with nuts and oranges, and more than one merchant had hung mistletoe in their doorways and evergreens in their windows. It was lovely and festive and, although Hampstead boasted a few shops that decorated for the holidays, Eliza had never seen anything like it. She resolved to go for a walk along those streets in the next couple of days to have a closer look at some of the displays.

How Eliza wished her mother could have seen this. Mum had loved Christmas, and one of the last happy memories Eliza had of her mother was last year's trip to see the Christmas decorations on Hampstead High Street.

They had admired the window displays, bought all the necessary ingredients for their plum pudding, and then Mum had pulled her to a bench built around one of the huge oak trees by the well. She had pulled out the silver locket holding a lock of her father's hair, the one her mother had worn daily before she had married Horace, and put it around Eliza's neck.

"That's the last I have of my Jack," she'd said with a sad smile. "Wear it for me, but make sure Horace never sees it. He'd filch it from you and give it to that whore of his."

Eliza's hand crept under her cloak to check for where she had pinned the locket to the shoulder straps of her chemise. Sometimes it felt like that smooth bit of silver was the only thing keeping the image of her mother's broken body at the foot of the stairs at bay, the only thing that stood between Eliza and despair. She knew she was able to wear it openly, now that Horace was no longer there to take it from her, but she still couldn't quite trust her safety and, until she did, she would keep the locket right where it was.

FROM PICCADILLY THEY TURNED EAST into a warren of smaller streets until they reached the huge market in front of the opera house, commonly known as Covent Garden, even though there had been no gardens in this area for several centuries.

It was a large, cobbled area, covered in market stalls and one rather grand permanent structure, housing the more affluent traders and craftsmen.

They left the coach outside the gates, and Henry took Eliza's arm while Roberts and William followed behind. It was no doubt a risk bringing her to such a crowded place. But Henry reasoned that with the three of them ready to protect Eliza, this would also be an opportune moment to draw out Wilkins, if he was indeed still after her.

But mostly, Henry wanted to put a smile on his fair companion's face.

Eliza had never seen so many people in one place. The sights, sounds, and smells made up an almost celebratory atmosphere. It was noisy with all the vendors vying for the shoppers' attention and joking good-naturedly with their customers in their thick cockney accents. The stalls were covered with colorful canapés, and as far as Eliza could tell, anything one could possibly desire was for sale somewhere in this market, from sweet apples to small mountains of exotic spices and dried fruit, to bales of wool and silk cloth, to books and cheap trinkets, as well as shoes, hats, and furs. It smelled of roasted chestnuts, mulled wine, and unwashed bodies, and someone, somewhere, was roasting meat.

The cries of the hawkers were underscored by the occasional

sounds of a fiddle, an old English ballad, and even the distant strains of a bagpipe. Henry explained the best musicians would be at the plaza in front of the Opera House, where the Punch and Judy show was and where the acrobats performed. He promised they would stop there later after they were done shopping.

Sir Henry insisted on freshly roasted chestnuts to munch on while they explored. They meandered through the seasonally large crowd. Representatives of all social strata could be observed perusing the stalls—the market was one of those rare places where the classes mingled naturally, all drawn by the festive atmosphere and the bargains to be had.

They bought cone-shaped bags of sugar plums and candied almonds for Mrs. Tibbit, some delicate doll clothes for Emily's favorite doll, a length of lovely white-on-white sprigged muslin for Eliza to practice her sewing upon, and, of course, the gloves and muff they had come for.

The gloves were soft gray leather and slid onto Eliza's fingers like a second skin. Not that she could bear to wear gloves in a place where every stall seemed to hold something that just had to be touched or smelled to be fully appreciated. The muff was, at least to Eliza's mind, a decadent creation, made of gray rabbit fur and covered on the outside with red velvet.

Rubbing the soft fur against her cheek, she thanked Sir Henry for the handsome gift. But, afraid she would lose the lovely thing in the crush, she let the vendor wrap it for her and handed it to William to carry.

Henry watched Eliza explore, and smiling to himself, relaxed into the experience.

The two servants took the opportunity to do a little Christmas shopping of their own and were soon laden down with purchases. It seemed prudent to send Roberts back to the coach with all the packages and then meet them in the plaza before the Opera House, where the buskers and acrobats performed.

On the way to the plaza, they cut through the big market hall, where Eliza admired a hat in a milliner's shop. Henry saw the fur-trimmed gray hat with the dark red ribbons and was about to suggest they go in when she hustled past him and pretended to be impatient to see the acrobats. Obviously she was embarrassed about the money he had already spent on her, but the hat would go perfectly with Eliza's new muff and cape and would make a splendid Christmas present, even if he couldn't be there to see her unwrap it on Christmas morning.

Henry hadn't seen anybody who looked remotely how Eliza had described Wilkins, and he felt confident no one had followed them. So he called to William to stay close to Eliza and ducked into the small shop to buy the hat.

As soon as Eliza stepped into the plaza she felt exposed, vulnerable. She couldn't have explained why; it was just a cold prickle at the nape of her neck, and she told herself to stop being such a ninny and that both Sir Henry and Roberts would be back in a trice. Besides, the burly William stood right next to her, sharing his sugared doughnuts with her, so she was hardly alone. But the prickle of warning would not go away.

They had worked their way into the crowd to get a better look at the tumblers, and so while William marveled at a girl cartwheeling on a tight rope, she looked around her, unable to dismiss her feeling of unease.

There were no familiar faces in the crowd, but the handsome gent in the dapper rust-colored suit and the brown top hat behind her had an odd glint in his eye when he said to no one in particular: "She's a pretty pigeon."

The smile he bestowed on her made her skin crawl, and the thought that this creature was ten times worse than Horace occurred to her. But before she could nudge William or cry out around her last bite of doughnut, a broad, callused hand closed over her mouth and a beefy arm pulled her backwards through the crowd. Then the stench of onions and rotting teeth threatened to overwhelm her when Wilkins's voice whispered in her right ear, "Come along, Liza, play time's over! I come to collect what's mine."

Eyes wide with panic, Eliza tried to get William's attention by the sheer force of her will. She scratched at Wilkins's hand as he dragged her mercilessly backwards and kicked at the dapper gent who had parted her cloak to grab her around her waist and kept smiling at her as if they were playing some sort of game.

Within seconds, she couldn't see William anymore and knew herself to be lost if she couldn't alert anyone to her plight. She swallowed the last bit of doughnut lodged in her throat and bit down as hard as she could on Wilkins's fat, dirty middle digit. He bellowed and cursed, but let go of her mouth. By this time they were out of the crowd, and she was being dragged between stalls toward a dark little lane beyond. Eliza threw her head back in desperation, head-butting Wilkins in the process, and screamed with the full force of her lungs.

"HELP! HENRYYYY!!!! HE...AHHH!"

Her scream for help turned into a cry of pain as Wilkins cuffed her around her ear, and the other man's hand grabbed her breast in a viselike grip and twisted her nipple with excruciating efficiency. "Shut up, bitch, or I'll tweak the other one too!"

Fear froze any further sound in Eliza's throat as she looked into the man's pale, menacing eyes. The smile creeping over his face was pure evil. The vise grip around her nipple relaxed, and his hand started to massage the pain away. She thought she would be sick on his polished boots.

"See Wilkins, it's always a question of findin' the right mo'ivator. Soon as we're in me alley, she can scream all she likes, no one will take no notice."

With that, he turned her and grabbed her around her waist as Wilkins's fist closed around her upper arm on the other side. His stupid grin held the promise of more pain to come.

"Right ya are, Mr. Hobbs."

Now that she could see they were only one stall away from said alley, Eliza knew with blinding clarity she had to make one last stand. Neither Henry nor William could come to her aid if they didn't know which way she'd gone.

She fervently wished she had ignored the doctor's advice and donned her stays just for today. They would have offered some protection from Hobbs's evil fingers. But there was nothing for it: she ignored all the fear pooling in her belly and used the fact they were practically carrying her to pull up her knees and slam down her booted heels on both her captors' toes. In the same movement, she twisted her arm out of Wilkins's slackened grip and turned under Hobbs's arm to head back toward the stall behind her.

"SIR HENRY! HELP!"

She managed to grab the canvas of the rickety stall and upend a table full of brass oil lamps. They clattered to the ground, making an unholy racket, before a merciless hand grabbed her hair right at the nape and yanked her back. Then his hand closed around her other breast, and the white hot fury of pain he inflicted on her rendered her helpless. The pain had left her no breath to scream, but the stall holder's anger lent her hope he might remember her if Sir Henry came to see what the commotion was all about.

Hobbs hauled her through the last row of stalls and into the alley.

THE ALLEY WAS DARK AND stank of sex and human refuse. Farther into the shadows, one could just make out girls for sale loitering against the walls. This was obviously Hobbs's kingdom and he didn't expect anyone to dare follow him here. He pushed Eliza forward. "Crikey, the bint 'as more spirit than what's good for 'er. Now she's got matching fucking marks on 'er titties. 'Ow am I supposed to sell 'er if she can't show 'er tits?"

Wilkins's laugh was mirthless and derisive. "She'll have plenty more marks by the time I'm done with 'er. I owe 'er a few just for today, never mind that that nob took what was mine."

Hobbs, suddenly all business, stopped to square off with Wilkins, keeping an iron grip on Eliza's arm. "Stop whining, ya snifflin' pillock. Virgins are overrated anyways, she'll still be young and tight. But get this straight: this one's trouble as-is and the only reason I'm still 'ere is 'cause the good Sir Henry owes me a pigeon. So fuck 'er all ya want and I won't even say anythin' if ya prefer the wrong 'ole, but put another mark on 'er and ya'll 'ave a hard time gettin' your twenty quid off me. Are we understood?"

Wilkins planted his feet, squared his shoulders, and yanked Eliza closer to his side. He extended his neck to get farther into Hobbs's face and narrowed his eyes. "I'll do with 'er what I want and I don't know what ya're complainin' about. Ya're getting 'er all broke in. Since 'er fine gent has already done half the work, all I have to do is make sure she knows one cock's as good as the next and that gin takes the edge off. That's what you said. Besides, a deal's a deal."

As the pain subsided, Eliza started to follow their exchange and finally found enough breath to voice her disgust. "Fucking bastards! You think I'm Sir Henry's whore, and now you," she indicated Wilkins with her head, "are going to force yourself on me and then sell me to this demon here out of revenge? Because you think I gave Sir Henry my virginity, instead of guarding it faithfully so you could be the first bastard to rape me?"

Her eyes flashed angry fire as she looked from one to the other, questioning whether she had all the facts straight. Hobbs assumed a calm, almost gentle demeanor, making Eliza cringe with apprehension. "Come, come now, pigeon, of course he's had ya. Ya've been living in 'is 'ouse and 'e's famous for 'is great big cock and 'is liking for the ladies. So we're going to let Wilkins 'ere 'ave his pound of flesh and then . . ."

At that moment, Sir Henry emerged from between two stalls with a pistol firmly trained on Hobbs. Eliza wanted to sag in relief, but was all too aware one man against the two of them on Hobbs's turf was probably a very bad idea, so she shook her head at Henry to warn him away. He nevertheless smiled reassuringly and stepped forward. "Ah, but I'm not done with Miss Eliza yet. So if you would step aside, Mr. Hobbs."

Hobbs turned to him with a grin and raised his hand, also holding a pistol. "And why would I? This 'ere is my world."

Henry nodded and seemed to think for a moment. "True enough. But you see . . . " He indicated a low roof behind Hobbs, where William was just coming into view with a rifle trained on Hobbs. "This here is William, and he would like nothing better than to put a bullet in your head for hurting his girl. Daisie, you might remember her? I persuaded you to leave her in my care?"

Hobbs was a businessman at heart and had no trouble realizing when a deal was no longer to his advantage. He released Eliza from his grip, lifted his hat, bowed with a flourish, and then retreated farther into the alley, all the while keeping his gun at the ready, just in case.

Wilkins, stunned by this development, yanked Eliza back to him before she could step closer to Sir Henry, and furiously shouted after Hobbs, "You lily-livered bastard! Ya're supposed ta 'ave me back."

Hobbs fixed him with cold, hard eyes. "She ain't worth the trouble. Get yar twenty quid off 'im. He obviously enjoyed her, so he might as well pay. And a word of warning, mate—if 'e still wants 'er, you won't get 'er off 'im. He can be a right 'ard bastard." The pimp turned and walked away.

Wilkins took a moment to assimilate what Hobbs had said, then turned to Henry to rail at him. "I paid for a virgin and ya bloody ruined 'er! So if ya want 'er back, it's gonna cost ya."

Henry regarded him for a moment. "I'm willing to gift you fifty pounds if you will sign a contract that says you give up all rights to Miss Eliza and you will never come near her again."

Eliza quickly calculated—Wilkins had only valued her as long as she was a virgin, and he would let her go more readily if he thought her spoiled goods. What Eliza found troubling was that Sir Henry was about to buy her. Her heart sank further as she realized fifty pounds was not a sum she could hope to repay anytime soon. Her only consolation was that being owned by Sir Henry was infinitely preferable to being owned by Wilkins.

Wilkins agreed to the deal. "All right. But show me the money first."

Henry handed his gun to Roberts, who had appeared behind him, and retrieved a crisp fifty-pound note from his wallet, holding it up for Wilkins to see, right there in a Covent Garden back alley. Eliza couldn't make up her mind whether it was the bravest or the stupidest thing she had ever seen anybody do.

"There is a scribe in the market, so if you let Eliza go with my man here, we can have the contract drawn up for you to sign. William and I will witness it."

Wilkins thought about it for a few seconds, but eventually let go of her arm. Henry took Eliza's shaking hand, held her close for a moment, then handed her over to Roberts. He met her eyes and gave her a little smile, hoping to reassure her. "Wait for me in the carriage. I won't be long, and then you will be rid of him once and for all," he whispered to her.

Eliza returned a shaky smile and nodded.

CHAPTER EIGHT

ELIZA HAD KEPT HER WITS ABOUT HER WHILE confronted by the two villains, but now that Sir Henry was fighting her battle for her, she shook so badly her legs could barely carry her. Roberts took her elbow and gently guided her through the market to the carriage, where she spent a tense half hour waiting for the business to be completed and Henry to return.

Roberts put a cup of mulled wine in her hand, which settled her nerves somewhat, but she still jumped when Henry opened the carriage door. Sliding onto the seat next to her, he drew her into his arms, only to pull back immediately when she cried out in pain as her breasts came into contact with his chest. "Good Lord, Eliza, where are you hurt?"

She indicated her nipples, flaming scarlet with embarrassment. "Hobbs . . . he twisted them . . . really hard." Hot tears shot to her eyes at the memory.

A gentle hand touched her cheek, and Henry lightly kissed her forehead. "He will never touch you again, I promise."

Eliza leaned into the kiss and thanked her lucky stars she was sitting here with Henry and not in some hovel with Wilkins or—God forbid—Hobbs.

She raised weary eyes to him. "I don't think I'll be able to bear your touch on my breasts for a while."

Henry was momentarily stunned. "You what?" As he slowly began to comprehend her meaning, he was chagrined. "You think because I didn't correct . . ."

Eliza did something she had never done before: she cut him off. "You bought me."

Anger flashed in Henry's eyes, and his words were hard and clipped. "I did not buy you! I merely bought your freedom; there's a difference. I do not believe one human being should be allowed to own another. I know it goes on, but I don't condone it, and I certainly have no wish to own you."

Eliza collapsed into a tearful heap and breathed, "Oh, thank God."

Henry's expression softened as he thought back to the scene in the alley and realized how things must have seemed to Eliza, especially considering how men in the past had treated her as an object to be bought and sold. He gently took both her hands into one of his and lifted her chin so she would look at him. "Eliza, my sweet. When I heard you scream earlier, my heart stopped, and when I saw it was Hobbs who was dragging you toward his alley, the blood froze in my veins. All I could think of was how to get to you, and how you could get away from them. I allowed them to think I had made you my mistress to free you, without thinking of how you might feel, and I apologize. I certainly do not expect you to become my mistress. It never entered my mind you might think I was buying you. Please accept that my only goal was to secure your freedom from those miscreants."

She gave him a watery smile and shook her head as if she couldn't believe she had ever doubted him. "I should've known you're not like that. Forgive me."

His smile broadened. "There is nothing to forgive."

She held his gaze and willed him to grasp her sincere appreciation. "Thank you for coming after me, for rescuing me once again. When they took hold of me in the plaza, I knew I somehow had to make noise, create a commotion so you would know where to look for me. I hoped you'd come after me, and you did. I owe you so much! How can I even begin to repay you?"

His response was simple: "You don't owe me anything. You are my friend and I only did what I would do for any of my friends."

She laid a hand on his cheek and stretched up to press a soft kiss to his lips. When she winced as the fabric of her chemise chafed her nipples, his gaze dropped to her breasts. "He really is a rare bastard. Turn around and lean on my shoulders so I can hold you. I think we both need that right now."

Eliza turned around and did as he said, grateful for the comfort of his arms. He leaned his cheek against her hair, placed the contract Wilkins had signed into her hands, and prayed she would soon realize it truly was over and she was free to do as she pleased.

Upon their return to Cavendish Square, Henry led Eliza into the library, settled her on the sofa before the fire, and sent William to find Mrs. Tibbit. But just before the door closed behind William, Henry thought better of it. "Wait, William, you had better send in Daisie as well. Hobbs hurt Miss Eliza in a way she might know how to treat."

William's face hardened. "You should have let me put a bullet in the bastard."

Henry raised his shoulders in helpless frustration. "Yes, well, I would've liked to have done that back when we got Daisie out. Unfortunately the authorities like Hobbs because he keeps a lid on the turf warfare in the area and thereby makes those streets safer for the rich who like to play in them."

William snorted in disgust. "Whores and politics." He closed the door with a sharp click, underscoring his anger with the situation.

"Quite," Henry muttered between clenched teeth.

Eliza watched the exchange with interest, noting there had been nothing of the usual master/servant attitudes in the way the two men talked to each other. She knew Daisie, a chambermaid in the house, and she knew Daisie was William's girl, but what had this all to do with Hobbs? She was intrigued. "William hasn't always been a footman, has he?"

Henry threw her a quick assessing look. "Indeed not, he was a rifleman in the same company as Daisie's brother, Dix. I was helping with the organization of the supply lines from England to the Spanish front lines, and their company was assigned to me. When Dix found out his mother had died and Daisie was snatched by Hobbs to be put on the streets, he went half mad with grief, rage, and worry, and since I was on my way back home, I requested Dix as my escort. We came back here and got Daisie out."

Eliza remembered what Hobbs had said about Henry. "So that's why he said you owed him a pigeon: Daisie was one of his girls." Eliza knew the cheerful chambermaid and shuddered at the thought of what she must have endured.

Henry nodded grimly. "She was barely sixteen, and in a bad way when we found her. She needed time to heal, to try to put the whole ordeal behind her, but had no skills and nowhere to go. Dix and I were under orders to return to Spain posthaste, so I engaged her in my household and left her in Mrs. Tibbit's care."

The realization she was not the first girl Henry had rescued and brought to his house further calmed Eliza, and Daisie's plight distracted her from the horrors of the day.

"How did William come to be in your employ?"

Henry grinned at the memory. "William was injured on the march to Paris some time later and was sent back to England. Once he was able to walk again, he came to visit Daisie on Dix's behalf and fell madly in love with her. The war was over by then and the army didn't want him back, so he needed a job. And I needed a footman."

The simplicity of his reasoning made Eliza smile. "You like helping people, don't you?"

He smiled back. "I told you, I take care of my friends."

Just then, Mrs. Tibbit bustled into the room with a tea tray in her hands. She set down the tray, poured for them both, and measured out some drops on a spoon for Eliza. "Here, love, from what William told us, you've got bruises again. Daisie will be here in a jiff and once you've had your tea, we'll take you upstairs for a nice warm bath."

Eliza took a deep breath and let out some of the tension in a sigh. Mrs. Tibbit's motherly concern was exactly what she needed. The tea was comforting, but as much as she appreciated it and the warmth of the fire, she was impatient to go upstairs and rid herself of her unforgivingly chafing garments. Luckily, she didn't have to wait long before Daisie entered to announce her bath was ready. Then she inquired quietly, "Where did 'e 'urt ya, Miss Eliza?"

Eliza blushed again and answered in a hushed voice, "My breasts . . . he twisted the nipples."

Daisie blanched. "Both of them?"

Eliza nodded, tears standing in her eyes again. Daisie took her hand and squeezed reassuringly. She sat herself down next to Eliza on the sofa, completely forgetting where she was and who else was in the room. "It'll be all right, love." She patted the younger girl's hand and turned to Mrs. Tibbit. "Do we 'ave any green cabbage, ya know, the one with the smooth leaves?"

Mrs. Tibbit looked like she wanted to ask what the cabbage was for, but then thought better of it and turned to William who stood just inside the door, waiting to be of assistance. "William, see whether Cook has green cabbage."

Daisie turned her attention to William. "I saw the ice man this mornin'. Tell 'er to take off two of the big leaves and chill 'em for ten minutes. It works better that way."

They all looked at her for elaboration. Daisie looked embarrassed for a moment, then relented. "It's a trick one of the girls learned of a midwife. There's somethin' in the leaf that stops the swellin'. The leaves are cool and soothin', and when ya stick them on under yar corset, they stop the chafin'." She blushed and looked at her feet. It was still hard to talk about that part of her past.

But when she looked up again and found William's eyes, he gave her an encouraging nod and smiled. "Don't you worry, Dais, I'll bring them upstairs when they're nice and cold."

He left for the kitchen, and Mrs. Tibbit took charge of Eliza, ushering her and Daisie upstairs.

ONCE THE DOOR CLOSED BEHIND them all, Henry let out a heartfelt sigh and poured himself three fingers of scotch. He had made mistakes today, and they could have been disastrous for Eliza.

Good God, had he lost his edge?

He should've known Hobbs would sniff out an opportunity like this, and he had failed to anticipate it. Worse, he had arrogantly thought to draw out Wilkins so he could deal with him and then had left Eliza's side.

In Spain, such carelessness and lack of foresight would have cost him the mission, if not his life.

And still Eliza thought him a hero. Him, a hero, what a joke. She was the truly brave one, and he would do his best to make sure she never suffered again.

However, they had all survived, and Eliza was shot of that clod Wilkins. At least he had managed to turn the situation around. Still, perhaps he should stick to managing his holdings from now on and start acting his age. Wasn't that what his grandmother kept telling him?

He sank into the armchair by the fire and drained his glass. Letting his head roll back over the rounded edge of the backrest, he felt the tension drain out of his body.

Bloody hell, what a day. And tomorrow he would have to take the gray two-year-old to Avon and get into the Christmas spirit.

He looked forward to seeing Emily and Grossmama, but he didn't think he could stomach the duchess's annual twelve-night party. He would come back on Boxing Day and spend New Year's with Eliza. It might be his last chance to enjoy her company before she got herself a position and they had to say their goodbyes.

He didn't want her to leave. Quite the opposite, he wanted her in his bed, but he liked her too much to seduce her. She had been forced into enough situations of a similar nature already. If they were ever to be together as lovers, he wanted her to choose him, not give in to him.

WHILE HENRY WAS LOST IN his thoughts by the fire, Eliza, with her hair loosely coiled into a bun and pinned to the top of her head, was helped into a warm bath and sank into the rose-scented comfort with a grateful sigh. Above her head, Mrs. Tibbit and Daisie exchanged worried glances as they assessed the burgeoning bruises on Eliza's arms and breasts.

Mrs. Tibbit gently lifted the arm that had, until two days ago, been kept in a sling, and examined a darkening bruise around Eliza's upper arm. "This looks nasty, dear. How does the rest of the arm feel?"

Eliza opened her eyes and glanced at her abused limb. "It's a good job he grabbed me up there; any lower and he might have broken it again." She raised the other arm to study the matching bruise there, then rested back down against the curved lip of the bath and closed her eyes, the deep furrow between her brows evidence of how much pain she was in. "It aches, but it'll be all right. I'm more worried about these." She indicated her breasts, careful not to touch them. "They hurt like the devil."

Daisie hugged her own breasts in an unconscious gesture of sympathy. "Let's get ya washed and out of the bath so we can do some'ing for those as soon as Will gets 'ere with the leaves."

Mrs. Tibbit, seeing Daisie had things well in hand, departed to see to dinner, promising to return with a tray for Eliza. Once the door pulled shut behind her, Eliza turned to Daisie to ask the question most urgently on her mind. "After Sir Henry rescued you, did Hobbs ever come after you again?"

Daisie met her eyes, and Eliza read sympathy and complete understanding in their depth. "I worried abou' that for years, but 'e never did. I guess it's like Will says: Hobbs is clever and brutal, but 'e don't go out of 'is way for no one, not even if ya make 'im angry."

Eliza thought about that for a moment. "So you think I'm safe?"

"As 'ouses! As long as ya don't go walkin' into 'is alley, that is." Daisie saw the doubt in Eliza's eyes and tried to explain. "Think abou' it, 'e don't care abou' us, we're just pigeons to 'im. He can get another one on the next corner and there's no fuss; 'e don't care, but 'e ain't forget-tin' neither. You and I aren't important enough for 'im to bother with. He'll wait for Sir Henry to get 'is revenge."

Yet another thing Eliza would owe Henry for. But at least she didn't have to worry about Hobbs. Daisie's assessment was right; Hobbs struck her as an opportunist rather than a dog-in-the-manger type. And his attitude toward women was such that he probably didn't think them worth taking revenge on beyond what he'd already done to her.

So while she climbed out of the bath and Daisie helped her dry herself, it slowly but surely sank in that she was indeed free.

Horace had obviously lost interest the moment she had defied him by crawling out of the coal chute. After all, he had been paid, and that was all he cared about.

Wilkins had accepted money for her and signed a contract. And Hobbs was only interested in revenge on Sir Henry.

It was over. The nightmare that had started with her father's death seven years ago was over. It had taken her mother's death and her own willingness to die rather than submit to the fate others had arranged for her, but she was free.

Eliza reached for the locket still pinned to the shift she had been wearing earlier and wished with all her heart she could do something for her mother. But all she could think of was to wear the locket for her and to endeavor to live the best life she could. Turning to Daisie, she asked, "Could you find me a ribbon so I can wear this?"

Daisie was by the chest of drawers looking for a nightgown that could be laced tight in the back, but turned to admire the locket in Eliza's hand. "Oh, that's lovely."

"My dad gave it to my mum a long time ago."

Handing her the nightgown, Daisie took the wet towel out of Eliza's hand. "The one that sold ya was yar stepdad, right? There's ribbons in the top drawer."

She slipped the nightgown over Eliza's head and went back to the chest of drawers to select a thin, light blue ribbon. She secured the locket onto it and handed it to Eliza so she could tie it around her neck. Eliza smiled her thanks and turned to the mirror to see how it looked. It felt good to finally wear it out in the open.

A knock on the door heralded the arrival of the chilled cabbage leaves. The relief was immediate as the smooth, cool leaves molded onto her abused breasts to form a barrier against any chafing garments. After Daisie pulled the laces tight in the back of the nightgown to hold the cabbage leaves in place, Eliza sank into the chair by the fire and let the relief wash over her.

Thank God this day was over.

Thank God for Sir Henry, and for cabbage leaves.

THE NEXT MORNING, ELIZA HAD just been fitted with a fresh set of chilled cabbage leaves when Henry strolled into her room, followed by Mrs. Tibbit, who carried an enormous breakfast tray. He wore buckskin breeches and tall riding boots, and his brown wool waistcoat was buttoned up all the way, but he had yet to don a jacket.

"Mrs. Tibbit said you were up, so I thought we might break our fast together before I depart for Avon."

Eliza smiled her welcome as he looped a companionable arm around her shoulder and kissed her temple.

"How are you this morning? I hear Daisie's treatment is a success."

Eliza let him lead her to the small table Mrs. Tibbit had pulled in front of the fireplace and was currently setting for two. "I have a whole new appreciation for cabbage, although I may have to don a corset today to hold the bloody stuff in place." She frowned down at her breasts and gingerly moved the left cabbage leaf back up to where it did most good.

Henry's lips twitched in amusement. "I'd offer to help, but somehow I don't think you would appreciate the gesture."

Eliza blushed, realizing what he was watching her do, but grinned back at him. It was lovely how he could see the amusing side of everything. It certainly was one of the reasons she liked his company so much. "Let's sit and eat. The less I move, the better my chance these things will stay in place."

Pulling out her chair for her, he seated her with genteel ceremony. "By all means! But tell me, how is your arm and how did you sleep?"

Eliza watched him sit and spread his napkin on his lap with a graceful economy of movement. Then he held the dish of eggs for her so she could serve herself.

"My arm aches, but it will be fine. And as for sleep? I had worried I would dream of the day's events, but I slept like a newborn babe, and feel much restored for it."

Henry handed her the cup of tea Mrs. Tibbit had poured for her. "I'm very glad to hear it. I have always found sleep to be the best medicine." He reached for her hand and looked at her with a tenderness she longed to explore, now she knew she had a choice in the matter. "I have to go to see my daughter today, but I leave you in good hands, and I would not be leaving you here if I thought you were in any kind of danger. I want you to take this time to recuperate and get past all this. When I get back after Christmas, we will talk about what you want to do with your future."

She turned her hand up to hold his and gave him a crooked smile. "I'm not sure a fortnight will be enough time to get over six years of misery, but I am eager to get on with my life."

Her glib remark made Henry frown, so he added, "That's not what I meant, silly."

She shrugged, but he saw the pain in her eyes and squeezed her hand reassuringly. "You are welcome here for as long as you want to be here. I am certainly in no hurry to lose your company."

She swallowed her tears and smiled again, wishing she could crawl into his arms and just stay there until she was brave enough to face the world on her own.

They chewed their eggs in silence for a few moments before Henry pointed to the locket on her neck. "You are wearing the locket. Will you tell me about it?"

Her hand came up to rub the engraved silver piece between her thumb and forefinger. "It was my mum's. My dad gave it to her when he asked her to marry him, and she gave it to me just before she died. It's the only thing I have left of them."

"And you have been wearing it pinned to your undergarments so

Horace couldn't take it away from you." He chuckled at her surprised look. "Mrs. Tibbit told me she found it pinned to your corset after I first brought you here, so it's an easy assumption. I take it your wearing it openly now means you know in your heart this whole horrible muddle is truly over."

Eliza nodded. "It occurred to me last night that Horace must have washed his hands of me as soon as he realized I was gone. Why else would Wilkins have teamed up with Hobbs to find me? I bet Horace told him to go to hell rather than pay him back. All he really wanted was to get rid of me anyhow."

It was Henry's turn to nod in agreement. "That's the conclusion I came to. And I am quite certain Hobbs will not bother to come after you: it's me he wants. But just to be on the safe side, I had William call in two of his old army chums to make sure you and Daisie are safe whilst I'm in the country. They are both good men. You can trust them."

Eliza swallowed a fork full of eggs and sipped her tea before she looked up again. "Thank you for looking after me. I can't tell you how much it means to me."

Henry gave her hand one last squeeze before he let go to devote himself to his breakfast. She looked so young and vulnerable in her voluminous, quilted white dressing gown, and he longed to fold her into his arms. Of course he couldn't, considering the reason for the cabbage leaves.

CHAPTER NINE

WHILE SIR HENRY BEGAN HIS TWO-DAY JOURNEY to Avon, his daughter outwitted her long-suffering governess in order to join her male cousins on their annual excursion to Woodborough to purchase presents for their parents and siblings. This was an unescorted outing, restricted to the Redwick boys, Julian, Andrew, and Bertram, but Emily had no time for such restrictions. As long as no one outright forbade her from attending, she saw no reason to stay behind.

Woodborough was a small village with little to recommend it except its picturesque setting and proximity to the Avon estates. Besides a pub that had hosted many generations of Redwicks, it also boasted a shop offering soaps, sweets, and other trinkets produced by local artisans.

This was the third year Emily had managed to talk Bertie and his older brothers into bringing her along. She was, after all, a superb horsewoman and would not complain about the hour-long cross-country ride. In fact, she was the one leading the charge, her only regret being that Fanny, her beloved pony, could not jump the taller fences. But since her fifteen-year-old cousin Andrew was so rotund he could barely sit his horse, her pony's short legs served to preserve his dignity.

Emily's blue eyes shone with excitement and the thrill of having achieved her freedom for the afternoon. Her long white-blond hair was somewhat contained by a hat, but it still whipped behind her like a flag. At almost twelve years of age, her slender frame showed no signs of the woman she would become, but she sat her pony admirably in her deep blue riding habit.

They entered the village, flushed and smiling from the vigorous ride, and headed to the stables behind the pub, where they left their mounts.

Emily removed the bridle so Fanny could nibble on the hay. The animal nickered and rubbed her head on the girl, then made to nibble her hat instead of the hay.

"Fanny, you devious beast! Don't you dare destroy my hat. Aunt Hortense went on for a full hour after you ate the flowers off my bonnet." Emily dodged out of the reach of the pony's determined teeth and closed the gate to the stall before turning back. "I'll tell you what. You be a good girl and I'll bring you back some mint pillows."

The pony nickered again and moved her head up and down as if to say yes, which made Emily laugh. She ran to catch up with her cousins, skipping up to Bertie, who at fourteen fought pimples and a cracking voice, but still had the distinction of being her preferred partner for any and all adventures. She got there just in time to see her oldest cousin, Julian, turn into the high street the wrong way. "Where is Julian going?"

Bertie tried to maintain a superior mien but couldn't keep the awe out of his voice. "He brought all his presents down from Oxford with him, so he is meeting James Halsy for a drink in the pub."

Emily's eyes went wide with awe, but it didn't take long for her curiosity to override all else. "Do you think they will let me in the taproom, seeing as we will have to go find him later in there?"

Bertie met her eyes, his reflecting his own eagerness to explore the bastion of adult masculinity that was the pub. He put his hand on her arm to slow her and nodded at Andrew's back. "We'll have to get rid of him."

Emily's eyes sparkled with mischief. "Well, that's easy. Just send him to the bakery for apple turnovers to eat on the way back. It will take him at least half an hour to sample all their cream cakes."

Bertie gave her a conspiratorial grin before he urged her down the street to the shop.

The bell chimed over their heads as they entered the colorful haven of Mrs. Beal's wondrous establishment. The boys had decided earlier to pool their resources so they could buy bigger gifts. Silk scarves for their two older sisters, a princess puppet for the youngest, a lacquered trinket box for their mother, and so on. Since this arrangement had the added benefit of letting them divide the present-buying between the two of them, they completed their shopping in record time.

Emily was studying a selection of rose-scented soaps when the two boys came up to her. Bertie nudged her with his elbow to get her attention. "We're going across the road to get a purse for Father from the saddle maker."

Emily nodded absently. "I won't be long. I just have to decide which soap to get for Grossmama and then find the lemon drops for Papa. Do you think Grossmama would like the one shaped like a rose or the one with the pink rose petals inside?"

The two boys shrugged simultaneously and hurried toward the door before she could ask them any more impossible questions. Bertie threw over his shoulder, "Don't go running off before we get back."

Emily finally looked up and grinned at Bertie before she called after them, "Are we getting apple turnovers for the way back?"

Andrew's face instantly brightened at the thought of a trip to the bakery. "I'll go get them and meet you back at the stables. Bertie can come back and escort you."

Bertie answered Emily's conspiratorial grin with his own and almost ran into a tall, immaculately dressed gentleman in his hurry to get out the door.

Emily had already turned back to the rose-scented soaps, so she wasn't aware of the gentleman's presence, nor the speculative glance he sent after Bertie, nor the way his cold gray eyes settled on her.

The stranger studied her intently as she made her choice and added the rose-shaped soap to the basket hanging from her arm. When Emily moved to the boiled sweets, displayed closer to the counter in the center of the shop, his eyes traveled up and down her still-childishly flat form with a hint of disdain, but lingered with approval on her shiny blond hair and her delicate profile. He quietly circled to the shaving supplies, from where he had a perfect view of her expressive face.

The tall stranger smirked when she picked out a lemon-shaped tin filled with lemon drops and longingly eyed a similar tin in the shape of a raspberry.

At that moment the shopkeeper bustled from the back room with an assortment of silk ribbons fluttering from her hands. "There you are, deary. Those are all the remnants I have at the moment. I can let you have the lot for sixpence."

Emily turned her attention from her favorite raspberry drops and gave Mrs. Beal a bright smile. "Oh, those are just perfect. I can make all kinds of sashes and hair bands for Delia's dolls and still have enough left over to put pretty bows on all the presents."

Mrs. Beal finally noticed the gentleman who had selected a san-dalwood soap and was slowly making his way toward the counter.

"Just so, Miss March. Can I help you, sir?"

The stranger waved toward Emily. "Carry on serving the young lady."

Mrs. Beal gave him a grateful smile and started to make a list of all the things Emily had selected, adding up the purchases before wrap-ping all her treasures in parchment. "That'll be twelve shillings and sixpence. Will that be all for you today, Miss March?"

Emily carefully counted out the money, pulling one coin after an-other out of her purse, but was interrupted by the stranger. "March? Would you, by any chance, be the daughter of Sir Henry March?"

Emily had not previously paid any attention to the gentleman, but now whirled to face him. "Do you know my papa?"

The stranger removed his hat, revealing dark hair, receding just a little from his brow, and bowed elegantly before her. "I am Lord Astor. I am pleased to make your acquaintance, Miss March. Is your father with you?"

Emily blushed with the knowledge that she had left the safety of the estate without permission. She opted to evade the question. "I came with my cousins."

Remembering her pony, she turned back to Mrs. Beal. "Oh, and can I get a cone of mint pillows?"

The shopkeeper turned to get the mints off the shelf behind her while Emily dug in her purse for the appropriate coin but came up empty. Lord Astor, who had watched her every move, realized her dilemma before she could voice it and laid a staying hand on her arm.

"Allow me, Miss March."

She turned innocent eyes to him, and he leaned down to whisper conspiratorially, "I won't tell your papa if you don't."

Lord Astor handed Mrs. Beal payment for the sweets and his soap, and Emily curtsied prettily but moved half a step back. "Thank you, sir."

Mrs. Beal winked at Emily and handed her the mint pillows. "Aren't you lucky, miss."

Just then the bell above the door chimed, and Bertie urged from the door, "Come on, Em, they only have three kinds of cream pie today."

The unmistakable signs of annoyance flitted across Lord Astor's impassive face, but he quickly controlled his reaction. "May I trouble you for one mint pillow? I find myself craving something sweet."

Emily opened the bag with a practiced flick of her wrist and thrust it toward the lord. "By all means, sir. You paid for them." Then, turning to Bertie, she called, "I'll be there in just a moment, Bertie."

Lord Astor waited until he had her full attention once more, then slipped the mint pillow between his thin lips and speared her with his arctic gaze. "Until we meet again, Miss March."

Emily couldn't quite ignore the icy shiver running down her spine, but adventure awaited and Bertie was safety, so she bobbed another curtsy, grabbed her parcel, and rushed out the door in Bertie's wake.

Lord Astor nodded to the shopkeeper, who indulgently smiled at the antics of the young. Slipping the soap into his coat pocket, he left the shop. Outside his eyes quickly found the two youngsters rushing toward the pub. The smile playing around his lips would have frozen the blood in the veins of a hardened criminal. "Enjoy your freedom,

Miss Emily March, it won't last for very much longer."

Then he turned into the alley behind the shop, handed the groom holding his horse a small purse, and took the reins. "Well done. Tell Ostley he may attend the next event."

THE WEEK FOLLOWING HENRY'S DEPARTURE passed quietly. Eliza missed Henry from the moment he left for Avon, but did her best to keep busy. She continued her sewing lessons with Mrs. Tibbit and took to helping Daisie with her duties. With the master of the house not in residence, the two girls made short work of it.

That left plenty of time to engage in knitting, sewing, and embroidering their Christmas presents in front of the fire in Eliza's room: a knitted throw for Mrs. Tibbit, an embroidered chemise for Daisie, a cardinal red apron for Cook, and personalized handkerchiefs for the men of the household. They embroidered a horseshoe for Roberts, a bumblebee for Joe the gardener, and a gate with two crossed lances for the two footmen, William and Thomas.

Whenever the weather allowed, William and his army mates escorted Daisie and Eliza on walks around the neighborhood. The men were rough around the edges, not unlike the men Eliza had grown up with at the inn, but they always treated her with kindness and respect. Eliza was certain their behavior toward her reflected how much they respected Sir Henry.

Their little group went to take a closer look at the shop windows on Oxford Street, listened to the choir practice for the Christmas service at St.-Martin-in-the-Fields, and saw the nativity scene at Westminster Cathedral.

On Sunday, Daisie and William took Eliza to service at St.

George's to look at the grand ladies who frequented the little church in Mayfair. They sat in the back pews and watched the society matrons in all their Sunday finery file in.

William knew most of them by name and pointed out the most important dames to Eliza. Of course there were gentlemen too, but they were mostly clad in somber grays and blacks. In Eliza's eyes, none were as handsome as Sir Henry, so she paid them no mind.

The ladies' ornate gowns fascinated Eliza: crafted out of the finest wool and velvet, trimmed with lace and fur, matched with exquisite hats, and worn with such grace and poise. Eliza thought she had never seen anything more lovely.

One lady in particular caught her attention. She was of medium height and clad in a high-waisted, deep blue velvet gown with a matching full-length spencer over it. Her soft blond curls were covered with a black lace mantilla, and she wore no jewelry except the teardrop pearls on her ears. There was nothing ostentatious in her dress, but everything about her, her face and figure, her bearing and smile, was exquisite. What really set her apart, however, was the way in which everybody seemed to treat her with a measure of respect, and, at the same time, made sure not to come too close to her.

Eliza nudged William and nodded in the direction of the lady in blue. "Who is she?"

Daisie followed the direction of Eliza's gaze and sighed dreamily. "Ain't she lovely! And she's only the daughter of a stable master. Gives a girl 'ope, don't it?"

Stunned, Eliza directed her questioning gaze at William, who chuckled and explained quietly, "She is the Earl of York's mistress. The story goes that 'e noticed 'er when she was just thirteen, and was so moved by 'er, 'e 'ad 'er educated in the same school his sisters 'ad gone to. Then, when she came 'ome from school at sixteen, 'e made 'er 'is mistress and later took 'er with 'im to the continent on his various diplomatic missions. Apparently, she's as smart as she's lovely and 'elped 'im build the alliance that finally defeated the Corsican monster. There is many a politician who listens to 'er advice, and even the Regent attends 'er political dinners."

Eliza shook her head in astonishment. "I thought all mistresses were like Millie—you know, the one who wouldn't take no for an answer?"

William chuckled at the memory of Henry's ex-mistress invading the house.

Eliza continued to study the lovely lady in blue. "This woman looks more regal than the duchess over there."

William looked thoughtful. "Well, most mistresses are money-grabbing 'ussies who don't mind spreadin' their legs in exchange for a nice life. But then there are women like 'er. No one will ever confuse 'er for a painted actress, will they? I bet the earl finds more 'appiness in 'er arms than 'e ever did in 'is arranged marriage." William gave a stern nod to underscore his pronouncement and turned his attention to the service about to begin.

Eliza watched the Earl of York's mistress and wondered if she, Eliza, a mere tavern wench, could make Sir Henry happy. Somebody should.

ON CHRISTMAS MORNING, ELIZA WOKE to a hatbox holding the hat she had admired in Covent Garden. She didn't have to read the note to know it was from Sir Henry and wore it with pride to Christmas services, along with her locket on its new finely-wrought silver chain. Mrs. Tibbit and Daisie had presented it to her at breakfast and explained that the entire staff had chipped in to buy it for her. Eliza thought it the most perfect gift she had ever received, not that she had received many in the past six years.

Christmas dinner was a cheerful affair in the big warm kitchen at the back of the house. Outside the kitchen window, a steep embankment led up to the side lawn. Late in the afternoon, the icy rain had turned to snow, lending a surreal quality to the back yard. The snow crystals were caught in the lavender and rosemary just beyond the windows and sparkled in the light of the candles. "Christmas lights for the fairies," Eliza's mother would have called it.

Cook and Mrs. Tibbit put their best foot forward, and everyone who held a position in or around the house gathered at the kitchen table. It was covered in fine linen, decorated with gilded walnuts and pine cones, laden with veritable mountains of delicious food, and lit by at least a dozen beeswax candles.

Sir Henry insisted his staff should eat as well as he did on feast days, and had he not been at Avon, he and Emily would have joined them in the kitchen.

The room smelled of duck roast and mince pies, and the wood fire in the hearth accounted for only a fraction of the warmth in Eliza's heart. These people gathered around the table had taken her in, healed her, and continued to protect her. Although one could argue Sir Henry had ordered them to do those things, they had also welcomed her into their midst out of the goodness of their hearts. They made her feel like she belonged, and that soothed her soul.

Not even the vicar in Hampstead, who had known her all her life, had been willing to help her. In fact, he had lectured her on obedience rather than offer his protection from a known wife-beater. Sir Henry and his household didn't face Horace and his cronies on a daily basis, but still.

Looking at all the friendly, cheerful faces around the table, Eliza realized this was her first real Christmas since her father had died. She missed him, and she missed her mother even more, but she knew they would want her to enjoy this moment and make the best of this new chance at life.

So she smiled through her tears, held on to her locket, and tried to think of something she could do to repay the kindness her new friends had shown her. It would have to be profound, she decided. And for Sir Henry, it would have to be personal. The only thing of value she possessed was her virginity. Perhaps she ought to give it to Henry; he had made it quite clear he desired her. As for Eliza herself, her dreams were filled with the possibilities his gentle touch had conjured.

AFTER CHRISTMAS DINNER WAS OVER, the dishes had been washed, and the china returned to its rightful place, Eliza and Daisie took the last of the mulled wine up to Eliza's room to have a cozy good night chat.

Settling into the armchairs before the fire, Eliza noticed a strain around Daisie's eyes. "You all right, love? You look a bit peaked. You didn't argue with Will, did you?"

Daisie leaned her head against the backrest and closed her eyes as she savored the warm wine. "Na, Will and me are good."

She sighed heavily. "It's Christmas that gets me down. It's been eight years now, but it don't matter 'ow long. Me mum died the end of

November. Three weeks later, Hobbs snatched me right off the bloody Bow High Street and took me up to 'is cottage in Hampstead . . . for trainin', as 'e calls it. By Christmas Day I was some toff's present to 'imself."

It was a touchingly prosaic description of the personal disaster that Christmas had been for Daisie. But somehow the monotone of her voice and her closed eyes, as if she were unwilling to face the ugliness of those memories, spoke more clearly of the horrors she had endured than any number of tears could ever have communicated.

Eliza knew despair, had seen it clearly in her mother's eyes, and when Daisie's eyes opened, she saw it there. She took a deep swallow of wine, hoping it would take the edge off her own memories, but Daisie continued. "I know I'm safe from Hobbs and perverts like that toff, but some things you just can't un-know. And you would 'ave to un-know them, 'cause you sure as shit can't forget them."

Her mother's desperate screams reverberated through Eliza's mind. "No, you sure can't."

They were quiet for a while, each unwilling to burden the other with further details of their private pain. But somehow their silence was a comfortable one because it was shared.

And then, into that silence Daisie said the one thing they both wished for: "I wish I could kill the bastard."

Eliza raised her glass for a toast. "I wish I could dance on Horace's grave."

Daisie smiled her approval, but added, "I don't just mean for revenge. If I wanted revenge, I'd tie up that toff and shove one of 'is bloody toys up 'is lordly arse." The despair in her eyes had turned to anger. "I wanna stop Hobbs so he can't make any more girls do things so 'orrible they shrivel your soul."

Eliza had looked into Hobbs's eyes and knew for a certainty the man had no humanity left in him. She also knew, no matter the pain Horace could inflict, Hobbs was far more dangerous. According to Henry, he was also untouchable, at least in London. And that was when she remembered something Daisie had said earlier. "Dais, did you say Hobbs took you to Hampstead?"

"Yea,'e 'as a cottage there. He takes all the new girls there. His toff friend gets first crack at them, specially the virgins. The rest 'e introduces to the trade at The Silver Fox. By the time 'e brings them back to town, they feel so dirty, they don't wanna see their families ever again, even if they 'ave any left."

Eliza thought about that. "I suppose that's where he met up with Wilkins. Daisie, after Hobbs tried to kidnap me, I overheard Sir Henry and William talking about why they can't just put a bullet in his head."

Daisie sighed. "I know, the London magistrates think 'e's the lesser evil and turn a blind eye. And every year 'e gets richer and more untouchable."

Eliza was beginning to see this more clearly. "You think he pays them off?"

Daisie's bitter little chuckle left no doubt as to what she thought. "I'd stake me soddin' life on it."

Eliza thought it probable Hobbs had the magistrate in Hampstead in his pocket too, but still, he had to be more vulnerable there than he was in London, so why had they not looked for him there? Then all of a sudden it made sense. "You never told William or even Sir Henry about Hampstead, did you?"

Daisie only shook her head, and the sadness in her eyes bore witness to how much it cost her to keep her secrets.

"Why not?"

"Sir Henry never asked, and I didn't 'ave the 'eart to tell Will. He knows I was a whore and that's bad enough."

"But what if we could stop Hobbs once and for all? Would you tell Will about the cottage and The Silver Fox?"

Daisie nodded slowly. "If I thought it really would stop 'im, then yea. But I can't tell 'im about the toff. You get 'anged for shootin' a lord, don't matter what 'e's done."

Eliza couldn't argue with that; no doubt some of what Daisie had endured was dangerous for William to know. She would bear that in mind when she talked to Sir Henry about it. Would the connection to Hampstead be news to him, or had she just given her friend false hope?

CHAPTER TEN

IT WAS WELL AFTER TEN IN THE EVENING ON the third day of his travel from Avon when Henry finally stepped into the foyer of his house on Cavendish Square. He was cold, tired, and hungry, but unwilling to rouse his already sleeping servants, so he made his way to the kitchen to find some food and set water to boil for tea.

The eighty-mile journey had taken him three days rather than the usual two due to the frigid temperatures holding the home counties in an icy grip since Christmas day. Emily and her cousins had been delighted with the white Christmas, turning Avon's front lawn into a snowball reenactment of Waterloo. But the muddy roads had been frozen into bone-jarring ruts, and the snowy blanket covering them had only increased their treachery.

Henry was happy to be home and savored the peace of the sleeping house. The fire in the stove had been kept burning and the kettle was full of water, so tea would be on hand shortly. Henry cut himself a few slices of crusty white bread and leftover ham, spread them with butter and grainy mustard respectively, and ate while he waited for the kettle to boil. One never knew how satisfying a meal could be until one was truly hungry. Once tea was made, he added a couple of Mrs. Tibbit's mince pies to his tray and made his way to the library so he could spike his tea with the good brandy.

The fire in the library was burning behind its protective screen. Henry picked up his correspondence from his desk and sank gratefully into his favorite chair before the fire. Warm enough now to shed his coat and boots, he slurped his brandied tea and enjoyed his cousin's Christmas letter from Vienna.

He must have nodded off, but was startled awake by the great clock in the foyer striking midnight. Bowing to his body's need for rest, Henry decided to leave his boots where they were and headed to his bedroom on stockinged feet.

He lit a taper in the hallway and had barely made it to the bottom of the stairs when a bloodcurdling scream rent the quiet of the house.

All traces of Henry's sleepiness evaporated as he determined the scream had come from Eliza's room. Taking the stairs three at a time, he burst through her door and found her sitting bolt upright in bed, trying to catch her breath, her eyes still wild with fear and confusion.

Henry quickly ascertained there was no intruder, no real danger of any kind other than those remembered from the past, and sat next to Eliza on her bed, enfolding her in his arms. "It was a nightmare, sweetheart. You are safe."

Eliza was shaking as she clung to him, but her head was filled with the chant, *He is here, he is here, he is here!* The warmth of his embrace chased her fears away until she was finally able to speak. "You're back!" She hiccupped a last sob and dried her tears with the back of her hand, then buried her face even deeper in his neck. "I feel much safer when you're home."

The tickle of her breath on his neck felt like home, and her sleepy scent teased his nose as he pulled her even closer and buried his face in her hair.

Eliza had never been far from his thoughts over the past ten days, but he hadn't realized just how much he'd missed her. His hands made slow soothing circles on her back, and he enjoyed the weight of her against him while she slowly calmed herself.

Henry used his free hand to light the candle on Eliza's nightstand with his taper. The fire had been banked, so the room was rather chilly. His seeking fingers found a woolen wrap at the bottom of the bed and draped it around Eliza's flannel-covered shoulders, never breaking their embrace.

Eventually Eliza sighed and relaxed in his arms. "I hate nightmares."

"About the inn?" he asked, reassuring her with one little question that she was understood.

"Trying to get away from the inn."

Her head was still nestled against his shoulder, so he couldn't see her face. But he knew the powerful fears that caused her nightmares, so he gently laid his cheek against her temple and waited for her to tell him of it.

"I couldn't get out of the cellar. The coals kept slipping from under my feet."

She shifted back a little so she could look up at Henry. "Then I was on the road and my feet felt like they were stuck in molasses. I had to scream to wake myself up." One corner of her mouth turned up into a half smile. "And then you were here."

Smiling, he answered, "I'm glad I got back in time."

"It seems you are forever rescuing me."

Her eyes were full of warmth, and Henry's smile turned into a grin. "What can I say? You are my favorite damsel in distress." He placed a gentle kiss just to the side of her mouth. "Better?"

"Much."

To illustrate, she disengaged herself from his embrace, but instantly missed the warmth of his body, the strength of his arms. Still, she stacked the pillows so she could lean against them and smiled up at him. "How was your Christmas? How is Emily?"

Taking his cue from Eliza, Henry scooted down to the end of the bed and leaned against the footboard, one angled leg resting on the feather bed, the other dangling to the floor. "Christmas was nice and Emily delightful, as always. She named her horse Adonis, and promptly won a race against her favorite cousin, Bertie, and his big bay gelding."

Eliza giggled, and Henry found the sound most reassuring. "She is a bit of a tomboy, your Emily, isn't she?"

A broad grin split his face. "Much to my grandmother's delight and the duchesses's chagrin. It's chilly in here! Let me build up the fire for you."

Henry moved over to the fireplace as he spoke and started coaxing the flames back to life. He was glad for a task that needed doing. Eliza looked absolutely adorable sitting up against the white pillows, surrounded by a halo of dark curls, her eyes now shining brightly. His body had stirred as he had embraced her, and he longed to draw her back into his arms and kiss her with all the tenderness and passion he felt for her.

"How was your Christmas, Eliza?"

Eliza's voice was soft and warm. "Quite wonderful, actually. Thank you for my beautiful hat."

Henry chuckled as he finished up with the fire and rinsed his hands with some of the water kept warm on the hearthstone. He heard the rustle of linen from the bed and imagined her snuggling back down under the covers. Reaching for a towel drying on the fire screen, he straightened, still facing the fire. "You are very welcome. I can't wait to see it on you."

"I will wear it for you the next time you take me out." Her voice came from right behind him; he felt her arms coming around his waist as she hugged him from behind.

Eliza laid her cheek into the hollow between his shoulder blades and let herself melt against him. His hands came up to cover hers resting on his stomach, and she could sense him waiting to see where this was going. Smiling, she rubbed her cheek against his spine. "I missed you so very much," she whispered. "Stay with me, Henry."

He lifted his arm and turned in her embrace so he could return it. His hands landed lightly on her shoulders, one traveling up to delve into her riot of hair, the other stroking down and coming to rest at the small of her back. His arms tightened around her, and this time his body not only sheltered her but also left her in no doubt that, physically at least, he was more than willing to take her up on her offer.

He spoke into her hair, and the warmth of his breath sent delicious tingles all the way down her spine. "You, in my bed, would indeed be splendid, and I won't pretend I don't want you."

She wiggled a little in response. "Yes, that would be quite ludicrous."

He smiled down at her, then turned serious. "Eliza, I know you are still a virgin and I don't want to take that from you."

Laying her index finger against his lips, she blushed deeply. "I want to be with you, want to know what it feels like to lie with you."

Henry's blue, blue eyes darkened with passion. Put like that, he had no further objection to spending the night with her. He bent at the knees, grabbed her around her hips, and lifted her high above himself so she had to look down on him. "So be it, my delectable libertine."

The grin on his face was so full of delight, Eliza knew she would never regret giving herself to him, even if she did feel some trepidation about what was to come. She hugged his head to her unbound breasts and felt him nestle into the valley between them. He breathed her in as he carried her back to her bed. There, he let her slide slowly down his body while he kissed his way up her neck and chin to her mouth.

Back at the inn, a patron or two had managed to stick their tongue down Eliza's throat before she could get away, but this was different. Henry's lips played with hers, gently brushing from corner to corner, nibbling and tucking and covering her mouth softly. His tongue touched her lips and then, once she opened her mouth hesitantly, her tongue. He encouraged her to play with him, rather than just dominating her or demanding from her. It was slow and gentle and playful and so very, very good. Eliza lost herself completely in Henry's kiss.

All the while, his hands caressed her back until, without breaking the kiss, he stepped back half a step and ran his hands up along the sides of her body to untie the bow holding together the lacing at the front of her flannel nightshirt. When he had loosened the ribbon enough, he brought his hands to her neck and slowly pushed the shirt off her shoulders and down her arms, caressing the naked skin he revealed. Finally, the nightshirt slipped all the way to the floor to pool around her ankles, and he stepped back to look.

Her body, like her face, was fine-boned and exquisite. Her breasts were high and round, but no more than a handful. Her waist dipped in pleasingly, and she had the beginnings of a tiny belly he found reassuring. She had been so very thin when he had first brought her to his house, but now there was strength in her graceful curves. He thought her just about perfect. "You are even lovelier than I imagined you would be."

She blushed and covered her embarrassment over her nakedness by reaching out to undo the buttons of his waistcoat and then his shirt. He undid his cuffs and dropped the gold-and-carved-ivory cufflinks on her bedside table. The gesture was oddly domestic; had he been visiting a mistress, he would have put them in his pocket to avoid having to search for them later. This was special. This was Eliza, and he knew beyond a shadow of a doubt that she was, and would always be, his friend.

Henry let both waistcoat and shirt slide off his shoulders and drop to the floor. But he stayed her hand when she moved to unbutton his placket. Her hand trembled in his, and he realized just how nervous she was, despite her bravado. He lifted her hand to his lips, kissed her palm, and smiled into her soft brown eyes.

"No need to rush, sweetheart."

Eliza rubbed her hand along the stubble on his cheek, enjoying the roughness of it on her palm, and smiled back. "Can I not see you?"

"Of course you can, if you want." There was just a hint of challenge in his eyes.

She swallowed and nodded. "I want to see you."

Henry undid his placket and peeled off his buckskin breeches, undergarments, and socks in one economical movement. The boyishness of it made her smile, despite her nerves.

When he straightened and stood completely naked in front of her, she let her eyes trail from his face over his chest and arms to his belly, and then they rested on his cock.

He was lean, muscled and well-formed all over, and once she had looked her fill, she stepped closer to let her hands wander over the smooth skin of his chest. Her fingers played in the sandy tufts of hair growing around his nipples and trailed down to the curly nest around his cock. It was thick, heavy, fully erect, and pointing straight at her. It bobbed up and down in excitement under her perusal, and she looked up at him with a mixture of amusement and trepidation. "Rather like an excited puppy."

Henry laughed out loud, his eyes dancing. "Don't mind him. He is rather single-minded, if not to say simpleminded."

Eliza knew the basics but had no idea what to make of his comment. "What . . . exactly does he want?"

Henry pulled her gently into the warmth of his embrace and relished the feel of her nipples grazing against his naked chest and his member coming to rest against her belly. He nuzzled her temple and whispered in her ear, "He wants to be deep inside you, losing himself in the pleasure of it."

He had meant it as a tease, but she barely held back a gasp, taking him at his word. She smiled bravely and lay down on the bed, spreading her legs slightly, and waited for him to lie on top of her.

Henry looked at her puzzled for a moment until understanding dawned, then he regarded her with a rueful grin. "By all means, let's get under the covers."

He lay on his side next to her and pulled the coverlet over both of them, then stroked a reassuring hand across her belly. "Eliza, my sweet, my cock might be in a hurry, but I intend to savor you. I want you to enjoy what we are doing." He raised an eyebrow and held her gaze, willing her to understand.

Her relief was so obvious, he had to stifle another laugh. But then she turned into his arms and initiated their next kiss, and he filled his hands with the softness of her breasts, and time ceased to exist.

Eliza reveled in the closeness and the warmth of it all while Henry trailed open-mouthed kisses down her throat. She felt his tongue trace small circles along her collarbone, sending shivers down her spine and moisture between her legs. When he reached her breasts, he sucked her hardened nipple into his mouth with increasing pressure until she gasped and arched into him. All the while, he let his hands glide up and down her back in a measured caress, reassuring her it was safe to give herself over to the startling sensations he elicited.

Eventually his lips returned to her mouth, and he challenged her with a carnal kiss so deep it seemed to touch her very soul. He coaxed her lips open wide and explored the deepest recesses of her mouth with his tongue, foreshadowing the joining of their bodies.

Eliza never would have thought such an invasion of her being could be anything but revolting, but she found herself thrilled to the core and breathless with anticipation as to what he would do next.

Henry waited for Eliza to relax into the kiss and then let the hand on her back trail lower to caress the smooth curve of her bottom and down her thigh to her knee. He hooked his hand under it and pulled up her leg so he could lay it over his thigh and pull her whole body flush against his. Then he stroked his hand back up to her bottom and down the crease between her cheeks to her sex.

Eliza, gently caressing his back, momentarily froze at the unfamiliar sensation of her whole body being in such intimate contact with another, being touched so intimately by another, but when his fingers remained light and teasing, she answered his embrace with her own, bringing their bodies even closer together. There was something marvelously comforting in being skin to skin with another human being. Eliza resumed caressing Henry's back and, encouraged by his near purr, let her hand travel lower, over the curve of his buttocks.

Henry's heart sang with the joy of feeling her respond to him. He caressed her folds and teased her clitoris until she was wet and ready for him.

Eliza could barely draw enough air into her lungs as Henry's fingers explored her most secret places. It felt strange but at the same time so unbelievably good. With her face pressed into his neck, she breathed in his maleness with short pants.

His voice was soft when he asked, "Do you ever touch yourself here?"

Eliza blushed so hard he could see the rosy hue on her shoulder, and nodded into his neck.

"So you know what an orgasm feels like."

It wasn't quite a question, but she felt an answer was required. "That tingling feeling that makes the world go away for just a moment?"

He chuckled at her accurate, yet somewhat inadequate, description of the most powerful pleasure known to man. His fingers continued to tease over her clitoris and dip lower to circle her entrance and then back up to her nub in a hypnotic cycle. "It's more intense when you share it with another person."

She huffed out a laugh, acknowledging just how much he affected her. "You don't say!" She took in a shuddering breath as he continued his ministrations and extricated her face from his neck so she could look at him. "Do you think I can get there the first time? With the pain, I mean."

"I certainly hope so and promise to do my very best."

She shivered as his tongue circled the shell of her ear while his index finger circled her clitoris, eliciting a gasp. That gasp became an outright moan when he let his finger slide to her opening and in a couple of inches, until he was halted by the membrane across her entrance. Eliza was startled, so Henry stilled to let her get used to the sensation of being filled. "This is where I will put myself." He pulsed his finger just a little. "I suppose I can either go slow and try to push through as gently as I can, or seat myself with a couple of swift strokes to get it over with. What do you think would be best?"

Eliza's sheath was tight around his single digit, but he could feel her relax into the sensation, so he added a second finger. She inhaled sharply, but when she could breathe normally again, she said, "Fast, I think. Get it over with."

Henry gently stroked in and out of her a few times and kissed her just below her ear. "Brave, as always."

And with that he rolled her underneath him, pulled her bent leg higher over his hip, replaced his fingers with the head of his cock, and pushed in until he could feel her maidenhead.

His cock was so much bigger than his fingers had been. Eliza felt so full, it seemed impossible to push more of himself into her. But even as she thought it, her body yielded to his and the passion started to build again. His slippery fingers stroked up to her clitoris and circled over the tight little button until her breath turned into frenzied little huffs.

Then Henry pulled her folds wide so he would stroke against her clitoris as he moved inside her, slid both forearms under her shoulder blades, and hooked his hands over her shoulders to brace her against him.

Eliza held on tightly, but kissed him too, so he would know she was ready.

Kissing her back, he looked deep into her eyes. When she nodded in answer to his silent question, he pulled back a little and thrust into her. A scream broke in her throat as he followed the first thrust in quick succession with a second and a third before he stilled to give her time to adjust. She was so tight it was almost painful for him too, and she seemed to have trouble catching her breath.

"Breathe, sweetheart, breathe!"

The first moment of entry had felt as if he were ripping her apart, but then his lips brushed tender kisses over her eyes, cheeks, and neck, and his hands stroked her shoulders and massaged her scalp until her breathing slowed and her body relaxed beneath him. The pain receded, and in its place a powerful sense of connection and belonging filled her whole being.

As she stretched and softened around him, Henry was struck by the profoundness of the moment and buried his face in her neck to savor it. "Oh, Eliza."

His voice was rough and full of awe, and Eliza, who was no less affected, answered his caresses with her own as he kissed her deeply and held her close. Eventually she hooked her second leg over his hip, opening herself completely to him, indicating her readiness for the next stage.

As he started to move inside her with deliberate slowness, he braced one elbow under her shoulder and moved his other forearm down under her lower back to make it easier for her to flex her hips up into his thrusts. He taught her the movement, and once she had caught on to the rhythm, he increased the speed and depth of penetration.

Eliza could only marvel at her own body. All traces of pain had vanished, her body craved to be filled, and she was eager to experience that complete loss of control alongside Henry.

Henry relished her pleasured pants as she met his thrusts and arched her breasts toward his chest to feel him against her. He increased the speed steadily, but kept a tight rein on his need to thrust deep into her with the full force of his passion. But when she writhed repeatedly against his pelvis in an attempt to stimulate her clitoris more fully, he lost all control and buried himself to the hilt with a sharp thrust, knowing that that would give her the friction she sought.

Eliza gasped and lost all rhythm while the arm under her hip turned into a band of steel as he set a pace so fast and hard there was no room for anything except to open herself and receive him deeply into her body.

The tingling started in her fingertips and soon took over her whole body. She gave herself up to the storm of passion he unleashed on her and was rewarded with an implosion of all sensation into her vagina. The spasms of her orgasm clenched with such force around his raging cock that he shouted with triumph. And then the spasms radiated through Eliza's whole body and she was pure, throbbing, keening sensation. Not even in her wildest dreams had she ever imagined such pleasure.

Henry continued on for several more thrusts before he held himself deep, deep inside her, clutched her to him and pulsed his orgasm into her as shudders racked his whole body.

It took a while for them to find their way back to earth, their breathing heavy, their pulses still racing. But eventually they both calmed, and Henry became aware of her hand languidly stroking up and down his back. He needed the reassurance of her tender caress and rewarded her with another soul-deep kiss. "God, that was great." He kissed her again, then shifted up a little so he could look into her eyes. "How are you, my sweet? I wasn't quite as gentle as I'd intended to be."

Eliza tried to clear her dry throat, her voice hoarse from panting and keening. "I don't have words for how I feel. I don't even have a frame of reference to compare this to, but 'great' somehow is not quite adequate."

Henry stroked down her nose with his as amusement sparkled in his eyes. "My brain is a little addled at present. Give me a moment, and a drink perhaps, and I'll come up with a better word."

She ran her tongue over her dry lips and sighed. "Oh, water! I could kill for a glass of water."

But just then an aftershock quaked through her and her sheath clenched around his still-hard length, and it felt so right to be connected to him like this.

He was about to pull out of her to get her some water, but she didn't want him to leave, she needed him still, so she held him in place with her legs. "No, please. I'm not ready to let you go just yet."

Henry chuckled and reseated himself inside her, being himself in no hurry to leave the comfort of her body. "Careful, sweetheart, if you do that a few more times, it's going to take a while till you get your water."

Her eyes went wide, and she stared up at him in awe. "Oh, you mean . . . ?"

"Yes, I mean!" He kissed her gently. "But I don't think I should. You are going to be sore as it is."

They lingered there for some time until one last spasm expelled his softening member from her body. He rose, and with a small towel, tenderly cleaned between her thighs. After bringing her some water, he climbed back into her bed. She was all sleepy, well-loved woman as she welcomed him back, but there was also a little surprise in her eyes. Henry looked at her and grinned. "What? Did you think I would let you wake up by yourself after what we just did together?"

Eliza let out a satisfied sigh as he folded her into his arms, and together they drifted off to sleep.

CHAPTER ELEVEN

IT WAS AFTER EIGHT O'CLOCK IN THE MORNING when the light of day finally penetrated the gloom of a gray dawn. Henry stirred to the sound of someone cleaning out the fireplace and, since that was a familiar early morning sound, thought no more about it until he became conscious of the soft, warm female next to him.

Eliza!

She had become his last night, and he was damned if he would let her go anytime soon. He slipped his arm over her hip to hug her sleeping form to him and softly kissed the side of her face. She smelled musky and sweet and, while he nuzzled that spot behind her ear, his morning stiffness turned into the real thing. But then another noise from the hearth pulled him sharply back to reality.

The sound of movement from the bed brought up Daisie's head, and she startled when she faced Henry across the sleeping Eliza. But then, to Henry's surprise, a grin split her face. Clearly the maid approved of Henry's presence in Eliza's bed.

"Will said you was back," she said in a stage whisper so as not to wake Eliza, and Henry grinned right back at her.

He kept his own voice down. "Morning, Daisie. My thanks for seeing to the fire. Could you organize a bath for Eliza and let Mrs. Tibbit know there will be two for breakfast?"

Daisie didn't miss a beat. "Just what I would suggest. Shall I 'ave a bath drawn in your rooms too?"

"Perfect."

Eliza stirred, and he returned his attention to her while Daisie laid another log on the fire and discreetly left the room. Henry nuzzled Eliza's temple as she stretched in his arms and slowly blinked awake.

"Good morning, sleepyhead. How do you feel?"

Eliza wrinkled her brow as she assessed her body in order to give an in-depth answer. "Warm . . . cozy . . . wanted . . . oh, and just a bit sore." Her satisfied grin attested to the fact the soreness didn't mar her memory of the night before, and Henry hugged her a little closer to him.

"To be expected. A warm bath will help with that. Daisie is already seeing to it."

Eliza cuddled deeper into his embrace. "I liked what we did last night."

Henry brushed a brown curl out of her face and gave her a lopsided smile. "Good! Because I want to do it again."

She laughed, wiggling her hips against his fully engorged manhood. "I know!"

Planting a swift kiss on her mouth, Henry backed out of her embrace and swung out of bed. "Easy, woman! Bath and food first, I think. Have breakfast with me downstairs, say in an hour?"

To be sure, they had shared meals before, but the circumstances had been profoundly different. It was one thing for them to be lovers, but quite another for him to acknowledge their relationship openly. He read the question in her eyes. "I want to spend time with you, and I don't care who knows I've shared your bed, but if you don't want anybody to know, I will understand."

He held her gaze, willing her to be his for more than just one night. If she asked for secrecy, he knew, she would not let him look after her for long, would not stay with him indefinitely.

Eliza considered this. As his lover, getting a respectable position in another house would be very hard. But she couldn't deny what was between them, couldn't pass up the chance to be with him, no matter the consequences. "I'll have breakfast with you."

A slow smile spread over his face and lit his eyes with the same warmth he saw in hers. He bent to plant another kiss on her mouth. "Splendid! I'll see you in an hour."

With that, he pulled up his breeches, fastened a couple of strategic buttons, and strolled to the door. There he paused and gifted her with another brilliant smile before making his way across the hall to his rooms.

An hour later, Eliza quietly entered the breakfast room at the back of the house, garbed in her soft blue wool dress, a delicate hand-knitted shawl wrapped around her shoulders. The ivory color offset the sky blue of her gown beautifully. Her hair was twisted into a soft knot at the back of her head, and little curls had been allowed to escape all around her face, giving her appearance a sophistication she was sure she didn't possess.

Henry was seated at the head of the table, partially obscured by the *Times*. As soon as he heard Eliza enter, he put down the paper and rose to seat her. His hair was still damp from his bath, but he presented the very picture of the affluent gentleman about town. His neckcloth was carefully tied and held together by a gold pin, his black trousers fit perfectly, his Hessians gleamed, and his dove gray waistcoat and slate blue jacket brought out his blue eyes.

Eliza drank in the sight of him, but couldn't help picturing what lay beneath his clothes, and neither could she help the blush spreading over her cheeks. Henry brought both her hands to his lips, but grinned at her wickedly as he leaned in and confided, "You look lovely, but not quite as lovely as you were last night."

He kissed the spot just below her ear for emphasis while she turned crimson to her hairline and squirmed a little. Then she swatted his shoulder, which made him laugh and enfold her into a quick embrace before he pulled out a chair and seated her to the right of him.

On the table were three silver-domed serving plates, pots with tea and coffee, and a linen-covered basket with fresh scones.

Henry removed the silver domes to reveal eggs, sausage, and bacon, as well as fried mushrooms and tomatoes. Eliza briefly wondered where in the name of God Mrs. Tibbit found tomatoes in the middle of winter, and then proceeded to fill her plate with a little of everything.

When she also selected a scone, Henry pushed the butter and jam close to her plate. "Plum jam to your liking?"

"Mm-hm, yes. I'm starving."

"So I see, my sweet." Then, with another wicked grin, he added, "Lovemaking is known to increase one's appetite, you know."

Another deep blush suffused her cheeks, but there was a sparkle in her eyes when she retorted, "You seem rather pleased with yourself this morning, sir."

Now it was his turn to blush, but his lips twitched when he asked, "Tea or coffee, my lady? Or both?"

She grinned at the "my lady" and held out her cup. "Tea, please.

And you, too, look rather handsome this morning. Is that a side effect of lovemaking too?"

His laugh was soft and melodious. "Most assuredly. Cream?"

They ate in silence for a while, smiling at each other over their forks and tea cups as they attempted to get comfortable with their new intimacy.

Henry watched Eliza lick her lips after her last bit of scone and, lifting her hand, took great care to kiss every one of her fingertips. "Would you like to come for a walk with me down Bond Street to do a little shopping?"

Eliza pulled his hand to her face and snuggled her cheek into his palm. "I would love to come for a walk, but I have no need for the shops."

Henry stroked his thumb along the curve of her cheek and regarded her thoughtfully. "Yes you do. I want to take you to the theatre and the opera, perhaps even a ball or two once people get back to town for the opening of Parliament, and you have nothing to wear for that."

Eliza's eyes grew big and round. It had never occurred to her he would want to take her out; show her off, even. That certainly would publicly brand her as his mistress. But hadn't she already decided she didn't care about the brand as long as she got a chance to be with him?

"The opera?" she finally whispered. "Covent Garden?"

He smoothed his knuckle along her jaw and smiled his most beguiling smile. "Yes, my sweet. Covent Garden."

"Maybe just one dress for the opera," Eliza conceded.

Henry grinned at her as if she had granted him some great boon. "Splendid! Let's go visit the most extravagant modiste with the most outrageous French accent we can find."

That earned him a laugh and a kiss to the palm of his hand—he couldn't remember when he'd last been this happy.

HENRY HAD TO TAKE CARE of his correspondence before they could leave, so it was past noon by the time they entered Madame Clarise's establishment on Bond Street, a few side streets south of Oxford Street. Henry ushered Eliza through the mahogany and glass door, pointing out a luminous dark orange silk in the shop window.

The shop was quiet so late in the year, and they found Madame bent over her books. But as soon as she set eyes on Sir Henry, she came toward them beaming a delighted smile, wearing a demure yet supremely elegant blue gown. However, it was the way she spoke that was most remarkable. Her H sounds remained stuck at the bottom of her throat, all Y's were impossibly drawn out into endless E's, syllables of words were oddly separated from their counterparts, and many words were drawn up at the end in an unanswerable question. "Sir Henry, so wonderful to see you again. I heard you were spending Noel with your dear grandmère, but here you are, and you brought me a lovely young lady to inspire me. How thoughtful of you."

She beamed again, this time at Eliza, and Eliza had to bite the inside of her cheek to stop herself from laughing out loud at Madame's outrageously fake French accent. She glanced over and met Henry's laughing eyes. Oh, how lovely it was to be able to share a joke with him. He winked at her and smiled, then drew her closer and turned back to the modiste. "The lady needs something stunning to wear at the opera."

Madame's mouth formed a perfect O of delighted surprise, and her hands made a coquettish imitation of clapping in front of her face, while her eyes gleamed with satisfaction at the expectation of a large order. "How exciting, you are taking Mademoiselle to the premiere of *Don Giovanni*? You are so lucky, *ma petite*. And, of course, you must be the most stunning creature there. Only the best, the most *jolie* for Sir Henry. I know!"

Then she turned to Henry with a pained expression. "But the premiere is ten days away. Are you not taking Mademoiselle to the performers' New Year's Ball? Oh, but you must! A fairy land is being created on stage and throughout the auditorium, and everyone will come as disciples of the Fae King. It will be such gaiety."

Henry watched Madame's antics with a bemused smile. She had just turned the one-dress order into a two-dress order, and he fully expected to be paying for ten dresses before she was done. And that was partly why he had brought Eliza to Madame Clarise's establishment. She was not only a great modiste, but the most gifted saleswoman Henry had ever met, and he needed help getting Eliza to let him spoil her.

"Eliza as a fairy? I do think I want to see that." He smiled down into Eliza's expectant eyes. "You would look stunning in shimmering, translucent greens and turquoise." Of Madame he inquired, "Could you make such a dress by Friday, Madame?"

Madame Clarise's response was immediate: "But of course. And Sir Henry is right, translucent jade greens and turquoise. And you must have silver wings of the most sheer fabric ever made by human hand. Oh, and you must wear your lovely hair down with crystals shimmering in it like dewdrops."

She rushed to pull out a flat drawer in one of the big chests around the shop and took out a wooden box holding a set of hairpins on a green velvet cushion. The crystals at the end of the pins were expertly cut and backed with silver so they winked almost as bright as diamonds, and instead of two prongs to be pushed into a fastened-up style, there was a little spiral, perfect for winding around a loose strand of hair.

"Your curls are natural, Mademoiselle?"

Eliza nodded absently as she picked up one of the delicate hair pieces. It caught the light from the chandelier overhead and sparkled. "Just like a dewdrop in the sun."

When she looked up at Henry again, her eyes were filled with longing, and Henry knew she wouldn't argue about his buying the dress or going to the ball. He motioned to Madame Clarise. "You had better measure Miss Eliza whilst I take a look around for fabrics to consider."

Instantly Madame Clarise became the consummate professional she indeed was. She led Eliza to a fitting room, calling for her assistant to bring her tape measure. There Eliza was divested of all garments except her stockings, bloomers, and chemise, and the assistant was sent off to find a particular French-style half-corset Madame deemed essential for the design she had in mind for the fairy dress.

Once the corset arrived, Madame took off Eliza's chemise as well, explaining that the corset was meant to be worn next to the skin. The corset would make her decent and hold her assets in place, while the absence of a chemise allowed the design of the dress to be sheer over the shoulders.

Eliza wasn't sure she was bold enough to wear such a garment, but once the assistant brought in the bolts of green and turquoise chiffon, silver-blue shimmering organza, and a liquid silver satin for the underdress, Eliza was quite sure she couldn't exist without the dress.

She forgot all about her near nakedness until Henry strolled into the fitting room, several bolts of fabric balanced on his shoulder, a pattern book under his arm, and some lace samples in his hand.

Eliza startled and crossed her arms over her exposed chest, only to realize she wasn't wearing any petticoats.

Henry let his appreciative gaze travel up and down her body and grinned. "You have nothing to hide, my sweet. And Madame Clarise already knows you are mine." He deposited his burden on a worktable and strolled over to examine the corset more closely. Henry let his fingers travel over the deliciously exposed swell of Eliza's breasts, shaped by the clever corset. "I definitely approve of this."

There were no laces, and his fingers itched to unhook a few of the tiny hooks in the front and run his tongue down into the valley between her breasts, but he could see and feel Eliza's unease at being touched in so public a setting, and so he brought his hand up to brush a curl out of her face and kissed her cheek. "Be easy," he whispered and stepped back.

A deep blush stained her cheeks, but Madame gave her no time for further embarrassment, draping fabrics over her to test against her skin and against each other, soliciting Henry's opinion at every turn. Henry had a few ideas of his own and showed Madame the fabrics he had chosen and the patterns he thought would suit Eliza.

"The orange silk trimmed with the copper velvet for a formal afternoon gown, and I like this pattern with the square-cut décolletage for the opera. I found this almost bronze silk lace I like for the overdress, with the cream satin to go underneath. What do you think, Madame?"

Eliza listened to them, overwhelmed by the sheer number of beautiful fabrics around her. She could not have chosen amongst them if she had tried.

Madame, meanwhile, couldn't quite believe her luck at securing such an order on a dreary late-December day, but recovered quickly. "Your taste is exquisite. My only concern is that I will have to order more of the lace to complete the dress, and it may take two weeks for it to arrive from Paris." Her apologetic tone was accompanied by a speculative gleam in her eyes. "But won't the Mademoiselle need morning and walking dresses?"

Henry pretended to think for a moment. "Of course, two of each, made from the finest wool or silk. She also needs a cape to go with the opera gown and a fur-lined silver cape to go with the fairy dress. And then she needs matching slippers, and let's not forget silky underthings, and that intriguing corset she is wearing."

Henry's eyes gleamed with amusement as he watched the modiste's overblown reaction to each new item he ordered. He was certain Eliza would henceforth be treated with the utmost courtesy by any merchant on Bond Street. "I will leave my lovely Eliza in your capable hands, Madame, and return for her within the hour."

With that, he strode from the room, leaving Eliza no time to protest the order he had just placed. All she could do was stare at the closed door and then give herself up to the experience at hand.

HENRY MADE HIS WAY ACROSS the road to Harold Cross & Sons, jewelers to the king. It took some time to convince Mr. Cross that a fairy had no need for jewels the size of robins' eggs, but he eventually found a gold necklace and bracelet set, made up entirely of delicate grape leaves, and returned to Madame Clarise's with his purchase in his pocket.

Henry firmly believed a beautiful woman should have a pretty dress or two, and a pretty dress demanded nice jewelry. And he had never known a woman who didn't like getting presents. Eliza might not think she needed or deserved gifts, but if Henry had anything to do with it, she was going to get used to receiving them.

He reentered the dressmaker's establishment and found the assistant packing some of his purchases for Eliza into boxes. The girl looked up at the tinkle of the doorbell and smiled at him. "Miss Eliza is almost ready; Madame is just measuring her feet for the dancing slippers. We finished choosing all the fabrics for her wardrobe." The girl moved to the door to the fitting rooms and held it open for him. "If you don't mind, please come this way. Madame asked for you to take a look."

Henry smiled, realizing the crafty modiste had positioned her assistant to head him off upon his return so she could get his approval on everything she was about to make. He could hardly refuse to pay for a garment he'd personally approved.

He followed the assistant to a workroom where the chosen fashion plates had been neatly lined up with the fabrics to be used. Henry went over the assembled order with the confidence and speed of a man who was no stranger to shopping for women. He substituted a pale green silk for a moss green velvet and approved the entire order. He also made sure the assistant knew where to deliver everything, and as a sign of goodwill, settled the bill for the items ready for immediate delivery.

By the time he entered Eliza's dressing room, she was closing the last button on her blue dress, which seemed to fit her even better than before. The assistant nodded to Madame, who in turn beamed at Sir Henry. "It is such a pleasure to work with your beautiful Miss Eliza. I will bring the fairy dress to you on Friday no later than two o'clock so we can make any necessary alterations. All your other garments we will get to you before the end of next week, *n'est-ce pas?*"

"Except for the lace you have to order from Paris."

Madame patted his arm with a coquettish smile. "Oh, Sir Henry, you have such a good memory! Of course, you are right. And I regret to say that I cannot guarantee when I can complete it, but it will be such a stunning gown. I'm sure you will find a special occasion for Mademoiselle to wear it." Madame winked at Eliza conspiratorially.

Eliza had a hard time keeping her mirth under control as Madame said her goodbyes. But she had to admit, when it came to fashion, she had complete faith in Madame's ability.

Henry stepped up behind Eliza. "Did you enjoy yourself, my sweet?"

"How could I not? I feel as if I stepped into a fairy tale."

Henry grinned, satisfied with her answer, and whispered in her ear, "You are still wearing the corset!"

She sent him a cheeky smile over her shoulder and accepted the cloak he draped over her. "Does that meet with your approval, my lord?"

"Oh, most definitely." He directed her toward the door. "Time to get you before a roaring fire so I can peel you out of all these layers and inspect it once more."

She laughed up at him, still giddy from her shopping spree. "I do believe you are planning to corrupt me further, sir."

His eyes turned dark with desire. Bending close, he lowered his voice. "I'm planning to thoroughly debauch you and you will enjoy every second of it."

Eliza's eyes widened and she blushed furiously, then she swallowed and whispered, "You better get me home, then, before I melt into a puddle right here."

Henry threw his head back and let out a delighted peal of laughter as he led her out onto the street. "As first attempts at bawdy flirtation go, you hit the mark dead on, sweetheart." He drew her hand through the crook of his elbow, held on to her hand, and smiled down at her. "We are going to have so much fun together. There are so many things I want to show you and do with you."

"Lead on, then," she said through a grin and set a brisk pace for Cavendish Square.

CHAPTER TWELVE

DESPITE THEIR BRISK PACE, THEY WERE HALF frozen by the time they reached Henry's house, and since they had missed lunch, Henry ordered high tea to be brought to his sitting room.

William took their hats and helped peel them out of their coats.

"Are there fires laid in my rooms?"

"Yes, sir. And in the library."

Henry took Eliza's hand to lead her upstairs. "Good. Have extra wood brought up. Oh, and William, Madame Clarise is sending over some boxes. Have them brought to Eliza's room."

William winked at Eliza, making it clear he, too, approved of their new relations. "Will do."

Eliza barely had time to smile back before Henry dragged her up the stairs.

"And no one is to disturb me until further notice," Henry threw over his shoulder.

Lifting her skirts with her free hand, Eliza did her best to keep up. She was a little flushed and out of breath by the time Henry closed the sitting room door behind them and twirled her into his arms for a heated kiss.

"God, I want you!"

Eliza blushed and, a little shy, nuzzled into his shoulder. "I like it when you touch me and kiss me. And I like when we flirt. I suppose that means I want you too?"

He chuckled and held her close. "My want for you is a little more carnal, more focused on the act itself, but let's stick to the flirting till after tea. I'm hungry for just plain old food, too."

He led her over to the fireplace and rubbed her still-freezing hands.

Eliza had never been in this room before. She'd helped straighten out his bedroom but had never penetrated this far.

The room was spacious and bright, despite the winter gray outside the three tall sash windows. The walls were a creamy beige, the skirting and intricate crown molding brilliant white. The drapes were light blue velvet, and the armchairs in front of the fireplace and the sofa were covered in dark leather with big brass studs holding it in place.

There was a small writing desk in front of one of the windows, too delicate to be a man's desk, but the chair in front of it was sturdy and it obviously held pride of place. Eliza admired the mother-of-pearl inlay and thought that perhaps it had belonged to his mother. There were a number of beautifully rendered foreign-looking landscapes decorating the walls, and over the fireplace hung a picture of a bay stallion— Henry's favorite horse perhaps.

Bookshelves lined the walls, but most of the books seemed to have made their way into stacks on the floor, next to what was clearly Henry's favorite armchair by the fire. The polished floorboards were almost entirely covered by colorful Persian rugs, the most luxuriant of which was laid before the fire.

Eliza could picture Henry sprawled in the chair reading, his stockinged feet stretched toward the fire on the intricately patterned carpet.

As if he had read her mind, Henry urged her to the armchair opposite the one that was so obviously his. Once she was comfortably seated, he knelt before her to unlace her half boots and take them off so she could warm her feet. Eliza gratefully dug her toes into the soft wool of the carpet. "I imagined the magic carpet, in that story you read to me, just like this."

Henry gave her toes a little rub and smiled up at her. "I suppose it would have been very similar. The story comes from the same part of the world as the rug."

Then Henry went to take a seat in his favorite chair and pulled off his boots. He caught Eliza eyeing the stack of books by his chair and grinned. "Mrs. Tibbit despairs every time she comes in here, but I know exactly where everything is, and I like it that way."

Their cozy moment was interrupted by William, who came to drop the requested wood in the brass holder by the fire. On his heels followed Mrs. Tibbit with the tea tray, and they gratefully accepted the cups of tea she handed them and helped themselves to ham sandwiches and warm scones with clotted cream and plum jam.

For Eliza, there was nothing quite like tea and scones still warm from the oven on a cold winter afternoon. Besides the appeal of the food itself, the fare reminded her of happy times with her mother.

Mrs. Tibbit's friendly smile comforted her further, but that good lady's eyes held a question.

"Can I get you anything else?" It was a routine inquiry, but Mrs. Tibbit's intent gaze told Eliza it held more than its usual meaning, and it was directed at her. It seemed Mrs. Tibbit was in need of reassurance from her. The worthy housekeeper did not seem shocked that Eliza had become Sir Henry's lover, but she cared enough about her to want to make sure she was happy with her new status.

Eliza gave her friend her very best smile. "I'm perfectly content."

Mrs. Tibbit nodded her understanding and beamed at her with obvious relief. Sir Henry clearly held a place in her heart, and a conflict between her employer and her protégé would have placed a strain on her loyalties.

Henry, who had been too intent on his food to observe their little interplay, swallowed the last of his sandwich and washed it down with a swig of tea. "This will do very nicely till dinner. Thank you, Mrs. Tibbit."

He turned his attention to the scones, but not before he caught the look she sent his way. It conveyed something along the lines of "Be good to her, and clean up your room!" He smiled warmly at his housekeeper and longtime friend. "Don't worry, Tibby, she will come to no harm in my care."

Mrs. Tibbit mumbled something that sounded suspiciously like "She better not" and exited the room. But there was a spring in her step, and when she turned to close the door quietly behind her, he saw the smile on her face.

"I think Mrs. Tibbit approves of you taking me to your bed," Henry said when they were alone.

Eliza blushed furiously, but held his gaze despite his obvious amusement. "Or maybe she just approves of me being warm and well fed."

Henry's grin grew bigger. "She might at that. She has taken quite a liking to you."

So many in his household had become friends to her over the past weeks, and she was grateful beyond measure. It filled her with a warmth deeper than any fire could give. Henry, however, was not done teasing. "She could just be happy I'm no longer spending my money on a Drury Lane light skirt." He turned tragic eyes on her. "She never approved of Millie."

Eliza hadn't approved of Millie either, but was she really any different than Millie now? "In that case, she won't be so happy when the boxes from Madame Clarise start arriving."

Henry looked chagrined. "Why ever not? She will be happy I'm spoiling you a little."

She was truly embarrassed now. Once Madame Clarise had started draping fabrics over her, she had forgotten about the expense of it all. "You spent too much. I shouldn't have let you." She raised solemn eyes to him, and he knew he'd taken the joke too far.

Depositing both their plates on those handy stacks of books, he dropped to one knee, and took both her hands. "Eliza, my sweet, listen to me. I am a very rich man and no one is going to reproach you for accepting a few gifts from me. Not even you!" Winking at her, he placed a kiss on the tip of her nose.

She had to smile just a little at that, causing the dimple in her right cheek to make an appearance, which he then had to kiss too.

"I want to spoil you; it makes me happy to see your eyes shine with pleasure. And I like seeing you in pretty things. So the gifts I give you are really for me too. You understood that with the corset, that's why you are still wearing it." He let his eyes roam over her breasts and her narrow waist, so admirably shaped by the French garment.

She giggled at the way he ogled her. "I do like the way that corset makes you look at me. I like looking pretty for you."

His eyes grew soft and tender. "You are stunning."

He let his hands trail up the side of her body and opened a few strategic buttons on her dress so he could admire the naked swell of her breasts framed by the corset. She could see his eyes darken with desire, but when he looked back up at her, his expression was thoughtful. "I like to see you happy, Eliza. In fact, I want you to tell me whenever there is something I might do for you. And I don't mean just clothes and such." He gazed at her more seriously now. "For instance, I could look into the situation at the inn for you. It may well legally belong to you if your father left a will to that effect."

She nodded. "I did wonder why Horace was so eager to get rid of me. I don't like that he has my father's inn. But then again, I don't think I could ever go back after all that happened to me and my mum there."

"I'll have my lawyer look into it, and maybe we'll send William up there to have a look around the inn to see if we can find the original will."

Eliza turned this over in her mind, warming to the subject. She really did not want Horace to get away with all he had done. "If there's a will, it would be in my mum's papers in the trunk in the private sitting room at the back of the house. He never touched them, since he doesn't know his letters, so they might still be there."

Henry watched her as she stared into the fire, her brow furrowed in thought. "Tomorrow I'll send William and one of his mates. If it's still there, they'll find it."

She turned her serious brown eyes back to him, a crease between her brows. "Thank you, Henry, but if you were to do something of this nature for me, I would rather you did something to stop Hobbs. Horace is awful, but he's nothing compared to Hobbs. That one's a monster."

Henry nodded, huffing a sigh of frustration. "I quite agree, but there is nothing I can do about him at present. As long as he restricts himself to the city of London, he is protected by the city magistrates he pays off and the Lord Mayor, who is deathly afraid of an out-and-out war amongst the crime lords."

Eliza gave him a long, considering look. If she told him about Daisie and what had happened in Hampstead, William might find out. But then again, Daisie had said she would tell him if there was a chance it would do any good. "Could you get to Hobbs and deal with him if he went somewhere else?"

Henry's eyes sharpened in an instant. "Only if he does something illegal and the local magistrate is willing to cooperate or at least look the other way."

Eliza nodded her understanding and took a deep breath. "Hampstead. He takes the girls new to the trade to Hampstead."

Henry pulled a low stool over and sat directly in front of her, knee to knee. "How do you know?"

She laced her hands together in her lap and lowered her eyes to them. "That's where he took Daisie. He has a cottage there. The girls stay there and he makes them work at The Silver Fox."

He covered her hands with his, his voice urgent now. "How do you know this?"

Eliza met his eyes, silently imploring him to understand that there was more to this than she could say. "Daisie told me."

Henry looked confused. "She never told me, and I don't think she told William or he would have shot the bastard already."

"She couldn't. Apart from not wanting William to know what happened to her, she's afraid he's going to get himself hanged for killing a lord if he finds out."

Henry made a hissing sound as he sharply pulled in air between his teeth. "That bad!"

The two words conveyed a wealth of understanding. Henry knew Daisie had been a prostitute, and he knew William knew. So it followed, whatever Daisie didn't want William to know about was far and beyond what the average whore had to endure from her customers, and her pimp.

"Daisie said it's one of those things you would have to un-know because you couldn't possibly forget it."

Henry bowed his head and squeezed her hands tighter. "What does Hobbs have to do with this lord and how do you know all this?"

Eliza turned her hands under his and laced her fingers through his, seeking comfort as much as needing to stop him from storming out in search of Daisie. "I asked Daisie about Hobbs and she mentioned The Silver Fox. And then at Christmas, I noticed she wasn't quite herself, and she told me in confidence why Christmas was so hard for her." She looked at him intently and squeezed his hands. "I know you will have to talk to her if you think you can get Hobbs in Hampstead. And Daisie said she would tell you all she knows and even take you there if it helps put the bastard away. But please talk to her when William isn't around. She doesn't want him to know what happened to her there. It was that lord who did things to her. Hobbs gives him first refusal on all his new girls."

Henry nodded his agreement, lifted their entwined fingers, and bowed his head to kiss her hands. "I will wait until William has gone to the inn." He continued with new fervor, "There is a very good chance we could get to Hobbs in Hampstead. One of the magistrates is old and complacent, but he certainly wouldn't take bribes from the likes of Hobbs. The other is an old chum of mine, so we might actually get some local support."

Eliza smiled at him. "Will you let me help?"

Henry shook his head in disbelief but grinned. "Certainly! It's your home turf; your help will be much appreciated. But you will have to promise to stand aside if I deem it too dangerous for you."

Her smile broadened, but there was a hard edge to her voice. "I want to get the bastard. And yes, I will follow your lead. I don't want to need rescuing again."

Henry understood. He understood her need to regain some control over her life by taking revenge on at least one of the people who had hurt her. And he understood the lingering fear that would accompany her well into the future. Wrongs had been done to her and her mother that needed to be righted.

But he also understood that right now she needed to be distracted before the black clouds of her past overwhelmed her. So he cocked an eyebrow at her and gave her his most lascivious smirk. "I'll rescue you any day!"

She gaped at him for a second, completely thrown by the sudden change in his mood. But the comment was accompanied by such an exaggerated ogling of her barely covered breasts that the joke became obvious, and she whacked his shoulder in mock outrage before she dissolved into laughter.

Her response emboldened him to bury his face in her pushed-up cleavage and blow raspberries on the tops of her breasts. By the time he dug his fingers under the short corset to tickle her sides, she was squirming and screeching with laughter. She had no option but to wiggle out of the chair to get away from his evil fingers, and they landed in an undignified heap on the plush carpet in front of the fire.

Henry laughed just as hard as she did, as she tried to ward him off with her hands and feet. He decided not to risk one of her naked feet connecting with his groin, pinned her middle to his chest, and exploited the fact her dress had ridden all the way up her thighs by continuing his tickle assault on the backs of her knees.

Her giggles turned into frantic gasps. "Mercy, mercy! Henry, stop! I can't breathe!"

Henry took his hand from her knees, but kept her pinned against him. "What do I get if I desist?"

Her frantic giggles slowed to a chuckle. "A kiss?"

He regarded her for a moment, then moved his hand back to her knee. "Mm, tempting, but I think I prefer you squirming against me."

The breath rushed out of her as his hand resumed its assault. "No, no. Stop! Stop! Stop! I'll let you take off my corset."

His hand stilled and he pushed slightly away from her, glaring at her in mock horror. "Miss Eliza! Shocking, simply shocking!"

But his gaze was drawn to the nipple of her left breast. It had escaped the confines of the corset and tempted him in all its pink, flushed glory. His eyes grew dark with desire as he drew in a sharp breath. "Deal!"

Then he dipped his head and sucked that nipple deep into his mouth, making her groan, her tickle-sensitized body arching with appreciation.

Henry took his time worshiping her left breast, then stood her on her feet to divest her of every last stitch of clothing while she unbuttoned his waistcoat and pulled his shirt over his head.

Her touch was still unpracticed as she stroked her hands up his forearms and biceps to his shoulders and leaned in to kiss his nipples.

There was no demand or hidden agenda, just a woman wanting to touch him. It struck him that it had been a long time since a woman's touch had been caring and not just arousing.

Once she'd unbuttoned his pants and pushed them off his hips, he pulled his socks from his feet and laid her back down on the carpet. Then he reached over her to throw another log on the fire. Henry thoroughly enjoyed the way her arms came around his waist and hugged him to her naked breasts. She felt so good in his arms; the way they came together was so natural. In short, she was a revelation.

Henry smiled down at her, trailed his fingertips down her face, and kissed her forehead, then the tip of her nose, and finally captured her lips in a kiss so slow, lush, and deep, it literally curled her toes. From there, he trailed kisses down her throat, over the swell of her breasts and down to her side.

He let his tongue tickle the spot where his fingers had tortured her earlier, then his mouth wandered farther south, over her hip, down her thighs to her very toes.

She gasped when he kissed the arch of her foot and giggled when he sucked one of her toes into his mouth, but was so caught up in the eroticism of it all, she didn't protest.

From her toes, his journey took him up the inside of her leg. He pressed his tongue to the hollow behind her knee and trailed open-mouthed kisses up her thigh to caress the dark curls at the apex of her slender legs. He breathed in the scent of warm, ready woman and sighed a contented sigh when her fingertips started to massage the scalp beneath his short hair.

When he pushed her thighs wider and parted her tender flesh with his tongue, however, she made a startled noise and tried to lift his head up and squirm away.

"You will like this, I promise. Just let me show you."

Eliza did not know enough about sexual intercourse to anticipate what Henry intended. She only knew that this felt even more intimate than what they'd done the night before. But his touch did feel good, so she let him have his way. Pushing her fingers back into his hair, she kneaded and tugged while his tongue found her clitoris.

He teased her with soft licks and his lips gently sucked, but he soon graduated to alternating those light touches with the rasp of his teeth.

The sensations he elicited were new and unexpected, almost over-whelmingly wonderful, and Eliza had absolutely no idea what was expected of her. Her breath came fast and heavy. She didn't know whether to gasp or sigh; hold still or push herself into his kiss; pray for him to stop or beg him to take her all the way to—where, she did not know.

Thankfully, desire took hold of her and all thoughts fled as her hips bucked uncontrollably and the need for completion drowned out all other considerations.

Henry restrained her movements gently, reveling in her body's re-sponse and the uncensored noises escaping her lips. He sucked and licked and kissed and probed with his tongue until she was keening with pleasure and the need to come. Then he inserted two fingers into her vagina and curled them up to stroke the secret spot inside her. He did not stroke in and out of her, mindful of her residual soreness from the night before. He just filled her and stroked his fingertips over the sensitive spot.

From his position between her thighs, he watched her throw her head back on a breathless sigh and then her whole body arched.

The tingles spread all through Eliza's being, dissolving into an orgasm gentle and strong all at once, an all-encompassing embrace.

Henry watched Eliza until the last spasm had rippled through her body, and extracted his fingers before he crawled up, trailing open-mouthed kisses over her belly and between her pert breasts. His tongue slid up her neck and over her chin and in between her parted lips, where it met with hers. It was a soft kiss, full of appreciation and silent wonder.

Henry gathered her pliant, sated body in his arms and allowed his full arousal to be cradled between her thighs, but made no move to take his own pleasure. He just held her, letting her drift back to earth gently. They remained like that for long minutes until she finally opened her eyes and smiled. "I did like that!"

Henry smiled against her temple where he was placing a lingering kiss. "Mm-hmm, I noticed."

She shifted slightly so she could wrap her arms around him more fully, and became aware of his erection. It didn't take her long to realize he had given her pleasure, but had not taken his own yet. Letting her hand drift down his side to his groin, she stroked him tentatively. He covered her hand with his, encouraging her to wrap it around him tightly and stroke up and down.

"Mmm, that feels good."

His hand fell away, but she continued to stroke him, adding her thumb to caress over his smooth head on every upstroke. He let out an appreciative groan and closed his eyes. Still, she was unsure as to what to do or expect next, so she asked, "Will you put yourself inside me?"

He didn't open his eyes, just nuzzled her hair. "No, my sweet, you are still sore and I don't want to hurt you."

Her hand still stroking him, she assessed her body for a moment and had to agree with him. She appreciated his thoughtfulness, which made her want to give him pleasure even more. "Can I give you pleasure the way you did to me?"

He gently kissed her temple. "You are giving me pleasure right now, sweetness."

She smiled, and pulled on him just a little as she squeezed the head of his penis and was rewarded with another groan. He rubbed his nose along her neck while his hand massaged her breast.

She wiggled her leg free from under him and slid halfway down his body. Her hair had escaped its pins by now, and Henry reveled in the feel of it dragging over his chest.

Almost at eye level now, Eliza took a closer look at his manhood. It was proud and strong and thickly veined, the head pink and smooth. She used her free hand to investigate the strange skin sack below his member. The elliptical shapes inside it moved between her exploring fingers, and Henry moaned with pleasure. "Can I kiss it and make you feel the way you made me feel?"

Henry's eyes flew open, and he met her gaze. "You don't have to."

Eliza was slightly perplexed by his answer. "I want to. What do I do? Teach me."

Henry framed her face with his hands and caressed her cheeks with his thumbs. He searched her eyes, torn between wanting her mouth around him and not wanting to overwhelm her. As always, her eyes were unguarded, and in them he saw nothing but curiosity and genuine warmth.

He trailed one of his thumbs across her bottom lip and dipped it inside her mouth. She instinctively sucked and let her tongue play with it.

"What you are doing to my cock feels very good! Your lips and tongue on it would feel even better. But, Eliza, it is an acquired taste. So if you find it less than pleasing, stop."

She wrinkled her brow in puzzlement. "You did it for me."

A huge grin spread over his face. "Ah, but I find it hugely erotic to kiss a woman's nether lips and watch her find her pleasure."

A smile transformed her face as she realized she hadn't been the only one who had enjoyed his carnal kiss. She winked at him. "Well, who knows, perhaps I'll acquire a taste for it."

He laughed out loud. "Oh, I so hope you do."

Her grin was downright wicked as she slid farther down his body and used her tongue to wet his head before she fit her lips around his cock and gently sucked. Henry drew in a shuddering breath and gathered her hair at the nape of her neck so he could watch. He guided her to use her hands in tandem with her mouth and marveled at her adventurous spirit. And when his pleasure came to crisis, he lifted her gently away from him and spilled himself into his shirt. Then he pulled her up and over his body and kissed her passionately.

Eliza reveled in his appreciation. "I take it you enjoyed that." Her smile held a hint of triumph.

Henry's eyes danced with amusement, and he cocked a brow. "I take it you acquired a taste for this?"

She giggled and blushed, and he rolled her under him, chuckling at her sudden shyness. But then she cleared her throat and her blush spread all the way down her neck. Henry had a sudden feeling there was more to it than her being shy. "Out with it, sweetheart," he commanded.

"Well, what I just did, would that be what Wendy the barmaid called givin' a bloke a suck?"

The unexpected crudeness left him speechless for a moment, then a snort of laughter shook his entire body.

He nodded but couldn't quite leave it at that. He caressed her lower lip with his thumb and placed a tender kiss on each corner of her mouth. "Technically that is a crude term for what you did for me. But we are lovers and that makes it different."

Eliza's expression turned thoughtful. "It does," she agreed. "I am quite certain the only thing Wendy liked about sucking someone behind the shed was the extra money it earned her." Her brow furrowed as she remembered the baseness that had surrounded her at the inn. "Poor Wendy, she really had no idea, did she?"

The smile she gave him was so pure and joyous it almost seemed like a miracle, considering what he knew she had endured. He asked himself once again how she had managed to survive the inn with her innocence intact.

"God, you make me happy, Eliza." Even while he said this, he was struck by sadness. In her question was a reminder that he couldn't hold on to this moment forever. Happiness, even one as pure and uncomplicated as theirs, was fleeting.

The hint of longing in his expression gave Eliza pause—and she knew without a doubt that she was not the only one who had encountered the ugly side of life. They were kindred spirits. They needed each other to redress the balance.

She pulled him down to her and hugged him fiercely. "I never knew I could be this happy."

CHAPTER THIRTEEN

THEY CUDDLED AND DOZED IN FRONT OF THE fire until the gray afternoon light outside the windows turned to night and the fire lost its blaze.

Henry helped Eliza dress and encouraged her to go find out what Madame Clarise had sent so far, so he could catch up on his correspondence and decide how to run the mission to Hampstead.

Eliza found every surface in her room covered in boxes of all shapes and sizes, and Daisie waiting with gleaming eyes to help her unpack them. There were drawers, shifts, and petticoats made of silk and the finest lawn; a full corset, covered and lined in rose-pink silk; and a whole box full of French silk stockings and garters of various colors. The box holding an ivory satin nightgown and a matching wrapper with goose down framing the neckline made Eliza blush. But when the next box contained a confection made entirely out of silky gold lace, she buried her head in her hands and groaned. "Oh Lord, I'm not sure I'm cut out to be a fancy woman."

Daisie, who'd been lovingly folding lacy underthings and placing them in the chest of drawers, came to look over Eliza's shoulder. Her eyes widened, and she brushed past Eliza to lift the delicate garment out of the box. "Crikey, Liza! He ain't no skinflint, that's for sure."

That broke the tension and Eliza dissolved into breathless giggles. "A skinflint?"

"Well, 'e ain't. There's a whole wardrobe 'ere, all the finest things, and them are only the underthings."

Eliza looked around herself at the sheer mass of beautiful garments no one except Henry would ever see, and it dawned on her these were the things he had bought for her to wear just for him. That thought was exciting rather than embarrassing and made her look at the lacy negligee in a different light.

She took the garment out of Daisie's hands, let the candlelight play through the lace, and imagined the way Henry's eyes would darken with desire when he saw her in it.

Daisie, meanwhile, lifted the lid off the last box and gasped.

Eliza turned, and together they lifted out a shimmering bottle-green silk gown in the very latest style. The bodice was fitted down to the waist, with a deep v-shaped plunge in the front, but not so immodest that she would need a fichu. From the bodice, the dress flared out into a full skirt, but the sleeves were entirely fitted down to the wrist and devoid of the usual puffed sleeves. The gown was beautiful, but it wasn't one Henry had ordered for her. She looked in the box and found a green lace shawl several shades lighter and kid leather slippers dyed the same color. It wasn't until Eliza turned over the lid that she spotted the note from Madame Clarise.

Madame begged for Eliza to accept the gown and slippers as a courtesy since it would take several days for her own choices to be completed, and the gown should fit her well enough.

Eliza grinned at Daisie as she handed her the gown so she could get changed into it for dinner. "Madame sure knows how to sell her wares. She is already working on me to come back and order more. Too bad for her I only really have use for one dress at the time, and Sir

Henry already ordered a dozen for me."

"As I said, no skinflint, our Sir Henry." Daisie chuckled. "Makes ya wonder who ordered this dress and then couldn't pay for it."

Eliza giggled. "Whoever it was has very good taste."

Eliza washed, and Daisie helped her into the green dress and brushed out her hair. The small velvet box with the hair crystals was on the dresser, and neither Eliza nor Daisie could resist trying them out. So when Eliza went downstairs to find Henry before dinner, she was resplendent in the green gown and sported three crystals in her hair, clustered over her right ear.

WHILE ELIZA UNPACKED HER NEW treasures, Henry called for William. He was to go to Hampstead and retrieve any official-looking papers from Eliza's mother's trunk, then find out what Horace knew about the legal ownership of the inn.

It was agreed William would take two other men and set out in the morning. Once they were done at the inn, they were to go on reconnaissance to The Silver Fox to find out more about Hobbs's dealings there, and hopefully locate the cottage Daisie had told Eliza about.

It was a good thing William had learned in the army to take orders without question, as Henry would've been hard-pressed to explain how he knew about Hobbs's Hampstead operation.

William was to stand back in all things since Hobbs knew him and Wilkins might remember him, but he was experienced in the art of intelligence gathering and could be trusted implicitly. There simply was no better man for the job, as far as Henry was concerned.

William's first order of business was to ask Eliza for a detailed description of the inn's interior so he could look for her mother's trunk.

He caught up with her on the way to the library, and she sat herself at Henry's desk to draw him a map of the ground and first floor of the inn.

Once armed with the floor plan and a description of Horace, William went off to the pub to round up his mates for the trip to the country.

HENRY FOUND ELIZA STILL SITTING at his desk, the bottle-green silk of her dress making her pale skin glow in the candlelight. A few gentle curls had been allowed to escape from her loose chignon, making her look lovely and soft. She was deep in thought, drawing the feather of a quill through her fingers.

Henry studied her for a moment from the threshold while affixing his gold watch chain to his deep blue velvet vest and adjusting the cuffs of his fashionably fitted charcoal evening jacket. Dove gray pantaloons, black patent leather shoes, and a snowy white cravat completed his man-about-town evening attire.

Eliza looked up at his approach, but instead of soft thoughtfulness, there was determination in her eyes. "Henry, if the inn does belong to me, will you help me kick out Horace?"

Henry smiled, relieved she was willing to fight for what was meant to be hers. "I fully intend to kick him to kingdom come whether provisions were made for you in the will or not."

She let out a heavy breath and returned to watching the feather slip through her fingers. "Thank you! The thought of him getting away with what he did to my mum and getting the inn in the bargain doesn't sit right with me."

Henry found it troubling she made no mention of the cruelties she had suffered at the brute's hands. "I saw what that sorry excuse for a man did to you, and I'll see him rot on a prison hull for the rest of his natural life just for that."

Eliza looked up at his fierce tone, his eyes intense with encouragement and protectiveness rather than any sort of menace. Grateful to know Henry would avenge her, even if she was mainly seeking justice for her mother, she nodded. "True. Then there is what he did to me."

Henry took the abused feather out of her hands and pulled her up and into his arms. "We will deal with Hobbs first because he is the bigger threat, and I want to know more about this mysterious lord. But I promise you, you will see justice for yourself as well as your mother, even if I have to mete it out myself."

He placed a kiss on her forehead for emphasis as her fingers played with the folds of his neckcloth. "My champion as well as my knight in shining armor, are you?"

He gently rescued his cravat, tipped up her chin, and waited for her to meet his eyes. "Always. Now, let me show you how to waltz, so I might dance with you tomorrow." He moved her hand onto his shoulder, placing his palm between her shoulder blades, and drew her other arm out to her side.

A slow smile crept up her face, finally reaching her eyes. "Oh, the fairy ball."

Henry watched as the smile transformed her face and chased the troubled shadows from her eyes. He started to sway her back and forth, getting her used to matching his movements. The shimmering green silk displayed her figure to perfection, and he could hear the enticing whisper of the silk undergarments.

"Yes, the fairy ball." He grinned. "Did Madame Clarise send this dress?"

Eliza smiled up at him. "She did. Daisie thinks it was made for someone with a similar figure who never picked it up." Eliza's smile widened to a cheeky grin. "She sent it to compensate for not being able to complete one of mine today."

Henry answered her grin. "And in the hope I would like it so much on you I would order more just like it from her."

Eliza nodded, still swaying gently in his arms. "She is one smart businesswoman."

"She is indeed. I wouldn't have thought to put you in bottle green, but it does marvelous things for your skin, and the cut is very becoming—the latest fashion straight from Paris. I might have her make one in a dark rose silk for you."

Eliza's eyes went round and she shook her head violently. "Oh no, no, no you won't. She will charge you twice as much next time if you bite right away."

Henry burst into laughter. "It would seem Madame Clarise is not the only shrewd businesswoman of my acquaintance."

Eliza shrugged unapologetically. "I was raised to run a profitable as well as respectable inn one day. It's not my mother's fault the place went to seed."

Henry pulled her closer and laid his cheek against hers. "Your mother did a marvelous job."

Eliza took a deep breath, let herself sink into his arms, and accepted the offered comfort gratefully. "She was wonderful."

Henry let her rest against him for a little while longer and then stepped back into waltzing position. "Now let's get back to your dance lesson. When I start counting, start with your right foot back and follow my lead."

He made enough space between them so she could look down and watch his feet to better follow him, and started to dance.

"One, two, three—count with me, it will help. One, two, three . . ."

Half an hour later Eliza had stopped watching their feet and was smiling at Henry as he led her through a series of twirls. And when Mrs. Tibbit announced that dinner was served, Henry waltzed Eliza all the way down the corridor and into the dining room, much to his housekeeper's delight.

AFTER A COMPANIONABLE DINNER, HENRY kissed Eliza good night, told her not to wait up, and made his way to White's, where he was almost certain to find Robert Pemberton at this hour.

He was not disappointed.

Robert's primary estate was located between Hampstead and the village of Finchley, a mere ten miles from London. But being a viscount, he had duties at Parliament, so he kept rooms on St. James's, across the street from White's and within easy walking distance of the House of Lords.

Robert was ensconced in a quiet corner with another patron and a bottle of brandy, and engaged in an animated conversation. The other man was half hidden behind his armchair, but as soon as Robert noticed Henry coming toward him, he swatted his companion's knee and nodded toward Henry, then beckoned Henry to come join them.

"Guess who just made it back to the shores of Britannia, Henry?"

The other man stood and turned. Henry's eyes lit up at the sight of his long-absent friend, and a broad grin split his friend's face. Allen Strathem was well-built and of more than average height. He had pleasant, even features, wavy brown hair, and vivid green eyes. At present those eyes sparkled with pleasure.

Allen's age was hard to judge, but he was certainly the youngest of the three men, and while his eyes seemed to hold the wisdom of ages, his smile was carefree.

Henry stopped in his tracks, studying his friend's smiling face, shaking his head slightly and chuckling to himself at some private joke. "Allen, you are a sight for sore eyes. How were the wilds of Canada?"

Allen pulled a disgusted face, which seemed to inspire Robert to join in Henry's amusement. "Dull as an auctioneer's catalogue. Not a conspiracy to uncover, nor a villain to foil."

Henry barked out a delighted laugh. "Still full of beans. Well, I might just have something to get your blood pumping again."

Allen joined Henry and Robert in their mirth and pulled Henry into a backslapping embrace. "That's so much better than the 'I told you so' I expected." Then more quietly he added, "What are you involved in? Can you say here?"

Henry took a quick look about the room, noticing the interest their boisterous greeting had garnered. Most members were already returning their attention to their own conversations, but Henry's gaze collided across the width of the room with the cold stare of Lord Astor, who studied him as one might study an insect. Henry nodded a cold greeting, knowing Allen would notice the direction of his gaze. "Apparently not."

Allen instantly diverted the attention of the room to himself. "Waiter, a glass for my friend. Let's raise a toast to old times and catch up. I have been in the wilderness for a year, have mercy on me."

Henry and Robert answered with easy laughs and more backslapping. They settled down for drinks, all three of them now conscious of the chilling presence across the room.

Henry deliberately took a seat where Lord Astor would not be in his line of sight, but felt the man's attention on him until he departed for the dining room half an hour later.

Robert, who watched the man exit, shook his head in exasperation. "I don't know about you, Henry, but I still like him for De Sade."

Henry kept his voice down, but there was more than a hint of frustration in his tone. "Not that we could ever prove anything. What's common knowledge, however, is that he was one of my father's friends. That alone makes him somebody to be extremely wary of."

Allen raised a quizzical brow. "Is that why he seemed to skewer you with his eyes?"

Henry laughed a mirthless laugh. "No, his personal hatred of me has more to do with Cecilia choosing to run away with me rather than take up with him. Come to think of it, he became friends with my father after that."

Henry turned to look at the seat Astor had vacated and noted his cigar was still smoking in the dish on the table. He himself had used that trick once or twice if he wanted a reason to reenter a room to catch somebody unawares. He caught Robert's eye and turned to Allen. "I can't believe you went all the way to the Americas and didn't even shoot yourself a bear."

Allen didn't miss a beat. "Oh, it wasn't for lack of trying. But it's not like hunting a fox where you set your dogs, gather your friends, ride out to the sound of the horn, and at the end of the day gather in a cozy lodge, eat well, and drink even more. Out there you have to track the beast for weeks, with no one but a native to keep you company, and not a creature comfort in sight. Frankly it's tedious. So once I could no longer see the forest for all the trees in it, I told my guide to take me back to where we'd started and leave the bear be."

During Allen's animated speech, Henry kept watch out of the corner of his eye, and sure enough, Astor retuned for his cigar, swept his virtually colorless eyes over the group in the corner once more, and departed as silently as he had slipped in.

A chill ran down Henry's spine as he realized Astor might well be the lord to whom Hobbs had sold Daisie. Astor's father, the Duke of Elridge, owned Oakwood House, the largest estate in Hampstead, making Astor a distinct possibility. Henry had long suspected Astor could be De Sade, the most dangerous and hated English traitor of his generation, but he didn't have a shred of evidence.

Dubbed by the French "De Sade Anglais," and with access to information on the highest level, he had sold countless military secrets and had thereby caused the death of thousands of men. De Sade was an extremely skilled spy, who had eluded capture in the field and had never left a piece of evidence behind, at least as far as the agency knew, but he had one fatal flaw.

De Sade Anglais had earned his name on account of his sexual practices. The spy's extreme sexual habits seemed not to have troubled the French authorities since they had raised no objection to him leaving a trail of traumatized blond and blue-eyed ex-virgins all over their country. Meanwhile, the English intelligence services—of which Henry and his friends had been prominent members during the Napoleonic wars—had used his proclivities to track him and try to build a case against him. But when he disappeared from France without a trace right before Waterloo, they had to admit defeat.

Henry and his colleagues had found evidence De Sade had returned to England, but all their witnesses were in France, and the evidence had been dismissed as hearsay. They had sought, but never found, victims of the man's proclivities in England, and thus had never been able to prove anything. It led them to assume De Sade was too clever to indulge in his unsavory practices anywhere close to home. But if Henry's hunch was right and Hobbs turned out to be the connection, then perhaps they could prove Astor was De Sade after all, or at least prove he was a sexual deviant and, as such, dangerous to society.

All this churned through Henry's mind as he sat and chatted easily about Allen's exploits in the Canadian wilderness. He needed to talk to Daisie to see whether there had been proof living right under his roof all along. And he needed to find out why Astor had been so interested in their conversation.

It was time to gather what information he could and take action, so he invited his friends to his house for a late breakfast the next morning, then headed home through the dark streets of late night Mayfair.

CHAPTER FOURTEEN

HENRY WAS SOMEWHAT PUZZLED NO ONE FOL-
lowed him home. Perhaps Astor had bought their happy reunion and
had lost interest. Still, he rose before dawn to tell William to make
certain he had lost any possible tail before he made his way north to
The Cat and Fiddle.

With dawn being so late during the winter months, Henry found
he had no further need for sleep, so he ordered coffee to be brought to
his sitting room, informed Mrs. Tibbit he expected guests for breakfast, and asked her to send Daisie to him.

Daisie entered with the coffee tray some fifteen minutes later.

It was obvious from the apprehension on her face that she had a
good idea why she had been summoned. But when Henry looked at
her more closely while she poured coffee for him, he saw resolve in
her face too.

"Pour yourself a cup and sit with me, Daisie." He indicated the
armchair opposite his in front of the fire.

Despite her astonishment, Daisie curtsied. "Thank you, sir."

Henry smiled reassuringly and waited for her to serve herself.
"You know why I want to talk to you, don't you."

It was a statement rather than a question, but she answered it anyway. "When William told me last night he'd be takin' some of 'is mates
with 'im to go to Eliza's inn, I figured you'd be wantin' to hear all about

what Hobbs is up to in Hampstead."

There was a hopeful note to her statement that was not lost on Henry. But he also noted she placed her coffee cup back on the tray. "Indeed, I do want you to tell me all about Hobbs's activities there, and I need you to tell me where the cottage is you told Eliza about."

He knew how hard it would be for Daisie to talk about what had happened to her, but he had to know. His scalp had been itching ever since he'd heard about this lord and then seen Astor last night. He knew deep in his gut he was on the verge of something big, and over the years Henry had learned to trust his gut.

"But, Daisie, first I need you to tell me about this lord Hobbs sold you to."

Daisie's whole body stiffened and her eyes filled with dread.

"Daisie, if this lord is the man I suspect he might be, he is more dangerous than even you can imagine, and I want to make sure he hangs for the things he has done."

Daisie looked at him with haunted eyes. "I don't know if that toff is the same one you're lookin' for, but if you go after 'im and Will finds out what 'e did to me, I need you to promise 'e will pay no matter what, 'cause I can't 'ave me Will goin' to the gallows for shootin' no lord."

Henry knew William was in love with Daisie, but until this moment he hadn't known how fiercely Daisie loved him back, how much she wanted to preserve the life they had built together. "I give you my word. William will not suffer the consequences of what you tell me, nor will he suffer for helping me get Hobbs, or this lord."

He met her gaze steadily, and Daisie took her time assessing his sincerity. Finally she nodded and took a deep breath, willing herself to calm so she could tell Henry what he needed to know.

"That man, he raped me in ways . . . Sir Henry, 'e did things . . . 'e made me do things . . . " She trailed off, lost in a fog of torturous memories.

Henry covered her tightly laced hands with one of his. "Daisie, look at me." He waited for her to meet his eyes. "You don't have to tell me all the despicable things he did. But I need to know: did he leave a mark on you?"

Daisie blanched. "How did you know?"

Henry couldn't help his excitement despite her distress. Could this really be it, the link that could finally unmask De Sade Anglais?

Daisie swallowed and indicated the underside of her left breast.

Henry could barely breathe. All the other victims they had found alive had marks on the underside of the left breast. "Can you show it to me?"

She didn't respond but started to unlace her bodice. She pulled up her chemise and held it up together with her breast to reveal the mark on the underside. Three black dots marking the corners of a triangle. It was a crude tattoo but it was undeniably the same mark Henry had seen on the other young women De Sade had tortured.

He nodded to indicate he had seen what he needed to see. Daisie righted her clothing, then her whole body slumped in defeat. Her voice was flat and barely audible when she spoke again, and Henry had to strain to hear her. "He called it me memento for bein' a good playmate."

It took him a moment to assimilate what she had said, but then Henry could only stare at her in shock. None of the French victims he had talked to could ever tell him anything beyond the fact he was a foreigner and possibly English. None of them had spoken any English, and De Sade had never spoken to them in French. They had assumed it was part of the torture—no communication, no hope of convincing him to stop. But he had spoken to Daisie and used the communication to torment her. Could it be De Sade didn't speak French?

The very reason Astor had never been fully investigated was the fact he didn't speak French. He'd never learned; not French, not Latin, not Greek, nor German nor Italian. An actuality that had been verified by his masters at Eton and his dons at Oxford. In short, he was singularly untalented when it came to learning languages. This circumstance had led him to a commission in the army rather than going into the church, the traditional choice for the third son of a duke.

Henry reeled. It seemed the very reason Astor had eluded them all this time could be the way to tie him to the persona of De Sade in the end.

But before Henry could apprehend his old nemesis or even talk all this over with his friends, he had to get more facts from the one witness who had ever spoken to De Sade. He needed Daisie to describe her attacker and the things he had done to her.

But as soon as Henry turned his attention back to Daisie, he realized she was distraught beyond all reason. What he saw before him was not the confident, contented woman who lived and worked in his house, but the crumpled remains of a broken fifteen-year-old.

Henry knelt in front of her and tried to lift her head so he could see her face, her eyes. "Daisie, it's over. He can't get to you now." He rubbed his thumbs over her cheeks, still holding her head up, but she refused to look at him.

"I tried everythin' to wash off them marks. Even tried to scratch them off."

She finally met his eyes, but what he saw in them was not hurt and fear, but shame. Shame so deep it gnawed at her very soul. The words came slowly, but once she started it was as if a dam had broken and she had to tell him all of it.

"There's somethin' wrong with me."

Henry shook his head. "No, Daisie. He did terrible things to you, but you survived."

It was her turn to shake her head. "You don't know! That man, 'e is like a devil. He had devil's eyes, all cold and dead inside, and 'e did do terrible things to me. Hobbs took me to The Silver Fox up in Hampstead after 'e snatched me off the Bow High Street. I didn't know it then, but 'e parades all 'is new girls for that lord whilst 'e is 'avin' a pint, and if 'e calls for another, Hobbs blindfolds the girl and takes 'er to the dungeon. Hobbs's pigeons call 'im Lord Pain and 'e goes for blond, blue-eyed virgins, and Hobbs knows it, so that's what 'e gets for 'im."

Daisie gathered herself for a moment.

"So Hobbs drove me out of Hampstead. Not far, but it was real quiet like. No voices, no animals, just night birds, and the last bit we had to walk. He took me up a few steps and into a buildin' and then down a long stairwell, and then 'e told me to sit and wait for me first client. I was already so scared I almost peed meself, but I did peek at where I was once Hobbs was gone . . . and then I wished I hadn't. Lord Pain was there watchin' me, smilin' and tellin' me to take off the blindfold and 'ave a good look around and askin' me what I thought it was all for. I was shakin' in me boots when I saw all them chains and whips and 'ooks and canes, and toys that looked like cocks but much too big, and I could only shake me head. But he liked me scared, and laughed and said not to worry, 'e was gonna show me how every single one of them things was used, and if I was a good playmate I would like it."

Henry had gone completely cold, but kept holding Daisie's hands and stroking them with his thumbs, somehow certain she needed the human contact to get her story out.

Daisie swallowed and continued in the same monotone voice.

"And show me 'e did. 'E took off all me clothes and locked them away, and then 'e chained me to some hooks in the ceilin', and once I couldn't 'old meself upright any longer, he tied me with some rope over a bench. 'E beat me with whips and canes and chains. Stuck hooks through me skin and pulled on it until I thought 'e was gonna skin me alive. 'E raped me in every way a man can rape a woman except the normal way, 'urt me in ways most people can't even imagine, stuck things inside me and needles through me most sensitive parts and even strung me up by me 'air. I screamed and begged and screamed some more until I was spent and could beg and scream no more, and gave in.

"And that's when 'e stopped, took me out of the bonds and took all his devilish toys off and out of me and took me to the bed 'e had standin' in the other room. 'E pulled me legs wide open, pushed through me barrier and buried himself deep inside, and I was so relieved that the pain was ebbin' away from that and from before, that when he rubbed me gentle-like to make me come, I did."

Tears of shame flowed freely down her cheeks at her admission.

"He liked that and told me I was a good girl and that I'd pleased 'im, and then 'e gave me the tattoo, to remember always that I liked what he'd done to me. Like I could ever scrub the shame of that from me mind or me soul. I was there for three days, and at the end of each day of pain 'e made me come. So you see, there is somethin' very wrong with me, that I could like what he'd done to me."

Henry was quiet for some time. He was no expert on the human mind, but he knew she had in no way wanted or enjoyed what that monster had done to her. Her response must have been completely involuntary, like some kind of defense against the pain her body had endured.

The physical scars of her encounter with Lord Pain might have healed, but the mental torment continued. He had read the Marquis De Sade's book and knew of his assertion that pain could heighten pleasure, but did that last pleasure justify the pain? He felt totally inadequate to help the tortured woman in front of him.

Nevertheless, he pulled her into his arms, cradled her against his chest, and tried to explain what he thought had happened to her when she was in Lord Pain's dungeon.

"Daisie, listen to me! There is nothing wrong with you, it was just your body trying to cope with all the pain that man put you through. You didn't want what he did to you, not the pain and not the other part either. You did what you had to do to survive: you gave in. This is the same man I was tracking in France, where we found dead girls with wounds indicating they had suffered similar tortures to what you described. We only found marks like yours on his victims who were still alive. My thought is: if you had not come, he might not have let you live."

Daisie let herself rest against him, too spent to do anything else. "For a long time after, I thought it would 'ave been better if I 'ad died in that dungeon."

Henry gently rubbed her back, reminded of one of his men who had admitted to him that he thought their fallen comrades had it better because they no longer had to live with the awful memories. "You don't mean that, Daisie. I know you love William and you enjoy his attentions, don't you?"

Daisie wiped at her eyes and sat back a little so she could look at Henry. "Yes, 'e is gentle and lovin'. But still I can't help thinkin' I must have wanted what that man did to me, and what kind of a monster does that make me? I might not 'ave wanted it, but my body did."

Henry looked at her earnestly. "Daisie, you had no choice, and your body did what it had to, to survive the pain. Can you forgive yourself for surviving?"

Daisie had never thought of it that way. "You think me givin' in was me way of survivin'. I can understand that in a way. But what about when I want it rough? Will, 'e doesn't mind, but 'e doesn't know why, and I think if 'e knew why, 'e'd hate me."

This was a very unusual conversation to be having with an employee, and a female one at that, but Henry still held her and tried his best to put into words the things he knew to be true.

"No, he wouldn't. He would want to rip that man apart and he would feel guilty for enjoying something so similar to the torture you endured, but you two have been lovers for a long time. He wouldn't love you any less. It's very normal to be a little rough from time to time. There are even some books written about how pain can heighten pleasure. Not pain like that man inflicted on you, but more subtle things that heighten the whole body's awareness. Maybe wanting it rough with a person you can trust helps you to make sense of your memories, so you don't have to remain tormented by this your whole life."

People dealt with trauma in strange ways. Henry had witnessed that often enough on the battlefield. Soldiers rocking back and forth over the dead body of a friend, cursing God, only to walk off the field some time later, refusing to speak the dead man's name ever again. Others would hack their way through the enemy, then walk off the battlefield seemingly unaffected, laughing, gambling and whoring the night away, then break down days or even weeks later, crying like a babe at the sight of a lame bird.

Daisie nodded slowly, her brow furrowed in thought. "I was so scared when I was there. I knew 'e was evil and I knew what 'e was doin' was wrong and 'orrible, but 'e was the one hurtin' me and 'e was the one who could make it stop, and then 'e made it better when I gave in, so I gave in. Maybe now I want to control the hurt. And the hurt is so much less than the shame. And I am ashamed for doing anythin' so 'e would stop hurtin' me."

Henry wished he could erase what had been done to her from her mind. "You really only did what you had to do to get out of that dungeon alive."

Daisie had calmed considerably, but still clung to Henry, finally looking up at him with hope in her eyes. "So you think I need to forgive meself for givin' in to the bastard, and then maybe I won't feel so terrible?"

Henry smiled down at her and brushed a strand of her hair behind her ear. "That's exactly what I think. Can you try to do that for me?"

She nodded and tried valiantly to smile, heaving an enormous sigh. Then she rested her head back down onto his shoulder. Henry did not know what else he could say or do to help her, so he just held her and let her draw strength and comfort from him.

They stayed like that for a long while. Henry watched a pale sun climb over the rooftops across the square, and still he held Daisie, letting her gather herself, letting her find her way back to the woman she had become over the past eight years.

Eventually Daisie drew herself up and out of his embrace and straightened her bodice with a more confident smile. "Thank you, sir."

Henry sat back on his heels. "You are most welcome. I'm sorry I had to put you through this."

"I never told no one about this before, but I feel better for it, so don't you be sorry."

Henry gave her hand a reassuring squeeze and stood so he could lean against the mantel. "I do believe what you told me will help us go after this lord and bring him to the gallows at last. And I don't want to put you through any more pain, but do you think you could describe him for me?"

Daisie took a deep breath and nodded. "I remember 'is eyes. So cold and dead, they didn't even 'ave a color. They were kind of murky like the Thames in winter. He was tall and thin but strong, wiry like. He had dark hair, kept long, and he wore it in a queue. And 'e 'ad a scar on 'is shoulder, big long slash it was."

She indicated her right shoulder, and Henry growled. "He was wounded at Salamanca. Son of a bitch."

Henry seethed with frustration. Why had no one ever bothered to check Astor's military record, his deployments, his absences? He knew Astor had bought his commission late into the Peninsular campaign and most of De Sade's activity in France had been between 1809 and 1811, but still, if he could match dates to Astor's absences, it would give the Old Man ammunition to have Astor investigated.

Daisie gave him a long, assessing look. "You sound like you know who it is."

"I have a very good idea, but until now I could never persuade my superiors of the validity of my hunch. I have to check and cross-check my facts because this man has very powerful relatives, but I think I finally have enough to persuade my commander to let me lay a trap for him."

She didn't know what he had in mind or who his superiors might be, but she squared her shoulders and gave him a sharp nod. "I'll help. Just tell me where, when, and what you need."

"We won't do anything until William comes back with more information. But in the meantime I will enroll the help of some friends I can trust, and see what kind of assistance I can expect from the powers that be."

Daisie stood and gathered their cups. "Do you want me to bring you some fresh coffee, sir?"

Henry watched her thoughtfully. "No, thank you, Daisie. I'll have some with my breakfast when my friends arrive. You go take the day off and take care of yourself."

Daisie wrinkled her nose. "With Will out of town, I'd much rather carry on. Besides, I wanna meet that Madame Clarise and 'elp Eliza get ready for the ball."

Henry understood all too well how staying busy could be a salve for one's hurt. "In that case, why don't you organize a bath for Eliza and bring us some hot chocolate to her room?"

Daisie gathered the tray, and Henry walked with her to the door, but held her back for a moment with a hand on her arm. "And Daisie, if you want to talk or need anything, anything at all, come to me."

Daisie gave him a shy smile. "I will! Thank you."

She turned into the corridor and made for the servant stairs while Henry headed the other way to Eliza's room.

CHAPTER FIFTEEN

ELIZA WAS STILL ASLEEP WHEN HENRY SLIPPED into her room. She was nestled deep into her feather bed, and he stood there for a while just looking at her, reflecting on all he had learned in the past hour.

The pale morning sunlight filtering through the heavy drapes gently illuminated what could be seen of Eliza's face. She seemed so peaceful in her sleep, so young and innocent, and so very beautiful. He shuddered to think what would have happened to her if he hadn't found her on the road into Hampstead.

But he had found her, and she was safe, and somehow that knowledge calmed him, enabled him to think. The implications of what Daisie had told him and what he now knew to be true were horrendous. Astor was indeed the spy De Sade and a monster.

Astor had been Henry's nemesis since Astor had done his best to make Cecilia his mistress. Despite Astor's status, Cecilia had taken Henry to bed. And when they ran away together, they thought they had seen the last of Astor.

Not so. A year later, Astor had been at his father's house when Henry had come begging for help with his infant daughter in his arms. His father had advised him to "take his bastard to the next workhouse where it belonged." And then he had forbidden his wife, Henry's mother, to help them.

Henry had always felt guilty for the difficulties he had caused Cecilia. But now it seemed he might have saved her from a far worse fate.

"Oh merciful saints!" Henry went ice-cold with dread. Astor knew about Emily! And he knew how much Henry cared about her. Henry had even turned away from his father because of her.

Emily was barely twelve years old, but she already looked like her mother: blond, blue-eyed, and delicate. Henry refused to even think about what that monster could do to her; that way lay madness.

Thank God Emily was protected in the ducal household. He would write to his cousin to warn him of the possible danger. But she couldn't live sheltered at Avon forever. Eventually she would be attending finishing school to help her find her place among the elite, and then she would come to town for her season.

Grim determination settled over Henry as he watched the peacefully sleeping Eliza, her need for protection as palpable to him as his daughter's. He had saved Eliza and she was now under his protection, but it had been sheer luck he had been in the right place at the right time.

His chances of protecting Emily were much better since he had stumbled across this information and could see the threat clearly. He realized the value of anticipating the events of the future, no matter how frightening. Figuring out a conundrum and knowing when to take action was something the Old Man had taught him well.

Astor would have to die, one way or another, before Emily left Avon.

His decision made, Henry turned his attention back to the woman before him. His woman, for now.

Eliza was lying on her stomach, both her hands resting next to her head on the snowy white pillow. Her hair had escaped its braid and fell all over her face. Only a sleep-rosy cheek was visible, and one of her curls stirred with every breath she took. The simple sign of life was oddly reassuring to Henry. Warmth, peace, and beauty—these were the perfect antidotes to what he had just encountered and what he would have to do. He needed to touch her.

Henry pulled off his jacket, toed off his shoes, and quietly made his way over to the window to pull back the heavy curtains and let in the pale winter light. Then he slipped into bed beside Eliza and pulled her warm sleeping form into his arms.

She stirred and turned toward him so she could nuzzle into his chest, but did not open her eyes. "You're here."

Henry stuck his nose into the riot of curls surrounding her head and inhaled deeply. "Good morning, my sweet."

She rubbed her face along his chest to his shoulder and opened her eyes just a crack. "Do I need to get up?"

Henry pulled her head back onto his chest and threaded his fingers into her hair to hold her in place. "Not yet. Just let me hold you for a while."

Eliza snuggled closer to him, instinctively trying to give him comfort. "What's wrong, Henry?"

His arms tightened around her. "I talked to Daisie just now."

"Oh, bad?"

He sighed heavily into her hair. "Bloody awful. Incomprehensible really, what that man did to her."

"How is she?"

"Wounded. Ashamed. Afraid William would turn from her if ever he found out. Afraid for William if he insisted on avenging her. Confused by her own reactions and so very hurt, I don't know if anything will ever be able to take away that hurt."

Eliza drew her arms tighter around him. "Probably not. Some things cannot be forgotten, even if they are forgiven eventually. But she's strong."

Henry kissed her hair and stroked a gentle hand up and down her back. Her kind of wisdom came from experience, and Henry wished he could have shielded her from it. "And she is determined! In fact, she is quite a woman. William is a very lucky man."

Eliza smiled and leaned back in his arms so she could look at him. "Are we going after the lord then, too?"

"Yes. I'm almost certain the lord who tortured Daisie is the same man who did this to countless French girls and sold military secrets to the French. I could never prove it before, but now I think I can."

Eliza turned into Henry's shoulder and took a long inhale, drawing in his scent. Coming up for air, she said, "Good. Daisie needs someone to fight that battle for her."

He kissed her forehead and looked at her very seriously for a while. "I'm not just doing it for Daisie and justice."

"What do you mean?"

Henry braced himself. "This man holds a grudge against me and he knows about Emily. I will not be able to ensure her safety until he no longer roams free."

Eliza pushed up onto her elbow, clearly troubled by this revelation.

"This will be very dangerous and I will need all the help I can get, but because of this new and additional danger, I'm not at all sure you or Daisie should come to Hampstead."

Eliza's brow furrowed. "It seems to me this will be most dangerous for you." She shook her head, then thought better of it and shrugged. "But I said I would follow your lead. I still want to go, but if you think it's too dangerous . . . Is there any other way for me to help?"

Henry was pleased with her restraint—it almost swayed him in favor of taking her along after all. In spite of, or maybe because of, all she'd been through, Eliza had an inner strength in the face of injustice that continued to impress him. "Will you have breakfast with me and my friends so you can tell them about Hampstead and we can plan? I would invite Daisie as well, but I don't think she is in a fit state to tell any aspect of her story to strangers at present."

"Of course I will," she agreed earnestly. "I want Hobbs off the streets, and if this lord is doing to other girls what he did to Daisie, then he must be stopped, especially if he is a danger to your Emily. Now that we know, we simply can't stand by and let him continue."

Determination marked Henry's countenance. "Quite right."

Eliza's expression turned more hopeful. "Once he is brought to justice, perhaps Daisie will be able to feel safe in this world again."

Henry dipped his head to kiss her tenderly, then stroked her hair out of her face and marveled at the compassion in her beautiful brown eyes.

Daisie wasn't the only one who would feel safer in this world without Astor in it.

Eliza continually impressed him. He had made her his mistress, but she was also his friend, and now she would be his partner. She was barely eighteen, but he had respect for her, and that was more than he could say of any of the women he had bedded in the past.

Henry pulled her back down into his arms, and they held each other for a little while longer, until a knock at the door heralded the arrival of the requested hot chocolate.

LEAVING ELIZA TO HER BATH, Henry went downstairs to tend to his correspondence. He had just read through the last of the morning's mail when he heard Robert's jovial baritone from the foyer.

Henry had hoped for a few minutes alone with Robert to gain his cooperation as a magistrate in Hampstead. It wouldn't do to rely on his status as trusted friend to get his help. If Robert knew all the facts and deemed it necessary to take action, he would make the mission his own, and Henry had learned a long time ago that Robert's help was invaluable.

He strode into the foyer with his hand outstretched in welcome. "Robert! A good morning to you."

Robert shook his hand with a broad grin. "The same to you, Henry! I admit to being curious about this bit of action you mentioned."

Henry gestured his friend toward the breakfast room and signaled the footman on duty to bring them coffee. "Come have a cup of coffee with me whilst we wait for our adventurer."

The breakfast room was a warm, sunny room done in various shades of yellow from butter to sunflower, and also had the additional benefit of being at the back of the house where the garden was surrounded by a tall wall. It assured no one who was not trusted would come within earshot, or even sight of them, during their meeting.

As Henry poured for his friend, he asked, "Are you aware that Eliza, the girl I found half-dead on the road, is from The Cat And Fiddle just outside of Hampstead?"

Robert's eyebrows rose in question. "No, I wasn't. That used to be a decent inn to go for a pint and a game of darts, but the proprietor died and the widow let it go to pot."

Henry suppressed the urge to growl at his friend. "That's not quite what happened, but for now, let's just say Eliza is the daughter of the innkeeper you knew. She and her mother went through hell after her father's death."

Robert held up his hands in silent apology. "You can tell me the entire story another time, just give me the facts for now."

Always to-the-point, Robert could ever be depended upon to consider the facts and form an opinion based on the rationale of the situation. Henry took a sip of his coffee and gathered himself.

"The facts as they are known to us are as follows: I encountered Eliza on the road into Hampstead in mid-November. Her stepfather had sold her to a man named Wilkins, and her refusal to go with him had earned her a brutal beating. She was locked into the cellar but managed to escape up the coal chute."

At the mention of Wilkins, Robert's expression grew thoughtful, but he let Henry continue.

"I saw her on the road, realized she was seriously hurt, and offered my help. She had nowhere else to go, so I took her here. A month later, once she was finally well enough to leave the house, she was snatched right out of Covent Garden market."

Robert's brows rose in astonishment as Henry continued.

"Thankfully Eliza managed a bloodcurdling scream before she was dragged into an alley, so we could give chase. It turns out Wilkins had dealings with a man named Hobbs. He helped Wilkins find out where Eliza was. Apparently, once it was clear she was under my roof, this Wilkins assumed she was no longer a virgin and sold her to Hobbs, who is a well-known pimp and was all too happy to steal her from me since I rescued one of his 'pigeons' some years ago."

Robert knew who Henry referred to and could no longer contain himself. "Bloody hell, the same swine who stole Dix's sister and pressed her into prostitution? And his name is Hobbs? I know of some cretin named Hobbs, who I'm certain offers girls at The Silver Fox, but so far I have failed to catch him *in flagrante*."

Raising his brows, Henry waited for Robert to catch up. Robert did not disappoint.

"The same Hobbs, then."

Henry nodded. "Fortunately, once Hobbs found himself eye-to-eye with William and me, he gave in almost immediately and walked away from his deal with Wilkins, whom I paid off later."

Robert stirred two heaped spoonfuls of sugar into his coffee and connected a few more dots. "And Wilkins is the miller? A rare brute whose second wife died not too long ago, under suspicious circumstances, I might add. But there is nothing I can do if it's the husband who is doing the beating."

Henry nodded once more, barely containing his disgust. "The same. Eliza says Wilkins and her stepfather, Horace, are best friends, birds of a feather she calls them. She knew about Wilkins's wives and had no doubt she was running for her life when she climbed out that coal chute."

Robert smiled at the pride in his friend's voice when he talked about this girl. "She sounds like quite the woman."

Henry smiled to himself. "She is a mere slip of a girl and only eighteen, but she has more backbone than I have ever seen in a woman. You will meet her in a short while. What I need to ask you, my friend, is whether you will help us go after Hobbs on your turf, since he is untouchable within London city limits."

Robert's response was immediate and definitive. "It will be my unmitigated pleasure. Never had much patience for bribery."

"Good show!" Henry exclaimed. "I may also need your help in dealing with the stepfather, but there is much more to this." Henry trailed off, looking at Robert meaningfully. Robert tried to will him to go on, but Henry only stared right back at him, making Robert near crazy with curiosity. "I shall wait for Allen and Eliza."

Robert held his gaze for a short while longer, then grinned. "I suppose all will become clear in good time?"

The line had been a running joke between them when working together to unravel the secrets the French had tried so hard to keep out of their hands. Henry returned the grin, as they fell right back into their old rhythm, then grew somber. "You have no idea how right you are. You and I have been puzzling over this particular murky problem for the better part of ten years."

Robert had a sudden sinking feeling he knew exactly where this was going. "You have my undivided attention."

Just then the door opened and Eliza entered, urging both men to their feet. Henry moved toward Eliza, took her hand, kissed it, and turned toward Robert to introduce her. "Eliza, this is my friend Robert Pemberton, Viscount Fairly. Robert, this is Eliza Broad, my houseguest."

Eliza smiled nervously at the thought of addressing an actual lord, but managed to sink into a graceful curtsy. "My lord, it's a pleasure to meet you."

Robert stepped forward, took her hand to raise her out of the curtsy, then bowed over it, flawless in his observance of the polite pleasantries. "The pleasure is all mine, Miss Broad."

They assessed each other for a moment. Robert found himself pleasantly surprised by her steady gaze and frank appraisal, while Eliza couldn't help but admire the viscount's undeniable beauty. He reminded her of a picture of the Archangel Michael in full battle armor—he was everything she would have expected a true blue blood to be. But she also found his perfect manners cold and his classic good looks intimidating, and so she stepped closer to Henry and the comfort of his familiarity.

"Call me Eliza if you would, my lord."

Henry's hand at the small of her back had made her brave, but she blushed furiously nevertheless. Robert had neither missed her step into Henry nor her blush. For once Henry had managed to get himself involved with a woman who was loyal as well as innocent, and had backbone. Knowing how unprecedented this was and how important it could be for Henry, he smiled his first true smile since Eliza had entered. "Only if you will call me Robert."

The viscount's reply deepened Eliza's blush, but the smile accompanying the offer prompted her to reassess her judgment of the man. He was not cold; he was cautious. He had reserved judgment, but somehow she had proven herself worthy, and now that he had accepted her, she knew without a doubt he would be a friend to her if ever she needed one. She bowed her head to indicate she would indeed call him by his Christian name, then turned to Henry. "Didn't you say you were expecting two friends?"

"That would be me."

At the sound of the smooth, cultured voice, Eliza turned to the

door, where Allen had appeared. The stranger was clad in riding attire made entirely of soft, tan doeskin, not just his breeches but also
his vest and the short riding jacket. The unusual attire brought out the
moss green of his eyes and set off his sun-kissed skin and the brown
of his wavy hair against the white of his cravat.

"Allen Strathem at your service."

He bowed over her hand, and she curtsied, observing the pleasantries, but when she looked up at him, his eyes sparkled with silent
laughter. She liked him instantly.

CHAPTER SIXTEEN

ALLEN TURNED TO HIS FRIENDS, RAISING A HAND to them in greeting. "Henry. Robert. Let's not make the lady wait for her breakfast."

Both Henry and Robert burst out laughing. Allen looked at them, astonished. "What? I'm starved!"

Henry, his voice still full of laughter, returned, "You are always starved, whelp." Then, taking Eliza's hand, he gestured. "This is Miss Eliza Broad, by the way."

Allen blushed slightly as he realized he had not waited for her to be introduced, but recovered instantly. "Have you broken your fast yet, Miss Eliza Broad?"

She shook her head, but before she could answer in words, Allen took her other arm and led her toward the breakfast buffet. "By all means, then, let's fill you a plate."

Eliza turned amused eyes to Henry, who returned her gaze with equal amounts of mirth and whispered *sotto voce* in her ear, "We had better feed him or he will go from merely frantic to positively cantankerous, like a two-year-old."

Allen threw Henry a look of mock hurt, which was rather difficult considering he had half a pastry stuffed in his mouth. "Who are you calling an infant, old man?"

"No talking with your mouth full, there is a lady present."

Allen sketched a quick bow in Eliza's direction and indicated his still-full mouth in apology for not apologizing verbally.

Robert shook his head. "You have been in the wilderness for too long."

Allen took his plate, piled high with eggs, bacon, and mushrooms, grabbed two scones with his free hand, and swallowed the last of his pastry as he moved around the table to find a seat. He heaved a long-suffering sigh. "You are not wrong there."

Eliza had followed their antics in silent astonishment, and finally dissolved into delighted laughter. They all three turned to her in unison, then looked at each other, grinned, shrugged, and went back to piling their plates with food.

Henry led her to the table, put his plate down, seated her to his right, and winked. "Could be we all spent too long in the wilderness."

Renewed laughter shook her shoulders. "You three are like the Collins brothers when their Da isn't around."

Robert winced. "Ouch, not the Collins brothers."

Allen's eyebrows lifted. "You are familiar with these paragons?"

"I certainly am. They are the menace of Hampstead, otherwise known as 'the triple threat,'" Robert reported.

Eliza's eyes grew wide. "You really do know them. Are you the one who is a justice of the peace there? Did Henry tell you that we need your help?"

Robert bowed his head with a bemused smile. "Guilty as charged. And yes, he did. But let's eat first and deal with business later. Both Allen and I think much better with a full stomach."

Henry couldn't help himself. "Oh, is that why I had to do all the thinking on the Peninsular campaign—not enough rations?"

Allen shrugged irreverently. "No, we just figured we'd let you get on with it, seeing as you were so very good at thinking, and it took all our efforts to find enough food to keep the meat on our bones."

Robert nodded wisely. "Besides, you were the one with a bee in your bonnet about proving to the Old Man and Wellesley that battle plans should be kept secret even from the Admiralty."

Henry instantly rose to the bait. "Well, as soon as they did, we started winning. That proved it as far as I'm concerned."

"Yes," Allen placated. "We all know it was you who put it together and almost caught De Sade."

A dark cloud crossed Henry's face. "Yes . . . almost."

Eliza's head snapped up. "De Sade, the one we've been talking about? You've been after him for all these years?"

Henry nodded to her while holding Robert's questioning gaze.

But it was Allen who blurted out, "Good Lord, how does she know about De Sade?" His worried eyes searched Eliza's face before his shocked gaze locked onto Henry's.

Henry knew what he was thinking and shook his head minutely, then took Eliza's hand and squeezed it reassuringly before he turned to his friends. "I have new information on De Sade, and Eliza is the one who brought it to me. I spoke to the witness directly this morning, and I believe I finally have enough evidence to convince the Old Man that Astor is indeed De Sade."

"Son of a bitch, how?"

Robert looked just as disturbed as Allen. "Is the witness also a victim?"

Henry laced his fingers through Eliza's and held tight. "Yes."

There was a brief pause before Robert gathered himself to ask the next question. "Who is it?"

"Daisie."

"God damn it!"

"Hell and damnation!"

Their eyes held so much sadness, Eliza knew without a shadow of a doubt they knew what Astor, or De Sade, had done to Daisie. She looked at these two men who were so inflamed with the injustice of what had been done to her friend and so many other girls. They were like Henry in so many ways, it was easy to see why they were friends. And it was good to know there were more men like Henry in this world.

"Thank you, both of you, for supporting Daisie."

Allen smiled at her. "Believe us, we know: anybody who comes into contact with the darkness that man creates needs a few good men on her side."

Eliza nodded and turned back to Henry. Quietly, she prodded, "Tell them about Astor and Cecilia and what you fear for Emily."

Henry sighed deeply, kissed her forehead, and drew away slightly, but kept hold of her hand. He fixed his friends with a gaze that made them sit up straighter and focus their full attention on him.

"You know about the animosity between Astor and me and that it goes back to Cecilia." Henry ran his left hand across his face in an attempt to gather himself. "I thought he had gotten his revenge after he turned my father against me, but it occurs to me now that he wasn't satisfied with that. I could never quite put my finger on it, but over the years his ill will toward me seems to have muted into anticipation. He is always observing me, lurking in shadows, watching me. The trouble is, he knows about Emily, and from what I have learned from Daisie this morning, I now believe he may well be planning revenge through her."

There was dead silence in the room, leaving Henry's last statement hanging in the air like a specter. Both Robert and Allen knew the exuberant, smart-aleck tomboy that was Emily. Both would give their lives to protect her. She was Henry's heart.

No one spoke, no one moved, and food remained unchewed in Allen's mouth until Robert spoke aloud what Henry had concluded earlier.

"He has to die."

Henry's shoulders relaxed somewhat, relieved he would not have to face this by himself.

Allen swallowed the mouthful with a curt nod and demanded, "Tell us everything you've uncovered."

And with that, a jovial breakfast amongst friends turned into a war council. Henry and Eliza relayed every last bit of information they had about Astor and Hobbs, and Eliza was called upon to answer questions about Horace and Wilkins and their possible involvement.

As the morning turned to afternoon, they moved to the library so Robert and Eliza could pore over a map of Hampstead and the country around the small town. Between them, their knowledge of the area was reassuringly complete. Robert knew all the great houses and estates and the town itself, whereas Eliza knew every farm and bridle path. Between them they found three possible houses that could be Hobbs's cottage, identified as possibilities because neither of them knew who lived there.

Possible locations for Astor's dungeon were more difficult to pinpoint, and eventually Henry went in search of Daisie to find out if she had any specific recollections of her trip there. But all she could say for sure was the wagon ride had taken no longer than forty minutes, and they had travelled no faster than a walk on a rutted dirt road. They had climbed a steep, long hill, then left the cart behind to walk the last few yards through eerie silence before ascending a number of steep steps, and finally going down a long flight of stairs to the underground location.

In the end, Henry drew a three-mile radius around The Silver Fox, but none of the structures along that line seemed in the least promising.

In France, most of the victims had been taken to remote cottages, but Robert and Eliza could account for all similar locations in Hampstead. Besides, what Daisie had described was more akin to a garden house, and the only one they knew of was the Greek pagoda on an island in the ornamental lake behind Oakwood House, an estate belonging to the Duke of Elridge.

Hobbs would have had to walk Daisie down a hill and across a bridge to get there, and the sound of water would have been unmistakable. Henry very much doubted Astor would locate his torture chamber so close to the house his father owned and which Astor was known to frequently visit. A covert operator, Astor would never disregard the first rule of subterfuge by keeping anything incriminating in or around his home.

Henry was about to give up on finding Astor's dungeon—Hobbs would just have to lead them to it—when Allen asked, "What about graveyards, more specifically a mausoleum? They are remote, frequently on a hill, and most have stone steps."

Henry's expectant gaze rested on Robert, but it was Eliza who eyed the map with renewed interest. "There's one on the heath." She let her finger trail over the area on the map that represented Hampstead Heath.

Robert joined her and pointed to a remote area some distance from the border of Oakwood House. "There is indeed. And it is on a steep hill, within our radius, and has a small, fenced graveyard around it. The monument is a round classic structure with several steps and columns all around it. The mausoleum itself is small, but who knows what could be beneath it."

They all looked at the spot he pointed to on the map. Henry slowly nodded. "That should be the first place we check when we get up there."

"This will be a cat-and-mouse game," Robert said, "and in order to know when to pounce, we need to know every move our two targets make. In order to get Astor and be able to tie him to De Sade, we need to catch him *in flagrante* in his dungeon. In order to know when he will have a woman in there, we will need to wait for Hobbs to bring him one."

Though supremely uncomfortable with the idea of delivering some poor innocent into Astor's hands, Henry could not find fault in his friend's logic. "Agreed. We need to tail both Hobbs and Astor, and if we want the Old Man to sanction this, we had better ask for his help. Besides, Astor knows all of us and is probably familiar with our men, so we will need an experienced agent unknown to him. I will take it upon myself to pay the Old Man a visit before I escort Eliza to the Fairy Ball tonight. Robert, are you taking Millie?"

His friend grinned. "Certainly! Millie spent wads of my money having matching costumes made for us."

Eliza looked at them, bewildered. One second they were discussing putting a girl at the mercy of Lord Pain and now she was supposed to go dancing. "We're still going to the ball?"

Henry looked at her with intense eyes, and she suddenly felt naïve and out of her depth.

"It is imperative we attend. As men of leisure about town, both Robert and I are expected there. If either one of us didn't attend, it would raise eyebrows; and if both of us are absent, it will tip off Astor that we are up to something. The last thing we want is for him to pay us more attention than he has so far." He kissed her hand, willing her to understand. "Madame Clarise was engaged to make you a fairy dress specifically for this ball, and she is coming to fit it today. Consummate businesswoman that she is, she will know if her creation made it to the ball to be duly admired, and anybody could be using her for information. If we hope to have a shot at catching Astor unawares, we have to go."

Robert added, "And because the event is organized by the demimonde, there is a good chance Hobbs will hear of our attendance or absence, and he already has a wary eye on Henry." Robert considered for a moment how she might feel about what he was about to say, but thought it best she understood all considerations. "Besides, the best way for Henry to keep you safe is to claim you as his for all to see. It will also reassure Astor to know Henry is busy with a new mistress."

Eliza mouthed a silent "Oh" and nodded. "You might be right with regards to Hobbs; he backed out of his deal with Wilkins the moment he realized Henry was willing to fight him to keep me. But Astor wants to hurt Henry. Don't you think he could decide to do it through me?"

Henry looked a little taken aback. "My apologies, Eliza. You raise a valid point we would do well to bear in mind: this undertaking is not without danger for you." He kissed her hand again. "You don't have to go tonight if you are uncomfortable with the risk."

Troubled, she shook her head. "No, no, that's not what I meant. I want to go, to help. In fact, I need to. I know I'm being naïve, but I feel like helping you with this somehow makes up for not being able to help my mother." She hung her head and trailed off. "I don't mind the danger. I was just thinking out loud."

All three men were staring at her now, but it was Robert who put into words what they were all thinking. "You are not being naïve. We all do this for a reason: we are all making up for something. And as to you speaking your mind, your observations are completely valid, and one of us should have thought of the possible danger you might face. We are, after all, the ones with the experience in this arena."

"As for tonight," Henry pointed out, "Robert or myself will be with you at all times, and as far as I know, Astor is not yet aware of your connection to me, so you should be safe from him for now."

Allen addressed the brandy in his snifter. "Let's just be grateful you are neither blond nor blue-eyed."

His comment seemed to somehow settle the subject to everyone's satisfaction, and Henry turned to him, intent on organizing the surveillance on their targets. "Is Rick still with you?"

Allen spread his hands wide, indicating his unusual get-up. "Can't you tell?"

Henry smirked. "Consider it a rhetorical question then. What did he do, hunt the deer and tan the hide himself?"

Allen looked a little sheepish. "Not exactly. He bought this leather off the women of an Indian tribe we came across while wandering around the wilderness trying to find out what the French were up to. He told me he had never seen finer quality or felt softer leather, and after he presented me with this suit, I had to agree."

Allen held out his crooked arm so everyone could feel the quality of his jacket's leather. His sheepishness intensified. "He sort of persuaded me to go into business with him, and we came back with a whole cargo hull full of fine Indian leather."

Both Henry and Robert exclaimed simultaneously, "Again?"

Allen grinned and shrugged. "Ah well, at least if this one fails I'll have a lifetime supply of fine leather at my disposal. Apparently you can make all manner of things out of the stuff, from shirts to cushions to shoes to bedspreads to carriage upholstery."

The banter continued, and although Eliza was still puzzled by the swift change in mood, she was beginning to understand. What they had done together and were about to engage in was filled with so much danger and darkness, they had to keep the light alive for each other.

As for going to the ball, now she knew it was a ruse, she would put her heart and soul into it. It occurred to her that Henry's whole life was a ruse, carefully constructed to avoid scrutiny by the very people he investigated.

His image of the womanizing spendthrift who cared for nothing but his pleasure did not match her experiences with him. She had wondered about that before, but now it made perfect sense. He had built his image on the wreckage of his affair with Cecilia and it had served him well.

While she mused about the things hidden beneath the glamour

of high society, the men made plans for the rest of the day. Allen, who was the only one not known to Hobbs, was sent to The Crown in Covent Garden, where Hobbs held court. He was to establish an around-the-clock tail on the pimp. Once given his purpose, Allen departed to collect his man and head east.

The door had barely closed behind him when a footman appeared to inform Eliza that Madame Clarise had arrived to attend to her. Eliza had never been to a fitting before, so she was a little lost as to what she should do.

Henry noticed her hesitation and started giving the orders for her. "Thomas, escort Madame and her seamstress to Miss Eliza's room and make sure they have all they need. Then go tell Daisie—she was keen to help. Miss Eliza will be up in a moment."

Thomas departed, and Henry turned to Eliza. "I will be up as soon as we finalize our plans and I have written a quick missive to my cousin."

She blushed at the idea of him coming to watch her getting in and out of her dresses, but acknowledged his statement with a shallow curtsy. Then she turned to Robert. "It was a pleasure meeting you. I trust I will see you tonight, Robert."

Robert bowed over her hand once again. "You shall indeed, and the pleasure was all mine." Then, with a little wicked smile she knew had melted a thousand hearts, he added, "Save me a waltz, oh fairy princess."

Eliza looked to Henry to see what his reaction was to losing one of the three dances she would be able to dance due to her ignorance of quadrilles and the other refined dances that made up a proper ball, but Henry only smiled at her renewed uncertainty.

"It's not a formal occasion. At this ball, all the dances are waltzes."

Understanding dawned. The actors, dancers, artists, and women of ill repute that made up the little section of society commonly known as the demimonde did not adhere to the same rules as high society, and as Henry's mistress, she was now a member of the demimonde. To her surprise, it didn't bother her in the least. In fact, there was something freeing about it.

She smiled at the two men and headed for the door.

CHAPTER SEVENTEEN

ELIZA REACHED HER BEDCHAMBER AND OPENED the door to an explosion of colorful fabrics, frantic activity, and an open-mouthed Daisie. Madame Clarise clearly ruled her fashion empire with an autocratic hand, no matter which space she colonized for her purposes.

Mostly-completed dresses and undergarments covered every surface in the room. Three seamstresses sat ready to do their mistress's bidding around a table close to the sparse winter light streaming through the windows. A plethora of ribbons fluttered in the breeze of activity, and a delicate pair of silver fairy wings hung from a corner of the clothes press. But there was no time for Eliza to take in the riches before her; Madame Clarise's unchecked enthusiasm demanded her immediate attention.

"Mademoiselle Eliza, how wonderful to see you again."

The exuberant dressmaker bussed both Eliza's cheeks, then held her at arm's length by her shoulders. Madame took in Eliza's blue gown and, with a gesture of Gallic disdain, commanded her minions, "Oh, *mon Dieu! Vite vite*, help me get these rags off her."

Before Eliza could formulate a protest, she was pulled to the fire and divested of her gown and underdress. But as soon as Madame took in the French corset and the silk petticoats Eliza wore underneath, she was all smiles again. "Good girl! We French always know best how to reveal a woman's assets."

Eliza smiled at the English dressmaker claiming the French as her countrymen. "It's very comfortable, and the hooks in the front make it easy to put on."

"And get out of, *n'est-ce pas?*" Madame winked, and Eliza blushed deeply, which made Madame laugh uproariously. "Oh, I can see why Sir Henry is besotted with you. That blush is adorable."

All traces of coquetry evaporated in an instant, and her charming smile turned all business as she fixed her assistant with a stare that clearly announced playtime was over. "Now, Marie, hand me the rose silk. Let's deal with the morning and walking dresses first."

Madame guided the heavy silk gown over Eliza's head with practiced ease, ordered her assistant to close the buttons in the back, then walked around Eliza, and with a critical eye assessed every aspect of the fit. She pinched the dress in a few places to mold it better to Eliza's form and pinned it in place. Then she lifted it off her again and tossed it across the room at one of the three seamstresses, who caught the gown and started to stitch without so much as a flinch.

Eliza caught Daisie's mesmerized stare and couldn't suppress a giggle. An answering grin spread across Daisie's face, her eyes dancing with amusement. Eliza was glad to be able to provide her friend with a diversion from this morning's trials.

Gown after gown was tossed over Eliza's head, pulled, pinched, and pinned into place, then ripped off again, and piled onto the table by the windows where the seamstresses worked. By the time Madame ordered Eliza stripped to her drawers, Eliza felt more like a rag doll than a valued customer. She was so exhausted from all the pulling and pushing, not to mention the meeting that had come before, she didn't even think to object to Madame's commands until she saw Daisie look at someone behind her with a startled expression.

She reflexively crossed her arms over her naked breasts and looked over her shoulder to see what had caught Daisie's eye, to find Henry grinning back at her.

"Seems I made it just in time," he quipped while Madame sank into a deep curtsy.

"Sir Henry, what a pleasure!"

But before Madame could launch herself at him, he waved her off. "Don't mind me. Carry on."

Eliza saw the little smirk on Madame's face as she turned back to her assistant, and when she looked at Henry again, he winked, and she was struck by the realization he was not here to ogle at her—well, not exclusively anyway—but to reinforce the fiction that he was nothing but a rogue wastrel, intent on debauching his mistress. He was here to maintain a cover for all of them, and she would do her part to help. She let her arms drop, giving him a tantalizing side view of her breasts, and returned his wink right in Madame's line of sight. Henry's grin widened and he mouthed, "Good girl!"

Daisie had divested her of all her petticoats, and Madame had her ease a fabulously soft silver-gray satin underskirt over Eliza's head. The garment slid down Eliza's body like flowing water, but as soon as the skirt had settled over her hips, Madame ordered harshly, "No drawers."

And Henry drawled from the other side of the room where he was leaning a hip against the footboard of her bed, "My sentiments exactly!"

Eliza was torn between amusement and mortification, but obediently held up the narrow skirt so Daisie could remove her drawers. Out of the corner of her eyes, she caught Henry tilting his head to the side to get a better view of her bottom and almost laughed out loud at his expression of rapt attention.

Daisie busied herself lacing up the silver-gray satin corset Madame had instructed Eliza to climb into and chose that moment to whisper into Eliza's ear, "What's the matter with Sir Henry? I've never seen 'im like this."

Madame and her assistant were absorbed in lifting a shimmering garment out of a box on the bed and had not noticed the exchange, so Eliza answered, "Shh, just play along."

Then she winked at her friend, and judging by the wicked grin on Daisie's face, there was no need to explain further. After all, Daisie was fully aware of the meeting that had taken place earlier. "Ah, gossip! Can be useful, that."

Eliza nodded sagely and went back to throwing coy smiles over her shoulder at Henry as the dressmaker and her assistant approached with the gown.

The gown was an exquisitely layered flurry of blue, green, and turquoise chiffon and shimmering silver organza. As the dress settled over Eliza's body, it became clear it was just wide enough to slip over her head and shoulders without having to be laced in the back, but tight enough to follow her curves and sheer enough to let the silver-gray underskirt and corset shine through.

The dress was made up of three overlapping paneled layers that played against each other. Instead of sleeves, the panels ended in points with tiny crystals sewn onto them. Madame took those points and tied them in a simple knot over each shoulder and let the sparkling ends play down Eliza's arms. The dress had a simple v-neck plunging right to the edge of the corset and flared out into a full skirt, ending again in points. Eliza realized these, too, had tiny crystals winking from the hem, and still more crystals glistened from the folds of the dress, randomly placed like dewdrops.

The shape of the skirt reminded Eliza of a bluebell, and she loved the way it swished and flowed around her as she walked to the mirror. She had no doubt it was designed to draw a man's attention.

Henry's sharp intake of breath let everyone in the room know it had the desired effect.

Madame retrieved the wings from the clothes press and showed Daisie how to tie them. The silver ribbons coming over her shoulder crossed between Eliza's breasts and met up below them with the lower ribbons that had been brought forward. They were twisted together, crossed in the front, and then tied at the back.

The artfully tied ribbons added a Greek feel to the gown, but also raised its hemline above Eliza's ankles. The ensemble was completed by sheer silk stockings, tied Roman sandals made of the same silver satin as the underdress, and a silver-lined, jade-green velvet cape with a tasseled hood.

But Eliza couldn't ride in the coach with the wings; they would have to be tied on at the opera house. So Henry decreed Daisie would accompany them, eliciting excited squeals from the maid.

Her mission completed, Madame gathered her assistant, begged Henry not to hesitate to call on her in the future, and swept out of the house, leaving her seamstresses behind to finish the remaining gowns. In her wake, a calm descended on the room that finally allowed everyone to take a deep breath.

Henry came up behind Eliza, who was still mesmerized by her own image in the mirror. "It's exquisite and you look exquisite in it. But it's also quite scandalous. Are you ready to expose yourself to the world like this?"

Eliza leaned into him, as much for warmth as to show her appreciation of his concern, and smiled. "What's scandalous is that I'm your mistress, but I find I'm quite unconcerned about scandal. I'm more concerned that I might freeze to death."

She threw a quick glance in the direction of the seamstresses by the window. He smiled his understanding at her in the mirror and bent to kiss her neck. "Don't worry, I shall keep you warm, and these affairs usually overheat pretty quickly." Then he motioned to Daisie. "Come help Eliza into a warmer gown and then bring us some tea to my sitting room."

WITH THE FICTION OF HIS dissolute nature successfully maintained, Henry departed for his apartment to change into formal afternoon attire for his visit to the Old Man.

To everyone else, the Old Man was the mysterious, omnipotent figure who always knew far more than they did and only told them what they needed to know in order to complete their mission. But to Henry, the Old Man was his mentor, almost a surrogate father. Still, the reason for today's visit made him more than a little nervous. So much depended on the Old Man sanctioning this mission.

Ten years ago, in Portugal, when it had become clear to Wellesley and his staff that the British campaign was being hampered by espionage, Wellesley—now the Duke of Wellington—brought in the Old Man to organize a countermeasure. The Old Man in turn had recruited Henry, who had been on Wellesley's staff at the time, and, by and by, six others who formed independent cells for the purpose of counterespionage.

They created covers for themselves and continued in their military positions, but their true purpose was to find out where the leaks in the admiralty were coming from and who exploited them, and to feed those agents false information. They also were entrusted with carrying secret dispatches and coordinating with the Portuguese and the Spanish Guerrillas.

Quite a few of the agents knew each other—it was essential to their mission that they did—but only the original seven knew who the Old Man was and were sworn to keep his secret to their dying day.

Henry tied his snow-white cravat and tucked the ends into his proper gray wool vest, retrieved his watch from the dresser, and threaded the chain through his buttonhole before he headed back into his dressing room.

Preparedness being nine parts of success, he checked that his Oberon costume, a veteran of three previous costume balls, had been properly aired out and pressed. Then he shrugged into his fitted gray dress coat, smoothed down the black velvet lapels in front of the mirror, and ran his brush through his short sandy hair. He had shaved that morning, so his chin and sideburns looked presentable enough, but he would have to shave again before the ball to spare Eliza's delicate skin.

He smiled at the thought of sharing her bed again tonight, or perhaps he would invite her into his bed instead. But first he had to warn her about the kinds of things she was sure to hear about him from others at the ball. She was his friend as well as his responsibility, and he would be damned if he let her walk into this situation without all the armor he could provide.

He grabbed his top hat when he heard Eliza enter the sitting room and walked out to meet her.

She was back in her serviceable blue wool dress and looked up from surveying the volumes on his bookshelf by the window. "You look very dapper."

He winked. "Well, yes. One can't visit with one of the grand dames of society in anything but the correct attire for the occasion."

Eliza frowned in confusion. "I thought you had to go see someone in charge to get another person to shadow Astor."

Henry smiled, but his eyes were serious. "Indeed I do. But Eliza, I think it best for you to forget you ever heard mention of the Old Man. As far as you and everybody else is concerned, I am about to pay a visit to my godmother."

Eliza looked at him for a moment, then nodded and sat on the chaise longue, her hand pressed against her forehead. "Oh Lord, do I have a heap to learn about all this sneaking around. I'm glad you told me; I might have blurted that right out in front of someone who could have told Astor or Hobbs."

Henry sat next to her and drew her against him, mindful of his pristine cravat. "That is precisely why I am telling you now. So far, we have been amongst friends, and you did fabulously well with Madame Clarise earlier." He kissed her temple to underscore his words. "I know you will do well tonight, but there are some things you should know before we go. You might be subjected to crude comments from my so-called friends, and jealous speculation from some of the women."

She looked at him, slightly alarmed. "What do you mean?"

He heaved a sigh and locked eyes with her. "I have a reputation in this town, one I have carefully nurtured over the years. As far as society is concerned, I am a ladies' man. I like variety and I'm not afraid to pay for it. Over the past six years, I have never been without a mistress, and I rarely keep one for longer than three months. I am always upfront and generous with the women I engage to provide me with intimacy and companionship, and when the time comes, I hand them off to another affluent man waiting in line, or I provide the lady with enough funds to tide her over until she finds another protector."

Eliza couldn't help but fear he was telling her what would happen when he grew tired of her, and swallowed hard to subdue her panic. But she held his gaze and straightened her spine, resolved to deal with whatever life had in store for her.

Henry was quick to reassure her. "Those are the facts as far as society is concerned. However, and I need you to believe me when I say this: none of this applies to you! You are not a professional like all those other women were. You were my friend before we became lovers, and I'm well aware of the gift you gave me when you surrendered your innocence to me."

The relief on her face was obvious, and he was glad to be having this conversation. Not just so she would be prepared, but also because he had a sudden longing to tell her how he felt.

"Eliza, my sweet, there is no time limit on what is between us. The affection I feel for you goes far beyond simple desire, and I can't imagine a circumstance under which I would want you to leave."

Eliza gave him a shy smile and nuzzled into the hand he had cupped around her face. "I like you too, Henry, very much. You have already shown me so much more of life than I would ever have seen at the inn, especially the good things. You make me feel valued and safe."

He brushed a soft kiss over her lips, thanking her wordlessly for her trust. "You are the first woman to inspire trust and affection in me since Cecilia broke my heart the day she had my infant daughter delivered to me." He leaned his forehead to hers and let out a long breath. "I could understand why she succumbed to the pressure put on her to return to her husband, but to simply abandon our daughter, that was cruel."

Eliza stroked her hand over his head and kissed his cheek. "Perhaps she had a good reason to send Emily to you. Did you ever ask her?"

He shook his head. "I haven't spoken to her since she walked out of our rooms in Belgium on her husband's arm."

Eliza wanted to say more, to encourage him to find out Cecilia's motives and heal this lingering pain. But Daisie entered the sitting room with a loaded tea tray, reminding them both she was now part of their plans for the ball. Hobbs could be amongst the guests, so it was imperative they find a way for Daisie to remain undetected.

Henry had secured a box at the opera house, and Daisie assured them she would be happy to see the spectacle from there, but Henry was reluctant to leave her by herself. It would be much safer for her to hide behind a masked costume and join them whenever they left the box. To that end, Daisie was dispatched to the attic to look through the trunks of clothing his mother had stored there, and he hadn't had the heart to get rid of.

Henry poured Eliza a cup of tea and urged a slice of fruitcake on her before he helped himself. "So you know not to take anything derogatory you might hear tonight to heart, don't you?"

She smiled. What he'd said earlier had given her confidence. It felt good to be wanted. "Yes, Henry, I promise not to listen to any of the gossip, and if I do, I will not let it upset me."

"And if I happen to pat some dancing girl's bottom?" He gave her a teasing grin, and she slapped his shoulder in mock outrage.

"I shall slap your hand away and put myself in between you and her bottom."

That got her a laugh. "Perfect! Just what a jealous mistress would do."

Satisfied with her reply, Henry urged her to rest on his chaise longue for the rest of the afternoon, pressed a kiss to her forehead, and excused himself to go on his visit.

HENRY STEPPED OUT OF HIS house into the waning winter light and headed toward Brook Street and the house of his godmother. He was certain to find Lady Greyson at tea with her bosom friends at this hour of the afternoon.

Once ushered into the drawing room, he kissed her cheek affectionately, accepted a cup of tea, and chatted amicably with the assembled matrons until the salon had cleared. Lady Greyson was a formidable woman and one of the very few people who actually knew what Henry had done to earn his knighthood.

There was no need for him to tell her why he had come. Lady Greyson was astute enough to know her godson had not appeared in her salon on New Year's Eve because he had a hankering to kiss her wilting cheek one last time for the year. Henry thanked God the lady was not only skilled at clearing a room, but also secure enough in his affection for her that she wouldn't be offended by the ulterior motive for his visit.

As soon as the butler had closed the door behind the last departing guest, she waved Henry out of the room, and he departed, blow-
ing her a kiss. He let himself out of a set of French doors at the back
of the house, hopped over the wall at the bottom of the garden, and
stepped into the tiny square of no-man's-land between all the neigh-
boring gardens. It was a peaceful little forgotten wood in the midst of
the bustling metropolis, and Henry paused for a moment, inhaling the
crisp winter air.

He knew it was no coincidence that all seven cell leaders had either relatives or friends living in houses abutting the tiny no-man's-
land, but it still seemed surreal every time he made his way through
Lady Greyson's backyard to a meeting.

After scanning his surroundings carefully, he removed a brass key
from his pocket and headed to a wooden gate at the bottom of a garden whose house fronted onto Grosvenor Street.

Light spilled out from behind the drapes of the library windows,
and Henry tapped out a predetermined series of knocks on the French
doors, then waited for the sound of a bell before he slipped another
key into the lock and let himself in.

CHAPTER EIGHTEEN

HENRY RETURNED FROM HIS CLANDESTINE meeting satisfied and in time to share a light dinner with a rested Eliza before they both retreated to their rooms to change for the ball.

Henry took his time to don his costume, knowing Eliza would need more time than he. He bronzed his face, neck, and forearms with a theatrical powder and eventually headed downstairs to await the ladies.

The chandelier in the foyer was lit, making it easier to check his appearance in the mirror there.

He liked this costume, and not just because he liked the character of Oberon or because *A Midsummer Night's Dream* was one of his favorite plays. From the pointed shoes, gold embroidered silk stockings, and tan velvet breeches to the flowing, ruffled silk shirt, long tan velvet vest embroidered with gold, and the glittering powder on his face, the whole outfit made him feel just a little bit naughty. It seemed to him, if one was going to put on a costume, one might as well give full measure and enjoy the freedom a costume could afford.

He placed a gold-dusted laurel crown on his head and was in the process of arranging his forest-green velvet cloak around his shoulders when he heard Eliza and Daisie come down the stairs. Henry turned, and his breath caught.

Eliza stood on the stairs, turned half away from him, talking to

Daisie, who held her wings and cloak. The blue, green, and silver fairy dress was as exquisite as he remembered, but the bright light from the chandelier made the crystals wink from its folds and sparkle from Eliza's dark hair. Her hair flowed in loose, luxurious waves around her shoulders and down to her waist. She truly looked like a fairy princess.

But as ethereal as she appeared, the silver ribbons wound around her exposed ankles to hold up her sandals were downright arousing, and Henry had to momentarily look away to get his wayward body under control.

By the time he looked up again, Eliza had turned to him, and her excited smile was no less arousing than the sandals. "Henry, you look wonderful! Oberon?"

"Indeed, my Titania, although you are more fairy princess than queen."

She smiled as she took in all aspects of his beautiful costume, and the man in it, and he fancied an ember of desire sparked in her dark eyes.

"I'll be a young Titania, then."

He moved to the foot of the stairs and held out his hand to her. As she stepped off the last step and placed her hand in his, he pulled the necklace and bracelet set he had bought for her out of the pocket in his vest.

Before Eliza could protest, he clasped the bracelet around her wrist and stepped behind her to affix the intricate chain of golden leaves around her neck. "This should make you feel a little more regal."

Eliza's hand flew to her mouth as she looked at the delicate piece of jewelry on her wrist. When Henry moved back around to face her, lifting his hands to caress her arms, she looked at him with tears in her eyes. "This truly is fit for a fairy queen. I don't know what to say."

Henry smiled and took her to the mirror, admiring her reflection. "Say 'thank you' and that you will wear them for me. They suit you so very beautifully."

Standing behind her right shoulder, he kissed her temple and let his finger trail along the golden leaves circling her neck. The metal glowed on her skin and accentuated the silver and green of her dress. Looking for her cape, Henry's gaze traveled over Eliza's shoulder to where Daisie stood in an elegant but old-fashioned dove-gray silk gown.

"So you found something in my mother's trunks?"

Daisie grinned and twirled for him to show off the 1790s full skirt and cinched waist while holding a beaked three-quarter mask to her face. "I'm a woodland dove, rather than a soiled one."

The joke was accompanied by a swing of Daisie's hip, making Henry laugh and Eliza dissolve into giggles. Daisie's blue eyes shone with the excitement of attending the ball, and Henry was glad to see she had recovered so swiftly from the morning's ordeal.

Daisie stepped in front of the mirror, where Eliza had returned to reverently fingering her necklace. She threw a dark wool cape around her shoulders before she nudged Eliza with her elbow. "He's right, you know, them baubles look good on ya."

"They're so delicate! I just hope I don't lose them."

Her words were so quiet that Henry, who still stood within touching distance, could barely make them out. His voice was equally quiet as he stepped closer still, ran his hands up and down Eliza's bare arms, and whispered in her ear, "Delicate like you, my little fairy."

She leaned into his embrace for a moment before Henry stepped back to put her cloak around her shoulders and then led the ladies to the waiting coach.

THE BALL WAS SLATED TO commence at nine in the evening, and their little group had set out in plenty of time to witness the opening ceremony.

The organizers of this particular ball might not be part of high society nor have access to that world's wealth, but they certainly knew how to put on a show, and made good use of their talents to ensure all their events were special. The New Year's Eve ball was already a tradition, but this year's opening performance was rumored to be spectacular.

As expected, the streets were crowded with all manner of revelers, so their progress through Oxford Circus to Wardour Street and along Long Acre to the Royal Opera House was slow. Luckily, Henry's coach was spacious and comfortable, and the late December chill was kept at bay by several hot bricks spread under their feet.

Eliza's thin, sleeveless fairy dress would be a boon later in the evening when the opera house became uncomfortably warm. Henry was well aware how heated the dancing masses at these things could get, but for now he worried Eliza would be blue by the time they got there, so he wrapped her in lap blankets as well as his arms to keep her warm.

Eliza, on the other hand, was too excited to feel the cold, and even if she had given it a second thought, she would have suffered the cold gladly to wear a costume as stunning as the one Madame Clarise had made for her. But she loved Henry's arms around her, so she settled into his embrace and looked out onto the lively scenes around them on London's streets.

There were numerous mostly closed vehicles, filled with elaborately dressed ladies and gentlemen who could be admired through the windows of their conveyances. Many others were abroad on foot, some on their way to entertainments, and others out for a stroll to participate in the excitement of this night as spectators.

Daisie, being familiar with many London celebrities on sight, entertained both Henry and Eliza with her running commentary on those she could point out and their varying wardrobes.

It was a cold but clear night, and all along Oxford Street the New Year's Eve spectacle was illuminated, not just by the stars above and the lanterns of the conveyances, but also by the newly installed gaslights along the route.

This being only Eliza's second ride in a closed coach, she enjoyed the luxury of the ride itself, as well as being entertained by the multitude of sights along the way. Eventually, they made it to the line of coaches waiting to deposit their occupants outside the Royal Opera House.

Eliza helped Daisie secure her mask since it would be safest for her to be completely anonymous, but Eliza's wings would have to be dealt with once they were inside the theatre.

When they finally got close enough to the entrance, a footman stepped up to the coach and opened the door for them. The sight before them was almost like a mirage.

The entire facade of the Royal Opera House looked like a giant weeping willow, through which a procession of fairies and woodland creatures was ushered into the fairy kingdom. The whole building was hung with silk streamers of varying greens, and behind them a hollow tree trunk had been crafted over the main doors and up into the eaves of the portico.

Henry couldn't quite tell whether it was the anticipation of the night or the scene before them, but there was magic in the air, and he thoroughly enjoyed the amazed gasps coming from his companions as they took in the whimsical facade and the artful costumes around them.

The scenery artists and carpenters had truly outdone themselves, but the willow tree was nothing compared to the wonder in Eliza's shining eyes. He took her hand and threaded it through his arm, then winged out his other arm to offer it to Daisie. "Come on, you two, my box is right on top of the stairs. We will leave our cloaks there, and Daisie can help you put your wings on in relative privacy."

Eliza could only nod, and as he led them up the stairs to the cleft in the tree trunk, Eliza's hand slipped down into his. Loving the trusting gesture, Henry laced his fingers with hers, brought her hand up for a kiss, and pulled her close to him, keeping hold of her hand.

They stepped through the tree and into a nighttime forest, illuminated by thousands of tiny flickering lights, reminiscent of fireflies. Eliza took in the wondrous sight with utter delight while Daisie cooed excitedly.

"Look, Liza. What do ya call them bugs that glow at night again?"

"My dad called them glow-worms. Sometimes in summer they would be under the oak tree behind the inn, but I haven't seen one in years."

"I never saw no real ones, but this 'ere fairy forest sure gives me a thrill."

Eliza looked at her friend across Henry's broad chest and giggled at her slightly naughty undertone. Daisie's blue eyes sparkled behind her mask, and Eliza wished William were here to make the evening truly special for her friend.

Meanwhile, Henry made a mental note not to let either woman stroll through the shadowy foyer unattended in the later parts of the evening lest some drunken reveler pull one of them behind a fake tree and take advantage. He had no doubt both women would be able to deal with an overly amorous gentleman, but Eliza was his now, his to protect. He figured the best way to do that was to introduce her to as many of his acquaintances as possible before they got too drunk. So he ushered the girls toward the main staircase and led them up to his box, where he relieved Eliza of her cloak and held her wings in place while Daisie tied them on.

From up here they could see the pit had been cleared and roped off, and although the orchestra was in its usual place, stairs had been constructed on either side, going up to the stage. The stage was cleared except for the gently illuminated forest scenery, and a balustrade had been placed at the front of the stage, presumably to stop revelers from falling off the stage and onto the orchestra.

The forest theme carried on all along the front of the balconies and boxes, where every column had been turned into a tree, every partition into a thicket.

"Let's go back downstairs, ladies. The opening ceremony is usually best experienced from the pit where they perform."

Eliza's eyes were busy exploring the fairy forest all around them as well as the sumptuous interior of the famous opera house, trying to find where the bird calls echoing through the house came from. But ultimately she was more curious about the ceremony. "Do they perform something like a play?"

Henry considered for a moment while his eyes swept over the theatre below. "No, it's more like a fantasy parade. You will see."

The boxes and balconies below them were filling up fast, and Henry spotted Robert escorting Millie to one of the large boxes right by the stage. They were noisily greeted by a throng of colorfully costumed women, and the sight made Henry sigh gratefully, glad he no longer had to contend with Millie's giggling gaggle of friends.

He pulled Eliza in for a quick kiss. "Are you ready, my lovely?"

Eyes shining, she nodded. He led both women back down the stairs and under the balconies into the pit where a large crowd was forming behind the ropes. He found a spot with a view of the pit, the stage, and the ceiling, from which ropes and silk banners were being dropped.

Acrobats in fairy costumes tumbled from all directions into the pit, where they made a human pyramid to the amazed exclamations of the audience, then scrambled up the ropes and banners and performed all manner of feats ten feet off the ground.

While the acrobats performed, a slow drumroll started up like distant thunder, growing louder and nearer until it suddenly stopped. Into the utter silence, a staff thudded three times at the back of the theatre.

"Make room for the king and queen of the fairies."

The voice of the master of ceremonies boomed across the empty expanse of the pit. The acrobats scrambled to the ground and pulled the ropes and silks to the side, like a giant gateway for the approaching royalty. The procession making its way from the foyer through the pit to the stage was spectacular indeed. The royal couple was carried in on shields resting on the shoulders of four fairies each. Both stood barefoot in a layer of what appeared to be rose petals and held hands across the heads of their subjects. Henry bent to whisper in Eliza's ear. "That's Edmund Kean, the actor, as the fairy king, and his queen is a dancer by the name of Funny Grimes."

Eliza turned smiling eyes on him and teased, "I thought you were the fairy king tonight."

Amusement sparked in his eyes as his gaze swept the crowd. "I'm afraid I have a good deal of competition for the title." He considered her for a moment before he decided to push their flirtation further. "I fear the only place where I have any chance of ruling tonight is your bed."

She blushed beautifully, but kept her eyes on the fairies parading past them as she curtsied. "My liege!"

Henry's pupils widened, and his cock stirred. He knew it was all just a joke to her, but their little game was arousing nonetheless. He pulled her in front of him, doing his best to avoid her fairy wings and let her feel his hardness.

"Easy, minx. Don't distract me too much," he teased.

As the king and queen of the fairies proceeded down toward the stage, she wiggled her hips just the tiniest bit into his erection and turned her grinning face up to his. "Just a little bit then. I do have to be convincing as your mistress, after all."

This time he outright laughed, and judging by the number of curious heads turning in their direction, it wouldn't take very long before all of London was aware of her position in his life. "Behave and watch the show, my sweet."

She winked at him, laughter dancing in her eyes, then turned back to the spectacle in front of her.

The fairy king and queen were being carried up the steps on either side of the stage, and the procession of fairies followed behind, each carrying a lantern in the shape of a flying insect on a long stick, swaying to and fro as they moved. Once they were all on the stage, the king commanded, "Dance for me, my queen!"

The fae queen leapt from her high perch on the rose petal shield and was caught mid-flight by two male fairies and turned toward the gasping audience before they set her on her pointed toes gracefully and spun her into a pirouette.

Lilting music swelled from the orchestra as the three of them performed an intricate dance. The chorus of performers moved their lanterns in a carefully choreographed pattern behind the three principals before they joined them, one by one, until they were a flurry of pirouetting arms and fairy wings.

Eliza was mesmerized. She had never seen human beings move with such grace, in such intricate and exquisite harmony. It was the sort of beauty that made her lament not having the talent to create it, but also might just be the only true reason to continue to live in a world filled with pain and ugliness.

Her mother had made her believe such beauty existed, and when she was young she had seen it in the glow-worms under the oak tree and in a summer meadow. Henry had shown her the beauty that could be found in a book, a painting, and music, but not until this moment did she understand the human body itself could be an instrument to express joy, sorrow, and harmony with exquisite beauty.

The dance on the stage ended much too soon, and the dancers sank into floor-deep curtsies in front of the fairy king. He accepted their supplication graciously, and then turned to the masses filling the theatre.

"Dance and be merry, both fairy and mortal. The realm is open until the night retreats!"

The fairy king's words were still echoing off the walls when the ropes were removed and the audience became the participants, coupling up and filling the empty expanse with bodies swaying to and fro in the first waltz.

Henry spun Eliza into his arms without any further ado, and she only had time to see Daisie was being asked to dance by a woodland fairy before her line of vision was blocked by the sea of waltzing humanity. Henry whispered in her ear, "Don't worry, my sweet. I told her to make her way to the box at the left of the stage where Robert has taken up residence with his mistress."

Eliza's eyes sparkled. "The incomparable Millie, I suppose?"

Her cocked brow made Henry laugh. "Yes, my sweet, and you stole me from her, so be nice."

His swift sideways glance alerted her he had made the comment for the benefit of a gentleman dancing next to them, and sure enough, the gentleman in question swung his partner around so he could face them. He grinned broadly at Henry and then winked at her.

"New ladybird, eh, Henry?"

Henry inclined his head in greeting. "Indeed, Ellert. Millie was getting a little too obvious in her attentions to her favorite part of me, so I gave her to Fairly. By all accounts, she is enjoying his purse with equal enthusiasm."

Ellert laughed heartily at Henry's crude remark and turned his attention to Eliza. "Well, well, well, so you moved in and lured him away from the saucy strumpet. Can't say I blame him for being tempted. You are as pretty as a picture."

Eliza blushed. She didn't like the way the man looked at her, nor the way his eyes widened with lust when he saw her discomfort, but she managed a little smile. "It's a pleasure to meet you, sir." She declined her head and moved just a fraction closer to Henry, who tightened his arm around her waist protectively.

Oblivious, Ellert turned his attention back to Henry. "And not a hint of the East End. Where did you find her, you lucky dog?"

"Easy, Ellert! She's still new to this."

Ellert laughed while Eliza's ears burned. "I can see that. That blush is enough to give me a cockstand. Let me know when you are done with her; I want first crack."

Eliza stared at him in wide-eyed disbelief while his disgruntled dance partner kicked his shin. "Oy, I'm still 'ere."

The storm cloud descending on Ellert's face made Henry's shoulders shake with silent laughter and put the smile back on Eliza's face.

"Your servant, Melissa. And, Ellert, that might be a long wait. I suggest you buy Melissa something nice in the meantime."

That earned him a brilliant smile from the outraged mistress before she turned to her lover and whacked his shoulder. "Hear that, you pig? 'E knows 'ow to treat a lady."

They started to dance away. "Now hold on there, Lissa. I was just . . ." Then their words were drowned out by the music.

"My apologies, Eliza, but Ellert will ensure everyone here knows you are my new mistress."

They danced the remaining bars of the waltz. "Does she really not mind knowing he will leave her at some point?"

Henry led her through the crowd on the dance floor and toward the stage. "Melissa actually does mind, which makes Ellert even more of an arse. But most women like Millie only care that the men they tolerate in their beds make their lives easier than they otherwise would be."

Eliza looked pensive. "That's not why I invited you into my bed."

He softened and drew her nearer, to comfort as well as reassure. "I thought you weren't going to let anything you hear tonight bother you."

She shot him a look, unease still clear on her face. "I'm not. I just have a hard time comprehending such casualness about something so intimate."

He feathered a butterfly-soft kiss against her cheek. "I love that what we have is intimate. Being a mistress does not have to be about mutual exploitation. There are notable exceptions."

The orchestra struck up a new waltz, and he drew her back into his arms. He held her close and whispered sweet nothings in her ear while he cast his eyes about the room.

He found what he had been looking for and turned back to her. "Speaking of notable exceptions. Would you like me to introduce you to one of them?"

She smiled at him sweetly. "I would like that very much."

CHAPTER NINETEEN

HENRY THREADED HER HAND THROUGH THE
crook of his elbow and led her to the steps at the right-hand side of
the stage, where they would be able to converse with the people in the
boxes close to the stage. Most of them were empty now, their owners
preferring to dance the night away, but the box nearest the stage was
occupied by an elegant party of six who had apparently decided to
partake of refreshments before they exerted themselves.

Henry approached with Eliza on his arm and offered his greeting across the banister separating the box from the temporary stairs.
"Good evening, ladies, gentlemen. I hope this New Year's Eve finds
you in good health and in anticipation of a wonderful New Year."

He had addressed the whole group, but then turned to a middle-
aged gentleman standing behind a beautiful blond lady in a stunning
forest-green satin gown decorated with a spray of wildflowers. Flowers were also woven into her hair, and she smelled of jasmine. She
looked somehow familiar to Eliza, but she could not place her until
Henry spoke to the man behind her.

"York, I heard you were back from Paris. I hope the journey was
not too tiresome."

The Earl of York stepped forward to shake Henry's hand. "March,
it was a shame you couldn't make it. I always value your insight."

"Well, the war is over and I have four estates to run."

The earl heaved a sigh. "We all have to take care of the home front from time to time."

Henry chuckled and turned his attention to the beautiful flower fairy, whom Eliza now recognized as the lady she had mistaken for a duchess during Sunday service at St. George's.

"Sara, my dear, you are a balm to the eye, as usual."

"Sir Henry, what a pleasure to see you again, and how fortuitous I should meet you here."

"Oh, how so?"

She smiled graciously and extended her hand for him to kiss. "I have a small matter regarding which I would greatly appreciate your advice."

Henry kissed her hand across the partition and acknowledged her request with a nod. "May I make known to you Miss Eliza Broad." He guided Eliza into the foreground. "Eliza, this is Miss Sara Davis, the Earl of York's companion."

Eliza, thinking "companion" was a much more suitable title for Miss Sara Davis than "mistress," observed and admired the other woman's poise, and sank into the most graceful curtsy she could manage. "I am delighted to meet you, Miss Davis." Although she felt completely out of her depth talking to the exquisite creature in front of her, she managed to keep her voice steady and her gaze direct.

Sara nodded her acknowledgment, and Henry, who had kept hold of Eliza's hand throughout the exchange, elaborated: "Eliza is a guest in my house at present and is curious to know how a woman of merit might make a life for herself without the benefit of connections."

Sara Davis surveyed the couple in front of her carefully. Her shrewdness and superior intelligence were well-hidden under the veneer of beauty and graciousness, but nothing escaped her. Not the tender light in Henry's eyes when he looked at Eliza, not the blush on her smooth young cheeks, not the lilt of her voice or the manners and grace with which the girl had greeted her, and especially not the fact Sir Henry had never introduced one of his amours to anybody but other men.

"I would be more than happy to speak with you, Miss Broad."

Eliza stepped closer to the partition so she could clasp Sara's hand, her shyness receding behind her gratitude. Until this very moment she had not known how much she needed another woman to confide in. Daisie was her friend and her equal, and she knew how to please a man, but she had no advice to give on how to be a worthy companion to a man like Sir Henry.

"Would you really? I would be most grateful for your advice."

She offered a shy smile, and Sara patted her hand reassuringly. "Indeed, my dear. But I'm afraid this rowdy gathering isn't conducive to an earnest talk, so I shall call on you at Cavendish Square in a day or two."

There was true kindness in her eyes. Eliza could only imagine the honor a visit from Miss Davis represented.

"You are very kind and most generous, Miss Davis."

"Not at all, my dear, not at all."

Eliza straightened to turn toward Henry, who was again engaged in conversation with the earl, but noticed that Sara raised her eyes and declined her head in greeting to somebody behind her. Looking over her shoulder, she found Robert smiling down on them.

He bowed politely to Sara, but addressed Eliza. "Will you grant me this dance, oh fairy mine?"

She returned his smile with a little bemused grin as she took in his elaborate Roman costume. "Just so long as you don't expect me to join your circle of concubines, oh Lord Bacchus."

He laughed down at her before turning to Sara, who had followed the exchange with an approving smile. "Will you excuse us, please, Miss Davis?"

Sara waved him away. "By all means, Fairly."

Robert sketched her a half bow, turned back to Eliza, and drew her hand through his arm. "I give you my word, oh fairy, you shall be safe with me."

They both turned to Henry for approval, and when he smiled, they went to join the dancers below. Henry looked after them for a moment until Sara whispered to him, "You are being observed by our mutual friend."

Henry gave no indication of surprise at her statement or even that he had heard her, except that he instantly and smoothly turned back to his conversation with the male occupants of the box.

Henry knew Sara to be a skilled operative, and the fact she had never been involved in the hunt for De Sade made her the perfect choice to keep tabs on Astor. However, he didn't like that Astor was in attendance, nor that the very person who had been chosen to shadow him met most of the attributes his victims had shared. But then again, the Old Man was near infallible when it came to picking the right person for a task, so he would just have to trust his judgment.

As soon as he could, he excused himself and went in search of Daisie. She was masked and the crowd should shield her well enough, but he was concerned what it would do to her if she recognized her abuser. If she did see Astor and indeed recognized him, she should not be alone. On the other hand, Henry could not pass up the chance for a positive identification.

Henry found Daisie toward the back of the theatre, hugging the shadows. He knew instantly she was nervous about something and hoped she hadn't seen Astor already.

"What is it, Daisie? Come dance with me so we can talk."

Daisie made no move to leave the shadows. "I don't know, sir. Hobbs is 'ere. I saw 'im talk to them girls in the box with Lord Robert. And then I saw 'im leave the box with the one that was with Lord Robert."

Henry's brow furrowed. "Millie? I wonder how those two are connected. Come dance with me; he can't recognize you with your mask on."

Daisie stepped forward reluctantly, but let him lead her into the waltz. Over her shoulder, Henry spotted Astor on a balcony to the left of the stage. His attention was on a beautiful blond woman on the opposite balcony. Henry recognized her as a prominent actress from the Sans Pareil at the Adelphi Theatre, a Miss Clara Adams.

As much as Henry loathed to have to draw Daisie's attention to the man, he needed to know if Astor was indeed her attacker. He kept his voice low and calm. "Daisie, I need you to tell me if you recognize a gentleman, but I want you to remember you are safe with me."

Her hand tightened around his. She obviously had an inkling whom he wanted her to identify. "All right, where is 'e? You better get it over with, you're making me jittery."

There was no point in prolonging her apprehension. Henry swung Daisie around so she would have a clear line of sight to Astor. "There is a man up on the balcony behind me. He is staring at a woman across the way. Do you recognize him?"

She looked where he had indicated, and when she gasped in recognition, he turned her a quarter turn so her face would be hidden from Astor.

Daisie swallowed hard and looked at him with wide eyes. "It's Lord Pain." Her words were barely audible, and she shivered with dread. "I would know those eyes anywhere."

It was the confirmation to all his suspicions, and yet he could find no joy in it. There could no longer be any doubt that Astor was De Sade, and to underestimate him would put them all in peril.

Henry pulled Daisie closer to steady her and danced them slowly but steadily to the back of the theatre. His fingers stroked tiny soothing circles under her shoulder blade as much to calm himself as to comfort her. He knew he had to get her to a safe place, away from prying eyes, and then round up Eliza.

They had accomplished what they had come to do, and more, and with both Astor and Hobbs in the building, he could no longer justify placing either woman in danger.

He kept his voice low but infused it with as much authority as he could. "Daisie, listen to me very carefully. Neither Astor nor Hobbs know or even suspect you are here, and they would not know you in this mask. I will walk you through the foyer, and then I need you to go straight upstairs and to my box. I want you to stay in the shadows in the back so no one can see you from below. If anybody comes into the box, tell them you are not feeling well and keep your eyes down. Can you do that?"

Daisie held his gaze, and although it was clear she still felt panicked, he could also see strength and resolve straightening her backbone. "Yes, sir."

Then she startled as if she had realized something. "Where's Eliza?"

It was lucky Henry was already holding her rather tightly, so he caught her without missing a step and guided her smoothly back into the rhythm of the waltz. "She is dancing with Lord Robert, so she is safe for now, but I need to get to her before she runs into Hobbs."

Daisie nodded, glad someone had the wherewithal to keep her from dissolving into hysterics. "She needs to know that monster is 'ere too. And I think you should tell Lord Robert who 'is ladybird is keepin' company with."

Henry looked grim for a moment, but then his mouth quirked up in a half smile. "I have every intention to."

They reached the back of the theatre as the last strains of the waltz floated through the air and made their way to the foyer through the general confusion of couples streaming to and from the massive dance floor. There were so many people now, the dancers started to take over the stage. Add to that the general increase in intoxication, and things could get out of hand very quickly.

Henry escorted Daisie to the bottom of the stairs, where she turned to him and whispered urgently, "Go on now, sir. I'll be all right."

He bowed lightly to her, and she scampered up the stairs at a fast clip. Henry watched after her long enough to make sure she made it out of the dark foyer without being accosted and then turned to go in search of Eliza.

He opted to make his way to Robert's box along the left-hand corridor in a bid to avoid the crowds in the pit, but found even here his progress was hindered by milling people attracted by the refreshments offered. Not to mention a gauntlet of acquaintances eager to confirm the news of Henry's new mistress and to express their disappointment at not finding her on his arm.

Henry wondered, as he often did, if his acquaintances were truly so shallow that a good tidbit of gossip could make their night, even distract them for a few more. He had used society's fickleness to his advantage a good many times before, but he still couldn't quite believe just how truly vacuous some of its members were.

It took Henry close to thirty minutes to reach Robert's box, and when he entered to find Robert surrounded by Millie's gaggle of friends without either Eliza or Millie in attendance, a frisson of unease crept up his spine.

Eliza enjoyed her waltz with the stunning viscount, but by the time it ended, even the excitement of the ball could not distract her from her need for the retiring room. So when Robert led her from the dance floor and toward his box, she asked him, with no small amount of embarrassment, to direct her to the closest retiring room.

Robert indicated the last door to the right at the end of the hallway running around the outside of the auditorium. His box was a few doors down and across the corridor from the ladies' retiring room, so Robert left the door to the box ajar, trusting Eliza would find her way there once she had taken care of her needs, and went about trying to find where his mistress had gone off to.

In front of the mirrors in the retiring room, a few women adjusted their costumes and reapplied cosmetics when Eliza entered. The privacy screens were in some disarray at the back of the room, but she found one angled to shield her from the curious gazes of the other occupants of the room. She heard them giggle as she ducked behind the screen and hiked up her skirts to relieve herself, sighing as the pressure on her bladder diminished. Eliza silently vowed she would never again drink a whole pot of tea before going to a ball—if indeed she got the opportunity again.

The door opened and some of the giggling girls departed, and the quiet following their departure made Eliza strangely uneasy. But then she heard the rustle of petticoats out by the mirrors and knew she wasn't alone. Reassured, Eliza was just rummaging in her reticule for the square of newsprint she had stashed there so she could wipe herself, when the door opened again and a male voice hissed, "You alone in 'ere, Millie?"

It took Eliza a moment to realize a male voice was out of place in the ladies' retiring room. But before she could decide whether she should let whoever was out there know they were not alone, a voice sounding vaguely familiar replied.

"Yea, yea. What else do you want, Mac? It better not be a flyer; I'm entertaining tonight, you know."

The man chuckled, and Eliza froze. She was almost certain she had heard that chuckle before, and if it was who she thought it was, he'd better not find her. His next words confirmed his identity, and Eliza recalled where she had heard the woman's voice before, so she sank to her knees in an effort to remain hidden. What did Henry's last mistress—not to mention Robert's present one—have to do with Hobbs?

"I'm always up for a quick poke, love, but I need the good viscount pantin' for ya so ya can keep 'im out of me hair when I go up to Hampstead next."

"Shame he won't take your coin, then I wouldn't have to hump the boring blighter."

"What's the matter, Millie, 'e not spanking you 'ard enough?"

Millie bit out a harsh laugh. "That'll be the day."

"Talkin' about whips and chains, Lord Pain's 'ere. You can always get 'im to give you a proper seein' to."

"Not if you want me to babysit Fairly. He'd notice the bruises. What does His Lordship want?"

Eliza wondered whether Robert knew Millie was leading him by the nose. From what she had seen of the viscount, she wouldn't have thought it possible, but then again . . .

"He wants 'is special request. Says 'e saw 'er in the park and she's more than ripe for the pickin'."

"And you want me to get her for you?" Millie huffed her exasperation. "How the hell am I supposed to get her away from her clacking hen of a mother? The two of them are practically joined at the bloody hip."

"She's your friend, you figure it out."

"Ha! Two years I've invested with that woman and she still doesn't trust me."

Hobbs laughed, apparently having no sympathy for Millie's plight. "I guess she's smarter than we thought. So touchin' to find a mother who cares."

Millie let out a most unladylike snort. "Right, guarding the golden goose, more like. As long as the girl is with her, the father provides the coin for both the girl and Clara."

There was speculation in Hobbs's voice. "Did you ever find out who her fancy man is?"

"Na, her mouth is shut tighter then a fucking clam. But he's rich . . . you should see her house. Only the best for them two, lace and brocade everywhere and there's never any shortage of meat or sweets on her table. Sure wouldn't mind seeing their holier-than-thou arses taken down a peg or two."

Millie sounded harsh, full of hate and envy. Eliza shivered at the tone. Horace's voice had sounded like that, the last time she had heard it.

"Well, love, there's your chance. All you got to do is get young Stephanie out of the 'ouse by 'erself. Can't be that 'ard! Take 'er shoppin', buy 'er a few ribbons, then lose 'er in the crowd. I take 'er to 'is Lordship and he'll do the takin' down for ya."

"I guess I could persuade Clara to let me take her shopping for her birthday; she turned eighteen not two weeks past."

"There you go! Take 'er to the Emporium on Sloane Street, Clara won't want to make the trip to bloody Knightsbridge if she 'as to be in the theatre by six."

There was a pause. Eliza prayed fervently she hadn't made a noise to give herself away. They were discussing the kidnapping of a girl; surely Hobbs wouldn't hesitate to kill her if he found her. But apparently Hobbs had only been thinking.

"I wanna know why 'is Lordship is so obsessed with this one. It can't be 'er, she's not even 'is usual type. Not blond enough and not young enough; there 'as to be more to it. And why now?"

"Oh, get over yourself, Mac. You're always working an angle. As long as he pays me, I don't care what his motives are."

"And that, love, is why I run this town and you work for me."

She laughed and it almost sounded genuine. "Right, Mac, I'd better get back to it then. I'm sure by now the viscount is done dancing with that wee slip of a girl Henry dragged along."

Eliza heard the rustle of petticoats as if Millie was moving to the door, but Hobbs wasn't done yet.

"By the way, love. Why don't you play nicey nice to Sir Henry's new bint. Then when 'e gets rid of 'er, you bring 'er to me."

Eliza gasped. She immediately realized her mistake and slammed her hand over her mouth to stifle the sound, but apparently she wasn't fast enough.

Hobbs's voice was all of a sudden full of suspicion. "You sure there's no one in 'ere?"

The disinterest was audible in Millie's voice. "Meg and her whole stable were in here, but she herded them all out when I came in."

"You're getting careless, my girl."

Eliza heard footsteps come closer and did her best to make her breathing as shallow as possible. She worried Hobbs would hear her heart beating, it was hammering so hard in her chest.

"Come out, come out, whoever you are."

The singsong of his taunt chilled Eliza to the bone as she did her best to melt farther into the shadows.

Millie had no patience for this game. "There was no one in here, Mac. And if there were, she would have to have a fucking death wish to blab her mouth."

That seemed a sound argument to Eliza, but Hobbs's footsteps kept coming closer. "Better safe than sorry . . ."

At that moment, the door burst open and crashed against the wall. "Pardon me, Madam—"

Hobbs's footsteps stilled. There was a champagne hiccup and a stumble before the newcomer caught himself.

"And gentleman. Retiring room for both sexes, how very droll. Don't leave on my account, just need the chamber pot, don't you know."

CHAPTER TWENTY

ELIZA COULD HAVE KISSED THE DRUNK INTRUD-
er. Hobbs had stopped a couple of feet away from the screen she was
crouched behind, and she could hear Millie's skirts moving to the door.

"Toodle-oo," she trilled.

"Shit." Hobbs obviously didn't appreciate the interruption. But
with the drunk crashing around the room, he had no choice but to
retreat. "Ya're in the wrong place if ya're looking for the gents'. Millie,
show 'im the way."

Millie's footsteps leaving the room did not slow, and the man
seemed to be too drunk to care where he relieved himself.

"No need to trouble yourself, I'll just be a moment."

Actually locating a chamber pot seemed to be quite beyond him,
though. Eliza heard him weave his way from screen to screen until he
stood right at the opening to the nook where she was hidden.

The moment he came into view, Eliza was grateful her hand was
still over her mouth or another gasp would surely have escaped her.

Before her, disheveled and swaying, wearing another leather suit,
this one decorated with elaborate beading and fringes, stood Henry's
friend Allen. And when he saw her, he flashed her a brilliant smile and
moved behind her screen toward her.

"Ah, the pot."

As soon as he could no longer be seen from the room, he mouthed "close your eyes" to her. She complied, and within seconds she heard him relieve himself into the chamber pot.

Allen let out a satisfied sigh while the tinkling in the pot slowed, and on the other side of the screen Eliza heard Hobbs chuckle to himself.

"I guess I start 'earin' things in me old age." Then he walked away from them and out the door.

Eliza could hear the swish of Allen's leather suit, and then his hand touched her shoulder, and when she looked up at him he pressed a finger to his lips. They heard the door close behind Hobbs, and Allen peeked over the screen to make sure he was indeed gone, then helped Eliza to her feet. "My apologies, Miss Eliza. That rotter was so suspicious, it was the only way I could think of to convince him you weren't here, or at least not behind this particular screen."

Her legs were so weak she had to lean against him, and he obligingly wrapped his arms around her. But when her overtaxed brain put together why he was apologizing, she chuckled. "I grew up in an inn. Most drunks don't give a toss who they piss in front of. In fact, I want to thank you for warning me to close my eyes; it's much appreciated."

Allen laughed and pulled her closer. "If I couldn't see how good you are for Henry, I would do my best to steal you away from him."

She knew he was just flirting, but she felt a little spark that went beyond being grateful for his timely intervention, so she felt the need to clarify. "And if I didn't owe him my life twice over, I might even consider it."

Allen's amusement turned into a real smile. "Brave, loyal, beautiful, and sensible. Henry truly is a lucky man."

She blushed at his compliment and, since her legs had steadied under her, playfully pushed him away. "You forgot to add 'not easily duped.'"

He chuckled and pulled her out from behind the screen and toward the mirrors. "You stay here till you hear three knocks on the door." He demonstrated on the wall: three sharp knocks, separated by a full beat in between. "Robert should have whisked his wayward mistress to the dance floor by now, and I'm off to become Hobbs's new, best drinking companion." He winked at her. "I might even let him find me a girl."

She burst out laughing at the tease. "Oh! Charming, handsome, and fickle. You are indeed a bargain, aren't you."

It felt good to relieve the tension, but she wouldn't feel safe until Henry was back by her side. Allen must have seen some of what she felt, because he pulled up a chair and laid a hand on her shoulder to urge her to take a seat. "Henry will come get you as soon as I manage to drag Hobbs out of sight."

She looked up at him, some of her apprehension leaving her at knowing Henry was near, but now that she was calmer, questions started to form. "How did you know where I was?"

"I didn't. I lost Hobbs in the crowd and went up to the stage to see if I could relocate him. There I ran into Robert, who had misplaced his mistress but was surrounded by a pack of giggling hens. When Henry stormed into the box, demanding to know where you were, Robert realized you hadn't come back from the retiring room."

Eliza was more confused rather than enlightened by this speech. "So how did you end up coming to my rescue?"

"Well, I'm the only one not known to either Hobbs or Millie."

Eliza nodded thoughtfully. "That makes sense. But how did you know we were all here?"

There was a note of admiration in Allen's voice. "Ah, that's Henry in action for you. Within two minutes of knowing you might be in danger, he knew where Astor was, and had found out Millie was in the same ladies' room as you. It was clear you were held up in there in some manner, and so I was dispatched to eavesdrop at the door and intervene if necessary." His grin threatened to split his face. "I did, and then I did!"

Eliza squeezed the hand still resting on her shoulder. "You three are really good at this, aren't you? Thank you."

"You are quite welcome. I had better go so Henry can get you out of here. I shall see you tomorrow. From what I could hear through the door, you getting stuck in here may have been worth it."

He beamed at her, then crashed through the door and into the corridor beyond, back to playing the drunk.

The door slammed shut, and Eliza attempted to gather her scattered thoughts, but she was still slumped in her chair when the door opened and two women entered. The older one of the two sent Eliza a motherly smile. "Too much drink or too much dancin', deary?"

Eliza produced a tired smile and her best cockney accent. "A bit of both."

The women laughed and headed for a screen.

When the three knocks sounded, signaling the hallway was clear, Eliza heaved a dramatic sigh. "Christ, I 'ope that's me man ready to take me 'ome."

She headed for the door and slipped out to the sound of the other women chuckling. Hopefully, her little role play would be enough to cover her tracks completely.

HENRY TOOK ONE LOOK AT Eliza and knew it was time to call a

halt to the night's adventures. He wrapped his arm around her waist and pulled her close to him. "Lean into me, Eliza; it will stop all but the most persistent of my acquaintances from trying to engage us in conversation."

Eliza promptly wrapped her arm around Henry's middle and aimed a seductive smile at him. He returned a similar smile, caught the hand at his hip, and gave it a reassuring squeeze. "Excellent."

Tired and weary, but looking to all the world like an amorous couple, they negotiated the corridor in good time and were ambling up the stairs when Henry leaned down and whispered in her ear, "Giggle as if I just said something naughty. That's Astor coming down the stairs."

Eliza managed a coy giggle, playfully swatted at Henry, and took a surreptitious look at the lord with the cold gray eyes staring daggers at Henry as he passed. Once he was out of earshot, she stretched up to whisper in Henry's ear, "If looks could kill, you would be bleeding to death draped over the railing."

Henry made no attempt to see in which direction Astor had gone, but listened carefully to the direction of his clicking heels on the marble in the dark foyer below. "He must be up to something. He hasn't been this obvious in his hostility toward me in a decade."

"I think Ho . . ."

Henry cut her off with a kiss. "Not here. You will tell me everything at home whilst I ply you with hot chocolate and rub your feet."

Eliza rested her head on his shoulder. She needed the safety of Henry's arms and longed for the security of his home after her adventure in the retiring room and the malevolence of Astor's presence. "God, that sounds good. Take me home, Henry."

Henry nuzzled into her unbound hair. "I intend to, my sweet."

They reached the box, and Henry opened the door quietly. In the dim light inside the small space, he couldn't see anybody. "Daisie, are you in here?"

There was a pause, then a small, shaky voice came from behind a drape at the back of the box. "Here."

In front of that drape stood the sofa where they had left their capes. Henry was around the sofa in two steps and crouched next to where Daisie had crumpled to the floor in a miserable heap.

"What happened?"

There wasn't enough room for Eliza to wedge behind the sofa as well, so she knelt on it instead and leaned over the back. "You all right, love?"

Daisie's relief at seeing both Henry and Eliza was obvious. She tried a shaky smile, but her lips trembled uncontrollably. Almost an hour had elapsed since she and Henry had parted in the foyer, and she had not stopped shaking since. Her panicked eyes found Henry's. "Lord Pain! I kept an eye on 'im, but then 'e started lookin' up 'ere, like 'e could feel me lookin', somehow knew I 'ad talked about 'im. And then 'e left the balcony and I got so scared I hid behind 'ere."

Henry had taken possession of both her hands at the mention of her tormentor and squeezed them, trying to calm her. Daisie's pupils were dilated, her eyes unfocused as if she were in shock, and her voice was reed-thin, her cockney almost impenetrable.

"Did anything happen?" He was starting to get truly worried about her.

"He came in 'ere not three minutes ago."

"Did he see you?"

She shook her head in short, sharp jerks as if to shake out the mere idea of Astor seeing her, finding her. "No, I was down 'ere."

With a gentle hand under her chin, Henry turned her head and forced her gaze to his. When her eyes focused on his, he spoke again. "Daisie, he is gone. We passed him on our way up. And then I heard him exit through the foyer. He is no longer in this building."

Daisie nodded slowly and took a deep breath. "I was so bloody scared."

Henry rubbed her icy hands and watched her closely as the panic receded and her resolve returned. His voice was soft but firm. "I'm here, and as long as I am, he cannot touch you."

Her eyes remained focused on him, trying to accept his vow to protect her. Once her hands had warmed in his and her breathing evened out, he nodded to Eliza to get ready and crawled out from behind the settee. "We need to get you home."

Eliza had already taken the wings off her shoulders and pulled the heavy curtain aside. Henry extended his hand to Daisie. "Can you stand?"

Once Henry had Daisie on her feet, Eliza draped the gray cloak around her friend's still-shaking shoulders. Then she handed Henry his and wrapped herself in her own, while Henry kept his hand on Daisie's elbow to steady her.

"Come on, love. Sir Henry promised me hot chocolate, we'll share it." That earned her a little smile, and this time Daisie's lips did not tremble.

They got downstairs, through the foyer and into Henry's coach without any further incident and started the journey back to Cavendish Square in exhausted silence.

FROM DEEP IN THE RECESS between two columns, a tall, cloaked shadow separated itself from the darkness all around and stepped into the road to glare after the departing coach.

"Enjoy these days of peace, 'Sir' Henry. I promise they will be your last."

ONCE HE HAD THE WOMEN safely back within his own walls where he could protect them, Henry tasked Mrs. Tibbit with taking Daisie a cup of hot chocolate and tucking her into bed with a hot water bottle. Once the good lady had hustled Daisie to her room on the top floor, fussing all the way, Henry ordered the promised hot chocolate for Eliza and led her up to his rooms.

A cozy wood fire crackled in his bedchamber, and he led her to the Gobelin-covered high-backed armchair in front of it. Taking her cloak off her shoulders, he sat on the matching ottoman in front of her and removed her satin sandals.

A footman arrived with their chocolate and poured them both a cup of the hot goodness. Once the footman had retreated, Henry filled a porcelain basin with water from the pitcher warming by the fire and proceeded to wash Eliza's tired feet for her.

Who knew having one's feet washed could be such a singular experience? So intimate, so caring, and so utterly reassuring. Eliza let out a long sigh, leaned back, and closed her eyes. She could not have said why, but with his hands washing away the evening's adventures, she felt like she was indeed home and safe and capable of just about anything.

"Now, my sweet, tell me what happened in the retiring room."

Eliza allowed herself a long pause, during which Henry dried her feet and started to massage them with surprising skill. Eventually, she told him everything in meticulous detail, from the moment she'd entered the retiring room to the moment he had knocked three times, leaving out nothing except for Allen's flirtatious comments.

Henry kept working on her feet throughout and was silent for a long while after. Finally he released her feet to the carpet, took her empty cup from her hand, and helped her out of the chair. "You are a very brave woman, Eliza. You kept your head and remembered all the details. I am so very proud of you."

Henry's praise warmed Eliza from the inside, filled her with a glow she had rarely experienced in her former life. Except for her parents, she could not remember anybody ever telling her she had done anything right, much less well.

She blushed and bowed her head and leaned into him, clearly tired.

"Time for bed, my sweet. And tomorrow, first thing, I will put a man at Miss Clara Adams's house. If she has a daughter, I believe that is who Hobbs is about to abduct." He kissed her forehead, helped her disrobe, and tucked her into bed. He shed his own costume, made short work of washing off the remaining gold powder, blew out the candles, and joined her under the covers.

But when he pulled Eliza into his arms to tempt her into a little late night loving, she had already fallen into a deep sleep. Chuckling, Henry spooned himself behind her and settled in for the night.

HENRY AWOKE TO THE GRAY light of morning filtering in through the gaps around the curtains and the sweet weight of Eliza's head resting on his biceps. The cold winter light and the morning chill in the room contrasted sharply with the sleepy warmth of her body. Her backside was intimately cuddled into his groin, and her hand wrapped around the two middle fingers of his right hand, while his left hand cupped one of her breasts.

Henry savored the feel of his bedmate in his arms for a few moments. Eliza was still fast asleep, and even though Henry wanted nothing more than to nuzzle and burrow into her warmth, he recognized it wasn't fair to deprive her of sleep after the adventure she'd had the night before. At any rate, he was now wide awake with the day's challenges pressing on his mind.

Henry gently extricated himself from Eliza's sleeping form, wrapped himself in his thick, quilted dressing gown, stepped into his slippers, and went about stoking the fire back to life. Once he had achieved a cheerful blaze, he took himself to the library, where he dashed off a number of notes, summoning all involved parties to a meeting later that morning.

To avoid suspicion in case his house was watched, he sent his footman with all three messages to the alehouse as if fetching his morning ale. His man was then to send the messages via some of the exinfantry men frequenting the place and return, ale in hand.

In the meantime, Henry took his morning tea and looked through his mail. Before long, there was a tap on the rear library window, and Henry had the pleasure of shaking hands with one of his old comrades. Elijah was one of Henry's most trusted men, and the two of them conferred quietly through the open window.

Before the sun had time to break through the morning mist, the man was dispatched to watch over Miss Clara Adams and her daughter, if indeed she had one, and report all unusual activity.

The bracing morning air had cleared Henry's head, and he lingered in the library over his second cup of tea for some time, trying to work out why Astor was all of a sudden so openly hostile toward him.

He felt increasingly certain that whatever Astor was planning, it had something to do with him, but he couldn't figure out what the connection was. He was missing something, something crucial. The uncomfortable feeling that something important was staring him right in the face became more pronounced the longer he thought about it, but it didn't give him any further insight into what that something might be. Eventually, he banished the whole conundrum to the back of his mind, to be reexamined later as more facts came to light.

Henry thought it possible Astor was aware of his ignorance, counted on it, and enjoyed it with all the fiendish malice he was capable of. He was powerless to stop whatever injury Astor was about to do him, because he had no idea what it was.

Henry could only go by the information he had. He would try to block Astor's next move without jeopardizing the twin goals of eliminating Astor legally and for good, and getting Hobbs off the streets by any means necessary—as long as it happened outside of London's city limits.

It was a battle of wits, and so far Henry was swinging his rapier in the dark. But whichever way Henry looked at it, it was imperative Astor continued to consider Henry ignorant of any possible danger to him and his, and that prompted him to send Robert a second note to ask him to come incognito.

Having taken care of all that could be done for now, and knowing his guests would not arrive for several hours, Henry ordered fresh tea and took the tray upstairs to seek the comfort and warmth of his bed, and the woman in it.

CHAPTER TWENTY-ONE

ELIZA WOKE TO THE SMELL OF TEA AND A SOFT nuzzle against her cheek. Her eyes still closed, she stretched and hummed her contentment. So encouraged, the nuzzle moved from her cheek to her neck and into her hair, then turned into an embrace as Henry's arm burrowed its way under her shoulder and his other arm found its way around her waist. She stretched farther as their bodies aligned, enjoying the feel of his bare skin, and noted that his was cool next to hers. "You've been up already."

He kissed her gently on the mouth, drawing another *hmmm*, this one disgruntled. "And you used the tooth powder," she added. "Not fair."

Henry chuckled and kissed her again, this time teasing her lips open and stroking his tongue against hers. "I don't mind, but I'd be happy to keep the bed warm whilst you wash."

Her eyes were still closed, and she snuggled deeper into his embrace. "Hmmm, in a minute."

His hand traveled over her mussed hair. It still sported a few crystal pins—come to think of it, he had found one stuck to his thigh when he'd gotten out of bed earlier. His hand stroked farther down her back and over her bottom before he lifted her leg over his hip, nestling his erection between her legs, nudging at her opening. "A little tea perhaps? Or just sleepy coupling."

Eliza rolled her hips against him, arched her breast into the hand that now caressed it, and grinned, still refusing to open her eyes. Her voice was still rough with sleep. "Sleepy coupling, that sounds intriguing."

Henry nudged her chin up so he could trail his open mouth and tongue down her exposed throat and then dipped his head to suckle her pink nipple. He thoroughly enjoyed the warmth of her body lying so open and supple from sleep in his arms. "Sleepy coupling it is then, my lovely."

His fingertips traced up her inner thigh to her center. She was all soft and warm and moist, and he let a finger slip into her to gather more moisture to spread over her clitoris. He caressed her there until her breathing grew heavier and more erratic, then worked himself into the welcoming heat of her channel.

Their present position, side by side with her leg hitched over his hip, did not quite allow for full penetration and so he rolled to his back and pulled her on top of him. Then he held her hips steady and thrust up into her.

Eliza drew in a sharp breath, her eyes finally flying open as her hands grappled for purchase to either side of his head to steady herself. "Oh . . . there is nothing sleepy about this anymore!" she gasped.

Henry grinned at her wickedly. "Rise and shine, my sweet. I'm all up, and it turns out I need you awake for this."

Eliza tried valiantly to adjust to him being so deep inside of her in this position. "God, Henry, you feel wickedly big like this."

He had to smile at her breathless admission. She had no idea how pleasurable it was for a man to hear himself described like this. "And you are squeezing me wickedly tight."

She rolled her eyes, and he took pity on her. "Get your legs underneath yourself so you sit astride with one knee on each side of me."

He helped her lift her hips and fold her legs under her, then took her hands and showed her how to brace herself against his chest. "See, now as you kneel up or sit down, you can take as little or as much of me as you want. You are in control of how you ride me now."

Eliza knelt up a little and an "oh" of realization shaped her lips. But then she tilted her head quizzically. "Ride? Is that what you call it?"

He chuckled, holding himself still as she tried moving up and down on him. "Ride, swive, fuck, intercourse, tup. There are many names for it, but in this position, I think 'ride' is most appropriate."

She grinned broadly as she sank back down on him, eliciting a groan. "For obvious reasons."

Eliza continued to move on him, finding out what pleased her. "I like this way, and I like the name better than some of the others, but I can't figure out how I can ride and kiss you at the same time."

Henry took her cue and arched up to capture her lips in a brief kiss. "Ah, yes, kissing is a little tricky." He settled down on his back, but lifted one hand to cup her cheek, then let his fingertips drift down her neck to her breast. "But I can do this."

His hand settled on her breast, stroking and fondling, tracing circles around her areola and lightly pinching her nipple until Eliza arched her back in an effort to increase the pressure of his hand on her breast.

"And I can do this." Henry's other hand trailed down her belly, over her mound, and when his thumb settled on her clitoris, stroking tantalizing circles around it, she gasped and let her head fall back.

"Oh yes, definite advantage," she breathed.

She was absolutely gorgeous, abandoned as she was to her pleasure, her lips slightly parted, her breasts heaving, riding him with increasing fervor. Henry kept his hand on her breast, stroked his thumb down to where they were joined, and gathered more moisture to lubricate her nub for his touch.

She had given up on bracing herself on his chest and instead held onto his hand on her breast, reveling in her own sensuality. As she raced ever closer to the peak of her desire, her rhythm broke and her movements became erratic.

Knowing she was no longer capable of controlling her thrusts, Henry moved his hands to her neck and her hip respectively, but kept his thumb on her clitoris as he took over, bucking up into her from below, making her take more of him and bringing them closer to completion.

Before long, the lightning of orgasm wrecked her body with spasms of bliss and sent ripples of joy through her vagina that demanded he join her in the oblivion of pleasure, and so, amidst a chorus of moans and cries, he did.

As the last tremors raced through them, she collapsed onto his chest and he caught her in his arms, both of them gasping for breath but sated.

They rested for a while until Eliza stirred. "Do you think that tea is still warm?"

He stroked his hand up her back, hugged her to him, and leaned up to kiss her forehead. "Don't care, I'm having some anyway."

It was her turn to chuckle. "I suppose we wore each other out."

"You suppose correctly. But luckily we are English, so it's nothing a good, strong cup of tea won't fix."

ELEVEN O'CLOCK SAW THE ARRIVAL of a tall, soot-covered chimney sweep and his equally blackened assistant. The two of them made quite a stir in the kitchen, unexpected as they were in that part of the house, on a day when no chimney sweep was scheduled to service the flues. The chimney sweep turned out to be Robert, and he was promptly ushered up the back stairs so he could clean up and exchange his disguise with Thomas the footman.

At the same time Miss Sara Davis, magnificent in sky blue velvet the exact color of her eyes, her smooth blond hair pulled back from her brow and gathered at her nape in an elegant knot, left her hat and cape in the foyer and was ushered into the front drawing room, where Eliza waited to receive her.

Henry had detailed everything Sara needed to be informed of and had instructed Eliza to ask a series of questions that might shed light on Lord Astor's intentions. It was imperative Miss Davis should not be seen to visit with the man of the house, for more than one reason.

Eliza looked most charming with her dark hair piled high on her head in a loose chignon with ringlets escaping all around her face, and clad in a low-cut, high-waisted rose silk gown—one of the creations Madame Clarise's assistants had stayed until the wee hours of the morning to finish. Eliza had picked this particular gown not for comfort or warmth, but because it was sleek and stylish and the absolute height of fashion. It gave her the extra bit of confidence to steady her nerves.

The two women greeted each other with all the civilities and seated themselves on either side of the fireplace facing each other.

If anybody cared to look in on the ladies from the square, they looked exactly as ladies of a recent acquaintance, visiting with each other for morning tea, might look. They were elegantly dressed, politely poised and distanced, and charmingly engaged in conversation amidst the splendor of Henry's formal drawing room, and nothing in their expressions or demeanor gave away what their conversation might be about.

The visit lasted just under half an hour, well within the time limits set by polite society for a morning visit amongst ladies. Footmen brought tea, which was served by the hostess, and cakes were consumed.

In short, the setting and visibility of Sara's visit was designed to distract anybody who might be watching the comings and goings at Henry's house. By the time the ladies curtsied to each other in farewell, Allen had entered from the mews through the back gate and was chatting amicably with Henry in the library, where a Spanish wall had been moved in front of the windows overlooking the square to block all eyes from the street.

Meanwhile the chimney sweep—now curiously shorter by a couple of inches—left the kitchen and was seen hustling his assistant down the street and toward his next destination.

Once Sara had departed, Eliza gathered her sewing basket and left the fishbowl-like front parlor. Someone watching would have seen her ascending the stairs and could have seen her bedroom door opening, but they would not have spied anything beyond that. They most certainly wouldn't have seen her deposit her basket just inside her room and depart immediately to make her way down the corridor and toward the back stairs, where she ran into a freshly scrubbed Robert coming out of the back bedroom.

"Good morning, Miss Eliza. You are looking very lovely and rested this morning. I trust your adventures last night were not too taxing." He gallantly waited for her to come abreast with him, offered her a smile, and bowed slightly. "No lasting effects, I hope?"

Eliza smiled back at him, grateful for his easy familiarity.

Before she could answer, he indicated his head toward the back stairs. "I take it the war council will be held in the library?"

She took his offered arm, and they continued along the corridor to the stairs. "I survived just fine, Robert, thank you. And Henry is indeed waiting for us in the library."

Robert nodded and helped her down the rather steep steps with the unthinking gallantry of a true gentleman. "Was that Sara Davis I saw leaving just a minute ago?"

Eliza had an eager gleam in her eyes when she answered. "Indeed. She is watching Astor, and Henry had to tell her things and ask her some others. But she can't very well visit with him, so I talked to her instead and we created a nice little spectacle in the drawing room in the bargain."

Robert laughed at her obvious enthusiasm. "You are really enjoying this whole intrigue business, aren't you, my dear?"

She blushed and bowed her head, but the smile blooming on her face was pure irrepressible glee. "Is it that obvious? I must confess, I am having the time of my life."

The smile faded a little, and Robert didn't miss the look of pain briefly crossing her face. "But it's not just the intrigue, or making sure these men do not hurt any more women ever again," she added. "I relish the fact that somebody finally trusts me to do things, and do them well."

Robert eyed her thoughtfully as they reached the bottom of the stairs and turned down the back corridor to the library. "From what I heard, you proved yourself more than capable last night."

Her spine straightened with obvious pride at his words. "It looks like I overheard a good amount that might be useful before Mr. Strathem could come rescue me."

They had reached the library, and she smiled up at him as he opened the door and stepped aside for her to enter first. Henry and Allen stood by the window intently reading a document, and William looked over their shoulders with his back to the newly arrived.

Looking up, Henry waved them over. "Robert!" He acknowledged the viscount and then turned to Eliza. "William is back. He found your father's will right along with your mother's and the deed to the inn itself."

Eliza stepped forward and nodded toward William. "My thanks, William. Does Horace know you took them?"

William shook his head with a rueful smile. "Nah, the stupid bastard is too busy whoring the barmaids out and drinking the profits to take note of what goes on under his nose. It was like taking sweetmeats from a babe."

Eliza grinned at his description of Horace, but her voice was bitter. "Nothing has changed, then, since I left. He's none too bright, but he's smart enough to only pick on those who are weaker than him."

Henry came to her side and draped a comforting arm around her. "Well, thank God he wasn't smart enough to burn your mother's papers. In your father's will, the inn is written in as your dowry, and your mother's will confirms it—although it is your father's will that is notarized and will therefore stand. It's very clear: you inherit the inn in the event of your mother's death no matter if she has remarried or not."

The news was good, but Eliza couldn't find joy in it. Pain twisted in her belly. "She should have told him. Maybe he wouldn't have killed her."

Henry saw the anguish in her eyes and pulled her into a tight hug. "Perhaps he did know and that's why he sold you. Now he seems to think you are so afraid of him you won't come back."

She pulled out of his embrace and wiped away her tears while her eyes spat fire. "Fuck that, I'm gonna have his balls!"

Four pairs of male eyes snapped to her, stunned at her unladylike outburst. Remembering the company she was in, she slapped her hand over her mouth, shocked at herself. She looked at them in turn, but there was no censure in their eyes. Robert looked surprised, Henry and William grinned, and Allen laughed outright. He stepped forward and knelt in front of her in mock fealty.

"My lady, may I pledge myself to present said balls to you on a platter?"

That got a laugh out of her, and she playfully shooed him away. "Oh, stop it, you know what I mean."

It was Robert who answered seriously. "We do, and you may count on us."

HENRY USHERED EVERYONE TO THE seating around the fireplace in the back of the library and took a seat next to Eliza.

The conversation swiftly turned to William's other observations in Hampstead. After liberating the documents from the trunk in the upstairs family parlor, they hung around The Cat and Fiddle long enough to make sure the only link between Horace and Hobbs was Wilkins.

Apparently there was no lingering bad blood between Wilkins and Horace over Eliza's disappearance. Wilkins had stopped in at the taproom on his way home while William and his comrades were there, necessitating William's quick departure through the back door.

William hadn't relished the prospect of freezing his arse off in the brutal English winter night, but as luck would have it, Wendy the barmaid had provided them with an unexpected boon. She was in the habit of taking her "gentlemen callers" to the little shed next to the back door, and one of the men she entertained, while William stood there keeping watch through the side window, tried to recruit her for Hobbs with promises of glamour and riches in London.

Wendy declined on account of her ailing mother, to whom she would be no help gallivanting around London—this prompted a quiet "good girl" from Eliza when William related it. William had deduced that if Hobbs had been in business with Horace, or had any reason to keep him on his good side, Hobbs wouldn't try to steal his girls, and therefore there was no need to waste any more time with Horace.

They observed the comings and goings for a little while longer, then decamped to The Silver Fox. There they rented rooms and settled in at the bar, where they spent some money Henry had provided them with and found out plenty about Hobbs and his operation.

The location of Hobbs's cottage, at the end of a lane on the southwest side of the village, far enough from its next neighbor that screams wouldn't be heard, had been almost too easy to learn from the pub regulars.

One of William's men was sent to look it over and found it deserted, as well as seriously lacking in any comforts, but there were signs it had recently been used. The cottage had two rooms apart from the kitchen, each with three cots in it. According to what William and his men had heard at the pub, Hobbs brought up to six girls there every month or so. The girls, some of them virgins and all of them new to the trade, were forced to watch each other service men "to further their education," and if one of them refused to do any of the things they were asked to do, they were spanked in front of everyone. The man who had been refused got to do the spanking with his own belt.

Some of the blokes at The Silver Fox got so excited telling William about their exploits with the "girls," it was obvious Hobbs's visits to Hampstead were the highlight of their miserable existence. It was quite enough to make a good man's stomach turn.

But what had brought William back to London wasn't what he had found out about Hobbs and the cottage, nor the fact that the pimp wasn't expected to visit for another three weeks at least, but rather another overheard conversation having nothing to do with Hobbs. William returned immediately to Cavendish Square to warn Sir Henry.

What he had—quite by accident—overheard was a liveried footman from Oakwood House relaying a message to a plain-enough-looking regular at the bar.

Apparently, "His Lordship" commanded the man at the bar to return to town and relate all comings and goings from 17 Cavendish Square to "His Lordship" at his address in town.

Not knowing about Astor and his connection to Henry as well as Hobbs, William first thought he'd heard the address wrong, but the man at the bar repeated it and then left immediately. William had been in the field long enough to know when to trust his instincts, so he left his mates at The Silver Fox with instructions to keep their eyes and ears open and made his way into town at first light.

Leaving his mount in the mews, William had paid a visit to his friend in service to the widow in Number 11 Henrietta Street, had left that house through the garden, and had arrived at home by hopping the wall from a neighbor's backyard. Once in the house, a quick look out the front had confirmed it: the man he had seen in Hampstead was already in place in the square.

CHAPTER TWENTY-TWO

THERE WAS A LONG PAUSE AFTER WILLIAM FIN-
ished. His report was precise and to the point, only occasionally colored with his personal opinions, and rich on detailed observations.
Eliza admired his ability to dig up information and piece together
the seemingly random, but it didn't make the picture he painted of
Hobbs's operation any easier to hear— after all, she could have been
one of those girls if Henry had not intervened.

However, the most worrisome piece of information William had
related was that Astor—for she had no doubt that "His Lordship" was
Astor—was now watching them.

Robert broke the silence in the room. "Well, I guess he knows you
are up to something. Do you think he suspects we know his identity?
Is that why you sent me the second message?"

Henry looked pensive. "I'm pretty sure he knows I suspect he is
De Sade, but he's also arrogant enough to believe I have no proof. So
no, I don't think that's why he's stationed his man outside my house.
And I sent you that message before I knew William was back."

The looks he got from the company ranged from puzzled to downright worried. Henry took a deep breath. "I have a theory. I think Astor is getting ready to do something to me, and seeing as he delights
in cruelty, he wants to know how I'll react, witness my pain. What I
can't figure out is how he is planning to hurt me with Emily safely in

the country."

There was a stunned silence in the room until Allen, ever the practical one, got up and went to the sideboard, pouring brandy for the men and sherry for Eliza. "What makes you think he wants to hurt you? I know you have history with him, but that was more than a decade ago."

Henry took a brandy from Allen and sipped. "A number of things, but mostly what Eliza overheard in the retiring room combined with Astor's attitude toward me as of late." Henry stared down into his brandy. "The whole debacle makes my skin crawl."

All four men in the room took simultaneous gulps from their snifters to fortify themselves. Then Robert sat forward, concern plainly written in his face. "Explain yourself, man."

Henry turned to Eliza, who sat next to him on the settee, and gave her hand resting in his an encouraging squeeze. "Would you please tell them what you overheard last night in the ladies' retiring room?"

Eliza nodded and addressed herself to the group. "As most of you know, last night I got stuck behind a privacy screen in the retiring room at the Opera House and overheard a private conversation between Hobbs and Millie."

Robert swore, realizing the significance of a connection between Hobbs and his mistress. But it was William, who was still uninformed about many things that had come to light since his departure for Hampstead, who interrupted. "Wait, what? What was 'e doing following you into the ladies'? I thought we dealt with the bastard!"

Eliza held up her hand to stop him. "He wasn't following me, he was following Millie."

William's eyes grew wide and then turned to Henry. "You mean that Millie? What 'as she got to do with Hobbs?"

Henry sighed. "Yes, that Millie! Eliza found out Millie is in Hobbs's employ. Apparently, they are as snug as two bugs in a rug." He snorted with a fair amount of self-derision, clearly not happy he hadn't picked up on that connection before.

Robert ground his teeth audibly and turned to Eliza. "Please, my dear, continue. I'm most eager to hear more."

Eliza smiled at him, appreciating his calm determination to get to the bottom of it all, despite how obviously disturbed he was by this connection.

"Indeed, my lord, there is much you all need to know." She proceeded to impart what she had learned the previous night with as much detail as she could recall. She told Robert how Hobbs had seized the opportunity when Millie was introduced to him because he wouldn't take Hobbs's coin, instructing her to distract Robert and keep an eye on him. Eliza also related that Millie had cultivated this Clara as a friend for two years in order to get close enough to her daughter so she could help Hobbs snatch her for Astor when the time came, and Millie's frustration at finding Clara a good mother and a conscientious chaperone.

Eliza also made sure everyone understood the kidnapping was a special order, placed by Astor at least two years ago, and that last night he had told Hobbs the time had come.

When she was finished with her report, William let out a low whistle, accompanied by Robert's resigned sigh. Allen, on the other hand, raised his glass to Eliza. "Well done, Miss Eliza!" He took a sip of brandy before he turned his attention to Henry. "But Henry, as far as I know, you have never had an affair of any kind with Miss Adams, so I don't follow your theory that Astor is trying to hurt you. What makes you think that?"

Henry shrugged, got up to walk to the mantel, and leaned his elbow on it, his brandy snifter dangling between his long fingers. "You are right there, I don't know Clara Adams personally, but she could be important to someone I know. I have asked Sara Davis to find out who her extremely discreet protector is."

Henry rubbed his chin with the back of the hand dangling his brandy. "I also took the liberty of dispatching Elijah to keep watch over the lady and her daughter, if indeed she has one."

William nodded in approval. "Elijah's sharp as a tack. If this Miss Adams is the one they were talking about, we will know soon enough."

Henry took a deep breath. "I know it's more hunch than fact, but Astor turned up last night, which is unusual in and of itself. Then he made damned sure I saw him staring at Clara Adams and, although the lady is attractive, we now know—and have it confirmed by Hobbs—she is too old to warrant such attention from him."

He exchanged meaningful glances with Robert and Allen. "I'm certain it was a taunt he was confident I wouldn't be able to read." Henry looked at William with a hint of apology in his eyes. "Then Daisie reported he'd come to my box just after midnight." He raised his hand to stay William, who obviously wanted to ask what Daisie had been doing at the Opera House. "And last but not least, when we passed each other on the stairs late last night, he looked at me with what I can only describe as a potent mix of malice, anticipation, and triumph."

Henry flipped the last remaining drops of his brandy into the fire, making it jump up with a bright orange flame hissing like a snake. "He is planning something and he expects me to suffer as a result of whatever he is about to do."

The assembled men knew better than to question Henry's hunches. Allen owed his life to one of those hunches, so it fell to him to express their feelings on the matter. "Son of a bitch. We'd better find out what the bastard is up to, then, and stop it."

William looked at each of the room's occupants and finally shook his head in defeat. "Would someone tell me who Lord Astor is? And what 'as 'e got against you, sir?"

Henry pushed away from the mantel and sat back down next to Eliza. "My apologies, William. There has been no time to fill you in. Daisie came with us to assist Eliza, and she was wearing a mask, so you don't have to worry."

William let out a relieved sigh, obviously not comfortable with Hobbs and Daisie having been in the same building. He nodded for Henry to continue.

"Astor is the Duke of Elridge's youngest son. He hates me because I ran off with Emily's mother when he wanted her for himself, and he's now our primary target because I recently got confirmation he is De Sade."

William's eyes bugged out. "Come again? A lord of the realm is that sick fuck Frenchy spy? . . . Crikey!"

Henry's amusement at his retainer's way of putting things was tempered by the knowledge of what Daisie had suffered at the hands of the "sick fuck."

"Indeed! I went to the Old Man as soon as I heard the eyewitness account. He advised that the only way to bring a lord of the realm to justice is to bring ironclad proof of his guilt, or kill him in the act of subversion before witnesses, and even then it would be preferable for the one who puts a bullet in his head to be a member of the peerage himself."

Allen turned to Robert, grinning from ear to ear. "I guess you are the man for the job. I have to say I am looking forward to witnessing Astor's descent to hell."

The answering grin on Robert's angelic face was surprisingly wicked. "Not as much as I will enjoy sending him there."

Henry cautioned, "We can only justify a killing if he resists arrest, and we can only arrest him if we catch him engaged in an act of subversion—murder, espionage, or sexual deviance at the very least."

Allen sobered. "You mean we actually have to let him get his filthy hands on this girl in order to be able to do anything at all about it?"

Henry headed for the sideboard to pour himself another drink. "That is precisely what I mean. The Old Man was very clear: Elridge's son cannot simply be assassinated. He needs to stand trial in the House of Lords, or we need a damned good reason for shooting him."

Silence settled over the group for a good while until Eliza could stand it no longer. "So what happens now?"

Henry stared into his brandy as if the spirit within could provide him with answers and guidance. "We watch and wait. We find the girl, and whatever we do, we must not lose sight of her. She is the key."

Allen set down his empty glass on the sideboard. "I take that as my cue to return to drinking with my new best mate."

Henry waved him out of the room. "By all means, but don't crowd him."

Allen smirked. "Don't worry, I have it well in hand, and even if I don't, Rick surely does." With that he bent over Eliza's hand to place a gentle kiss on it. "Stay out of trouble, fair Eliza."

She smiled, but before Allen got to the door, there was a brief knock, and Thomas entered with an unsealed note on a silver tray. Henry raised his hand to stay Allen's departure and took the note, which was short and to the point and contained no names. Henry felt a measure of pride at how well he had trained his men and how readily they fell back into the discipline when he needed them to. He turned to the young footman, not one of the old comrades, but a good man nonetheless.

"Who brought this?"

"One of them boys hanging around The Crown trying to earn a penny. Charlie, I think."

"Make sure he gets a penny and send him to the kitchen for some food."

The young footman grinned. "Already done, sir. Do you want him to carry a message back to Elijah?"

Henry assessed him for a second. "Well done, Thomas. No message, but tell the boy to go back to Elijah via a different route."

Thomas departed with his silver server, nodding at William on the way out.

Once the door had closed behind him, William met Henry's gaze. "That boy's coming along nicely, sir. Keeps 'is eyes and ears open, 'e does."

Henry nodded at the man who had once been his sergeant, pleased to have him still at his side. "I agree. Seems he knows how to put two and two together."

Allen, still hovering close to the door, ready to depart, broke their reverie. "So what was in the note?"

Henry strolled to the fire and absently tossed the note into the flames. "Confirmation! Miss Adams does have a daughter. And as luck would have it, this daughter has taken to her bed with a chill."

Allen let out a puff of air. "I hate to be ungallant, but good. She is not likely to go shopping with a chill."

Robert ran a hand through his perfectly styled locks, glad of the reprieve, while Eliza sagged back into her seat, relieved they would not have to face down Astor that day.

Smiling at Eliza, Henry exchanged glances with Robert and William, and clapped a hand on Allen's shoulder. "Quite. With any luck we will have a few days to prepare. Come for breakfast tomorrow. We should know more by then, and Robert will stay here for the time being."

Allen's eyes sparkled with mischief. "So this is to be our official headquarters even with the eyes in the square?"

A big grin spread over Henry's face, pleased Allen had caught his intent. They had played this particular game a number of times during the war. "Especially with the eyes in the square. What better place than right under the enemies' nose?"

Allen heaved a mock sigh and winked at Eliza. "I know, I know. Easier to avoid the eyes when you know where they are and to whom they belong." Allen strode out of the room, closing the door behind him. They could hear his steps retreat to the back of the house. Henry and Robert knew he would exit through the mews and circle around to take a good look at the watcher in the square before he took up his own vigil with Hobbs.

Robert turned to Henry. "So what do you need me here for, sir?"

Henry nodded his thanks to the viscount for acknowledging his position of command. "I need you to run headquarters whilst I take a drive up to Hampstead. Eliza, would you mind coming with me? I understand if you don't feel comfortable going there, but I could use your knowledge of the area."

Pride swelled in Eliza's chest at the thought of being useful once again, not to mention having Henry's confidence. She didn't give a second thought to safety, knowing Astor and Hobbs were under watch in town, and Henry would be at her side. She smiled her consent.

"As long as you let me rest on the way there, I'll be happy to help."

Henry returned her smile. "That can be arranged. I think we might both benefit from a nap. It could take hours of searching through possible locations before we find what we're looking for. It will give us an edge to know where the dungeon is and establish entrance and exit points if at all possible. Once we know, we can put one of William's men on it."

Robert furrowed his brow. "Wouldn't you rather I went? I do know the terrain and I know what we are looking for."

Henry assessed him for a moment seriously, but there was a twinkle in his eye. "You are right on both counts, and I'm sure Eliza would prefer not to run into Horace or Wilkins just yet, but we can't both leave town, and surely, my friend, you remember what you are like with a lock for which you don't have the right key."

Robert's eyes snapped to Henry's in annoyance, but a slow smile crept across his face. "Oh Lord, I'm never going to live that down!" He shook his head in defeat. "And you are right, Astor wouldn't leave a place like that open for just anybody to walk into."

William chuckled from the corner, and Eliza raised an inquisitive brow to Henry. Henry grinned at Robert, and the viscount nodded his consent, heaving a put-upon sigh.

Turning to Eliza, Henry explained, "Robert is a first-class officer and an even better spy, but when it comes to picking a lock, he has two left hands, I'm afraid."

Eliza looked at him for a moment, assimilating what he'd just said. "And you have no such troubles?"

It was Robert's turn to grin. "The lock Henry can't open within thirty seconds, and with nothing but a lady's hairpin for a tool, has yet to be invented."

Eliza glared at Henry in mock disapproval, but he only shrugged. "We all have to play to our strengths."

"Point taken, my friend." Robert sketched a bow toward Henry and Eliza. "Wrap up warm, then, and have a nice drive."

Henry indicated his desk by the window. "Make yourself at home. You know what to do." He then took Eliza's arm and led her to the door.

William followed at his heel. "Do you want me to come with you, sir?"

Stepping into the corridor, Henry indicated for Eliza to take the back stairs again. But before he let go of her arm, he paused for a moment, taking in her fashionable yet utterly impractical attire. "Get changed into your warmest clothes, several extra petticoats, that sort of thing. And walking shoes. But a stylish cape so it looks like we are going visiting. I shall see you in the front hall in half an hour."

Once Eliza had turned down the rear corridor, Henry turned to William. "Stay here; I need you to contact the rest of your boys and send them up to Hampstead. They will be under Lord Fairly's command."

William saluted smartly, and there was no hiding the eager gleam in his eyes. "Consider it done, sir!"

Henry grinned and clapped him on the shoulder. "And get some rest! God only knows when all hell will break loose."

CHAPTER TWENTY-THREE

HALF AN HOUR LATER, HENRY, IMPRESSIVE IN A many-caped greatcoat, helped Eliza into the waiting coach. She was wrapped in a beautiful gray fur cape, her burgundy hat shielding her face and her fur muff warming her hands. Getting into the vehicle, she did her best to hide her scuffed walking boots, hoping the watcher was too far away to notice.

The interior of the coach had been laden with hot bricks and soft blankets, ready for a lengthy drive in the January cold, but less than ten minutes later, they pulled up outside of Henry's godmother's house in Brook Street. They were ushered into Lady Greyson's house immediately and without question.

The lady herself was still abed, having celebrated the arrival of the new year a little too vigorously for her age, but the staff were swiftly informed that Henry didn't intend to disturb her rest.

The coach was sent to the mews, and the couple were led to the back parlor. They left through the French doors, which were promptly closed behind them to keep out the draft.

Henry and Eliza proceeded to the bottom of the garden, followed a tiny trail through the little wood to a gap between two houses on Davis Street, and crossed cautiously to the Brook Street Mews.

There they climbed back into the coach. Eliza noted that the red panels usually accenting the doors, box, and luggage compartment of Henry's coach had been replaced by plain black ones. The driver, Roberts, reassured Henry the watcher in the square had not followed them, nor had he communicated with anybody else to follow them.

They lowered the shades as the coach rumbled out of the mews to double back toward Oxford Street and Hampstead Road. Eliza snuggled into the right-hand corner, grateful for the hot bricks beneath her feet, the blanket tucked around her legs, and the cushion wedged between the window frame and her weary head.

Henry mirrored her actions on the other side of the bench seat, then laced his fingers through hers. "Sweet dreams, Eliza! Roberts will tell us when we get close."

Eliza closed her eyes with a soft smile on her face. "Thank you for letting me help, for trusting me with this."

Henry rubbed his thumb over the back of her gloved hand. "Thank you for being someone I can trust."

He raised his eyes to look for her reaction, but she was fast asleep. He smiled as a tiny snore escaped her parted lips, and his tattered heart filled with warmth for the woman next to him. She might have been born in an inn, but she wasn't just a pretty face. She had honor and strength, and she gave him hope.

HENRY STARTLED AWAKE AT THE sharp rap on the sliding panel behind the box. He moved up the blinds, and seeing they had reached the outskirts of Hampstead Village, he leaned forward and opened the panel.

"Take the turnoff on the right toward the heath and stop by the dirt track going up the hill there."

He closed the panel against the cold, and as he sat back, Eliza stretched and yawned. "Are we there already?"

"Not quite. We will try the mausoleum on the heath first since it's the most likely place and we have limited time. Roberts will take us as far as the dirt road, but then we have to walk."

She rubbed the sleep out of her eyes. "That's all right. It's not much farther than a mile, but it's uphill, so it'll get us warm."

The coach slowed as it turned right into a small lane, then veered left again and stopped.

Henry helped Eliza down, turning to Roberts. "Go to the coaching inn across from The Silver Fox, put up the horses, and wait for us there."

Roberts tipped his head with the whip in his hand and grinned in anticipation of a hot toddy and a warm meal. "Right you are, sir."

Putting his hand on the small of Eliza's back, Henry led her along the dirt track that wound up the hill and soon disappeared into the thicket of trees covering the Hampstead side of the heath.

The heath itself was a large expanse of open land, dotted with the occasional oak grove. Oakwood House sat to the north of it, and the little graveyard with the mausoleum they were heading for was less than a mile from the border to its grounds.

Henry looked around and took in the tree cover on this portion of the heath, stretching almost uninterrupted along the ridge. He mused that since he could not see their destination from the path and the place was easily accessible from Oakwood without a soul being any the wiser, it truly was an ideal location for Astor's purposes. He could only hope Astor had come to the same conclusion. It would make the task of finding his dungeon that much easier.

Henry briefly wondered if he would recognize the place once he saw it. It was naïve to assume he would find a similar scene to what he had encountered in France. This was Astor's permanent lair. He would keep it clean. Any equipment he had would be cleared away until needed, but surely there would be signs if he looked hard enough.

They walked in companionable silence for a while, and every so often Henry bent down to pick up a pebble. The third time he did it, Eliza could no longer contain her curiosity. "What are you picking up pebbles for?" She cocked a brow at him. "If you are planning on skipping them on the pond, I have to disappoint you; the pond is the other way."

Henry laughed and handed her the pebbles. "Put those in your pocket. You never know when you need a way to get someone's attention."

Eliza looked from the rounded stones in her hand back to Henry, and he could have sworn there were little devils dancing in her eyes. She surely was enjoying this adventure. "Don't tell me, you are going to cut hazel next and make me a sling shot."

Henry smirked, playing along. "That's not a bad idea. Would you know how to use one?"

She rotated the muff around her hand. "It's been a while, but I could manage." With that, she dropped the pebbles into a pocket in her cloak and took the lead up the steep incline.

Behind her, Henry lowered his voice so it wouldn't carry. "Simmer down now, Miss Broad. If someone should be up there, we want to look like dutiful mourners on our yearly visit to my sainted mother's grave."

Eliza heaved a sigh. "I guess if we don't find what we are looking for up there, we will be visiting my mother's grave in the churchyard."

Henry stepped up to help her over a rough patch of loose stones. "Yes, but I'm almost certain this is where it is. I just have to recognize it when I see it."

They reached the forested part of the track, and it took them a good ten minutes to climb to the top of the incline. From there, it was another ten minutes across open heath to an oak grove almost directly due north. The terrain had evened out, but they were still climbing.

They took the path around the trees, and when they turned the corner formed by the copse of trees, the mausoleum stood directly before them on top of the hill, with a perfect view over open heath down to Highgate Village.

There were about a dozen headstones surrounding the Greek-inspired structure, and a small wrought iron fence separated the consecrated ground from the heath. The location matched exactly what Daisie had described. The wagon would have to stop at the fence, one would have to walk the last fifty yards, and the mausoleum was five steep steps off the ground on this side.

Henry opened the low gate for Eliza to step through and tried to find the perfect grave for her to say her prayers: one from which she could see everyone who approached and at the same time could see the door to the interior of the mausoleum. That door was at the north side of the structure, facing yet another stand of trees, and Henry made a mental note to have a good look amongst those before he went exploring the interior.

Henry led Eliza to a marker between the mausoleum and the trees, and silently urged her to kneel as if in prayer. The gravestone belonged to one Elisabeth Holden who apparently had left her worldly woes behind ten years previous.

Henry removed his hat, bowed his head, and stood beside Eliza, seemingly in prayer as he scanned the area carefully from under his brows.

Just when Henry was satisfied they were alone, they heard the clip-clop of horses coming up the path. Eliza stiffened and tried to rise, but Henry gently put a hand on her shoulder. "Stay and keep your head down. It's better if no one recognizes you."

Remembering her promise to follow his lead, Eliza resumed her prayer position, but surreptitiously looked out from under the brim of her bonnet for the approaching horses. They caught glimpses of them through the bare trees now. Only one horse had a rider; the other was being led.

Henry patted Eliza's shoulder reassuringly. "Only a groom out exercising the horses."

But Henry noticed that Eliza, even though she kept her head bowed as he had requested, remained agitated under his hand.

"What is it?"

Eliza tried to keep her voice to a low whisper as the groom came cantering into full view. "I just remembered who Elisabeth Holden was. She was quite well-to-do, but she did not have a son."

Henry paused for a moment before his eyes caught the name on the grave they were paying their respects to. "My mother's sister, then, estranged if need be."

Henry felt her relax a little and nodded a greeting to the groom as he passed not fifty yards from where they were situated. The man, however, was distracted by the antics of the horse he was leading and made no sign he was aware of their presence. As fast as he had appeared, he disappeared behind the next cluster of trees and continued on toward Oakwood House.

As soon as the groom was gone, Henry removed his hand and turned to assure himself of the direction the man had taken. "Those were some mighty fine horses to be stabled in a residence Elridge never visits."

Eliza didn't understand what the presence of the horses could signify, but felt compelled to point out the obvious. "Isn't it more likely they are Astor's, since he stays there regularly?"

Henry stepped back from the grave and placed his hat back onto his head. "No, those were both purebred Arabians, the duke's favorite breed. Astor prefers bigger horses because of his height and weight."

Eliza looked up at him, still not sure what Henry was driving at. "What do you think it means?"

Henry shrugged his shoulders. "That the duke spends more time here than previously assumed. Beyond that, I don't know."

Henry rubbed the back of his neck, where his skin prickled with apprehension. If Elridge stayed at Kenwood and took pains to remain unnoticed since the locals were unaware of his visits, that raised questions about his possible involvement in the conspiracy against the crown. Henry's organization had known there had been a leak in the admiralty Astor had exploited; however, the war had ended before they could find its source.

But there was no need to trouble Eliza with these observations; their present situation was nerve-racking enough. The need to find the dungeon and deal with Astor in a timely fashion had to be their main concern. Still, the prickling at the nape of his neck urged him to assume they were dealing with more than just one mercenary younger son. Be that as it may, the task before him remained the same.

He turned toward Eliza and gave her a reassuring smile. "Stay here; I'm going to have a quick look around." With that, he hopped over the low fence behind them and disappeared amongst the trees.

Eliza was not at all sure about being left alone in the small grave-yard. But just then the gray snow clouds above the heath parted, letting through a few rays of the pale winter sun, painting the Greek columns around the mausoleum brilliant white. Her hand found the pebbles Henry had given her earlier, and she took heart. She was on her home turf, after all. She knew every path around here, and her local knowledge had just provided Henry with a better cover story.

However, that story would not do if she was found here alone and recognized. Why would she be kneeling at Widow Holden's grave? She got up and looked around. A lichen-covered rock just inside the fence beckoned, and she went to sit on it. Much better to say she used to come here with her mother. Most locals knew her story and would not wonder at her coming back to visit places where they had had good times together.

As she sat there enjoying the winter sun, she realized her new vantage point, besides being more comfortable, also afforded her a better view of the path in both directions. The door into the mausoleum was in full view to her left, and if she turned, she could see all the way down the hill to Highgate, should someone approach from that side.

About ten minutes passed before she heard a small noise behind her, and Henry stepped over the fence next to her.

"I take it you have thought of a better story should you be found by yourself."

Eliza smiled at his confidence in her. "I'm visiting places where I have happy memories with my mother, and I actually do have some here on the heath."

Henry chuckled and stroked a finger affectionately down her cheek. "Excellent! Honesty is always the best policy, especially when you are trying to deceive an adversary." His eyes made another sweep of the area. "I believe we are quite alone, and I couldn't find any hidden entrances or hatches close by, so I shall try that door now."

He nodded toward the metal door in the Greek structure before them, then took his hat off and stashed it behind the flat rock Eliza was sitting on. "Use one of those pebbles if you see someone coming."

Eliza watched with rising anxiety as Henry took the five steps up to the mausoleum door in two strides. After trying the door and finding it locked, he pulled out a slim tool and inserted it into the lock. Within seconds, the door opened and he disappeared into the dark interior, closing the door behind him.

Eliza took a good look around, making sure no one had observed Henry, and was struck by the peacefulness of the heath all around her. Was it truly possible a place of evil was just beneath her feet?

Sadly, life had taught her evil could be found just about everywhere. The true surprise was finding someone willing to stand up against it.

HENRY QUIETLY CLOSED THE DOOR behind him and stood for a moment to adjust his eyes to the almost complete darkness within. He had brought a little oil lamp, unlikely to be extinguished in a sudden draft, but just as he unscrewed the middle part to light it, he noticed dim light coming from the stairs descending from the small circular room he stood in.

He felt his way to the railing and down the steps. He counted fifteen of them until the staircase made a right angle and went down a farther five steps, and he found himself on a landing high above a large stone-paved room. The room was rather well lit by torches held on the wall in medieval-looking iron rings, and two servants were busy cleaning and dusting the various pieces of strange furniture strewn around the room.

The stairs leading down into the room along the wall to the right were open, so there was no way Henry could go down without being seen by the servants. Even standing where he was could lead to detection, so Henry dropped to the floor and crawled forward to the edge of the landing.

He did his best to stay out of sight, which curtailed what he could see of the room, but what he saw was quite enough to make him realize this was no ordinary catacomb.

On the wall directly opposite him was a bench Henry had no trouble recognizing as a spanking bench. He remembered them well enough from his days at Eton, but he had never seen one with restraints for the hands and pommels that would either keep the legs pressed together and the bottom high in the air or the knees spread apart painfully wide. Henry shuddered.

Next to it was a chair that looked almost like a birthing chair, except for its unusual height and the phallic-looking wooden carving sticking out of the middle of the seat. He could see the possibilities for this device with an adventurous partner supplied with a copious amount of oil for lubrication, but Henry seriously doubted Astor supplied any of his partners with anything that might make the experience pleasurable for them.

The strange furniture was intimidating enough, but what truly worried him were the chains ending in hooks and manacles. Some hung from the ceiling, others from big iron rings in the walls.

Henry was familiar with the uses for a spanking bench and had a fair idea how the chair would be used, but the chains were especially menacing. He fervently hoped he would be spared the sight of Astor using them on someone.

Along the opposite wall was an open set of double doors, through which he could see a maid stripping bloodstained sheets off an enormous, black-draped, mahogany four-poster bed. She grumbled as she worked, but Henry couldn't make out what she was saying. Apparently, neither could the middle-aged man who was busy with a bucket and mop, cleaning the floor in the main room.

"What are ya complainin' about now, Ducks?"

The woman turned to the open door, and Henry had to duck out of her line of sight.

"I said the only upside to this stinkin' job is that 'is Lordship orders new sheets for down 'ere, not just fresh. I don't think I could bear to wash the blood and muck off them sheets after 'e's had one of them poor girls in 'ere."

The man below kept mopping. "Ya think too much and ya sure as 'eck talk too much. We get paid well enough to do as we're told and keep our traps shut. And we get to play 'ouse in the dairy."

The disgruntled maid muttered a few more things under her breath as she dressed the bed with fresh linens, but couldn't hold back for long. "I 'ope I don't 'ave to wait on that trollop Millie again. Not only is she knobbed in the 'ead enough to like the stuff 'e does to 'er, but sometimes she comes to watch 'im torture them poor girls."

Her partner shrugged with supreme indifference. "It takes all sorts. Besides, she ain't the only one."

With that cryptic remark, he finished his mopping, picked up the bucket, and headed for somewhere below Henry's hiding place. The comment about Millie was ambiguous at best. Was she not the only one who liked it or not the only one who watched?

No matter; the objective to eliminate Astor remained the same.

Besides, something else had caught Henry's attention. They were "playing house at the dairy"? That could only mean they were living at the dairy. It was unusual for what were clearly menial servants to be allowed to live in a spacious dwelling of their own. The dairy would normally be profitably rented out to the farmer who worked the land; there had to be a good reason for these two to be living there. Hopefully Eliza would know who worked the Oakwood land and who lived at the dairy.

Henry had to try to see where the servants had entered the dungeon, for he was now sure of two things: this was Astor's dungeon, and no one built a room as elaborate and taboo as this one and did not think to have a secret entrance.

The maid in the bedroom finished fussing with the bed linens and extinguished the candles in the candelabra on the bedside table. She then picked up her feather duster and the soiled linens she had earlier rolled into a tight bundle and walked out into the dungeon.

With her no longer looking his way, Henry edged forward, trying to get a better look at the rest of the room. In the center, a little to the right, stood a long table with all kinds of leather straps and cuffs hanging off its sides and various chains hanging above it. The wall to the right was mostly blank, except for a torch and a sand bucket below it.

Against the wall to the left, however, stood two matching mahogany chests of drawers; a large gilded mirror hung above them, and in the closest corner was a doorway into a corridor.

The maid walked over to her partner, who had put his bucket and mop into the corridor to the left. She flung the bundle of linens at him. " 'Ere, put them in the furnace, love."

The man caught the bundle, but instead of going to dispose of it, had a good look around the room, checking they had done all they had been asked to do. "Are ya about done, Ducks?"

She started rubbing lemon-scented wax into the top of one of the two matching chests of drawers with strong, efficient strokes. "Just 'ave to polish them chests. Did ya oil the leathers?"

He rolled his eyes at her behind her back. "Did that right after 'e 'ad the last girl in 'ere. Doesn't do to let blood dry on leather, makes it 'ard and brittle."

He walked over to the bottom of the stairs, and Henry knew a moment of panic, but the man only took the torch there off the wall and extinguished it in the bucket of sand. He replaced it, then went over to the far side of the room and extinguished the torch there. By the time he had repeated the process twice more, the maid was finished polishing and the dungeon was dark enough for Henry to lean over the edge of the landing to have a look at the rest of the room.

What he saw directly below his hiding place made the blood freeze in his veins.

A large wooden X had been mounted on the wall, with manacles attached high and low on the beams for hands and feet. On a big rack next to it were all kinds of strange leather harnesses, coils of hemp rope, switches and canes of varying lengths and thicknesses, and every whip imaginable, from an enormous bullwhip to riding crops to a cat-o'-nine-tails with metal points. Henry had been in the army long enough to know what a cat-o'-nine did to a person's back. God only knew what a bullwhip would do to a woman's delicate skin. If these things were so openly displayed, Henry thought, bile rising in his throat, what sick toys were hidden in those chests of drawers?

This truly was a torture chamber. Henry could no longer see anything even vaguely erotic about the menacing setup below. This was the lair of a madman, and it was time he was stopped.

CHAPTER TWENTY-FOUR

THE TWO SERVANTS HAD MOVED INTO THE COR-
ridor, taking the last of the lights with them. Henry pushed down his
horror at what had occurred in this room and moved silently down the
stairs while pulling a compass from his coat pocket.

He made it to the door into the corridor in time to see the two
servants walk quickly down a long straight tunnel, and used the last
of the torchlight to read his compass. True north, toward Oakwood
land, and if memory served and his map was correct, where the dairy
was located.

Henry was just about to enter the tunnel himself to follow the pair
and find where it led when he heard the faint clunk of a pebble against
metal—Eliza's sign.

It only took him a second to make up his mind. Avoiding detection so they could catch both Astor and Hobbs in their own trap was
still paramount; he could come back later tonight and finish his ex-
ploration of the tunnel.

Henry made it through the now pitch-black dungeon and up the
two sets of stairs with astounding speed and cracked the door open
a few inches in time to see Eliza lift her arm to throw another stone.

She looked to the east and then nodded to indicate that whoever
was approaching couldn't see him exit the mausoleum. He slipped
out, relocked the door with his burglar's tool, and moved swiftly to

her side.

"A man coming up the hill from Highgate. Walking across the heath is a popular shortcut to Hampstead."

Henry helped her to her feet, and she leaned close as he retrieved his hat and then led her out of the gate.

"I think it's the curate from St. John's, and besides knowing me, he is a terrible gossip."

They reached the path back to Hampstead, and Henry took a moment to place his hat back on his head and thread her hand through the crook of his arm. "Let's stroll slowly. With any luck, he will join the path in front of us and go down the hill to the village. He might not even see us."

Henry could see Eliza was bursting to ask what he had found, but it was too dangerous with possible ears just beyond the trees. He patted her hand on his arm. "All in good time, my sweet." Then he leaned his head toward her, and reasonably sure he had found what they were looking for, she let out a breath.

They walked back at an easy pace, engaged in polite small talk about the heath and the people who lived on it. She explained that the Oakwood land was farmed by a local independent farmer with seven sons, who lived in a sprawling farmhouse on the other side of the heath. The dairy had stood empty for years and was said to be haunted. Henry could only shake his head to hear that such a trick still worked. But it was never very difficult to exploit the superstitions of the peasantry.

DARKNESS DESCENDED EARLY IN JANUARY, the last light of day fading into the shadow of night just as Henry and Eliza made it to the coaching inn.

Henry ordered dinner in a private parlor as well as a room for the night, and while Eliza was led upstairs to freshen up before they ate, he went to find Roberts in the stables.

The inn itself only sported ten guest rooms and one private parlor, but the taproom and dining room were busy late in the afternoon due to the food being decent and the post from the north coming through on its way to London. This was the last official change of horses, so the stables, unlike the guest accommodations, were quite extensive.

The express had already gone through, but the normal mail coach and the stage were not expected for another hour or more, so the yard was busy but not hectic. There were lanterns lit along the front of the stables, and light from the inn's windows illuminated the other side of the yard.

Henry found Roberts playing cards with some of the stable hands. They were grouped around an upturned barrel in a quiet part of the barn. It was an open game, thus no one even blinked when Roberts abandoned his hand, swiped the few pennies he had won into his pocket, and followed Henry into the yard.

Once there, Henry informed him they were staying the night and asked quietly, "Found out anything interesting?"

"Not much, except most of the lads here prefer a quiet card game to the ruckus at The Silver Fox."

Henry gave a satisfied nod. "Good, then they won't mind if we take out Hobbs."

Robert chuckled. "Might even get a few cheers. Hobbs 'as been trying to recruit local girls, and the boys are none too pleased."

That tied in with what William had reported from The Cat and

Fiddle. Hobbs was obviously trying to expand his business in Hampstead and was treading on local toes in the process.

Henry had just asked Roberts to go to The Silver Fox and tell one of William's men to meet him behind the inn at ten of the clock, when a man stepped out of the barn to address Henry. The closer the man got, the more satisfied his smile became.

"Excuse me, Captain? I mean, Sir Henry. It is you!"

Henry turned to him, and when he recognized the man's smiling face, he thanked his lucky stars for yet another good turn. "Riley, what in the devil are you doing here?"

Henry took in Riley's attire and the way the stable hands acknowledged him as he walked by. "Or should the question be, what is one of my sharpshooters doing as an ostler?"

Riley grinned from ear to ear to hear there was something the all-knowing Sir Henry didn't know. He closed the last few yards between them. "I grew up on a horse farm, sir. My sweetheart is the chambermaid here, and when the position came up, I jumped at it."

Henry shook his hand and gave him a friendly clap on the back. "I'm glad you found a good position."

Riley heaved a sigh, and there was a whole world of troubles communicated in it. It didn't matter what you knew or how well you had served your country, good positions were few and far between. "Aye, me too. But I miss the old days. I had a few bevies with the boys camped out at The Silver Fox and was hoping I might run into you sooner or later." He lowered his voice so only Henry would hear. "I know something's up, so let me know if you need anything."

Henry studied his face for a second, then nodded. "I could use two saddled horses at ten tonight. And keep an eye on my companion,

Miss Eliza, in room three for me whilst I'm gone."

Riley saluted smartly. "I'm on it, sir." Then a cloud crossed his eager face. "Wait, would that be Eliza from The Cat and Fiddle?"

Henry looked at Riley questioningly, waiting for him to elaborate.

"My Mary said she was staying at the inn with a fine gentleman."

Henry nodded, indicating he was the gentleman in question.

Shifting his weight nervously from foot to foot, Riley was obviously uncomfortable with what he felt he had to tell Henry. "Begging your pardon, sir, but you should know, she comes from a really rough place and her old man is a nasty piece of work."

Henry was a little annoyed at the way Eliza was being judged, but couldn't fault Riley for his honesty, so he placed his hand on the other man's shoulder and urged him a few more steps away from the bustle in the yard. "I'm well aware of her origins, and her stepfather is the reason she is with me in the first place. I found her two months ago on the road trying to drag herself away from The Cat and Fiddle. She was near starved and half beaten to death."

Riley hissed in a sharp breath and shook his head in disbelief. "Jesus, what did he do that for?"

Riley's reaction reassured Henry he had found the right person to keep Eliza's presence in Hampstead secret and her person safe in his absence. "She tried to refuse the man Horace had sold her to. A miller named Wilkins."

"Christ almighty! That cretin already put two wives into an early grave."

Henry was gratified to note that Riley was now firmly on Eliza's side. "Yes, so I hear. Can I rely on you to keep her presence here quiet? Wilkins has been paid off, but Horace may still hold a grudge against

Eliza and hurt her if he sees an opportunity."

Riley looked thoroughly disgusted. "Leave it with me, sir. I'll get Mary to stay with her whilst you're gone. I'll keep an eye on things."

Henry shook his old comrade's hand; there was nothing quite like having a man you could trust with your life at your side. It was re-markable how his old friends surfaced the moment he needed them. "Thank you, Riley. Your help is much appreciated."

Smiling, Henry stepped back into the light coming from the open door into the taproom and went to their parlor to wait for Eliza and his dinner.

ELIZA HATED THE IDEA OF Henry going back to the mausoleum, especially at night, but was relieved to hear one of William's men would be going with him and that they would be on horseback. At least they'd be able to get away quickly if need be. Henry had told her only in broad terms about the dungeon and the tunnel he thought led to the dairy, and she knew he wanted to see whether they could use it.

Still, there were plenty of reasons to fret. What if someone came upon them in the dungeon, or they got trapped in the tunnel? What if Astor found Henry snooping in his lair? They had had no message indicating the twisted master spy had left London. But what if he had, using subterfuge just like they had?

Eliza was glad for Mary's company and the set of cards she had brought to while away the time. They were up in her bedchamber, and Henry had tasked Riley to keep watch so no one would trouble Eliza.

Trust Henry to make sure Horace was kept well away from her, to think of her comfort and safety even as he rode out to court danger himself. She wished she could have gone with him, helped in some way, but all she could do was wait for his return.

Eliza had seen Mary in church almost every Sunday growing up. Horace had always hustled them away as fast as he could, stopping for no one save the vicar, so she had never actually talked to Mary before. As much as it hurt to remember her mother's plight, it was gratifying to discover someone from her world was finally willing to help her against her horror of a stepfather.

Mary was quiet, with a dry sense of humor, and she was wickedly skilled at playing cards. Eliza had lost nearly her entire stack of pennies by the time they heard the clatter of horses' hooves on the cobblestones below.

Eliza peeped through the gap between the curtains, but all she could see was Riley leading two horses into the stables. Not two minutes later, however, someone scratched at the door, and then Henry stood in the open doorway. He looked tired, mud-splattered, and dusty, but he was still in one piece, and Eliza was so relieved she flew right into his arms, no matter Mary's curious gaze.

Henry caught Eliza in one arm and closed the door quietly behind him with the other. He gave her a quick squeeze and kissed the crown of her head before he gently extricated himself. "Easy, sweetheart. Let me get out of this dirty coat first."

She grinned and stepped around him to help him out of the garment. "A little dust never bothered me." As she took a closer look, however, she realized it wasn't just dust, but a fine layer of soil all over him, and a few cobwebs were caught in his hair and the capes around his shoulders. "Dear oh dear, you look like someone used you as a feather duster."

Mary, who had quietly stashed her winnings in her apron pocket, clacked her tongue and took the coat out of Eliza's hands. "I'll take that and get it cleaned up for you. And I'll send up the tub and some hot water."

Sending a grateful smile in her direction, Henry pulled a shilling from his waistcoat pocket. "Thank you, Mary. And thank you for keeping Eliza company."

Mary curtsied with a big smile. "My pleasure, sir." Then she patted her apron pocket to jingle the coins within and her smile turned to a grin. "Definitely my pleasure. I made out like a bandit tonight."

Henry raised his brows, and Eliza laughed. "Mary is a regular card sharp. In three hours I managed to win the grand total of two hands."

Henry chuckled and offered Mary a mock little bow. "Well, I'm glad you found the evening profitable."

Mary was still grinning as she turned to the door, but Henry stopped her. "Do you think you could find me some brandy? I find I'm a bit chilled."

She curtsied again. "I'll be right back with it, and some more wood too."

She left, and Henry proceeded to remove his soiled jacket and boots. Then he bent over and vigorously rubbed his head to rid his hair of the spiderwebs, dust, and earth that had lodged themselves there. "Lord, I wouldn't be surprised if I brought a few spiders back with me. I'm sure that cellar hasn't been cleaned since it was built, and then I had to climb out a window to get my bearings."

Satisfied he had removed most of the grit from his hair, Henry straightened and removed his crumpled cravat. He shook it out and left it on the back of a chair. "The good news is, the tunnel indeed leads to the dairy, and I managed to leave a window in the back of the cellar unlatched. Now Robert will be able to go through the tunnel when the time comes and cut off Astor's escape route."

Eliza looked into his deep blue eyes and swallowed. They were really going to do this. They had found the dungeon. Henry had scouted it to the point where he was now planning who would enter, and from where, to spring the trap they were setting. Back in town their opponents were being watched, and more and more people were willing to help them.

Henry sank into a chair by the fire and pulled her onto his knees. "Everything is pretty much set here. We will go back to town first thing, and until we have figured out who Miss Adams's protector is or the girl recovers, there is nothing for us to do but wait."

Moments later, Mary came back with Henry's brandy. She also set a hot pot of tea on the table where they had played cards earlier and picked up Henry's soiled cravat. Riley and two other men brought in the tub and several pitchers of hot water shortly after that. When they had set up the bath in front of the fire, Riley saluted, Mary curtsied, and then the whole procession marched out the door.

Eliza helped Henry bathe. She washed his hair and rinsed him with warm water from the last pitcher, then rubbed his hair dry with a towel as he warmed himself by the fire, alternately feeding her little sips of tea or brandy. Half an hour later, they were cuddled together under the thick coverlet, and Henry had just enough time to kiss her brow before sleep claimed them both.

THE NEXT MORNING, ELIZA AWOKE to her pulse racing and the delicious sensation of Henry's mouth suckling on one nipple while his hands moved her hips into position. She opened her eyes to his smiling face just as he drove into her. She moaned at the now familiar and most welcome sensation of him filling her and half-closed her eyes in appreciation.

Equal parts affection and amusement colored Henry's voice as he slowly moved inside her. "Good morning, sweetheart."

She smiled and stretched out her sleep-locked muscles beneath him, rubbing her breasts into the hard muscles of his chest in the process. "Oh, a new wrinkle on sleepy coupling?"

"Mmm-hmm, it is the best sort of way to wake up."

Eliza's arms stretched high above her head, and Henry ran a possessive hand from her wrist down her arm and all the way to the firm mount of her breast. He savored the soft skin beneath his fingertips and the beautifully trusting way she gave herself to him. Their breathing grew heavier, and he hooked one of her knees in his elbow to open her wider so he could stroke deeper into her. Then he bent his head down and kissed her deeply.

They allowed themselves to sink into each other, their lips soft, their tongues caressing gently, their arms drawing each other close so they could revel in skin moving against skin. They loved each other in a slow, sensual rhythm until their passion built beyond tenderness and their movements grew more and more urgent, chasing each other into the oblivion of orgasm.

As their breathing slowed, Henry let go of Eliza's knee, but instead of moving off her, he wrapped both arms around her in a tight embrace and buried his face in her hair, kissing the tender spot just below her ear.

"I needed that after being in that horrible room yesterday."

Eliza had felt the emotional need in his touch and now heard the distress in his voice. Oh Lord, what was in that room to afflict the normally so cool and collected Henry? On second thought, perhaps she didn't want to know. How had Daisie put it? Some things, once you know them—or, God forbid, experience them—you couldn't un-know. It had to be horrible beyond anything she'd ever known for Henry to need her like this.

Eliza wrapped her arms and legs around him and held him tight until she felt the tension in his body ease. She was thankful she could help him in this way, at least.

CHAPTER TWENTY-FIVE

A GOOD WHILE LATER, HENRY WENT DOWN-stairs to order breakfast and organize their journey home, giving Eliza time and privacy to perform her morning ablutions. But what she found when she ran her washcloth between her legs had her call Mary to find her some clean rags.

In all the excitement of the past few days, she had completely forgotten about the imminent arrival of her courses, hadn't even noticed any of the cramps usually associated with their arrival.

By the time she dressed and got downstairs to the private dining room, however, she could feel the familiar twinges in her abdomen. She ate a light breakfast, but made sure to take some roast beef from the inside where it was still bloody, and her tea sweet and strong like her mother had taught her. But the thought of being rattled along in the coach for an hour or more filled her with apprehension.

Henry noted her unusual food choices and her slightly peaked looks, but didn't hit upon the cause for her behavior until they had left the stable yard behind and jolted over the first serious rut in the road. Eliza closed her eyes in despair and folded her arms protectively around her middle.

"Cramps, my sweet?"

She nodded, her eyes still closed.

"I didn't notice anything this morning. Have your courses started?"

Eliza's eyes flew open, and she threw him a slightly shocked side-long glance. How on earth did he know what ailed her, that any-thing ailed her at all? She had tried so hard to be inconspicuous. Then again, she supposed, as her lover, he would want to know when she was bleeding.

She felt shy talking about it, so she looked out the window. "They started right after you left."

Henry took one of her hands and squeezed it gently. "The ruts and the jostling make it worse, do they not?"

She nodded, still shy, but so very glad his voice held no irritation or derision, like she had heard in the voices of the men at the inn complaining about their women being "on the rag." Henry removed his left boot, which puzzled her greatly, and slid his foot behind her back to stretch it along the length of the bench. Then he pulled her forward and turned his body so his back rested against the side panel next to the door. "Come, sweetheart. Let's see if we can't make you a little more comfortable."

With sure hands, he pulled her to sit between his legs, urged her to put her legs up along the seat, and gently drew her back to rest against his chest, thereby cushioning her from the worst of the jostling. Then he draped a lap blanket over her, snaked his right hand under her cape, and cupped it over her lower abdomen. "Does that feel better?"

Eliza almost moaned with pleasure and relief when his big warm hand started to stroke slow circles over her sore belly. "Much! Please don't stop doing that."

Henry chuckled and pressed a kiss into her hair. "You just relax and let me take care of you. We'll be home in no time. Then you can curl around a hot brick, and Mrs. Tibbit will make you one of her herbals."

Eliza relaxed farther into his arms. "That sounds like heaven. How do you know so much about a woman's courses?"

"Let's just say I have lived more than a decade longer than you, and spent five years in the army. There are plenty of women who follow the drum, and their men are not always around when they are needed. Word got around fast that I had an infant daughter and that I'd taken care of her myself until my grandmother took her in. Many of the women following my regiment started to come to me when there was no one else to turn to. I'm godfather to twelve youngsters, and even had to help deliver a babe on the side of the road once."

Eliza contemplated the plight of the woman who had given birth on the side of the road. She could well believe people coming to Henry for help, relying on him. She did it herself, and she was almost ashamed she'd been nervous to tell him about her monthlies earlier.

"I didn't want to have to tell you earlier, about my courses, I mean."

"Why ever not?"

She blushed furiously. "I was embarrassed, remembering how the men at the inn used to talk about their women's time of the month." She turned her head up at him and held his gaze. "I'm sorry. I should have known you wouldn't be like that."

The trust in her eyes filled him with pride. She had seen so much that was ugly, and still, time and again she proved she could rise above her past and trust a man: more specifically, him.

He bent lower to brush a soft kiss on her lips. "Eliza, every time you put your trust in me and let me take care of you, you make me happy. It's a level of intimacy beyond the merely physical I haven't had with a lover in a very long time. So, thank you."

Her answering smile was nothing short of spectacular. He basked in it for a while, smiling back at her, but sobered when another thought struck him. Perhaps she shouldn't trust him as much as she did, since it was sheer luck he hadn't gotten her pregnant yet.

"I am also glad to know you're not with child. Not that that would be a problem; I promise I will take care of you and the babe if I do get you in trouble that way, but ..."

He paused, but Eliza didn't look at him, just encouraged him to say what he needed to say.

"But ..."

He nodded his silent thanks into her hair. "I cannot marry you and at the same time keep my vow to Emily."

That truly shocked her. Marriage between them was so far out of the question, it had never even occurred to her. He belonged to a class so far above her, she almost wanted to laugh at the idea. But she realized he felt guilty he couldn't offer her the security of his name, so she offered him her understanding instead.

Eliza turned in his arms to face him and studied him while she spoke. She laid her gloved hand against his cheek and waited for him to meet her gaze. "Of course you can't marry me. That would be worse for Emily's future than if you remained a bachelor. I know that, and I don't ever want you to worry about me in that way. If you hadn't found me and taken me in, I would be dead by now. And now you are showing me a life I never even dreamed could be possible, let alone for someone like me."

Henry's shoulders slumped in relief. He cared about this woman, he really did, but his daughter had to come first. That Eliza understood that and encouraged it made him respect her even more.

Eliza stretched up to kiss him, putting all the tenderness and gratitude she felt for him into it. Then a flash of mischief crossed her face. "Besides, I'm not quite as naïve as you think. If I ever learned anything from Wendy the barmaid, it's how to count the days of my cycle, and according to her, the week before the menses starts is the least likely for a woman to conceive."

A slow grin crept across Henry's face. How he loved that smart, practical, earthy side of her. "Did Wendy the barmaid also inform you as to what to do to avoid conception during the rest of the month?"

Two tiny lines appeared between Eliza's eyebrows, and her index finger tapped thoughtfully against her lips. "Well, Wendy said it was a complete waste of time to try to get men to wear French letters; they don't like them for some reason. Her favorite method is a sponge soaked in vinegar—but what exactly you do with it I could never quite work out. But Daisie swears by pennyroyal tea three times a day for the ten days before one's . . . "

She trailed off when Henry burst into laughter. Her eyes snapped to his, her eyebrows rising in a "what's so funny" gesture. He shook his head fighting for composure.

Should he enlighten her about the sensation-blocking properties of a length of sheep gut or the potential hazards of vinegar in the most sensitive part of a woman's body during a vigorous bout of lovemaking? No, her naiveté was just too endearing. Still chuckling, he pulled her close and pecked a kiss onto the tip of her nose.

"You are a treasure. I think we will go with the pennyroyal tea. Daisie seems to know what she's doing."

Eliza was still a little peeved he was laughing at her, but how could she be angry with him when he called her a treasure and kissed her?

So she leaned back in his arms and gave herself up to the soothing warmth of his hand circling over her abdomen.

DESPITE HENRY'S BEST EFFORTS TO keep her comfortable and the journey proceeding relatively smoothly, the frozen ruts in the winter-damaged road had jostled Eliza into exhaustion by the time they reached Mayfair. Roberts drove the coach directly into the mews behind the house, and they entered through the garden gate to avoid the watcher in the square.

Since nobody knew when to expect them home, Henry had to knock on the library window to get Robert's attention, but as soon as William had let them in through the French doors in the music room, Eliza was ushered up the back stairs into Henry's sitting room and installed on the chaise longue. A velvet-wrapped hot brick was placed against her back and one against her stomach, so she could curl herself around it as a steaming herbal brew of Mrs. Tibbit's secret recipe was set in front of her. Never had Eliza been swaddled in such luxuries in honor of her courses, and she wanted to cry with gratitude.

While Daisie and Mrs. Tibbit fussed over Eliza, Henry went downstairs to debrief with Robert. The viscount informed him everything had been quiet. A second man had appeared in the square to relieve the watcher for the night, and the first watcher had returned this morning. But as far as they could figure out, there were no others posted around the back or in other parts of the neighborhood.

The doctor had been called to attend to Miss Adams's daughter, and according to one of the housemaids, the girl was miserable but in no real danger. It seemed it would be some time before Millie and Hobbs could put their plan into action.

Henry was glad of the reprieve, hoping they would find out who the girl's father was before anything happened to her. Robert hadn't heard from Sara Davis yet, but she had been seen striking up a conversation with Miss Adams at the apothecary.

Henry told Robert what he'd discovered in Hampstead and his growing suspicion that others apart from Astor might be involved. Whether that involvement pertained to the espionage, the sexual aspects of the equation, or both, remained to be seen.

They decided to make detailed maps and floor plans of all the places they might have to follow Hobbs and Astor into to detain them or—in Astor's case—catch them *in flagrante* and save the girl. At least, Henry very much hoped they would be able to save the girl.

They called a war council for the following morning, for the purpose of making a preliminary plan of attack so everybody would know where to go and what to do, in case they had to suddenly move fast.

That was one thing they had all learned during their years on the continent: intelligence gathering could be a slow and at times tedious process, but it paid to be prepared in case there was a need for immediate action. Having a plan was always helpful, even if in the end they had to heavily improvise.

Once they had concluded their business, they joined Eliza in Henry's cozy sitting room for a light lunch, and Robert, who was the only boy amongst five sisters, indulged in some gentle teasing, calling Eliza the pampered princess of Cavendish Square.

The afternoon passed pleasantly with Eliza reading and dozing as the men played chess and mulled over various plans for the coming confrontation.

After the sun had set on yet another dull, gray January day, Henry used the cover of darkness to slip out the kitchen door and walk over to Grosvenor Street to report to the Old Man. He hoped to get some eyes on Elridge, who surely would be in London soon for the opening of Parliament.

THE TWO DAYS FOLLOWING HENRY and Eliza's return from Hampstead were taken up with making plans for what might occur once Hobbs kidnapped the Adams girl. Beyond that, Henry, Robert, and Allen prepared in meticulous detail for any other eventuality they could think of.

They all agreed they had to let the kidnapping happen in order to set up Astor. Too many people had suffered at his hands already, and with the war long over, there was no hope of proving his treason. Neither one of them liked the idea of putting the girl in harm's way, but there seemed to be no other way to get the irrefutable proof Parliament would require to try a duke's son. To that end, they had to stay well back in order to avoid arousing suspicion.

Henry and Robert placed their watchers in strategic positions so as not to miss any sudden move by any of the players involved, but they refrained from continuously shadowing Astor or Hobbs. Certainly Astor was too experienced not to notice being tailed, and they figured Hobbs was savvy enough to notice pretty quickly as well.

Luckily, Millie was instrumental in the abduction and vain enough to expect men to follow her, so as long as they didn't lose sight of her, they could be relatively certain not to miss the big event.

Just to be on the safe side, Henry recruited one of his ex-lovers, whom he knew to have no love for Millie, to keep tabs on her in places where their watchers could not follow, so Robert could go to Hampstead to oversee the preparations for their plans.

That evening, Robert stepped out of Henry's kitchen and into the cold, clear January night disguised in William's footman uniform. He walked across Mayfair undetected and slipped back into his rooms on St. James's Street. Once there, he was gratified to hear his man had told anybody who cared to listen that he had a cold, effectively deterring all questions as to Robert's whereabouts.

The next day, still sniffling and sneezing, Robert took Millie shopping and asked her to join him in Hampstead, where he told her he was forced to go in order to fulfill his duties as the magistrate.

Having no intention of leaving town or catching Robert's cold, Millie picked out the biggest, most expensive broach she could find, assured him she would be waiting for him when he got back, and sent him on his merry way, congratulating herself on how well she had handled the viscount.

An hour later, Robert was on his way north, fully recovered from his cold, and Millie was spotted first meeting with Hobbs and then visiting Miss Adams.

In the meantime, Eliza thoroughly enjoyed her indisposition, spending her days reading and being pampered on the chaise longue in Henry's sitting room, and her nights being tucked securely against the curve of Henry's body while his hand warmed her belly.

It was astounding how quickly she got used to sharing a bed with a man, especially during this time of the month. But spooning her back to Henry's front, sharing the warmth of his body, hearing his even breath as he slept peacefully, not only made her feel safe and secure, it felt right and natural.

She knew the world judged her for what she shared with Henry, but the same world had turned its back on her when she had needed help, so she couldn't bring herself to care. This man holding her securely in his arms had helped her without knowing her, and was now showing her more tenderness than she had ever known, so her loyalty lay with him no matter the consequences.

Eliza attended the planning meeting the day after their return and reported all she had seen in Hampstead. After that, her only task was to review the maps and floor plans Henry and Robert had drawn up. But by Thursday Eliza felt fully restored, so when Henry suggested a morning visit with Sara Davis, she was more than ready to leave the confines of the house.

Henry attempted to draw the watchers' attention by setting off on foot to join some acquaintances at Tattersall's, where the year's first crop of horses had arrived, but the watcher didn't follow him, confirming Henry's opinion that there were others around to pick up his trail.

Eliza emerged from the house an hour later, looking every inch the fashionable young woman in her sage green and ivory silk dress and spencer, trimmed with dark ermine and wearing a matching muff and hat. A dark fur cape was draped over her shoulders against the January chill. She was handed into the coach by William, who then hopped onto the footman's seat in the back, and they set out for Sara's residence in George Street.

She arrived around eleven, the perfect time for a friendly morning visit, and was ushered up the stairs to a drawing room that offered no opportunity for anyone to observe them unnoticed.

There Eliza found not only Sara Davis, who greeted her warmly, but also the Earl of York. Eliza curtsied as he rose from his seat by the fire and bent over her hand before he led her to a comfortable chair next to Sara's.

"Miss Broad, how fortuitous you should visit. We were just debating whether I would have more luck running into Sir Henry at White's or at Tattersall's. But now I can entrust you with the message I meant to convey."

Eliza arranged her skirts gracefully as she sat and did her best not to be intimidated by the Earl of York. She knew Henry had worked with him in the past and that she could trust him, so she didn't hesitate. "Sir Henry went to Tattersall's this morning to try to draw the watcher away from the house. But the man in the square didn't follow him, whatever that may mean."

York smiled at her. "It most likely means there are others, and someone else followed Sir Henry. Or it could be Astor only wants to know how Henry is going to react to whatever it is he has planned. Either way, I am glad I didn't go to Tattersall's; it is best we are not seen together."

Eliza smiled back at him and included Sara when she asked, "What do you want me to tell Sir Henry?"

She turned her attention back to York when she noticed Sara looking at him expectantly.

He grew serious. "Please let him know the Duke of Elridge arrived in town last night, minus one outrider whose horse had fallen prey to a rabbit hole along the road and is now laid up with a broken leg. This morning I managed to place one of my men on Elridge's outrider team, so we should get good intelligence of his movements."

Eliza nodded. "That's good. I know Henry is increasingly concerned about his possible involvement."

York heaved a heavy sigh. "So are we, my dear. So are we."

Henry had told Eliza what York and Sara had contributed to bringing about peace in Europe, so she could well understand the earl's frustration. To have to doubt the loyalty of such an important English peer was grave indeed.

The Earl of York stood and bowed to Eliza, then bent to kiss Sara's cheek. "Well, I leave you to discuss the other matter and shall return to my desk. The opening of Parliament is, after all, only days away."

CHAPTER TWENTY-SIX

AS SOON AS THE DOOR CLOSED BEHIND YORK, Eliza turned to Sara. "It's so nice to see you again. But as you might have guessed, Henry sent me to inquire whether you had any luck finding out who the girl's father is."

Sara shook her head and handed Eliza a cup of tea. "I'm afraid not yet. Milk or lemon? Sugar?"

Eliza took the cup. "Just milk, please."

Adding a swig of milk to Eliza's tea, Sara handed her a plate so she could help herself to food. Eliza chose a piece of fruitcake, but set it down, preferring to attend to the business at hand first.

"Sir Henry thinks it imperative to find out how he is connected to the girl. Since Henry doesn't know Miss Adams and therefore her daughter can't possibly be his daughter, he thinks the father is the link."

Sara looked thoughtful. "I was thinking the same thing. However, I don't know Clara Adams very well either, so I had to go through the servants. But they have turned out to be extremely loyal, and all I've managed to find out so far is that the girl has a bad cold and is called Stephanie."

Eliza let that percolate in her mind for a moment. She didn't know whether her opinion would be appreciated, but she voiced it anyway. "Millie said she's been friends with Miss Adams for two years and she still doesn't know who her benefactor is. And you say the servants aren't gossiping like they normally do. They must be paid very well indeed to school their tongues like that."

While Sara had to admit Eliza's assessment was spot on, she could also see that Eliza had more to say. "Go on."

Eliza shrugged. "Perhaps we should try to find out where the money comes from. Find a tradesman with whom the household does business regularly and ask them who pays the bill."

Sara Davis looked at Eliza speculatively, then a smile spread over her beautiful face, lighting her from the inside. "You are not just a pretty face, are you, Miss Eliza? I'm glad Sir Henry can see it and is making use of your abilities."

Eliza blushed and smiled with pleasure at being appreciated by someone she so admired. "Me too. I really don't want either of these men to hurt another woman."

Sara looked at her with concern. "They hurt you?"

"Hobbs would have done if Henry hadn't rescued me." Eliza clasped her hands in her lap as memories of that day in Covent Garden assaulted her.

Sara leaned over and covered Eliza's hands with hers in a comforting gesture. "But Sir Henry did rescue you and is continuing to keep you safe."

Eliza nodded and raised her soft brown eyes to Sara's. "He has saved my life twice already. I will never be able to do enough to repay him." Then a little smile stole into the corners of her mouth and made her eyes sparkle mischievously. "Besides, I really enjoy all of this cloak-and-dagger business."

Sara laughed. "You will do very nicely indeed."

The two women talked some more and finished their tea, so it wasn't until Eliza was in the coach on her way home that she asked herself what exactly she would do nicely for. But then again, what did it matter? As long as she was of use to Henry, she was well satisfied.

ELIZA REPORTED BACK TO HENRY over afternoon tea served in front of the rear fireplace in the library. While they consumed ham sandwiches and mince pies, she told him what Sara Davis had found out so far and what they had decided to do to get around the unusual level of loyalty displayed by Miss Adams's staff.

Henry knew how laborious and slow it could be to unearth someone's secrets, so he commended Eliza on their efforts, but had no expectation of finding out what he needed to know before the kidnapping took place.

He knew two things, however: he could not go to Clara Adams directly without jeopardizing his chance to finally bring down De Sade, and the girl's father was not only rich, but powerful. Money could only buy so much loyalty, and the loyalty of the servants in Miss Adams's household clearly went beyond that limit. It begged the question of how Astor had found out who the girl's father was. If Henry didn't thrive on intrigue, it would be enough to give him a headache.

As it turned out, they had plenty of time to ponder Miss Adams's secret as the week drew to a close without any improvement in Stephanie's condition.

In the meantime, there were more personal things to consider. On Friday, Henry asked Eliza to accompany him on a shopping expedition to find a suitable birthday gift for Emily, who would turn twelve on the thirteenth of the month, now less than a week away.

Hatchards on Piccadilly was their first stop. Eliza had spent a great amount of her time in Henry's library of late, but she'd never been to a bookshop, let alone one as large and well-stocked as Hatchards. She was a little awestruck by the rows upon rows of bookshelves tightly packed with every book imaginable. Her eyes shone with excitement at the thought of all the yet-undiscovered treasures in this place. But how one would ever find what one was looking for was a mystery to her.

Henry saw her awe as well as her confusion and explained the books were grouped into sections like fiction, poetry, or science, and that every section was alphabetically ordered by the name of the author. Eliza realized the shop was set up much like his library, but it wasn't until her eyes found the neatly painted signs naming the sections that she felt confident enough to venture forth. She quickly located the section housing fiction and informed Henry she wanted to go there first.

Henry laughed and motioned for her to proceed. "Why don't you look for something for us to read whilst I pick out a book for Emily."

Eliza eyes shone with pleasure as she took in the vast selection before her. "I might be a while!"

"There is no hurry, my sweet. Explore to your heart's content."

Henry left her by a display of newly published books and busied himself with looking for illustrated volumes of myths and legends for Emily. He then brought his favorites to a table near the front where the light was better so he could make a final decision. When he was satisfied with his selection, he went in search of Eliza.

He found her sitting on a stool, two books clamped under her left arm and totally engrossed in the reading of a third.

"Is it good?"

Eliza looked up briefly, then returned her eyes to the page. "I'm not sure yet."

Henry looked over the new publications, reluctant to interrupt her, but eventually took the volumes from under her arm and read the first title. "*Northanger Abbey* I have." He reached behind Eliza and placed the book back on its shelf. "If it's not in the library, Mrs. Tibbit may have it in her rooms." He turned his attention to the book still in his hand. "But this looks intriguing: *Ivanhoe*. It is about a knight?"

Eliza nodded without looking up.

Henry looked over her shoulder and chuckled. "You are reading verse without making fun of it? Now I truly am intrigued."

Finally looking up, Eliza shot him a reproachful look. "I didn't laugh at *Romeo and Juliet*."

Henry grinned from ear to ear. "No, you cried through two of my handkerchiefs! But that's Shakespeare. What's this?" Curiosity finally overriding patience, he took the book out of her hand to look at the spine, but it was as yet unbound and he had to turn to the front page to find the title and author. "John Keats—he is one of the new romantics, is he not?"

"I wouldn't know. All I know is, I like the way he says things. It doesn't seem very polished and there's nothing to swoon about, but it's heartfelt and beautiful in a quiet sort of way."

Henry looked from the book to Eliza and back. He read a few lines and had to agree with her: there was an unaffectedness about it that appealed. He held out his hand to Eliza and helped her up from the stool. "I'll have them bind a copy for you."

Henry led Eliza to the table up front to choose the book for Emily. Then they proceeded to the silversmith a few doors down where they found an enchanting charm bracelet with reminders of Emily's favorite hobbies: a horse, a musical note, and a book. Horses were Emily's first love, she played the piano, and she liked reading, like her father. There was also a castle, to represent where she lived, the obligatory heart, and a fleur-de-lis because her great-grandmother was a real-life royal princess. All the little silver charms were inlaid with colorful enamel, and Eliza could not think of a more perfect gift for a young girl.

They brought their treasures home, where Eliza wrapped them in printed muslin and colorful ribbons so they would be ready for him to take to Avon. The birthday festivities were set for Thursday the following week, and Henry hoped with all his might the whole De Sade affair would be over by then.

On Sunday, they finally got some welcome news. They attended services at St. George's and shared a pew with Sara Davis, who informed them discreetly that Stephanie was on the mend. That bit of information prompted Henry to send Thomas to Avon on Monday morning with the presents for his daughter and a letter explaining he might be forced to miss her birthday due to a very important matter he had to attend to. He told Emily he couldn't predict when his business would be concluded, and begged her forgiveness in advance in case he couldn't be with her for her big day.

He sent his daughter a thousand hugs and kisses, but also sent a message to his grandmother, whom he could rely on to make a fuss over Emily's birthday. Nevertheless, the mere thought he might have to miss Emily's day threatened to depress him. That particular day of the year was always difficult for him, but spending it with the one good thing to come from his entanglement with Cecilia always helped.

Then he recalled his hunch that Astor might somehow pose a threat to Emily, and that made it easier to sit and wait for events to unfold as Monday turned to Tuesday and then Wednesday without any public sightings of the younger Miss Adams.

Henry took Eliza for a daily morning drive to reinforce the image of the besotted swain he had presented at the New Year's ball. Not only did it afford them an opportunity to look out for the Misses Adams in the park, but it also explained Henry's presence in town during a week he traditionally spent at Avon with his daughter. He didn't know how much Astor knew about his habits, but he felt flirting in public with Eliza should be adequate cover.

The weather was exceptionally fine, and the roads dry and perfectly passable, especially for an experienced rider like young Thomas, so Henry was slightly worried when by Wednesday night he still hadn't returned from Avon.

On Thursday morning, Henry and Eliza went for their morning drive in the park and had the good fortune to observe not only Clara Adams taking the air, but also Stephanie. To top it off, they witnessed Millie running into the two women and striking up an animated conversation.

Henry drove home with the distinct sense that things were coming to a head. He welcomed the chance to put their plan into action and the sense of control that came with knowledge—only to find things had slipped out of his control as soon as they got back home.

The first sign events were not unfolding as he had anticipated was the presence of the large ducal traveling coach outside his house. Further unease spread through Henry's soul when he observed several pieces of luggage being removed and carried into his house.

Surely his cousin Arthur, seventh Duke of Avon, had no need nor desire to bunk with him; and his grandmother, the dowager duchess, always stayed at the ducal palace on St. James's Square. So there was only one person who would arrive in that coach and insist on staying with him. The thought of Emily arriving just as things were getting into motion made his heart sink.

He stopped the curricle beside the traveling coach, threw the reins to Roberts, swung Eliza down to the pavement in one swift motion and rushed her up the stairs with undignified haste.

As soon as they entered the foyer, his suspicion was confirmed when Emily shrieked "Papa!" and launched herself into his arms.

Henry let go of Eliza's hand and felt her trying to melt into the background so as not to intrude on their reunion.

Despite his trepidations about finding his daughter in London, or perhaps because of them, he caught her against his chest and enveloped her in a crushing hug, needing to physically reassure himself she was safe, at least for now.

"Happy birthday, poppet. What are you doing here?"

Emily peppered his face with great big smacking kisses. "Isn't it wonderful!" she gushed in breathless excitement. "Uncle Arthur had to come to town anyway, and Grossmama said we could come and stay until you are done with your business. After that, you can take us back, we can have my party then, and you won't have to miss it." She looked at him triumphantly.

Oh, bloody, bloody hell. Curse him for trying to be considerate and sending advance notice of his absence. Double curse him for telling his grandmother to indulge Emily's every wish. This was his own fault. He couldn't even hint at danger to the dowager, or ask her to take Emily back home. She would tell Avon, and then his exceedingly straitlaced cousin would do his damnedest to stop him from going after Astor, for fear the House of Lords would perceive it as a political vendetta against Elridge, Arthur's arch enemy.

All of this went through his head in the blink of an eye while he hugged his daughter against him and schooled his face to show nothing but pure delight. "That's incredible. I never imagined you would come to see me."

He set her down, and she stepped back with the biggest smile on her face. "That's what I told Grossmama. You constantly give me presents and I never have anything real for you except the stitchery Aunt Hortense forces me to make."

Henry grinned at her and teased, "But I like your stitchery, it's so very original."

Emily laughed uproariously. "You mean crooked, Papa."

Henry squeezed her hands, but sobered at the thought of his grandmother. At eighty-three, her age had to be considered, even if he was upset with her just now. "Is Grossmama with you?"

Emily shook her head, making her straight blond hair fly. "No. We arrived last night and she is still resting from the journey, so Thomas and Livy brought me."

Henry breathed a sigh of relief at the news the governess had accompanied his daughter, and Thomas had been on hand to protect her. "Ah, that's what young Thomas got up to. I was wondering where he was."

Emily giggled and skipped over to the window, from where she could see Thomas unloading the last of their luggage. "I stole him. He is very good with horses."

Henry couldn't quite stop himself from muttering, "Let's hope he is handy with a gun too."

Emily turned her beaming face back to him. "What was that, Papa?"

"Oh, nothing much, poppet."

Henry stepped behind her and used the opportunity to sweep the square with a practiced eye. Damn, the watcher was nowhere in sight. He looked over to Eliza, who had stepped to the other window, and saw her eyes widen with alarm as she surveyed the square. They both knew the watcher had been there when they had departed for the park. The man's absence could only mean he had deemed the arrival of a young girl in the ducal coach significant enough to desert his post in order to report to his master.

As much as his heart clenched with worry at the situation, he also recognized it for the opportunity it was. He needed to notify Robert, Allen, and Elijah, not only of the fact that Emily was now part of the equation, but more importantly to warn them that Stephanie's kidnapping was imminent, given what they had observed in the park this morning. This was his chance to do so without delay.

He smiled down at his daughter's expectant face and steered her toward the kitchen. "Does Mrs. Tibbit know you are here?"

Emily cocked her head to the side, assuming a pose indicating her infinite patience with her elders. "No, Papa. I just got here."

Henry bit back a grin. Another year or two and she'd be rolling her eyes at him. "Well, you had better go and make your presence known, then. And be sure to tell her to send a tea tray to the library."

Emily turned toward the kitchen, but as she did so, she spotted

Eliza by the other window and remembered her manners. She had seen Eliza enter with her father, but being excited about surprising him, had paid it no mind at the time. Now she bobbed a curtsy, prettily spreading her ankle-length skirts. "Oh, I beg your pardon, miss. How do you do?"

Eliza curtsied back and hoped to God Henry would have a good enough explanation for her presence in his house. Perhaps he wouldn't even introduce her, but simply send her to stay somewhere else while his daughter stayed with him. She knew Henry had to think of his daughter first, but she felt shaky inside at the thought of leaving him.

Eliza gathered her courage and smiled at the beautiful child with the big blue eyes. Her face was so open, every emotion on display, her whole demeanor carefree and innocent. Eliza had been like that once, and she decided right there and then she would do whatever it took to help Henry keep his daughter safe, even if that meant she had to be apart from him.

"I'm very well. Thank you."

To Eliza's surprise, Henry stepped to her side, taking her elbow to lead her farther into the foyer. "I have been remiss. Emily, let me introduce you to Miss Eliza Broad. She had an accident a while ago and is staying here until she is fully recovered."

Eliza almost sagged in relief at the realization she did have a legitimate reason to be in Henry's house, even if the thought of who and what had caused that accident still made her feel a little queasy.

Emily, who had studied Eliza's fashionable fur cape, dainty muff, and comfortable walking shoes with all the attention of a budding Bow Street sleuth, snapped her gaze back up to Eliza's face, intrigued by the mention of an accident.

Henry turned to Eliza. "Eliza, this is my daughter, Emily."

Eliza would have stepped back into the shadow where a mistress belonged, but it seemed Henry wanted her by his side, so she stretched out her hand. "I am so very glad to meet you, Emily."

Emily clasped Eliza's hand, but couldn't help herself, all sophistication and manners forgotten in favor of pure childish enthusiasm. "Was it a very bad accident? Did you break anything? My cousin Bertie broke his leg last year when he fell off his horse. But that was his fault; he should have known Hero wouldn't jump that gate."

Henry almost succeeded in suppressing a snort of amusement, and Eliza, suddenly very light at heart, made a valiant effort to answer in all earnestness. "Well, in that case, he almost deserved to break his leg."

A shadow moved across Eliza's face before she spoke again, but it was gone so fast that even Henry would have missed it had he not known her so well by now. Before he could intervene, however, she was smiling again. "I broke an arm and two ribs falling down the stairs," Eliza admitted.

Emily looked at her with wide eyes and pulled a grimace of sympathy. "Oh! Axel, the stable master, says ribs hurt like the devil." Then, remembering her manners again, she blushed and added, "I hope you are not in pain anymore."

Eliza had had a moment of panic when Emily asked her about her accident, but the child's comments had lightened her mood to the point where now she could barely contain her mirth and was grateful when Henry directed Emily to the rear of the house. "You had better go say your hello to Mrs. Tibbit or she will feel ignored. You can talk to Eliza again later."

Emily grinned, bobbed a curtsy, and skipped out of the foyer and toward the kitchen at the back of the house. Halfway down the corridor, they heard her call out, "Tibby! Tibby, where are you? I have come for a visit, and Papa wants to know if you have chocolate éclairs for tea."

Henry turned back to Eliza and smiled when he saw the grin on her face. Their shared amusement at Emily's antics created a moment's respite before reality once again intruded. His sure hands undid the clasps on her cape, took it off her shoulders, and handed it to her. He placed a quick kiss on Eliza's nose, and they crossed the foyer to take another look out the window.

Finding the square still empty, Henry put his hand at the small of Eliza's back and led her toward the library. "We should use the absence of the watcher to notify Robert and Allen of the state of play and warn them Emily is here. I will have to use some of my men to guard her."

Eliza nodded her understanding. "What can I do?"

Henry stopped in the corridor, considering. "Time may be of the essence. Would you write a note to Robert and one to Allen whilst I see to the delivery and talk to Thomas?"

Eliza smiled her agreement and continued on to the library, where she knew she would find paper and an inkwell. Henry watched her hips sway for a moment as she walked down the corridor and thanked his lucky stars she was with him. Then he turned and marched back to the front of the house.

He got to the foyer just in time to watch Thomas drag in the last of the baggage.

The young man put down the trunk he was carrying, closed the front door, and addressed his employer with a bow. "Sir, I know I was meant to come back straightaway, but when I heard in the kitchens at the castle that the young miss would be coming to London with the duke, I figured I'd best make the journey with them and keep an eye on her." Thomas looked uncomfortable and rubbed the back of his neck, trying to stand up to Henry's scrutiny. "Begging your pardon, sir. I know something is going on and that I brought her into some kind of danger, but your daughter is very determined. And after the old duchess said she could, there wasn't anything I could do to stop her from coming."

Henry sighed and relented. "I know, Thomas. And you did the right thing by offering your services and staying with Miss Emily. In fact, I commend you on your most excellent instincts."

Henry stepped closer, clamped a hand on the young man's shoulder, and waited for him to meet his eyes. "But that still leaves me with a dilemma. You see, you are correct, you did bring her into danger and something big is going on. So I have a question for you." Henry paused for a moment, holding the man's eyes. "Can you handle a gun?"

At first, Thomas didn't know what to think of his employer's question, but then a smile lightened his countenance as understanding dawned in his eyes. "My oldest brother was in the First Riflemen and made sure me and my brothers can shoot straight."

Henry took a deep breath and patted the man's shoulder; that made at least three people on his staff who could handle a weapon.

"Excellent." Henry looked around the foyer as if taking stock of his surroundings, then returned his attention to Thomas. "Leave the trunks for now. I need you to go to the stables and tell Roberts to get his most reliable stable hand mounted up to carry a message out of town."

Henry's eyes searched Thomas's before he continued. "Then I need you to find William and get him to arm you. Then both of you come to the library to discuss how best to keep my house and my daughter safe and secure until my current business is concluded."

Thomas's eyes brimmed with pride at being entrusted with such an important task. He stepped back, gave Henry a credible salute, and turned on his heel to carry out his orders.

CHAPTER TWENTY-SEVEN

TWENTY MINUTES LATER, THE RIDER WAS ON his way to Hampstead with the message for Robert. Charlie, the enterprising young man from the local pub, scurried away into the alley by the kitchen door, carrying a similar missive for Allen. Roberts himself headed off to carry a verbal message to Elijah, who was still stationed close to the Adams's residence, and Henry penned a note to his grandmother to thank her for bringing Emily to town.

Henry hated having to deceive the old lady, but for the sake of his mission, he couldn't afford to arouse her suspicion, nor his cousin's. Both Astor and Hobbs needed to be dealt with, as much for the sake of the local female population as for national security. Henry couldn't let his cousin's rigid sense of political honor get in the way.

Once the notes to Robert and Allen had gone out, Eliza took it upon herself to write a missive to Sara Davis asking her to tea the following morning, hinting at new developments and hoping her new friend might have some ideas of how to help Henry keep Emily safe while traveling around London. It seemed inevitable the girl would want to explore the sights, especially during her father's absence from the house. They could send footmen out with her, but Eliza knew from her experience at Covent Garden that they would be no obstacle to a determined kidnapper.

All the messengers were told to return to the house as inconspicuously as possible, since it had to be assumed the watcher would return to his post before long. As it happened, the last messenger had just departed when William entered the library, tea tray in hand, to report the watcher was just entering the square. William was followed by Thomas, who assured Henry that Emily was safely ensconced at the kitchen table, being spoiled rotten by a doting Mrs. Tibbit.

With Emily out of earshot and no apparent change in Astor's plans due to her arrival, it was now time to decide on the best and most efficient way to defend his home and all in it.

Henry had to go to Hampstead as soon as he got confirmation of Stephanie's kidnapping. He couldn't abandon the girl to the fate Astor had planned for her, nor could he leave the mission for someone else to complete. But there was also no way on God's green earth he would leave his daughter unprotected, so he had no choice but to divide his forces.

Henry invited William and Thomas to join him by the fire. Eliza rose from her seat behind his desk to leave the men to their discussion, but Henry motioned her to stay.

"Eliza, in the bottom left-hand drawer of my desk are some floor plans for this house. Would you find them for me, please?"

Eliza bent to find the papers while Henry poured tea for everyone and then turned to William, who stood at ease by the fire. "Will, please tell me you've kept up your target practice with Daisie."

William knew how serious their present situation was, but grinned with pride as he answered his employer. "Sure did, sir. She's almost as good a shot as me."

Thomas pursed his lips in a silent whistle, but Henry only nodded, expecting nothing less from William. "Good. Tell her to load her gun and keep it on her person at all times. I want her to stay as close to Emily as she can here in the house during the day, and at night she will sleep in her room until this is all over."

William was all business now. "I've already cleaned and loaded it for her, and I'll help her set up a pallet as soon as we're done here."

Henry smiled at his majordomo, for "footman" really didn't begin to describe William's role in his household. "You should have stayed in the army; you were one hell of a sergeant."

William shrugged dismissively. "Well, them nobs didn't want me, did they? Besides, I had me fill of idiots calling the shots."

Henry nodded in complete understanding. "Their loss is clearly my gain. You're in charge here when I have to go up to Hampstead. With Emily here and Astor watching us like a hawk, we will have to prepare for a possible intrusion into the house to harm her."

Both William and Thomas let out a few heartfelt curses, and Eliza, who had located the floor plans, joined them by the fire. "Do you really think Astor would harm Emily?"

Henry handed her a cup of steaming tea and rubbed the bridge of his nose. "She isn't his priority right now. But ultimately I am the target, I just know it, and Astor would hurt her to get at me, I can feel it in my bones."

Eliza swallowed visibly while William cursed some more, then took the plans from her and spread them out on the coffee table. "All right then! Let's make sure no one can get to the little princess."

William's resolute tone and practicality went a long way toward reassuring Henry, and they settled down to work through the problem at hand. Their first line of defense would be the locks on the house's windows and doors, so they decided to check those first.

Next they discussed the creation of an early warning system. Starting with the two doors in the library, Henry worked out a way to use a length of string to connect the door handles with the bell pull so someone in the kitchen would be alerted to an intruder and where he had entered, without the intruder realizing he, or she, had given themselves away.

They also decided it would be best to use the two most reliable stable hands to patrol the garden and mews. The night watchman would make them aware of anything unusual occurring at the front of the house.

But neither of these precautions guaranteed a trained operative wouldn't get into the house and up to Emily's bedroom, so it was imperative for someone to be stationed in the foyer, as well as on the back stairs.

Daisie was the last line of defense inside Emily's bedroom, but the men had no intention of letting an intruder get that far. William and Thomas could stay in town to guard Emily, but they would need to sleep at some point. Everything depended on the two guards in the two access points to the second story being alert at the small hours of the night, when an intrusion into the house was most likely.

Henry briefly contemplated asking Elijah to take over guarding the foyer as soon as Stephanie was on her way to the Emporium with Millie. But not knowing when exactly Hobbs would take Stephanie to Hampstead would make the timing of their trap for Astor impossible. The whole mission could be jeopardized, and that Henry could not justify.

Did Hobbs intend to stick to his usual timetable and bring Stephanie to The Silver Fox with his monthly crop of girls? Or was this job special enough to make an extra trip? He hoped that between Elijah following Stephanie, and Allen chumming around with Hobbs, they wouldn't lose the slippery bastard, and Henry would be informed of any and all developments.

In the meantime, they had to find more men to guard his household.

William scratched his head thoughtfully. "I suppose I'll be settin' up me own pallet in the corridor upstairs, and Thomas can kip in the kitchen so we know if the bells catch 'em out."

Henry studied the plans in front of him. It was a creative solution, using their resources to best advantage, and if the person to be guarded had been any other person than Emily, he would have thought it sufficient, but as things stood . . .

"That's good thinking, and you should both plan on those sleeping arrangements, but we need at least two sets of eyes open and alert and ready to shoot if and when something happens."

Henry looked at Eliza, assessing her, trying to make a decision. She had kept her cool under pressure at the theatre, but she wasn't a trained operative, and he didn't want to expose her to the kind of danger and depravity they would face in Astor's dungeon. On the other hand, leaving her behind seemed a waste of a valuable resource, and this way he could keep an eye on her personally. Perhaps he could keep her out of the dungeon itself until they had dealt with Astor and Hobbs.

"Eliza, I'll have to take the curricle to Hampstead. Would you come with me? The young lady may need a female on hand once we get her away from Astor. I don't hold out much hope she won't be traumatized."

Eliza looked at him with solemn eyes. She swallowed her trepidation at the thought of going down into that dungeon and nodded. "I'll be ready. And don't worry about me, I can wrap up warm."

Henry declined his head in thanks. "Good. That frees up Roberts to drive Emily, if need be, and guard the back stairs at night. But that still leaves us one man short."

Thomas had stayed in the background until now, taking note of what was decided and what needed to be done. But now he gave Henry a thoughtful, almost assessing look. "Sir, if I may. I might have a solution for you."

Henry turned to the young man. "Go on, Thomas."

Thomas gathered his courage and stepped forward. "Sir, my brother, the one who was a First Rifleman, he would be happy to help us out."

Henry liked the idea of another veteran in the house. "Oh, who does he work for? I may be able to borrow him for the time being."

Thomas shifted uncomfortably from foot to foot. "No one, sir."

"Why ever not?" And then it dawned on Henry. It wasn't an unusual story, but it still angered him when he heard about men who had given so much for their country, only to return to a society that prized bodily perfection above all else and consigned them promptly to the proverbial dung heap. "He was injured! How badly?"

Thomas's stance and tone was almost defiant. "He came back from Waterloo without his left leg and minus two fingers on his left hand, so no one will give him a job. But he's still the best shot I ever saw and he is loyal to the bone." Then, after a beat, he said in a more quiet voice, "He needs someone to give him a chance, sir."

Henry didn't even hesitate. "Is he in London?"

"Aldgate, sir."

Henry pulled a few coins out of his pocket and handed them to Thomas. "Go and get him! This is for a hackney cab, and be sure to bring him to the house through the mews. And tell him to bring his rifle."

Thomas beamed at him and took the coins. "Thank you, sir. You won't regret this."

Henry had never regretted a single thing he had done for his comrades, but he needed to meet the man to know where to place him most effectively. "How soon do you think he can be here?"

Thomas could hardly contain his excitement and waited impatiently to be dismissed by his employer. He was literally hopping from foot to foot. "I'll have him here by mid-afternoon."

Henry grinned at the young man's obvious eagerness. "Off you go, then, and come find me the moment you are back. But use your discretion with Miss Emily and any visitors we might have."

Thomas managed a "Yes, sir" before he rushed to the door, where he collided with Mrs. Tibbit.

The houskeeper looked sharply from one to the other when she saw both Thomas and William conferring with the master, and drew herself up to her full height. "Oh, that's where the two of you got off to. I was wondering who was going to open the door for Her Grace when she arrives."

Henry and William exchanged a chagrined look, and Henry gave his man a discreet nod. William bowed himself out of the room and turned to the put-out housekeeper, addressing her in the most proper English he could manage. "I shall see to it Her Grace is suitably greeted, but I don't anticipate her arrival before afternoon tea. Miss Emily said she was still resting after her journey."

Before the two servants could get into a discussion over who knew better how to run a gentleman's house, Henry stepped in. "Where is my daughter at present, and who is with her?"

Mrs. Tibbit caught herself, blushed furiously, and turned her full attention to Henry. "Begging your pardon, sir. Miss Holms took Miss Emily to the back garden to see if they could make snow angels in the old snow that's still lying back there, and then the young miss was hoping to persuade Miss Holms to escort her to the stables." She paused for a moment, then remembered her reason for coming to the library in the first place. "Oh, and lunch will be served for you and Miss Eliza in the breakfast room in fifteen minutes."

"Thank you, Tibby."

Mrs. Tibbit lost some of her starch at the use of her nickname and turned to leave. Henry stepped to the back window to check whether Emily and her governess were still in the garden. Finding them busy trying to make a snowman out of icy snow, he turned to William. "Would you mind escorting the ladies to the stables before they freeze to death out there? I will meet you there as soon as we've had a bite to eat." Then he turned to Eliza. "Come, my sweet. Let's go make ourselves a little more comfortable before lunch."

Eliza smiled and wound her hand into the crook of his arm.

The day progressed without further incident. In fact, all seemed so quiet and normal, Eliza was reminded of the calm before a storm. But the sun kept shining and the crows kept cackling their complaints in the bare tree outside the library window.

Henry spent the early afternoon with his daughter in the stables, where Emily visited with old four-hoofed favorites and made new friends. Eliza spent her time reading and waiting for messages, but only two arrived, and neither of them necessitated calling Henry back to the house.

The first note was from Sara Davis, announcing her arrival for morning tea at eleven o'clock the next day. The second confirmed the Dowager Duchess of Avon's intention to grace her grandson's household for afternoon tea. Hardly a surprise, but a source of anxiety for Eliza nevertheless.

Henry had introduced her to his daughter, so it stood to reason he expected her to meet his noble grandmother as well. Meeting another of Henry's relatives should have been a fairly simple thing, but as far as Eliza was concerned, she might as well have been asked to meet the queen. She decided not to dwell on the prospect; that would likely lead to a case of the vapors. She did, however, resolve to choose her wardrobe with extra care, and then she returned her focus to the task at hand.

Roberts got back, but had no further news from the Adams household.

At around three in the afternoon, Henry, Emily, and the governess returned to the house. Mrs. Tibbit whisked the girl upstairs for a hot bath to warm her back up after being out in the cold for so long. The good housekeeper also informed Emily she had pressed a pretty frock for her so she would be presentable for afternoon tea with the duchess.

Emily went upstairs grumbling that a cup of hot chocolate would have done the trick to warm her up. Furthermore, her Grossmama never placed much importance on such trifling things as pretty frocks when she had a heavily pregnant cat and an Arabian filly to report, but her objections fell on deaf ears.

SHORTLY AFTER EMILY HAD BEEN escorted up to her room, Thomas and his brother, Jack, came in through the kitchen. There they encountered Henry and Eliza in the process of making tea, since all the servants were busy fetching water up the stairs for Emily's bath. Henry bade the brothers enter and join them for a cup.

Jack had the drawn and slightly haunted look of an old warrior, but his handshake was strong and his gaze sure and direct. His leg was amputated above the knee, so he walked with the assistance of a crutch, but he managed it well.

It was clear the man before them had had all illusions knocked out of him; however, the world had not beaten him down yet. His pride kept him upright and it would not let him give up. Henry knew the type and liked him on sight. He suspected that whenever this man committed himself, he gave his all.

Over tea and a plate of sandwiches, it was decided Jack would be stationed in the foyer, by the front staircase, and would periodically patrol the front corridor from ten in the evening till the house awoke at five in the morning. During the same time period, Roberts would be stationed in the servants' staircase to secure the back of the house.

After Roberts had been informed of his new duties, William made sure all members of the staff who could handle a weapon were adequately armed, then the two night guards were sent to sleep for a few hours.

For simplicity's sake, Thomas offered his brother his bed in his room under the eaves, and went about setting up a pallet close to the bell pull board in the kitchen.

William went to hide his pallet in a closet on the first-floor landing, then both footmen returned to the foyer ready for the duchess's arrival.

Once all the arrangements to secure the house for the night had been made, Eliza went to her room to wash the day off her face. She rearranged her hair and attired herself in one of her most fashionable visiting gowns.

The gown was made of the deep orange silk Henry had admired in Madame Clarise's window and was bordered at the neckline, wrists, and hem with a reddish-brown velvet that made Eliza's eyes appear dark and alluring. The sleeves were slightly puffed at the shoulders, but tapered to narrow wrists secured with three brown velvet buttons. The waist was lower than the usual empire waist, and the skirt flared wider to fall in soft waves to the floor.

Daisie was busy elsewhere, so Eliza was thankful her corset was already laced tight and she could manage to fasten all the little velvet-covered buttons in the back.

She twisted her hair into a knot at the nape of her neck. It was simple enough to be modest, and because of the nature of her curly hair, it was still soft enough to be becomingly feminine. She finished off her toilette with the gold leaf necklace Henry had given her and gave her appearance a critical once-over in the mirror.

The young woman who looked back at her looked nothing like the tavern wench Henry had picked up on the way into Hampstead. This young woman looked fashionable and sophisticated, like she belonged in the house of a gentleman. Now if only she could trust that her manners and speech wouldn't let her down.

CHAPTER TWENTY-EIGHT

HER CONFIDENCE BOLSTERED BY THE BEAUTIFUL dress, Eliza draped a lacy cream-colored wool shawl around herself and went downstairs to await the exalted visitor in the front drawing room.

Henry arrived shortly after, clad in a blue-gray dress coat fashioned from superfine wool, cream-colored pantaloons, and an azure blue satin vest. He had made the effort to shave, and his shoes were polished to a high shine. The blue in his vest and around the room brought out the color of his eyes and made Eliza smile with appreciation.

He crossed the room to her and bowed over her hands. "I knew that orange would look stunning on you, particularly in this room."

She grinned. "I could say the same of you, Henry. We both match the decor quite well."

But despite the smiles, she couldn't stop fidgeting, giving her nerves away. Henry noticed and stepped closer to bring her hand up to his lips. "Don't be nervous, Eliza. My grandmother may be a duchess, but she is no prude and knows to value people for who they are. She also knows I would never introduce her, or Emily, to anyone unless I was assured of their merit."

Eliza bowed her head at the compliment. Then she straightened her spine and met his gaze. "I won't disappoint you."

Henry smiled and stroked her cheek. "You never do."

She held his gaze for a moment, reading what lay unspoken in his eyes. Far too many people, many of them women, had disappointed Henry, and she never wanted to be one of them. She turned her face into his palm and kissed it, until Henry stepped back and led her to the fireplace, where the two of them settled on one of the two sofas and used the time to review the day's events.

THE SUN HAD ALREADY SET and the square was draped in deep shadows when the formidable vision of Ruth Redwick, Prussian princess and Dowager Duchess of Avon, stepped from her town coach assisted by William and swept through the front door into the foyer.

There she removed her hat and gloves while graciously inquiring about the household. "You look positively rushed off your feet, William. Is my grandson keeping you busy?"

William took her hat and gloves and placed them on a side table. "He is indeed, Your Grace. But I like it that way." He helped her out of her dark blue fur-trimmed spencer.

She probed further: "I'm sure Emily's unannounced arrival has thrown the household into a tailspin."

William allowed himself a small grin. "She does liven the house up, Your Grace. She should be down in a moment."

She patted his arm knowingly as he led her to the drawing room door. "I'm sure she will have much to report on the content of Henry's stables."

That got a chuckle out of William as he preceded her into the room to announce her. "Her Grace, the Dowager Duchess of Avon!"

Both Henry and Eliza rose at the announcement. With a wide smile and open arms, Henry strode toward the old lady with the regal posture and the tight steel-gray curls surrounding her delicate face. Ruth Redwick took a few measured steps into the room and returned Henry's embrace with all the enthusiasm of a doting grandmother. "Henry, *mein Junge. Was sind diese Geschäfte die dich in London festhalten?*"

Henry bussed both her cheeks in the French fashion. "Oh, *eine schrecklich langweilige Angelegenheit.*"

Eliza couldn't understand their German, but their banter sounded easy and their manner with each other was affectionate. She stayed in the background, admiring the simple elegance of the duchess's high-necked dark blue gown, but the duchess spied her before long.

"Oh, how rude of me to speak my native tongue when you have a guest. Henry, where are your manners? Introduce me!"

Henry offered his grandmother his arm to lead her to his house-guest. Blushing furiously, Eliza sank into the deepest curtsy of her life.

Grandmother and grandson traversed the length of the elegant room at a measured pace. By the time they arrived in front of Eliza, her unpracticed legs were trembling and her head was bowed low.

Ruth Redwick might have been born a princess, but she abhorred ceremony. In fact, it was a major point of contention between her and her granddaughter-in-law, the current duchess. The dowager certainly didn't expect to be troubled with an excess of pomp in the house of her favorite grandson. "Goodness gracious, Henry, help the poor child up. My knees ache just looking at her."

Henry immediately held out his hand to Eliza and helped her out of her cramped pose, steadying her before he pulled her forward toward his grandmother. "Grossmama, may I present Miss Eliza Broad. Miss Broad had a series of rather traumatic experiences and is staying here until she is fully recovered."

It did not escape the dowager duchess's sharp eyes that Eliza moved a half-step closer into the shelter of Henry's body at the mention of those experiences. Neither did she miss that Henry kept hold of Eliza's hand while he introduced her. It had been twelve long years since her grandson had looked at any woman close to his own age without suspicion. Her Grace saw none when he looked at this one.

"Eliza, this is my grandmother, the Dowager Duchess of Avon and, aside from Emily, my favorite relative."

Her Grace's face spread into a very undignified grin, and Eliza, who had finally raised her head, had to smile. There was so much of Henry in the expression, Eliza couldn't help but like her.

She impulsively held out her hand, which the dowager duchess took and shook. "I am so very pleased to meet you, Your Grace."

The old lady noted the polite but warm greeting, the firm handshake, and the pleasant timbre of Eliza's voice, and she thought she detected the slightest hint of cockney in the girl's accent. Eliza possessed a delicate face and a pretty figure, but the accent didn't match the elegance of her gown, so the dowager duchess suspected Henry had supplied the latter.

"Oh, the pleasure is entirely mine, my dear."

Henry might have bought the dress, this Eliza might even be his mistress, but Ruth Redwick had a good feeling about the young woman with the soft brown eyes. She thought it most encouraging that the same softness was mirrored in her grandson's eyes when he looked at her. So she urged Eliza to take a seat next to her on the sofa and went about the business of getting to know her.

"I take it Mrs. Tibbit will arrive with the tea and something scrumptious presently." Chuckling, she added, "Chocolate éclairs if I know Emily."

Her Grace observed Henry finding Eliza's eyes and the two of them sharing an amused smile, and hope swelled in the old lady's heart. She turned back to Eliza. "I take it you have met my great-granddaughter?"

Eliza smiled a little nervous smile and played with the strings of her reticule, not at all sure a duchess would approve of her great-grandchild meeting her father's mistress. But she had to trust Henry knew what he was doing when he introduced her to his relations. "Yes, Your Grace, I did, and I do believe she mentioned chocolate éclairs to Mrs. Tibbit."

Mrs. Tibbit chose that moment to arrive with the tea trolley, laden not only with dainty little cucumber-and-ham sandwiches, but also a three-tiered cake tray, holding no less than three different kinds of éclairs. The traditional ones drizzled with chocolate, Henry's favorites glazed with caramel, and Mrs. Tibbit's specialty: chocolate éclairs filled with custard rather than cream.

As the good housekeeper rolled the trolley toward the little group by the fire, the three of them exchanged amused glances, and Eliza stopped thinking of the old lady as the Dowager Duchess of Avon and started thinking of her as Henry's grandmother. She busied herself with the tea tray while Her Grace exchanged pleasantries with the housekeeper.

"Mrs. Tibbit! Éclairs! You shouldn't have."

Mrs. Tibbit beamed at the dowager duchess. "Oh, it was no trouble, Your Grace. The little miss told me this morning Sir Henry had a hankering for them, and I know you like them. So, no trouble at all."

The housekeeper retreated, and Eliza inquired how their guest took her tea.

"Just a drop of milk, dear."

Eliza added milk and handed the tea to the old lady. Henry's grandmother carried her age well. Her hands and face were lined with fine wrinkles, but that made them no less delicate. Still beautiful, her eyes shone with kindness and keen intelligence, and her smile had a certain mischievousness to it that was youthful and most appealing.

Eliza handed Henry his tea and relaxed enough to bite into a tiny ham sandwich when the old lady decided it was time for her to hear Eliza's story.

"So tell me, dear, what were these distressing events Henry spoke of?"

Eliza panicked and shoved the rest of the sandwich in her mouth so she would have an excuse not to answer right away. She threw Henry a pleading look and prayed he would answer in her stead, since she had no idea what he intended his grandmother to know about her.

Henry did jump into the breach, but to her astonishment, he told his grandmother exactly what had happened. From finding her on the road outside Hampstead after her stepfather had beaten her within an inch of her life to Wilkins organizing her capture so he could sell her to a pimp to get his money back.

Henry didn't elaborate on any of the events, and he did not mention Astor or their business in Hampstead, but he left out nothing concerning Eliza's need for shelter in his house. All through his explanation he held his grandmother's gaze, but once he had finished his tale, he sent Eliza a reassuring smile and plucked a caramel éclair from the tray with his bare fingers.

"Besides, I truly enjoy her company." He bit into his éclair, chewed happily, perhaps even defiantly, and let the implications of that statement hang between them all in the room.

Eliza blushed crimson with the full fury of her mortification and glared daggers at Henry, wishing she could kick his shin for being so obvious.

The dowager duchess burst into a delighted peal of laughter. "Henry, you naughty, naughty boy. Well, pardon me for bringing Emily to town and spoiling the privacy of your love nest." Then she utterly astounded Eliza by patting her hand in a motherly fashion and winking at her. "Don't mind him, dear. He is terribly wicked for embarrassing you so, but he knows I'm not easily shocked. In fact, you should regard it as an honor. You are the first girl he has ever introduced me to, so he must think a great deal of you."

Eliza managed a smile and relaxed just a little.

Gesturing for Eliza to refill his tea, Henry elaborated, "As you can see, Eliza isn't some Covent Garden strumpet, so I have no qualms about Emily getting acquainted with her. But you know how people talk, and I really do have business keeping me in town, so it might be an idea to take Emily back to Avon sooner rather than later."

Eliza had refilled Henry's cup, fixed it to his liking, and tried to reconcile herself to the knowledge that Henry's grandmother now knew she was his mistress. But when he mentioned taking Emily back to Avon, she realized what he was doing and all her embarrassment seemed suddenly petty.

Henry caught her gaze and held it firm. "No offense intended to you, my sweet."

Eliza handed him his cup and held his gaze, trying to convey her understanding. "None taken. You are just trying to protect your daughter; I expect nothing less from you."

Her Grace let her sharp eye wander from one to the other and back again, wondering what she was missing, but ultimately decided the trust and affection evident between the pair was encouraging in itself. It certainly wouldn't hurt Emily to see her father happy in the company of a woman for a change. Sadly, the child had never witnessed a truly loving union between two adults since none of Her Grace's children or grandchildren had followed her example and married for love.

She heaved a sigh and directed herself to Henry. "I hate to admit it, but I am an old woman and my weary bones cannot make that journey more than once within the space of a week, so you are stuck with the little dervish for the time being."

Henry shrugged as if to say, *It was worth a try*. Eliza nodded at him reassuringly, and Her Grace had to admit she liked the intimacy of the non-verbal communication between the two, although she disliked not being able to work out the subtext between them.

Miss Eliza Broad obviously had neither family nor connections, and therefore Henry couldn't marry her, but at least his heart was no longer frozen solid.

In the midst of all these ruminations, Emily burst into the room. She was freshly scrubbed, her silver-blond hair curled into corkscrew ringlets and held back off her face with a comb. She was dressed in a white gown adorned with a blue sash and bows, and twirled her full skirt around her legs as she skipped toward them.

"Look, Grossmama, I match the room."

The dowager duchess opened her arms wide, smiling even wider. "*Komm her, liebchen*. You look absolutely lovely, especially in this room."

Emily threw herself onto the sofa and into her great-grandmother's arms. The dowager embraced her, then when she had sat back she patted her cheek and inquired, "So what did you find in your father's stables?"

Emily turned to Henry with a triumphant smile. "See, Papa, Grossmama cares far more about horses than a pretty dress."

She turned to Her Grace and launched into a detailed description of the new Arabian filly and a rapturous report on the winter kittens they could all expect in the next day or two.

Eliza watched the easy rapport between the three while they demolished the contents of the tea trolley over the next hour. It was nice to be with a family again, even if she didn't belong.

HENRY'S GRANDMOTHER LEFT JUST BEFORE the dinner hour, citing her need for rest as an excuse not to partake in the meal. Henry knew eating large meals late in the evening gave her indigestion, so he raised no objection despite Emily's vehement protests.

The rest of the evening and that night passed without incident, and when the sun rose over the rooftops of Mayfair, all seemed right with the world. Yet Henry couldn't rest easy. An innocent girl was about to be kidnapped, and he was still no closer to finding out why. Emily was possibly in harm's way, and the watcher in the square was still at his post.

The breakfast hour brought missives from both Allen and Robert. One reported another uneventful night of drinking and carousing with Hobbs, but promised to be extra vigilant in light of Emily's arrival. The other assured Henry all was in place in Hampstead. Having placed lookouts in strategic positions, Robert was confident he would hear about any major development without delay.

Henry had spent the night alone due to the presence of his daughter in the house, and had had plenty of time to contemplate his options. It was clear he had to deal with Astor in a way that would keep

Emily out of his reach permanently, and that meant her safety hinged on the success of this mission.

With that in mind, Henry took Emily on a morning visit to Lady Greyson, to recruit his godmother into helping keep Emily safe. He also felt he should let the Old Man know about his concerns for his daughter, in case something unforeseen happened. He hoped to find an opportunity to slip away for a time while Emily amused herself with Lady Greyson's collection of ugly, yapping lapdogs.

As luck would have it, they found Lady Greyson ensconced on her great divan with the Dowager Duchess of Avon at her side and surrounded by said ugly, yapping lapdogs.

Emily was instantly enraptured by a tan-and-black pug the size of a rat and barely managed a civil greeting for Lady Greyson and her great-grandmother. Her Grace, well acquainted with Emily's love for anything on four legs, saved the situation.

"*Guten morgen, liebchen*, bring the puppy and come sit by me."

Emily scooped up the little wiggling creature and rushed to her great-grandmother's side while Henry bent over Lady Greyson's hand and wondered how he could slip away.

"My felicitations on this fine morning. I hope the January cold does not bother your joints too much."

Lady Greyson tapped her fan over Henry's knuckles and grinned, then she winked at him, indicating she knew what he was really asking. "Poppycock, my boy. In fact, I was just about to suggest we kidnap the fair Emily and take her for a spin around the park while the sunshine lasts."

Henry sent a grateful smile to his godmother just as Emily let out an excited shriek. "Oh please, Papa! We could take Aunt Greyson's dogs for a walk."

"By all means, poppet. Why don't you take William and Thomas as reinforcements so the wolf pack doesn't wreak havoc with the ducks?"

MEANWHILE, ELIZA HAD MORNING TEA with Sara Davis and updated her on the state of play. After Eliza disclosed to her that Emily had arrived in London, that Henry considered her a target, and that the whole operation must now be handled all the more delicately, Sara promised to redouble her efforts to find out who Stephanie Adams's father was. She, like Henry, considered that to be the key to unraveling this entire sordid business and confronting Astor. But there was something else about this affair that didn't sit right with her. She shook her head and sighed.

"Eliza, my dear, I do believe this smells of politics in the most unpleasant way. And seeing as one of Elridge's sons is involved, I do think it prudent for Henry to find out what bills his cousin is working on at present."

Sara kissed Eliza's cheek, and before Eliza could ask her to elaborate, she swept out of the house in her haste to get to a meeting with the solicitor who paid the bills for the Adams household.

Having nothing further to do for the rest of the day, Eliza headed upstairs to shed her fashionable teal silk gown with the green piping she'd worn for Sara's visit, and changed into her marvelously warm burgundy wool dress. On a hunch, she added pantalets and an extra petticoat to her outfit and laid out her gray wool cape, a thick gray wool shawl, and her hat, in case they had to depart in a hurry. Then she headed to the library to read while she waited for events to unfold.

CHAPTER TWENTY-NINE

AROUND THREE IN THE AFTERNOON, CHARLIE
arrived to relay a message from Elijah, informing Henry that Millie
had arrived at the Adams household, and considering the carriage she
had left waiting at the curb, it looked like she planned to take Stephanie on an outing.

Eliza, who was the only one in the house to receive the message,
immediately handed a penny to the boy and sent him back to find
out whether Stephanie was indeed going to the Emporium. Then she
went in search of Henry to apprise him of the development.

She found him in the stables conferring with Roberts while they
watched Emily playing with the brand new kittens. Henry knew she
had news the moment Eliza entered the stables. He stepped quietly
toward her so they could talk away from Emily's sharp hearing, but
also so he could kiss her in private. He had missed her the night before, and Emily had already been at the breakfast table by the time
Eliza had come downstairs, so it had been almost twenty-four hours
since the last time he had held her.

Henry pulled Eliza behind the door of the tack room and claimed
her lips before she could voice any protests. But she had none. Eliza
melted right into his arms and gave herself to the pleasure of the kiss
until Henry reluctantly pulled back. "You look like you have news to
impart, my sweet."

Eliza nodded and steadied herself on his shoulders, her knees a little shaky after the passionate kiss, but keen to tell Henry her news. "Elijah sent Charlie to tell us Millie brought a carriage to take Stephanie for an outing, or so we assume. Elijah will follow them if Stephanie goes with her without her mother."

Henry listened intently and wound one of her loose curls around his finger as if it helped him to think better. A stony resolve settled over him as he straightened and held her gaze.

"So it begins."

An hour later, Henry had sent covert messages to both Robert and Allen, conferred with William about Emily's security, and ordered his curricle and horses to be kept at the ready, all without the watcher in the square being any the wiser.

Around five in the afternoon, Henry and Eliza opted for an early dinner with Emily. Thankfully, the pint-sized tyrant was tired from the day's adventures and showed herself willing to retire after her belly had been filled and her sweet tooth indulged.

The governess led the girl upstairs, Jack moved into his position in the foyer, and Henry settled in the library with Eliza to await further news. They were both clad in dark, practical clothing suitable for a cold January night, just in case they had to rush out at a moment's notice. Although Henry and Robert thought it unlikely Hobbs would break with old habits and take Stephanie to Hampstead this very night, there was no guarantee he wouldn't.

They had learned Astor chose his girls from the crop Hobbs brought to The Silver Fox every month, and Henry expected them both to want to stick to that cover. It was thought most likely Hobbs would take Stephanie to wherever he was holding the other girls he intended to break in this month and deliver her during his regular visit.

This theory was substantiated by the fact Astor was still resident in his townhouse and was currently at his father's mansion on Berkley Square, according to the man Sara Davis had following him. But one could never know for certain what the opponent's next move would be, especially not one as wily as De Sade had proved himself.

The first indication that not all was as they had anticipated came at the stroke of the quarter hour after six. Charlie stumbled into the kitchen, mud-splattered and out of breath, and was instantly ushered into the library. The boy ripped the cap off his head as soon as he spotted Henry and tried to wipe his dirty face with his sleeve, still heaving for breath.

To allow the boy a moment to compose himself, Henry turned to William. "Did anyone see him enter the house?"

William knew what Henry was asking. "No, sir, Jack has his eye on the watcher, and he hasn't stirred."

Henry breathed a sigh of relief. "Now is not the time to tip our hand."

It spoke of Henry's state of anxiety that he voiced the thought out loud, but it prompted Eliza to step close to his side, calming him somewhat. Henry turned his attention to the boy, noting the air of confusion about him, and could not stop his stomach from churning. "What news do you bring, Charlie?"

The boy shook his head and spread out his hands in a helpless gesture. "I can't find neither of them."

Charlie seemed to think that would explain everything, so Henry prompted, "Who can't you find and where can't you find them?"

Charlie shrugged, but his eyes brimmed with unshed tears of frustration. "Elijah, Miss Stephanie, that Millie trollop. When I got back to the Adams's 'ouse there was none of them there, so I 'opped a couple of cabs and got meself to the Emporium in Knightsbridge where Elijah said 'e might be headin'. But I couldn't find them, so I come back 'ere."

He let out a big breath, aware he'd let Sir Henry down, but not sure how or why. Henry ruthlessly tamped down his own sense of foreboding and reassured the boy. "You did well coming to tell me, Charlie. Did you notice anything unusual along your travels?"

Scrunching up his face in concentration, Charlie thought for a moment, then his eyes flew open. "The fake footman!"

Henry's keen eyes were on the boy. "Go on."

Charlie rubbed his head, trying to put his thoughts in order. "I sneaked in the Emporium to find them. They're all hoity-toity in there, don't like grubby paws on all them pretty things. I went all 'round till one of them clerks chased me out the back door, and there was more people back there than in front, so I 'ad a look-see. I reckon I saw Millie's coach, but it was too far, and then there was this boxy old coach. Big old ugly thing and it was rockin', so I took a gander inside, but this big burly bloke in a livery got me by the scruff of me neck and shoved me 'ard like. There was another one on the box with the coachman and one be'ind. Then the coach started movin' off and the burly bloke jumped on the board. But 'e was no footman. 'Is breeches don't match and 'is jacket was tight like. No toff who can afford liveries is gonna put up with 'im being that sloppy."

He gave his head a sharp nod to emphasize the rightness of his statement and looked from Henry to Eliza expectantly. Henry's lip quirked up just a fraction when his gaze met Eliza's, but their amusement was short-lived.

"You are quite right, Charlie. Did you, by any chance, see in which direction the coach went?"

Charlie nodded eagerly. "Sure did, gov. East they went, back to town."

Henry smiled at the boy, handing him a crown, and the boy beamed back at him. "You did well, Charlie. Go to the kitchen and have Mrs. Tibbit feed you supper. And tell her I said you can sleep by the fire there. Unless you have to get home, of course."

Charlie's eyes went as wide as saucers. "Thank you, sir."

William gave his employer a grateful nod and led the lad back to the kitchen.

Henry took a worried-looking Eliza by the hand and led her to the sofa. "Don't worry, sweet. Allen is on Hobbs, so he will find out where he takes the girl."

But that confidence was shattered less than ten minutes later when Allen's servant was shown into the room. The man looked utterly frazzled, though was trying valiantly to present a stoic countenance. Henry stepped toward him. "Good Lord, whatever happened, Rick?"

The man managed a bow in greeting and took a deep breath. "I'm sorry to be the bearer of bad news, sir, but Hobbs managed to ditch Mr. Strathem."

Allen was the wiliest of his operatives, which was why Henry had put him on Hobbs, and still the pimp had outwitted him. Henry could only hope Hobbs had simply intended to get rid of an inconvenient drinking companion for the day and was still unaware he was being shadowed.

"Report!"

Rick instantly calmed at the military command; he clicked his boot heels together and straightened his spine. "Sir. I've been tailing Hobbs and his bully boys, supporting Mr. Strathem's efforts. Yesterday I noticed a fancy carriage drive up to Hobbs's local, and he stepped up to it for a minute to talk to the fancy piece inside. Not his usual type of female; she was showy but classy."

"Millie, no doubt," Henry mumbled under his breath.

Rick, having no knowledge of the woman, merely continued his report. "After he came back into the pub, he seemed well pleased with himself and the world and sent some of his boys on an errand. Then he took the rest of them, including Mr. Allen, on a bender. They all got roaring drunk, and around six this morning he gifted Mr. Allen with one of his 'pigeons.' Hobbs helped himself to another one of his girls, and they both disappeared into private rooms. The rest of them passed out where they sat, and I went home assuming my employer would be right behind me. When he didn't get home right away, I assumed he took the girl up on her offer, which was unusual but not unheard of, so I went to bed."

Rick glanced in Eliza's direction, clearly uncomfortable with having to mention this in front of her. "I beg your pardon, miss."

Eliza waved him off. "Don't mention it. What became of Mr. Strathem?"

"The girl must have given him something."

Henry was pacing the room now, getting more agitated by the second. "Damnation! Where is he now and in what condition?"

Rick swallowed audibly. "He stumbled home about two hours ago, but it took a pot of coffee and a cold bath to sober him up enough to tell me that Hobbs slipped away."

Henry paced and rubbed the back of his head. Allen never drank on the job, so the drugging had to be deliberate.

Eliza fidgeted in her seat but finally rose to intercept Henry's path. "Something is not right. Hobbs is putting too much effort into this to treat her like all the other girls. Do you think he could be taking her straight to Hampstead?"

Henry paused long enough to squeeze her hand in reassurance. "I think we have to consider that possibility now." Then he went to his desk and pulled out the map of Hampstead and the heath, folded it, and handed it to Rick. "Has your master had time to acquire a fast horse yet?"

Rick, eager for somebody else to make the decisions, nodded in the affirmative.

"Go home, get the horse readied, and load his pistols. Then sober him up enough so he can ride, give him this map, and tell him to go to the mausoleum on the heath unless I send word otherwise before he is ready to depart."

Eliza headed for the door and into the corridor as she spoke. "I'll go and get our cloaks and have the curricle brought around. Are you sending a message to Viscount Fairly? I'll send word to the stables for a groom to get ready to carry it, if you like."

Henry smiled his thanks and nodded. "And send William to me. It's time to take out the watcher."

At that moment, Elijah stormed down the corridor toward the library. "No need, I've already taken care of him, and your man Thomas is out there waiting to intercept the man who relieves him for the night."

Eliza hurried to take care of her tasks, assuming Elijah's arrival meant their imminent departure. In the meantime, Henry fixed Elijah with a penetrating stare. "I do hope you didn't lose them too."

Elijah saluted promptly, knowing from experience that Henry was perilously close to unleashing his wrath upon somebody if things did not start going his way soon. "No, sir. I followed them to Tottenham Court Road and north to Hampstead Road, where they put a rider on the lead horse so they could keep up their pace in the dark. They are headed up Haverstock Hill and should be in Hampstead within the hour."

Henry stood and listened, assimilating the information given. Then he took up his relentless pacing once more and finally roared with frustration.

"Goddamn it all to hell. Why can't the bastard stick to his own bloody routine? There he is, dragging girls up to The Silver Fox once a month like clockwork for a bloody decade, then bloody Astor snaps his fingers and off he goes making a special bloody delivery. The stupid git!"

An appreciative chuckle came from the open door into the hall.

"I haven't heard you swear like that since Waterloo. Do you feel better for it, sir?"

Henry whipped around to face William, fury still blazing in his eyes. He gave his old comrade a curt nod, gathered the composure of command around him like a cloak, and addressed himself to all the men assembled. "Let's work this situation to our advantage. All is in place, so all this means is that we have to strike tonight instead of having a week to fine-tune everything. For the girl, this may be an advantage; at least she doesn't have to spend a week in Hobbs's dubious care."

Henry drew himself up to his full height, looked each man square in the eye, and cleared his throat. "Gentlemen! This is a big mission, an important mission. But we are professionals and we have managed this sort of thing before, so let's make a good job of it."

All three men stood to attention and saluted in unison. Henry acknowledged it with a nod and turned to each man to give him his assignment. "Rick, go and get your master on his feet as fast as you can. You best take one of my horses and go with him so he doesn't break his neck along the way."

"Yes, sir," was Rick's only reply before he hurried toward the back of the house and the mews.

"Elijah, you had best go with him and have Roberts saddle you a horse too. I need you to go to The Silver Fox and find out if they came through there. You know William's mates, they should still be propped up at the bar. Send one of them to Hobbs's cottage to see whether they took her there. If you still haven't found them, Riley is stable master at the inn across the road. Ask him and tell him we will likely need a room later, but to keep it quiet. I'll be heading straight to the heath, so meet me there."

"I've got it, sir."

And Henry knew he did. Elijah was the best tracker he had ever encountered. Even in the most obscure corners of Portugal and Spain he had always found what he'd been sent out to seek.

Henry strode to his desk, intent on writing to Robert and ordering him to the entrance of the tunnel. His gut told him this would all be finished by the end of the night, but what it would cost, heaven only knew.

"William, you know what to do."

"Yes, sir! Sir, wouldn't you rather leave Miss Eliza here?"

Henry heaved a great sigh, regarding William with solemn eyes. "Of course I would. But I dare not. She knows Hampstead and its people better than any of us. I may well need her. Not to mention Miss Stephanie. I still don't know who her father is, and another female may be the only way to salvage her reputation."

He dragged a weary hand over his face and took up his quill. "God, I hope we manage to spring the trap and get to the girl before he does something truly awful to her."

PRECISELY SEVEN MINUTES LATER, HENRY'S groom was mounted and handed a missive with the seal still sticky and warm. The young man had been apprised of the urgency of the matter and disappeared in a cloud of dust heading due north, while Henry handed Eliza into the curricle, swung himself up, and urged his team east on Mortimer Street and then north toward Hampstead Road as fast as he dared, considering the dark but still crowded streets.

When they crossed Regent Street, Eliza looked south, and thanks to the gas lamps there, could just make out the time on the clock tower in Oxford Circus. It was a few minutes before eight o'clock. She wondered briefly where the time had gone, and then she worried that three hours had already passed since Miss Stephanie had been abducted. How scared she must be.

It would take Henry well over an hour to drive to Hampstead in the as-yet moonless night. She didn't think Hobbs would hurt the girl for fear of damaging his merchandise, but if he took her straight to Astor, then she could be delivered to the monster at this very moment, and Eliza knew from bitter experience just how much pain could be inflicted in an hour.

They made good time as long as the front windows of townhouses and other dwellings illuminated their way, but once they reached the bottom of Haverstock Hill, they had to slow to a walk. Henry knew the road well enough, but the carriage lamps didn't penetrate much farther than the horses' heads, and without even a sliver of moonlight, he was putting his team at risk, even at this pace.

Eliza thanked whoever was up there looking out for battered women everywhere that the white pebble paths of the newly landscaped Regent's Park would be much easier to follow than this muddy road. At least Elijah and the messenger were making good time, but there had to be something they could do to get up the hill faster.

She turned her attention to the carriage lamp in front of her right foot. "Can you take out these lamps and carry them?"

Henry didn't know what she was thinking, but was more than willing to entertain suggestions. "Yes, there is a lever on the right side. You move it and then you can lift the lamp right out of the casing. But the top of these things gets deucedly hot, so you can't really carry them whilst they are lit."

Eliza lifted the lever and wrapped her scarf around the handle so she could lift the lamp out. Then she scooted herself back onto the bench, held the lamp on each side, and lifted it up as far as her arms would reach. The higher she held the lamp, the farther its beam reached and the easier it was for Henry to see the road.

"Clever girl! But it's far too heavy; you won't be able to hold it up for long."

"Just get us up the damned hill, Henry, as quick as you can."

Henry threw her a sideways glance, but deduced from the determined set of her jaw that there was no point in arguing. He urged the team into a trot. That of course increased the jostle of the curricle, which in turn resulted in the light beam dancing wildly.

"Try balancing it on your head to steady it."

Eliza did as he suggested. It only lowered the lamp by a fraction and much improved the stability of the light beam and her ability to hold the lamp for an extended period. They were unlikely to make up any time this way, but at least they weren't falling behind any farther.

Once they had made it up Haverstock Hill, they turned right into Downshire Hill Road and then left onto Willow Road. Henry drove farther north along the bottom of the heath till they reached the dirt path leading up to the mausoleum. They both looked out for a big, boxy, black coach that would surely have stood out in the bare landscape even in this moonless night.

The dirt path was horribly rutted, so they were forced down to a walk again, and since Eliza knew the way well enough, she lowered the lamp with a groan. She dropped the light back in its holder and turned the latch. Then she rubbed her arms to relieve her stiff muscles. Henry transferred the ribbons to his left hand and rubbed her stiff neck, which made her groan again, this time with gratitude. Mindful of the cold, Henry wrapped the scarf around her neck again. "That was a stellar idea! Thank you."

She let her head rest on his shoulder for a moment as he hugged her to him with his free arm. "Should we extinguish the lanterns altogether so they won't spot us from too far off?"

She could feel him nod as he turned to kiss her brow.

"Another useful suggestion, my sweet."

He slowed the horses to a stop, swung himself down, and extinguished the lamps before continuing on their way. Oddly, the absence of light made it easier to see in the black night.

CHAPTER THIRTY

IT TOOK A GOODLY WHILE TO MAKE IT ACROSS the marshy meadow and halfway up the incline to the heath on the rutted, frozen dirt path. It was there, half hidden by the bare trees along the incline, that they became aware of a lone rider flying along their path at a full gallop. Eliza wondered briefly whether they were being followed by the headless phantom, but Henry had a more practical explanation for the ghostly horseman.

"I do hope Elijah found out where Miss Stephanie is."

He let the rider catch up to them, and when he did, Eliza was relieved to find it was indeed Elijah. He reined in his snorting and stomping steed and lost no time addressing Henry. "Sir, the girl was handed over about an hour ago, according to the miller who took them from the road to the mausoleum in his cart. The man also said Hobbs didn't come back with him, so it stands to reason he is still there."

That explained why they hadn't seen the boxy coach Charlie had described, and it confirmed they were headed to the right place, but Hobbs still being in the dungeon would make it that much harder to apprehend Astor, and God only knew what it meant for poor Stephanie.

But Eliza had another question she needed answered. "Do you know the name of the miller?"

Elijah did his best to control the dance his terrified horse performed beneath him as they all resumed their trek up the hill. "He's a nasty piece of work by the name of Wilkins."

A sharp intake of breath was Eliza's only reaction. She made a small gesture to encourage Elijah to continue.

"One of William's mates is sweet on one of the barmaids at The Cat and Fiddle and has become familiar with the patrons there. Wilkins is a regular. So when Wilkins stormed into The Silver Fox in a huff earlier, Ned took it upon himself to find out what had put his nose out of joint. At first he said he couldn't talk about it, but a bottle of whisky soon loosened his tongue. Turns out he has a longstanding agreement with Hobbs to take girls up to the mausoleum in his cart. Normally he waits for Hobbs, and when they get back to The Silver Fox, Hobbs lets him have one of the other girls he brought that month in payment."

Elijah looked at the occupants of the curricle, wondering whether he had said too much, but Henry nodded for him to continue.

Henry was still undecided as to what they should do next, knowing both villains were in the dungeon. He wished with all his heart Allen were with them. The risk of Astor getting away if Henry went in by himself was just too great. Elijah continued while Henry worked the problem over in his head.

"When the miller got the summons earlier this afternoon, he was all excited at the prospect of the virgin Hobbs had promised him, but then Hobbs told him he would have to wait a week for his payment and dismissed him as soon as they got to the mausoleum. Mr. Wilkins had a few choice words to say about crooked cheats as he poured his heart out to Ned. It was pure luck I was there and close enough to hear it all."

Eliza was speechless, but Henry, having come to a decision, now clearly saw the need for action. "Thank you, Elijah, but I'm afraid your work is still not done for the day. I need you to ride as fast as you can to the dairy, where Viscount Fairly is waiting for my signal." Henry turned to Eliza. "You had better tell him how to get there, Eliza."

Contemplating Wilkins and how close she had come to having to endure him didn't bear thinking about, so Eliza turned to practicalities. "Just as you get to the top of this incline, there is a path that follows along the ridge to the left. Take it, and when you see the mausoleum up on the hill to the right, it is one more mile before you get to a turnstile. Just beyond it, on Oakwood land, is the dairy."

Henry picked up the explanation from there. "A tunnel runs from the dairy to the dungeon below the mausoleum. I scouted it and left one of the cellar windows open. Find His Lordship and, provided Astor has passed through, go through the tunnel to the dungeon as fast as you can. I will enter through the mausoleum in twenty minutes and hope like hell you are on your way. With any luck, I can stop them from harming the girl and hold them off until you and Viscount Fairly can get there."

Elijah tipped his forehead with a two-finger salute and was about to kick his horse into a gallop when Henry added, "And Elijah, shoot to kill if you have to. These men are too dangerous to let live if we can't apprehend them."

A dark look passed between the two men, then Elijah sped off into the darkness.

Henry and Eliza continued in silence up to the heath. Clearly they could not wait for Allen, but thankfully they still had the element of surprise. Hobbs's presence in the dungeon also made Eliza's participation in the mission more dangerous, but she had already proven herself useful, so he couldn't bring himself to feel guilty for bringing her. However, he did worry about her state of mind.

"Are you well? Does Wilkins's involvement trouble you?"

Eliza shrugged nonchalantly, but her eyes were bleak. "I always knew he was despicable. This just proves me right."

Henry directed his team onto the most direct path to the mausoleum. "And it explains how Hobbs got involved in your kidnapping in Covent Garden." Henry heard her sigh in the dark and pulled her closer to him again. "I am sorry, my sweet. Now is probably not the best time to remind you of that day."

That made her chuckle, and she leaned up to place a kiss on his neck just below his jaw. "It's all right, Henry. I'm not afraid of the dark."

They used this moment of closeness to draw strength from each other for what was to come.

A few minutes later, they reached a copse of trees, from which the mausoleum was just out of sight, and parked the curricle amongst the trees. Keeping to the shadows in the copse, they approached the structure while keeping an eye out for the man Robert had placed here. When they had made it to the edge of the tree line just opposite the mausoleum without encountering him, Henry hooted like an owl, but there was no answering call.

Since they had a good ten minutes until the time Henry had said he would go down into the dungeon, he bade Eliza stay put and circled to the back of the Greek structure to make sure no one else lurked nearby. He returned soon and whispered in her ear, "There is nobody on or around the building as far as I can see. I assume Robert's man followed Hobbs and Stephanie inside. I had hoped I could leave you out here with him, but seeing as he is not to be found, you have to come with me."

He handed her one of his double-barreled handguns and told her to keep it pointed to the ground until she was ready to fire. "I want you to promise, no matter what happens, or what you hear, you will stay on the stairs above the dungeon and in the shadows. You know what Hobbs is capable of."

Eliza nodded firmly. Although the dungeon inspired a sort of morbid fascination, she had no intention to go anywhere near Hobbs if it could be helped. But Henry obviously felt the need to caution her further.

"He is a choirboy compared to Astor. If Astor catches sight of you, he will use you against me in any way he can."

Eliza squeezed his arm through the heavy folds of his coat, trying to convey her sincerity. "I understand. I promise I will not make a target of myself."

Henry knew he could trust her judgment, and that gave him the confidence he needed to face down Astor by himself.

They linked hands and swiftly approached the graveyard surrounding the mausoleum. Henry swung Eliza over the low fence, and they raced up the steps to the door. There they paused so Henry could listen for what they might find on the other side. What they could hear was faint and came from far below, but that made it no less chilling. They found the door unlocked, and Henry carefully led Eliza to the stairs in the middle of the small round room. As far as he could tell in the pitch dark, there was no one else up here.

The agonized screams of a girl, punctuated by the crack of a whip, were clearly audible now, making Eliza's breath catch in her throat and Henry's blood boil with rage. He took her hand again as they started to descend the stairs toward the sliver of light coming from behind the wall far below them.

"Stay behind me and don't go farther than that landing until I tell you to."

Eliza squeezed his hand in response, and they made their way down the staircase as fast as the sliver of light and the uneven stairs allowed. The closer they got to the bottom of the stairs, the more heartwrenching the girl's screams and the more horrifying the now discernible dialogue between her tormentors.

"Crikey, Your Lordship! I've gotta hand it to ya, the canin' made me wanna fuck 'er up the bum, but that crucifixion thing ya're doin' to 'er now 'as me cock throbbin' so 'ard, I'm gonna explode in me breeches."

Astor's appreciative laugh was nothing short of demonic. "Don't be shy, Hobbs. Free your beast and show the lady how much you appreciate her little dance."

"Don't mind if I do." A chuckle accompanied the remark. "Should 'ave brought one of me pigeons along to suck me off."

"Next time, Hobbs, next time," Astor promised.

Henry and Eliza heard what sounded like a belt being unbuckled and dropped to the ground. The next crack of the whip was particularly vicious, followed by a howl of pain and hysterical crying.

Eliza whimpered behind Henry, and he whirled around to put a hand over her mouth.

"Stay here," he breathed, and cocked his pistol. Then he did the same for hers and disappeared behind the corner where the last few steps led down to the balcony landing above the dungeon.

From below came the unmistakable sounds of a man pumping himself to a noisy orgasm while Stephanie wailed in abject misery and the whip continued to inflict pain. It was almost hypnotic, the sound of the cracking whip, and when it connected with the poor girl below, it gave a fleshy thud that made Eliza's stomach turn. It dawned on her they likely had stripped Stephanie naked for it to make such a sound and for Hobbs to be so titillated.

"Cor, 'ow do ya keep goin' for this long," came Hobbs's breathless voice, making Astor chuckle.

"Discipline, my dear Hobbs, discipline. How can I entice a woman to submit to me completely if I fail to demonstrate superior strength of mind as well as body? Any man can beat a woman, but it takes a strong mind and discipline to make her submit. But don't worry, my reward will come when she does give in and I finally rip her virginity from her and bring her to orgasm at the same time. That, her final surrender, is what I strive for."

Eliza shuddered. Was this what Daisie had refused to talk about, this perversion of a woman's pleasure? She might as well have been listening to two demons discussing torture in hell. She had to bite her knuckles so she wouldn't make a sound as Hobbs laughed a far too knowing laugh at Lord Astor's comments. Then his laughter abruptly died.

"Oh oh, Sir Henry! 'Ave ya come to join in, or do ya intend to rescue the wench and put 'er in your own bed?"

"Step away from the girl, Astor."

Henry sounded furious.

Eliza crouched low and peeked around the corner into the dungeon. She made certain to stay in the shadows, but simply had to see for herself what went on below.

Astor stood in the middle of what truly looked like a medieval dungeon designed for torture, with a bizarre-looking chair, an even stranger bench-like object that had restraints attached, and chains hanging from the walls and ceiling, some with devices at the end of them looking ominously like meat hooks.

But nothing in that room was quite as frightening as the man in the middle, holding a massive black leather bullwhip ready to strike once more. Astor held the peculiar short-handled device out to the side, letting the yards-long, thickly braided tail snake along the flagstones. His eyes were cold and unreadable, like the leaden skies of winter, but he looked and sounded completely relaxed, as if he were discussing the weather at his club.

"Sir Henry, I do confess to being surprised to see you here. I didn't think I left you nearly enough bread crumbs to find me. But since you are here, do come down and have a look around."

Hobbs stood farther back to the right, well out of reach of the whip, were it to be wielded overhead, and his hand was still wrapped around his now flaccid member. Stephanie was out of sight, probably right below where Henry stood. He had his gun trained on Astor, tension and fury evident in the taut set of his shoulders, but caution kept him out of the reach of the whip.

"Step away from the girl and I might."

Astor cocked his head to the side and shot daggers at Henry from his heavy-lidded eyes. "Such righteous indignation from the man who consumes women like so many tasty treats. I almost feel insulted! But then again, what should I expect from Avon's beholden cousin and

Wellesley's pet?"

Henry did not miss the fact Astor had just neglected to honor the Duke of Wellington with his well-deserved title and insulted his father's most prominent political opponent. So this was not just a vendetta against him: it was political and therefore had wider implications. He would definitely have to ask his cousin what bills he was working on for the present parliamentary session.

"You can insult me all you want, but step away from the girl."

Astor made no move to comply, and Henry was contemplating shooting the whip out of his hand when Eliza cried out behind him, "Watch out! Hobbs!"

Henry whipped his gun toward the pimp and shot the gun out of Hobbs's hand before anybody could blink. Hobbs made a pained grunting noise in the back of his throat, but Henry paid him no further mind, and before Astor could do more than raise his whip, Henry's gun pointed back in his direction.

Unfortunately, the perverted spy seemed utterly unconcerned that Hobbs's attempt on Henry had been thwarted. "Tsk, tsk, do you have so few friends you had to bring your mistress? What do you expect the poor girl to do for you?"

At that instance, Eliza shouted another warning, and Henry turned just in time to see Hobbs raise his gun with his uninjured hand. Henry aimed and fired in one fluid movement, but then searing pain tore through the fleshy part of his palm right below his pinky finger, forcing the gun out of his hand. He thought for a moment his gun had backfired, but as Hobbs sank to the ground with Henry's bullet lodged in his black heart, Henry realized Hobbs had gotten a shot off before Henry's bullet struck him down. Stephanie cried out again below him, but this time with something that sounded akin to relief. Eliza behind him made a strangled noise, which Henry interpreted as relief Hobbs was dead and he was still standing.

Henry's voice, despite the pain in his hand, was full of satisfaction. "Eliza is here to watch my back!"

Astor ignored both the crying girl in front of him and Henry's comment and trained dispassionate eyes on the lifeless body on the ground. "I knew he would come in useful tonight. That makes two bullets you spent, March. I believe that puts me back in the position of power, don't you agree?"

Of course it did. Henry's gun was now empty, and the whip in Astor's hand was a formidable weapon. No doubt Astor had learned in Spain how to wield it to its full, deadly potential. He spared the now useless gun one last glance and hoped Eliza was smart enough to stay well back. He retrieved a handkerchief from his coat pocket and wrapped it tightly around his bleeding hand. The wound wasn't serious, but blood loss could weaken a man and there was no sense in giving Astor another advantage.

Henry knew he had to play a waiting game until Robert or Allen arrived, so he took the bait and tried to engage Astor in conversation. "It would appear so. But somehow I can't bring myself to feel anything but joy at the ending of this particular vermin's life."

Astor chuckled. "It certainly is no great loss. Excellent shot, by the way, March. You really should have joined us years ago. I suspect you would have fit right in." He shrugged with supreme indifference. "Birthright or not, it is too late now."

Henry used his teeth to pull the knot on his makeshift bandage tight and wondered what on earth he meant by birthright, but decided to focus on the sexual to keep the madman below engaged. "I think not. I like my women to feel pleasure, not pain, when they submit to me."

Astor smirked in the most patronizingly obnoxious way possible. "Ah, but you do like them to submit. I shall show you around and let you in on a few of my secrets once I have achieved my current objective. Come to think of it, you should come down here and watch. She really is the most delightful subject, and you might learn something." He turned his attention back to Stephanie and raised the whip, causing the poor tortured girl to cry out in panic.

Henry took a step toward the railing and closer to the business end of the whip, desperate to regain the man's attention. "What is your current objective, Astor? I still don't understand the girl's role in all of this."

Astor turned his attention back to him, his thin lips curved up into a chilling smile. "I admit to being impressed you found out the girl had significance in the first place. As for what it is, you will find out tomorrow when I have her delivered to her father."

"Who is her father?"

Astor wagged a reprimanding finger at Henry. "Patience, my dear March, patience. I will let you live just long enough to find out, I think."

Henry was beginning to wonder what was taking Robert so long. He had never considered how taxing it would be to hold a conversation with a lunatic.

"Well, as long as you are planning on killing me anyway, you might as well tell me now."

Astor's laugh tinkled maliciously through the dungeon. "Oh, come now, March, where would be the fun in that? I want you to be aware of all the implications as they pertain to you, and you won't be able to fully appreciate them until the game is all played out to the end."

Henry was momentarily unable to reply; the length to which this man was willing to go in order to achieve his revenge boggled the mind. Then Henry heard Eliza make another strangled sound, followed by two sets of feet coming down the stairs, and dread pooled in his stomach. Astor, on the other hand, seemed well pleased.

"Well done, Leech. So nice of you to join us, Miss Broad."

Eliza appeared at Henry's side, then was urged farther forward by a man with long, greasy hair. Henry recognized him as the male servant he had observed cleaning the dungeon on his first visit here. He was holding Eliza's left elbow in a vise grip, but her right was buried in the folds of her cloak, and Henry wondered if she still had his gun. Henry tried stepping closer to her, but Astor cracked the whip right over their heads, eliciting a terrified shriek from Stephanie below them.

"Stay right where you are, March, or the next one will mar her smooth cheek."

Eliza glanced back at him and locked her gaze to his for a moment. Henry was relieved to find no fear in her eyes, just bitter resolve. He gave her an almost imperceptible nod, which she answered in kind before returning her attention to Astor, who was waiting for her.

"From now on, you will attend me and me only, girl. I am partial to blondes, but I will make an exception for you. Bring her down, Leech."

Before the man could tighten his grip on Eliza, she raised her right hand, still clasping Henry's gun, and fired in Astor's direction while Henry kicked Leech in his side with all the force he could muster at such a short distance. Luckily, it dislodged the man's hand from Eliza's elbow and sent him careening into the wall, where he slid to the ground. Henry delivered another kick to the side of his head, rendering him unconscious, but when he heard the hiss of the whip followed by Eliza's strangled gasp of pain and the gun clattering to the ground, he knew he should have lunged for the gun instead, despite the injury to his right hand.

Eliza's shot had gone wide, and now the end of Astor's whip was choking the life out of her, and the demented bastard was attempting to pull her over the railing. "You little bitch! I'll soon cure you of your feistiness and whatever other bad habits you might have."

Eliza desperately clawed at the leather noose around her neck, and Henry lunged forward to keep her from being dragged over the edge. But it was clear the coil around her neck would kill her long before her body broke on the flagstones below. He had brought her here; it would be on him if she perished here. Henry had a horrible moment of doubt as he stretched to wrap his uninjured hand around the whip and pulled with all his might. But despite Henry's best effort, Astor kept inching them closer and closer to the edge of a deadly fall.

Suddenly, a long knife flashed from behind them to slash at the whip while strong hands reached around Eliza to help slack the braided leather cord choking the life out of her. On the third strike, Rick's hunting knife finally severed the whip's tail, and Eliza fell back against Allen, who lost no time ripping the deadly coil away from her neck. Henry seized the gun she had dropped.

But before he could raise the gun and fix Astor in his sights, a shot rang out below, and the whip that had been poised menacingly to strike once more went slack in Astor's hand. The cold fury in his eyes turned to a look of surprise, and then the light there died altogether as a slow trickle of blood escaped the hole in his forehead, and his body crumpled to the ground.

A moment of complete silence followed the death of the man now lying in the center of his dungeon. He might have been a master spy and a monster, but he had indeed been a man and not invincible, and as that truth penetrated the consciousness of all present, they released a collective sigh of relief. A surge of joy went through them as they acknowledged that they had indeed vanquished the enemy and survived.

Below, Stephanie began to sob and chanted between heaving breaths, "Oh, thank God! Oh, thank God! Oh, thank God!"

Robert's shocked voice drifted up from the dungeon floor. "Jesus Christ! Henry, we need a doctor!" There was a little pause and some shuffling while he addressed Stephanie. "Hold on, sweeting, I have to find the key to get you out of this thing." Then a little louder: "Henry, Eliza, are you well?"

Henry looked over to where Eliza struggled to breathe in Allen's arms. Allen had opened her cloak and pushed the material away from her neck, revealing the angry red welt circling her throat. Tears streamed down her face, and her breast heaved, but she was breathing, thank the good Lord.

"Eliza is injured, but we are well enough. Allen is here. Just take care of Miss Adams." Henry had locked gazes with Eliza as he spoke, then moved closer and pulled her into his arms. "I'm so sorry, Eliza. I almost got you killed. I am sorry."

But she wrapped her arms around him, pressed her wet face into his neck, and croaked, "No, Henry, Astor almost killed me. You saved me once again. You and Allen."

Then she reached for Allen and pressed a wet, teary kiss to his cheek. "Thank you!"

Allen threw a quick glance at Henry, gauging his reaction to Eliza's kiss. But when his friend nodded his thanks to him, Allen grinned and made a big production of returning her kiss. "You are most welcome, darling. Any time you need a knight in shining armor and the old man here can't quite manage it, just say the word."

A grin turned into a chuckle, and then they all laughed. Only laughter and the warm light of friendship could dispel the horrors of this dungeon.

CHAPTER THIRTY-ONE

WHILE ELIZA DRIED HER TEARS WITH THE SLEEVE of her dress, Henry lifted her into his arms to take her downstairs so they could deal with the still-sobbing Stephanie and the two dead men.

Eliza was still a little dazed from being choked, but when he lifted her, she protested, "Henry, your hand. Let me down!"

"It's nothing, my sweet. Just a scratch. Let me hold you."

At that, she rested against his shoulder and allowed herself the comfort of his arms. But because she was being carried and could look over Henry's shoulder, she was the first of their group to see Stephanie and the horror that had been inflicted on her.

Stephanie was naked, her dark blond braids in disarray. Her hands and feet were shackled to a wooden cross mounted on the wall so it made an X about a foot off the ground. Her eyes were bloodshot and red-rimmed from the trauma, and tears still streamed down her cheeks. The snot bubbles escaping her nose were currently being wiped away by Viscount Fairly's monogrammed handkerchief while he attempted to calm her with gentle words.

Spread-eagled on the cross, Stephanie's weight was barely supported by the tiny footholds beneath her feet. Robert shed his greatcoat and held it against Stephanie's torso to shield her from view, but there were enough angry red welts and cuts on her legs and arms to make it clear she was not only in severe pain, but would need her wounds treated before they could put clothes on her.

Eliza forgot all about her own and Henry's injuries and pushed on his shoulder to let her down. "Heavens! We have to get the poor thing off that cross!"

Elijah answered from across the room, where he searched the chest of drawers against the wall there. "I know, miss. But we can't find the damned keys, and Miss Stephanie can't remember where the monster put them."

He looked deeply affected by the girl's plight, rifling manically through drawers. Eventually he lifted a small clamp attached to a silver chain. "I don't even want to know what that's for. I'm only sorry the swine is already dead so I can't use it on his balls. Give him a taste of his own."

Eliza decided it was safer for everybody's state of mind to focus on finding the keys and headed for Hobbs's corpse. "Have you looked in Astor's pockets?" she croaked out, her throat sore and aching with every word after raising her voice a moment ago. She stooped to go through the pimp's pockets, but stilled when she remembered something. "Henry, Daisie put a satchel in the curricle with things in it I might need to look after Stephanie. Could you go and get it? I think she put it in the box."

Rick, who was still on the stairs and obviously reluctant to come any farther, offered, "I'll go fetch it, miss. I know where it is; we left our horses there too."

He turned to go up the stairs before anybody could protest, so Henry called after him, "Bring the curricle and the horses around whilst you're at it. The quicker we all get out of here, the better."

Meanwhile, Eliza had turned back to Hobbs and proceeded to empty his pockets onto his brown and red polka-dotted waistcoat. One by one, she dropped a penknife, a knuckle duster, and a purse full of gold coins—which she suspected to be payment for delivering Stephanie—on his lifeless chest.

Stepping up behind her, Henry noticed her fingers shaking. He crouched down next to her, covered the dead man's flaccid penis with the flap of his breeches, and stilled Eliza's hands with his. "Sweetheart, you don't have to do this. Why don't you go and help Robert calm Stephanie? I'll help Elijah find the key."

Eliza gave him a grateful smile and rose to go to the girl, who was still helplessly and painfully suspended on the bizarre cross. But there wasn't anything she could do for Stephanie the viscount wasn't already doing. Robert covered and supported her with one arm, talked to her in calm, low tones, and gently stroked her hair and face with his other hand. And he was succeeding in his effort to calm her. Stephanie clearly credited Robert with her rescue and therefore trusted him. Eliza saw no reason to drag the girl's attention away from the one person who made her feel secure, so she turned to searching the room.

Elijah had advanced to rifling through the second chest of drawers, Henry was now searching Astor's pockets, and Allen had opened the double doors on the opposite wall. Amazed she hadn't noticed them before, Eliza watched Allen for a moment as he searched through what looked like the devil's own bedchamber. It was all dark wood, stark white bed linens, and carved demons.

Remembering the task at hand, she turned her attention to the rack on the wall next to the strange cross. It held all kinds of devices used to chastise humans and animals. Considering what had happened to Stephanie in this room tonight, the contents of the rack were enough to make Eliza turn pale, but what made her shudder was the fresh blood on the cane that had been haphazardly stored there. Remembering what Hobbs had said about a caning, she stepped next to the girl and lifted Robert's coat a few inches away so she could inspect Stephanie's back.

Eliza drew in a sharp breath. Stephanie's skin from thigh to shoulder was crisscrossed with angry welts. The strikes had been laid out with military precision, all about an inch apart, and many of them had broken the skin. Tears pooled in Eliza's eyes as she looked up at Robert. "Robert, try not to touch her back when you hold her up." When his eyes met hers and she read the question there, she added, "He caned her."

Robert's face lost all color just like Eliza's had, then he shifted to hold Stephanie up from under her arms. "Keep looking for the key, please. She is growing weak."

Returning her attention to the rack, Eliza surveyed the lower ledges on which the whips and canes rested. When she found nothing there, she let her fingers trail along the upper ledge holding the implements in place. Oddly, she found not a speck of dust, but when she came to the end closest to the cross, she brushed against something cold, which clattered to the floor. She bent to pick it up and found herself holding a small iron key.

Eliza instantly stretched up to try the key in the manacle around Stephanie's left hand. The key turned in the lock with a snick and the metal cuff opened, releasing the girl's limp arm as she cried out in relief.

Robert draped her arm over his shoulder and murmured instructions to Eliza:

"Her legs first and then the other arm."

Henry called to the other men searching the room, "Elijah, leave the chests. Allen, bring something to cover this table so we can lay the girl down. I doubt she wants to go in that other room." While he issued orders, Henry rushed over to help Robert and Eliza take Stephanie off the cross.

Allen appeared with all the bedding rolled up in his arms and, taking Henry's hint, closed the double doors to the bedroom. Elijah helped him spread the coverlet over the table so the other two men could lay Stephanie on it.

Stephanie shook like a leaf, and there was no telling whether it was from the cold, the shock, the pain, or sheer exhaustion, but the moment Robert let go of her and stepped away so Allen could cover her with the sheets and Robert's greatcoat, she panicked.

"Don't leave me. Please, don't leave me here!"

All four men looked ready to pledge their sword arm to her protection for the rest of their natural lives, but it was Robert who drew her into the shelter of his arms and stroked her head reassuringly.

The rest of the men stepped aside to debate the best way to get Stephanie out of the dungeon. By the time they had decided Elijah would go for the doctor and bring him directly to Robert's house, Rick arrived with the satchel Daisie had packed.

From the contents of the bag, Eliza was quite certain Daisie had suffered similar tortures. There was a bottle of witch hazel for cleansing wounds and a jar of ointment promising to treat severe bruising as well as heal broken skin. There were also several rectangular pieces of soft lawn the size of a woman's back and a plethora of soft bandages of various lengths. Beyond that, the bag contained a nightgown, a pair of sheepskin slippers, and a light wool wrapper.

Eliza stepped to the side of the table opposite Robert and set out what she needed to tend to Stephanie's injuries. Allen had slipped back into the bedchamber and returned with a washbowl, a pitcher of fresh water, and some clean towels, and set them on the table next to Eliza. She mixed a few drops of the witch hazel into water in the bowl and dipped a corner of a towel in it, nodded at Robert to lift the covers from Stephanie's back, and started to wash her. Henry and Allen followed suit, proceeding to wash her arms and legs. Then they applied the ointment, covered her worst wounds on her back and buttocks with pieces of soft lawn, and turned her so Eliza could tend to her front.

It was a measure of how truly traumatized Stephanie was that she didn't even attempt to cover her modesty, despite the three men surrounding her. She just whimpered and held on to Robert with her hands and eyes. Eliza had never seen wounds like the ones the bullwhip had inflicted and very much hoped she never would have to again. Where Astor had struck her arms and thighs, he had let the whip curl around like he had done with Eliza's neck, leaving thick red welts behind. But on her belly and circling her nipples, the strikes were vicious little licks that had broken the skin and were deep enough they might well leave scars behind long after they were healed.

Eliza cleaned away the blood as best she could and applied the ointment, but suspected the two biggest cuts on the sensitive underside of Stephanie's breasts would need stitches.

She used the soft lawn to cover the wounds, then Robert and Allen stood the girl up so Henry and Eliza could wrap her in bandages before they dressed her in the clothes and slippers Daisie had had the foresight to pack. Lastly, Robert wrapped the coverlet around Stephanie against the January cold and hoisted her into his arms like a child to carry her up the stairs and out of the dungeon to Henry's curricle and the safety of his home.

Henry used the satchel to collect the things he had found in Hobbs's pocket and the odd signet ring he'd taken off Astor's finger. It didn't show his family crest like one might have assumed, but two snakes hissing at each other, and Henry thought it best to show the Old Man. Meanwhile, Allen bent to heft the dead lord over his shoulder, but Robert let out a growl every bit as fierce as one might hear in the lions' den at the Tower. "I'll send my bailiffs; leave the bastards."

Reminded that Robert was the magistrate for the area, they left the corpses behind and followed him out of the dreadful place. Allen only stopped long enough to secure the still-unconscious Leech's hands behind his back.

OUTSIDE, THE HEAVY CLOUDS HAD opened while the events in the dungeon had unfolded, and a thin layer of new snow blanketed the heath. Henry assisted Robert into his curricle with Stephanie still cradled in his arms, then turned to Allen.

"Will you take Eliza up with you?"

Allen offered his hand to Eliza. "Of course! Come along, darling. That doctor should have a look at your neck too. I swear that toggle on your cloak was the only thing stopping your windpipe from being crushed."

Glad of Allen's easy chatter, Eliza took his hand and let him boost her into the saddle. "I'm fine. I don't need the doctor, but I wouldn't mind putting some of that ointment on my neck."

"I will gladly assist you with that as soon as we get to Robert's house. Right after I get myself a stiff drink, of course." He winked at her and swung himself into the saddle behind her.

"Such chivalry." She chuckled, but let him pull her more securely against him, exhaustion finally taking its toll.

THE SNOW ON THE GROUND illuminated the night, and so they made it to Robert's estate on the other side of Hampstead in less than half an hour.

The phaeton parked outside the great house, where many lit windows shone in welcome, indicating the doctor had already arrived. As soon as they pulled up to the front, the main doors swung open and they were ushered inside. The house itself was bustling with activity, reassuring the bedraggled group entering the foyer that the nightmare was over.

The butler stood ready to welcome them in, and the doctor waited by his side. A matronly housekeeper sent maids to bring baths to the rooms they had readied for the guests and then waved Robert to follow her upstairs with the girl in his arms.

"Goodness gracious, m'lord, whatever happened to the young lady? Let's get her upstairs and the doctor can have a look at her." She bustled up the stairs, chattering all the way.

Henry put his hale arm around Eliza's waist to lead her up the stairs behind Robert and Stephanie, and waited for the housekeeper to escort her employer and his charge to the best guest room before he demanded her attention.

"Mrs. Mallory, would you be so kind as to show us to our rooms and see if Lord Robert's man could assist me? And tell him to bring some bandages. Also, could you please make sure my companion is brought a meal and a hot bath? Miss Broad, too, has been through quite an ordeal, so I rely on you to make her as comfortable as you can."

Mrs. Mallory instantly puffed up with pride and forgot all about the unseemliness of Sir Henry's arm around the young lady's waist. She clapped her hands to get the attention of her maids, and in her zeal to play the mother hen for an exhausted Eliza, she ended up putting the two into adjoining rooms.

Henry had his bath and ate a light meal before Robert's valet put two stitches in his palm and bandaged it competently. He then waited until he heard the maids clear away Eliza's bath before he knocked on her door. She sat up in bed, dressed in a sensible flannel nightgown, smiling tiredly at him, and stretched out her hand toward the jar of ointment Henry held. "I was hoping you still had that. How is your hand?"

Henry shrugged out of the dressing gown he had found in his room, laid it at the foot of the bed, pulled a spare bandage from the pocket, and climbed in beside her. "Well enough. Scoot over, my sweet. I'm going to take care of your poor, abused neck, and then I'll hold you all night so you can sleep."

Eliza smiled gratefully and moved her hair aside so Henry could tend to her. "Thank you, Henry. I was just wondering how I would manage to go to sleep after today. Your presence is most welcome."

"I thought you weren't afraid of the dark?" Henry teased while he laid the bandage around her neck.

Eliza wrinkled her brow as if trying to recall something. "Did I say that?"

She smiled, but there were shadows in her eyes. He finished her bandage, brushed her hair away from her face, kissed her gently on the lips, pinched out the candle, and pulled her down into his arms. As they settled into the cushions to sleep, he admitted, "I don't want to sleep alone tonight either."

THEY WOKE TO SUNNY SKIES and a sparkling blanket of snow the next morning. The whole world seemed to blaze with light in an effort to drive the shadows from their very souls. Eliza knew it to be a fanciful thought, but she was comforted by it nevertheless. She dressed in front of the window, looking out on the landscape she had grown up in, with Henry playing lady's maid. He laced and tied her corset, then held her petticoats so she could step into them easily, and finally lifted her wool gown over her head. Once he had closed the buttons going up the back of her gown, she turned to tie his cravat for him and buttoned his waistcoat.

Henry took the opportunity to drape her arms around his neck, pulling her into his arms and kissing her with a tantalizing mixture of tenderness and passion. "I'm sorry I have to hurry away. Tonight I will love you with all the care you deserve."

He pecked her on the nose and shrugged into his coat.

She smiled up at him, liking that he used the word "love," but not sure how to respond to it. "You always make me feel cared for."

She reached up to stroke her hand over his slightly stubbled cheek, and he pulled her in for another kiss.

"I very much care for you, and I promise I will always take care of you." He kissed her again before she could answer and then pulled her to the door. "Let's go break our fast, and then I have to drive back to town to report to the Old Man. We do have to address the fact that we killed a lord last night, not to mention he was the son of a very powerful Peer of the Realm."

Eliza let him lead her down the main stairs and toward a room at the back of the house where breakfast would be served.

"Would you please stay here with Stephanie until I return with her mother? I know Stephanie seems to have a preference for Robert, but I suspect it would comfort her mother to know a woman is with her."

It seemed they were the first to come down for breakfast. Henry handed her a plate so she could help herself to the dishes laid out on the sideboard.

"Of course I'll stay. I, too, want to make sure Stephanie is as well as she can be under the circumstances."

Henry pulled out a chair for her and set down his plate next to hers as she poured tea for them both. "You might also take the opportunity to tell Robert when you want Horace removed from the inn, since he is trespassing on your property. Robert is aware of the whole situation, so all you have to do is tell him when you are ready."

Eliza sipped her tea and thought for a moment. "But what do I do once I have removed him? Even if I wanted to go back there, he would come back for revenge, making life difficult for me at every turn."

Henry chewed his ham, then calmly stated, "You don't have to worry about Horace. Robert suggested putting him on a ship to Australia for what he did to you. All you have to decide is whether you want to go back or not."

Eliza turned to him fully, her eggs forgotten for now. "That's just it. I don't ever want to go back there—too many bad memories. But I can't let it just fall to ruin either."

Henry smiled, and she had an inkling he was glad she didn't want to return to her father's inn. "May I suggest you lease it to Riley and his Mary? It's just the kind of challenge he would love to take on. He is a good, capable man and would make the place respectable again. You would gain an independent income, and they would appreciate being their own masters."

Eliza gifted him with the most beautiful smile, dabbed a little fat from his lips with her serviette, and leaned in to kiss him right there at the breakfast table. "Why, Henry, you gave this thought, didn't you? It is the perfect solution, and I thank you. You really are the best of men. You saved me, took me into your house, gave me your friendship, and now you would give me my independence. I hardly know what to say."

He leaned his forehead against hers. "Say you will stay with me. That's all I want."

But before Eliza could answer him, Allen strode into the room with the air of a man on a mission. He lost no time heaping food on his plate. "Good morning, lovebirds. It's just gone eight; I'm surprised you are still here, Henry. Don't you have to go explain yourself to the Old Man so he can save us all from the gallows for slaying Elridge's misbegotten fourth-born?"

Henry kissed Eliza's cheek in farewell and stood. "Indeed. My curricle is being brought around as we speak. I shall return with Miss Adams later, and you, my friend, might do well to consider leaving the country for a little while. You are the most vulnerable of us three in this situation."

Allen only laughed. "Don't worry about me, old man. I fully expect to be sent on a wild goose chase to the dark continent by this afternoon."

Henry laughed right back, knowing full well his friend liked nothing better than the nail-biting adventures he termed "wild goose chases." "We shall miss you!"

CHAPTER THIRTY-TWO

LESS THAN AN HOUR LATER, HENRY ENTRUSTED his team to a groom outside Lady Greyson's house and was shown into her morning room, where the lady was in the process of breaking her fast.

Lady Greyson waved him to her side, offered her cheek for his kiss, and indicated the seat next to her. "Come fortify yourself with a cup of coffee before you go satisfy the Old Man's curiosity. We heard rumors, you know."

Henry dutifully kissed his godmother's cheek, sat in the seat indicated, and accepted the cup offered to him. "Oh?"

Lady Greyson chuckled. "Don't worry. Sara was here and mentioned you were not in town, so we concluded your mission had begun."

Henry could barely contain his excitement. "Did she tell you what she wanted to see me about?"

"No, dear, but she did say she left a message at your house."

Henry thought for a moment while he drank his coffee. "Could you send someone to retrieve that message whilst I'm in with the Old Man? It may be urgent."

The lady turned curious eyes on him. "Of course, my boy. But first tell me about your charming friend Eliza. Sara seems to think I will be called upon to train her before long."

Henry sat back in his chair and smiled at the woman who had taken the place of a mother in his life for the past eleven years. "Sara is a very smart woman. Eliza has already proven her worth. She is smart, seemingly unflappable, and has that most elusive of skills: the ability to work within the situation, whatever it may be. But most important of all, she has honor. So, yes, I would like you to take her under your wing."

Henry drained his coffee, set down the cup, stood, and bowed to his godmother. "But first I need to go report, then enroll the Old Man's help in keeping Robert and me from the gallows for killing a peer."

Lady Greyson's mouth dropped open in a most unladylike way. Then understanding dawned, and a wicked grin spread across her face. "If the peer you are referring to is Astor, all I can say is: good riddance!"

Henry was already in the corridor, but the "Indeed" he uttered under his breath was still clearly audible.

HE REENTERED THE HOUSE FORTY-FIVE minutes later and was handed a sealed note addressed to him in Miss Davis's hand. He broke the seal and unfolded the message. It contained only one sentence: "Avon pays the bills."

Henry stared at the parchment in his hand a good thirty seconds before a truly foul string of swear words rang out in Lady Greyson's elegant foyer, followed by a clipped command: "Bring my curricle around."

A footman swung the front door open, and the butler handed him his hat and held his coat open for him. "Right outside, sir. Your man William said the message was urgent, so I took the liberty to have your carriage brought around."

Henry nodded his thanks, pushed his hat down on his head, and bounded down the stairs and up into his curricle. He barely waited for the groom to get out of his way before he urged his horses into a near gallop. He did not know how his cousin had managed to keep a second family secret all these years, but he did know, with absolute certainty, that if Stephanie was indeed the Duke of Avon's daughter, and the world found out about her existence through these circumstances, there would be hell to pay.

There would be a mortifying scandal for the entire family, to be sure. Arthur might even be sufficiently angered by the fallout to force Emily from his home, but the true damage would be to his political career. He would lose allies in the House, the press would be merciless, and any bill he put forward or lent his support to would be doomed to failure.

Henry had almost made it to his cousin's ducal palace on St. James's Square when the truth struck him. Getting at him and threatening Emily had only been a sideshow, perhaps a fringe benefit for Astor. The real target was Avon and always had been. This was political in nature, and what Henry needed to do right now was stop Arthur from playing into the enemies' hands. His task was not to be the bearer of bad news, but to stop his cousin from reacting to said news and going to his secret family's aid.

Henry approached his destination at a more sedate pace, asked his team to be walked as if he was about to pay a courtesy visit, and was admitted by a wigged and liveried footman. But instead of waiting for the butler to announce him, Henry ran up the stairs and straight into his imposing cousin, who seemed to be in a hurry to leave the house.

"Bring around the unmarked carriage," rang out the sharp command, then on seeing his cousin he boomed, "Ah, Henry, good to see you. Grossmama is in the morning salon."

Henry took his cousin's outstretched hand, but instead of releasing it, he clasped Arthur's elbow with his other hand and drew him close so he would not be overheard. "Cancel the carriage and come to the study with me." When Arthur tried to pull away, he added, "Stephanie is safe! But someone is trying to discredit you by creating a scandal."

Arthur drew in a sharp breath, but held his composure admirably, then turned to the footman. "I won't need the carriage after all."

They proceeded down the corridor toward the duke's study, doing their best to appear unhurried, but as soon as the door closed behind them and Arthur had led Henry sufficiently far into the room to ensure the footman on the other side would not be able to overhear, he turned to him, barely containing his agitation. "How do you know of Stephanie, and what do you know?"

Henry went to the brandy decanter and poured them both a drink, despite the early hour. "Stephanie is the daughter of Miss Adams. She was kidnapped yesterday by an individual named Hobbs and brought to a man I have long suspected of being a French spy and, therefore, had under surveillance. As soon as we realized to whom the girl had been taken, my associates and I went to where we suspected she would be held and rescued her. Both villains died in the resulting confrontation. Stephanie sustained some injuries and is badly shaken, but she is safe now, and the doctor who saw her said she will be well soon enough."

Henry paused to gauge the other man's reaction. The blood had drained steadily from the duke's face ever since Henry had mentioned kidnapping. He was now as pale as a ghost, but the hands holding his drink were still steady, so Henry continued. "I just found out Stephanie is your daughter and that you have been looking after her and her mother for the past eighteen years."

His cousin heaved a great sigh. "Twenty, actually. Clara wanted a child of her own, and I could not deny her, seeing as I was filling my nursery, adding to it with disturbing regularity."

Henry could see it clearly now. "You did your duty with Hortense, but you love Miss Adams."

Arthur put down his drink untouched and started to leave the room. "And our daughter! With everything I have. So you have to understand, I have to go to them, scandal or not. Whether it will cost me my political credibility or not."

Henry stopped the duke with a hand on his arm. "What bills are you working on right now?"

Arthur looked at him with a fair amount of confusion, but answered the question. "Voting reform. We are trying to create a more representational system, shift some of the decision-making power to the House of Commons and elected officials. This Regency has gone on long enough, and I hope to spare future generations from having to endure another."

"And I take it Elridge is opposed?"

"Violently so! To hear him talk, you would think I'm trying to destroy the monarchy."

"Then we know who is pulling the strings behind the scene here."

Avon looked shaken by the notion a political opponent would stoop to kidnapping his daughter and hurting her. "How would he even know about them? No one outside of Clara's household knows about us."

"Then we will have to look at her household for the answer to that question, but not now. Arthur, will you trust me and do precisely as I say? I promise to get you and Miss Adams to your daughter, and with any luck, Elridge won't even find out you have left town."

Arthur only nodded and waited for Henry to continue.

"You will take Grossmama and go for a visit to my house. Put it about that I came to invite you to an impromptu birthday party for Emily. Write to Miss Adams right now, tell her Stephanie is safe, and ask her to go for a visit with Sara Davis. Once we can verify whoever is watching you knows you are at my home, you will slip out my back door, take my carriage, and pick Miss Adams up from Miss Davis's. Stephanie is in Hampstead with Fairly, so you can go see to her, leave her mother with her, and come back to my house before anybody is any the wiser, and tonight we will go to White's for good measure."

The plan was so simple, it might just succeed. Even Arthur, who knew nothing of subterfuge, could see that. "Thank you, Henry. I will do as you say." He moved to his desk and sat to write to his mistress. "I'm glad she is with Fairly. He is a good man."

Henry chuckled. "I am glad you think so. He may well need your support in the House of Lords."

"Oh? Why?"

"Last night he killed the man who hurt Stephanie."

"I will make sure to thank him for that. Who was it?"

"Lord Astor."

Arthur stopped writing and stared at Henry. "Good Lord, you suspected one of Elridge's sons to be a French spy?"

Henry returned his cousin's stare, all humor gone from his countenance. "From what I have learned over the past weeks and what I witnessed last night, I am certain he was the spy the French called De Sade Anglais."

Arthur's face turned ashen, and the quill snapped between his fingers, leaving no doubt he'd heard what the spy did to his victims. "Merciful God! And my Stephanie was in the monster's clutches? How badly is she hurt?"

Henry could barely bring himself to speak of it, but his cousin deserved to know the truth, and Stephanie would need her father's love and patience. "She was caned and whipped, but, Arthur, I got there before he could do his worst." Henry held his cousin's gaze and willed him to understand what he was saying.

Arthur searched his eyes and finally let the air out of his lungs, relaxed his shoulders just a little, and nodded. Then he picked up a new quill and returned to the task of writing to his Clara. "Expect us within the hour."

Knowing he had been dismissed, Henry left to make all the necessary arrangements to provide cover for Arthur's journey to Hampstead.

HENRY BARELY HAD TIME TO send messages to Lady Greyson, Sara Davis, and Robert to apprise them of the situation before the ducal carriage pulled up in front of his house. Lady Greyson followed shortly thereafter with all her dogs, and they all congregated in the drawing room.

Charlie, who had been stationed at the corner of Oxford Street, came by to report the duke's chaise had indeed been followed, and pointed out the fellow, who had positioned himself on a bench in the square. Arthur left through the back door to pick up his lady and go to Hampstead, while the rest of the adults did their best to make Emily believe this was indeed a party for her.

They whiled away the day with the dogs' antics, a lavish lunch, songs in the music room, a birthday cake with all of the staff gathering around to wish Emily a happy birthday, a nap for the old ladies, and a trip to the stables for Emily. By the time they reconvened in the drawing room for afternoon tea, it was five o'clock and the last of the daylight was fast disappearing.

They had just settled down around the tea trolley when the Duke of Avon walked back into the room with Eliza on his arm. He seated her with the air of a man who had just made a new friend and took the chair next to Henry. The two men didn't speak beyond a simple greeting and the confirmation they would meet in the smoking room at White's around nine that evening, but the companionable silence in which they consumed their tea and cakes spoke for itself.

AFTER TEA, LADY GREYSON AND the ducal party departed, and Emily was ushered upstairs for her bath. Eliza excused herself as well to freshen up and change before dinner, so Henry retreated to the library to see to his correspondence.

But he had only just sat down behind his desk and found the tin that housed his spectacles when William knocked on the door and told him Riley had arrived from Hampstead with a letter. Curious as to who other than Robert would send him a letter from Hampstead and have it hand-delivered, Henry waved his old comrade into the room.

The letter Riley handed to him wasn't sealed. In fact, it seemed to be more than one letter, written on several pieces of paper differing in size and texture. A piece of foolscap, the kind the lady of the house might carry in her pocket on a small pad to write out menus and such, was wrapped around the outside. Someone had written in pencil:

Please deliver to: Sir Henry March, Cavendish Square, London

"There was a shilling next to it when Mary found it under the pillow," Riley explained.

Henry knew the slope of the hand that had addressed the letter, but he still sought confirmation. Hoping for what, he did not know. "Who stayed in the room that night?"

Riley scratched the back of his neck, aware Henry was struggling with something he had no knowledge of. "A Lord and Lady Ostley, I believe, and they were there for two nights."

Confirmation then. Henry had trouble keeping his hands steady enough to unfold the foolscap. The last thing on this green earth he wanted to do was read a letter from Cecilia, but she had obviously gone to some trouble to send it, and it might tell him more about the threat to Emily, the one he was not entirely sure had been eliminated. So he put his resentment and the old pain coursing through him at seeing her hand aside and spread the four pieces of paper on his desk, to find where best to begin.

He glanced up to where Riley still stood. "Why don't you go to the kitchen and let Mrs. Tibbit feed you? I may need you to take a message back to Viscount Fairly."

Riley saluted and left the room, closing the door behind him, but Henry was already engrossed in the task before him. The foolscap had a note written in pencil on the inside. It was dated from the night before and was headlined:

Thank you! Thank you! Thank you!

That alone was intriguing. What did Cecilia have to thank him for and why had she suddenly turned up in Hampstead after a decade of barricading herself on her husband's country estate?

Henry's head swam with unanswered questions, but they all dropped right out of his mind when he unfolded the three large ultra-thin pieces of parchment, narrowly covered in tiny script and dated from the 13th of May, 1808. Cecilia had written to him four months after Emily had been born. She had cared enough to write to him, he had just never received the letter. What he would have given to have received it back then. He had needed desperately to know her reasons for abandoning Emily, but did he still want to know what she had to say for herself?

Yes.

It was as if his heart had suddenly been thrown a lifeline and he could not, would not, let it go, so he pulled out his spectacles and started to read.

CHAPTER THIRTY-THREE

13th of May, 1808

Henry,

I wanted to start this letter with "My dearest Henry," but I realize I lost that right when I walked away from you in Brussels. I am sorry I walked away from you, you will never know how profoundly. I am sorry I hurt you, and most of all, I am sorry I did not put my trust in you. You were and are far more deserving of it than my husband ever was, and I should have known that.

I know I hurt you with what you saw as my betrayal, and I cannot, will never be able to, take that hurt away. All I can hope is that one day you will read this letter and perhaps understand why I did what I did, even if it was the wrong thing for us all in the end.

I thought at the time it would be best for both of us if I went back with Ostley. I know you think I went back to him because of the comfortable life he could provide me with and your lack of money and prospects at the time. I admit that was part of my motivation to return to my dull rural existence, but it was your father who convinced me our elopement had the potential to ruin your entire future. You were not meant to be a lowly clerk in Brussels, and I did not want to be the one who held you back. You were so young, and you would have resented me for it sooner or later, just like I resented you for our lack of money.

Your father promised to reenroll you in university so you could finish your degree, and that in turn would gain you the freedom from his influence you so desperately wanted. He also promised, if I went back to my husband, he would help you weather the scandal our elopement had created.

Ostley, for his part, promised me all would be forgiven if only I came home with him. He even offered to give the child I was carrying legitimacy under his name.

I was naïve and more than a little scared to give birth in a foreign country, far from the comfort of my mother's arms, but I was stupid to believe him. I was stupid, and I should have known better. I had been his wife for four years before we eloped, and I did know better than to believe he would take me back without repercussions, even if he had not been able to get me with child in all that time and needed an heir.

He behaved like the perfect gentleman on the journey home, reinforcing the fiction of his forgiveness, but as soon as the doors closed behind us at Ostley Manor, he gave orders I was not to leave the house and certainly not the estate. Then he dragged me to his study and proceeded to do his very best to beat our child out of me. Every day, he summoned me to the study and beat me until he tired. But my precious baby girl held fast, and since she would not give up, neither could I.

He kept that up for almost a month before the housekeeper noticed my morning sickness and the absence of my menses and took Ostley aside. She told him she believed me to be in an interesting condition and, although I clearly deserved the beatings, it wasn't Christian to punish the innocent babe. The housekeeper had been with his family for decades and held a prominent position in the parish, so he did not dare go against her, and I was left alone from then on.

It was several months later and I had just started to hope Ostley would accept the child as his own after all, when Lord Astor arrived. When I had flirted with him in Oxford, I had not known he was acquainted with Ostley, so I first assumed his visit was on my behalf. But instead of gallantly fawning over me, he took one look at my pregnant belly and sneered at me in disgust. And when I attempted to host dinner for him like any woman would in her home, he told Ostley to send me to my rooms so they could talk business, since he wasn't going to take a pregnant bitch in payment. I was shocked and confused at his language, but the way he looked at me whilst saying it left no doubt as to whom he was speaking of, and so, after my husband sent me from the room, I went to the room above the dining room and opened the chimney flue so I could hear what they talked about.

What I discovered, kneeling in front of the cold fireplace and trying my best not to make any noise, made my blood run cold. Apparently, Astor is a prominent member of a secret organization, the purpose of which seems, at least partly, sexual in nature. Ostley had been introduced into it, but in order to gain full membership, he had to offer something another member wanted. Money does not seem to be an option with these people, it has to be something secret or personal, so he had offered me. That was apparently why Astor had paid attention to me in Oxford. He sought my acquaintance to decide whether he wanted to accept me as Ostley's offering. It turns out he had wanted me and had accepted the bargain the very night you and I eloped. However, I was now heavy with your child, and he no longer wanted me.

I realized right there on the cold stone floor why Ostley had come after us, why he had wanted me back, and why he had tried to rid me of my pregnancy.

Astor was furious that Ostley had not succeeded on that last count, and they argued for hours before Astor offered him a new deal. If the child was *a girl, she was to be given to Astor twenty-four hours after I delivered. She then was to be brought up to become his personal slave. Astor would accept her as offering, and he would consider it adequate revenge on me as well as you.*

I knew I could not risk telling you any of this at the time; these people were much too powerful and dangerous for you to deal with. But I could send my child to you and trust you to keep her safe, perhaps even love her, so that is what I did. I managed to send word for you to wait at the crossroads and bribed my maid to bring you the infant, no matter whether I lived or died. I delivered her, held her for a precious few minutes, and then wrapped her in a blanket and the soiled birthing linens before she was smuggled out of the house. Ostley was told it was a stillbirth, and I was distraught enough for him to believe it, until word got out you were taking care of your illegitimate daughter several months later. But by then Ostley had already arranged for one of his cronies to lie with me, and I am once again pregnant with his potential heir, so he seems to be letting it go. Or maybe he just does not want to admit to what he had planned to do with my daughter. Either way, neither I nor my unborn child seem to be in any danger at present.

— Cecilia

5ᵗʰ of December 1809

My son, and Ostley's heir, is now one year old, and although I am still a virtual prisoner on the estate, I find great solace in being the best mother I can be to the child I am allowed to keep. Thank God the boy is blond and green-eyed like Ostley, so it's easy for him to feel as if he truly were his father. Charles is as yet too small to take hunting or parade around the neighborhood on a pony, so he is left mostly in my care.

I thank God every day that I was able to send our daughter to you.

Thank you for taking her in. I know you did the best you could for her, and I hear through my mother—who is now allowed to visit me every month since I presented Ostley with his heir—that you named her Emily and that she is being educated with Avon's children whilst you serve king and country on the Peninsula. I am glad she is at Avon; your cousin is not likely to take any chances with his children, and the fact that he and Astor's ducal father are bitter enemies in the House of Lords will make it even less likely for Astor to gain access to her while she lives there. I have not heard from or seen Lord Astor since that night, and Ostley never mentions him to me. But I do not know what he does, or with whom, when he goes to town, so I do not know whether Astor is still a threat to Emily.

I do not know if or when I will be able to send you this letter. And if I manage to send it, will you read it? You have every reason to think me shallow, spoiled, and heartless. I can only hope that if you do read this, you might find it in your heart to forgive me, and perhaps you will tell our daughter that I do love her and did not abandon her without good reason.

Know that my feelings for you were true, even if they were not strong enough to withstand the pressures of the world around us. I wish I would have been stronger, wiser, but that is neither here nor there.

Forgive me, and perhaps if I am lucky, I will get a chance to ask Emily for forgiveness one day.

— Cecilia

The last lines of the letter had blurred, and Henry finally allowed himself to shed the tears he had stubbornly refused to let fall until now. There had been a reason, a very good reason, and he didn't know why it still mattered after all these years, but it did. He felt like he'd been punched in his gut, and it took him a while to compose himself sufficiently to read the note accompanying the letter. There was a new lightness in his heart. Cecilia had not abandoned their daughter; she had done her best to keep her safe. And, of course, she had not been able to write a better explanation within minutes of giving birth.

Even when she had left him in Brussels, she had not been entirely selfish. All he had believed to be true for twelve years was, in fact, not.

His world felt as though it had shifted on its axis, but he was as yet unsure as to what the repercussions of that shift would be, so he wiped his fogged spectacles, pulled the note forward, his hands still shaking, and read what Cecilia had written the day before.

Thank you! Thank you! Thank you!

And thank God you arrived when you did to save that girl and elimi-nate the evil that was Astor, and the other man you shot. I am relieved beyond all measure to have seen with my own eyes that Astor is dead and is, therefore, no longer able to harm Emily. Whether that means there is no longer any threat to her safety, I cannot say for sure, but I am sure Astor was the one who sought revenge through her.

I was brought through a tunnel from the Highgate side of the heath to that horrible cellar and forced to watch what they did to the poor girl through a window. It must have been some kind of mirror on the other side, because none of you could see us. There were three more men in that room besides Ostley. We were all told to wear masks, so I cannot tell you who they were, except one of them was very old and walked with a carved ivory cane. To my utter horror, they all enjoyed what they saw. And then they departed like ghosts the moment Astor was shot.

Ostley told me the girl is Avon's illegitimate daughter, and that she was chosen to punish him for helping you take care of Emily, in order to send a message to you. I hope this information will help you keep our daughter safe.

You must have a hundred questions, and if you really need to contact me, you can try to do so through my mother, Mrs. Winters, 15 Emery Way, Oxford. But please read the letter I enclosed first. It may give you the answers you seek. I know I am asking a great favor, but please consider that any contact between you and me would give Ostley an excuse to take my son away from me.

Thank you again, and may God be with you.

— Cecilia

ELIZA ENTERED SOME TIME LATER to tell Henry dinner was ready to be served, and found him bent forward over his desk with his head in his hands. The picture he presented was so utterly desolate, she rushed to his side and enfolded him in her arms. Henry shifted in his seat so he could pull her into his lap, and once she was settled there, he buried his face in the curve of her neck and sobbed.

Eliza held him tight and massaged his scalp until his shoulders stopped shaking and his breathing calmed. And while she sat there and comforted him, she read the note that started with *Thank you! Thank you! Thank you!* and was signed by Cecilia, and wondered what was in the rest of the letter to upset him so much.

As if reading her mind, Henry reached around her and wordlessly handed her the letter.

Eliza read the whole of it, her heart aching for what the poor woman had endured, and what her suffering must mean to Henry. By the time she finished reading, he had finally calmed enough to speak.

"Oh God, Eliza, I loved her so much, and then she left me, and I was so hurt. That day she had her maid leave Emily in the crossroads,

I hated her, and I realize now that that hate has kept me going."

Henry lifted his head far enough out of the curve of Eliza's neck to take a big breath and let it out slowly. "But I can't hold on to it any longer, and I don't know what to do with the love and betrayal that lie just beneath. I was too hurt to find out what happened to her. I abandoned her to her fate, and now it's too late to save her, and I still don't know how to move on."

Eliza drew a handkerchief out of a pocket and dried his face, then kissed the lids of his eyes. "But now you can forgive her. And once you can forgive yourself, you can start to trust your heart again, because, after all, you hadn't been wrong about her. She did love you, and she did try to do the best she could by you and Emily. She was a victim of circumstance as much as you were back then. The difference is, you rose above yours, and she chose to return to hers and now chooses to remain."

Henry framed her face with his hands and looked at her with wonder. "How is it that you, with barely eighteen years of life experience, can see this whole situation so clearly, and I, who have lived a decade longer, been to war, faced untold dangers, and raised a daughter, can only see the tragedy of it all?"

Eliza stroked his cheeks and smiled sadly. "Perhaps because I, too, had to make an impossible choice. But I got lucky and I chose you. You restored my faith in humanity before I could completely lose it."

Henry remembered the moment last November on the road into Hampstead, when she had chosen to leave all she knew behind and put her trust in him. "You chose the devil you didn't know: me."

She smiled again, and there was no sadness in it this time. "And I choose you again now. You asked me earlier today if I would stay with you."

He finally met her eyes.

She saw hope there, and it warmed her heart. "I will stay with you, love, until the day you decide it is time for you to find a wife and mother for Emily."

The smile suffusing his face was as radiant as the rising sun. He pulled her into a kiss full of hope and love and tenderness, and finally spoke against her lips. "Thank you, my sweet Eliza. Whatever is left of my heart is yours."

LATER ON THAT NIGHT, AFTER Henry had departed for White's to meet Avon, Eliza went up to Henry's rooms to nap while she waited for him, and found a book lying in the center of the bed.

It was a thin volume, beautifully bound in dark blue leather with silver lettering and a light blue silk ribbon for a bookmark. It contained a collection of poems by John Keats.

Eliza paused, remembering Henry's teasing when he had found her reading one of Keats's poems at the bookshop the day they had gone shopping for Emily's birthday presents.

Picking up the charming little volume, she opened the first page to find a dedication.

To my sweet Eliza,
You are my thing of beauty.
Yours always,
— Henry

THE END

⌒

THE STORY CONTINUES IN...

THE GENTLEMAN'S DAUGHTER

⌒

January 1820, Hampstead Heath

A gunshot reverberated deep within the hillside and startled the servant in the sedan chair awake. The man jumped up, disoriented by the dark, cold night around him. But as soon as he remembered himself, he kicked his colleague who slumbered under a heavy blanket next to the chair.

"Something's up, mate."

The other servant scrambled to his feet and straightened his wig just in time. Hurried footsteps sounded from inside the hill and his partner opened the heavy iron door. Four elegantly dressed figures spilled out of the portal set deep into the hillside. They were all masked, and one roughly pulled the only woman of the group along with him.

Another new arrival, completely dressed in black, motioned to the man holding the woman's arm. "Take her away and make sure she talks to no one."

The man complied instantly, dragging the woman further down the heath where a coach waited by the side of the road. They got in and the vehicle pulled away, just as another gentleman emerged from the dark tunnel and stepped out into the open leaning heavily on a carved ivory cane. He was bowed by age, but the mouth below the mask was harsh and unyielding. As the coach disappeared into the darkness, the old man ripped the mask off his face and threw it to the ground. Ignoring the servants, he fixed the other two gentlemen in a death stare, anger rolling off him in waves. "Let that be a lesson to you, arrogance leads to mistakes. March may act the fool, but do not underestimate him again. Astor is dead because he got careless."

He walked to the sedan chair and sank into it, some of the tension leaving his body. "As for you two, give me your rings and collect all the others. We won't meet during the customary mourning period. I'll send out the rings again when it's time to elect the next dungeon master."

Both men removed gold rings from their pinky fingers depicting two snakes hissing at each other, and handed them to the old man. They then pulled off their masks, stashed them in their pockets, and the young man bent to pick up the old man's from the ground. The one entirely in black stroked a weary hand over his face. He looked somber, perhaps even a little shaken, while the younger one shook with barely contained anger. He was tall, powerfully built, and from what could be gleaned in the darkness, handsome; but there was a dangerous glint in his eyes. "I can't wait to get my hands on the meddling fool's bastard and show her that she's indeed the whore she was born to be."

The old man turned his unsettlingly bright eyes on the young man and pointed his ivory cane at him. "You have yet to be elected dungeon master, and there are at least three ahead of you who want the honor! Do not embarrass me by doing something rash, you just saw where that will lead. In case it has escaped your notice, we did not achieve our goal tonight. March may well be able to prevent the scandal we need to discredit the reform bill. Besides, young Emily March is only twelve and apparently still flat as a board. As far as I am informed, most of us still like our women with tits and to be old enough to appreciate what's being done to them."

The young man, feeling properly chastised, hung his head. "As you wish, grandfather. I apologize."

The old man's eyes softened just a fraction. "Fiddlesticks, my boy."

He gestured for the two servants to lift the chair so they could depart, then turned to the man in black. "Tell Ostley it will be his responsibility to retrieve the March girl when the time comes. And if he succeeds, he'll earn the right to be in the dungeon when she's broken in."

"It shall be done, my lord."

Both men bowed as the sedan chair was lifted and the old man waved his cane in a dismissive salute.

"It better be. I will not tolerate any further mistakes. The Knights can't afford them."

The two men watched the chair until it was swallowed completely by the night, then the younger man turned to the older. "I don't understand why Sir Henry isn't one of us; his father was!"

The older man smirked and turned to head down the hill. "Ah, the older March was a true believer, having served Charles Stuart himself for a period of time in Italy. Sir Henry, on the other hand, hated his father, did well in the army and may still be serving the Crown. Besides, not everyone shares our sexual tastes and we never could find anything sufficiently damaging to force him into the fold. His failings are all right out in the open for everyone to see."

The young man shook his head. "That's unfortunate, he is actually very clever."

The older man chuckled. "You have no idea, you were too young during the war. He's a formidable opponent. But fear not, we will break him through his daughter."

February 1823, on the way to Avon

The day was rather spectacular for late February. Sir Henry March, accompanied only by his groom, piloted his curricle along a small country road toward Upavon and his ducal cousin's estate. He'd taken his hat and greatcoat off some miles back to let the sun warm him, and it did. The dry and unseasonably warm weather had left the roads passable, the riverbanks painted in crocus yellow and purple, and the bare trees shadowed with the first hint of spring. Sir Henry had high hopes the familiar beloved landscape in all its spring glory would cheer him, but so far, nature's exuberance had only served to highlight the melancholy holding his heart hostage.

It was out of character for Sir Henry to feel so low. At four and thirty he was in his prime, blessed with a considerable fortune and the respect of his peers. He enjoyed good health, and nature had favored him with a pleasing countenance, straight limbs, and the kind of charisma women found hard to resist. His eyes were blue and penetrating, his hair sandy blond and cropped short, and his smile engaging.

However, only three weeks had passed since he'd said goodbye to his lovely mistress, Eliza. There was no anger to carry him through the parting since her sacrifice was as great as his own, and so he could only miss her. He missed her smell, her smile, the way she twirled her long dark locks around her fingers while she read. But most of all, he missed knowing she would be there when he got home. To make matters worse, he had left Eliza with his friend and partner, Allen, who had returned from a foreign assignment with considerable injuries. And then, to honor his agreement not to see Eliza for six months, he had to trust another agent to investigate the Russian threat and to keep Allen and Eliza safe.

Henry had just passed through a sunlit oak forest, bright with early whispers of green, and was heading up the last rise before his descent into the Avon valley. He pulled up his grays on the crest of the hill overlooking the river and his cousin's ancestral castle in the distance. The horses bent their heads to nibble at some tufts of grass by the side of the road while Henry allowed himself a moment to take in the familiar vista.

The road ahead led down a sheep-studded incline and over an ancient stone bridge spanning one of the Avon River's arms. It passed through the charming hamlet of Upavon and disappeared into the forests beyond. The calmly flowing river below was bracketed by willows and hazel, shimmering silver where the sun hit the water.

The scene was utterly peaceful. Not even the river had any sense of urgency, meandering here and there along its gently sloping valley, bordered by farmland and wooded groves. Henry took a deep breath, wanting the calm of this place to penetrate every cell of his being.

He let his gaze travel back up the side of the hill to the edge of the forest to his right and paused. There, some distance away, where the forest abruptly stopped and the grassland began, a woman sat silhouetted against the horizon. She was seated on a portable stool and leaned toward a spindly easel as she painted.

The woman was half turned away from him, absorbed in her work and oblivious to his presence. Henry found that circumstance most intriguing. It left him free to observe her, as she observed the landscape, and just like that, his love of the land was shared with another and his loneliness somewhat alleviated.

Her figure was pleasing, and she seemed too young to be sitting at the edge of the forest by herself. Even from where he sat, the look of concentration on her profile was unmistakable. Her dark hair was brushed back from her face and held together at the nape of her neck with a sky blue ribbon. Curiously, there were also several brushes stuck in it, and some of the shorter, slow curling strands were unceremoniously tucked behind her ear. She wore a rather dowdy blue dress, and a large green triangular shawl was tied around her peasant style, to keep her warm and her hands free.

But what held Henry's attention was not her youth, or her looks, but the way she painted. Just now she blindly bent to wash out her brush in a preserve glass on the ground, then flicked it behind her to expel the excess water, whilst looking alternately at the scene before her and her unfinished painting. Then she quickly dipped her brush into two different pots of paint, swiftly mixed the color on her palette, held the palette up to check the accuracy of the hue and added a few self-assured dabs to her composition. She cocked her head to the side to check the effect, added one more dab, and moved on to paint the sky with a broader brush she pulled from her hair.

Henry couldn't see the watercolor from his perch on the curricle, but he was willing to bet it was good. Every movement she made proved she was put on this earth to paint and seeing her embrace her purpose was very attractive. Perhaps if he could find a woman who had a purpose he could understand and respect, married life might not be so bad. Eliza was right, he had to open himself to the possibility of meeting a woman he could at least like, if not love. He would never even have contemplated such a thing if she hadn't insisted they go their separate ways.

ACKNOWLEDGEMENTS

Let me begin by thanking Michelle Halket at Central Avenue Publishing for taking a chance on me. You are amazing and I appreciate everything you do. My thanks also to Molly Ringle for her inspired period word choices, and her thorough line editing.

My biggest thank you goes to my group of writer friends. This book has had a long and varied road to being published and without my Bookbesties I would have given up long ago. Thank you Kelly Cain, Cathie Armstrong, Amanda Linsmeier, and Jamie McLachlan.

The first person on my personal list of thank yous is my lovely critique partner and friend, Carmen Chancellor. Thank you for letting me bounce ideas off you, reading my pages, correcting them and gently letting me know when something needed work each week. You came into my life at precisely the right moment and now I can't imagine it without you.

My next salute is to Annemarie Levitt. Thank you for correcting all my funky spelling and finding those words where the spellcheck had suggested the wrong thing and I was too dyslexic to see it. In these days of COVID-19 I miss our afternoons drinking Adam's wine.

Bobby, you were the first person to encourage me to write again and pushed me to get on with it. I realize this is not quite what you had in mind but it is what came out.

A nod of thanks to Jeff, who introduced me to Carmen and asked the plot changing question: where is the body?

And then there are Daria, Conrad, Brendan and a bunch of others. Thanks for all your support.

Bianca M. Schwarz was born in Germany, spent her formative years in London, and now lives in Los Angeles with her husband and son. She has been telling stories all her life, but didn't hit her stride until she started writing a book she would want to read for fun. Her debut novel, *The Innkeeper's Daughter*, is that book.